"Through the eyes of a naive but gradually maturing Ben, we learn the socio-economic history of the times: the near extinction of the buffalo; the conflicts between farmer and cattleman; the far-reaching effects of the depression . . . The story stands on its own as a beautifully crafted and credible piece of work."
—*The Horn Book*

"Carter has done his research. His portrayal of the tedium, filth, and barbarism of the frontier is vivid and realistic." —*Entertainment Weekly*

"The reader can taste the dust kicked up by the herd in this action-packed adventure story about the Old West." —*Children's Book Review Service*

★"An ambitious, panoramic tale, Carter's impressive novel takes seriously its intent to portray the Old West as it really was . . . Vivid and enlightening, this is a fine piece of social history cast in the form of a very absorbing novel." —STARRED / *Booklist*

An ALA Best Book for Young Adults

Also by Peter Carter
BURY THE DEAD

BORDERLANDS

PETER CARTER

AERIAL FICTION   FARRAR   STRAUS   GIROUX

For Hugo Donnelly
A square dealer

Oh, give me a home where the buffalo roam,
Where the deer and the antelope play,
Where seldom is heard a discouraging word
And the skies are not cloudy all day.

BORDERLANDS

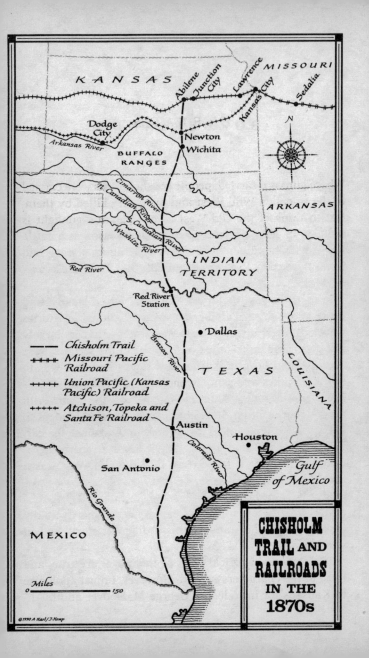

CHISHOLM TRAIL AND RAILROADS IN THE 1870s

PREFACE

Where guns are carried, people get shot. Guns were carried in the so-called Wild West and men were killed by them. But to think of the Old West as one gigantic gunfight is fantasy. In 1871, Abilene, in its busiest season as a cattle town, with hundreds of cowboys walking its streets, had fewer homicides than humdrum Merthyr Tydfil, in peaceful Wales.

In fact, the real history of the West was a steady, and rapid, move toward civil order. As the national territories were admitted into the Union as states—that is, largely self-governing units—the first impulse of the settlers, once counties had been organized and towns founded, was to build churches and schools and hire law-enforcement officers: sheriffs for the counties, marshals for the towns (with their deputies often, it might surprise British readers to know, called policemen), to enforce laws against the carrying of firearms, and, especially in Kansas, to enforce anti-drinking laws. It is fair to say that the Old West was a considerably safer place to be then than it is now—especially on Saturday nights.

Of course, before towns were organized—that is, legally recognized by the state—it was a different story. As you will see.

The obvious historical facts in this novel are true, and most of the characters existed. However, I must apologize to Kansans for introducing George M. Hoover and his liquor tent a year before he actually arrived in Dodge, and for donating a new railroad station, Bailey's Halt. I hope, too, that Texans will excuse me for endowing their state with a new county, Clement, and a new town, Lookout.

It might be of some interest that it was in Abilene, Kansas, where one Dwight D. Eisenhower spent his youth, going on to become twice President of the United States after being Commander in Chief of the Allied forces in the battle against the evils of Nazi Germany. He also vastly enjoyed reading Westerns!

GETTING
ALONG

■ O N E ■

Bo and me came out of Clement County—Texas, that is. Our pa was killed by Butler's Yankees in the War between the States, and our eldest brother, Keeler, lit out for California in '68 and we never did hear from him again. That left Ma, Bo, my sister, Flo, and me. There'd been two other kids, but they died young.

We had clear title to our land, although, when you got down to it, there wasn't much on it but scrub and a creek which dried up when you needed it most. Ma liked to call it our "ranch," but, then, she always was fanciful. Maybe it was because her folks hailed from Louisiana that she never did see things straight, mooning over some books by a feller called Walter Scott and naming Flo Florimella, which no one had ever heard of before, not around Clement anyhow, and calling Bo Beauregard de Quincy, would you believe. I guess I was lucky to get off with plain Benjamin, but, then, Ma never did take to me, perhaps because I was kind of small and raggedy, not like them knights of old, whoever the Sam Hill they was.

Then one day Flo, who I reckon had fanciful notions of her own, took off with a traveling man who sold women's clothes and notions. I didn't blame her none, because there sure wasn't nothing to hold a body in Clement County, but Ma had the vapors for a month, walking around like a ghost, although she came back to life when we got a letter from Flo saying she'd ditched the traveling man and got hitched to a storekeeper in Brownsville. She didn't give her new name, though.

So that left just the three of us, blistering in summer and freezing in winter, scratching for a living, growing a little corn when the weather and the bugs would let us, hiring out to anyone who had fifty cents, or anything else, come to that, not seeing a dollar bill from one year's end to the other, and now and then going off into the mesquite and getting ourselves a steer so's we could chew some beef.

But even that wasn't getting no easier. The way of it was, during the war millions of longhorns had gone wild, roaming where they willed, and picking one off with our old Spencer wasn't no harder than knocking over a jackrabbit. But times were changing. The war was over, them Yankees up North was starved for beef and down in Texas there was all them cattle wandering about, so some ranchers got the notion that they would take the cattle up there where the beefsteaks was wanted, and where there were dollars to pay for them, too.

That wasn't a new idea. Before the war, cattle had been trailed all over the entire United States, and afterwards, from the Southlands up the old Shawnee Trail through Missouri to the railhead at Sedalia. But then the settlers edged in from the West, filling up Missouri, and them sodbusters claimed the herds trampled down their crops and carried cattle fever, tick fever it was, although them farmers called it Texas fever, too, even though it didn't have nothing whatever to do with Texas, and they said fever killed their cows, and they got the herds banned. So things got pretty slack for a while, but then the Union Pacific Railroad came snaking across Kansas and a Yankee called Joe McCoy bought himself a ticket, got off at Abilene Town, Kansas, took a peek around, saw there was plenty of grass and water and not too many sodbusters, got himself elected mayor, and him and the railroad sent agents down to Texas saying, "Boys, bring your cattle to Abilene and we'll rail them off to Kansas City and Chicago, and it's cash money on the barrelhead." And he kept his word, too, which is where that saying comes from, "the real McCoy."

Well, the Texans weren't maybe bright—not much brighter than John D. Rockefeller, that is—but they got the message loud and clear, so they rounded up the cattle and walked them north to Kansas, and a steer worth maybe two or three dollars in Texas, if you could get that, would bring thirty or forty greenbacks in Abilene. And that was fine and dandy because the herds could go up the Chisholm Trail, where there weren't no farmers, the only snags being that it was five hundred miles longer, crossed ten rivers, and went slap through Indian Territory.

Still and all, the cattle went, by the million, and I ain't kidding, and them big ranchers, and the small ones, too, started to see them wild steers and cows as just so many dollar bills on four legs and started branding them and it became a mite harder for two country boys to cut themselves out a beeve because that was rustling, and you could find yourself doing the Texas rope dance for that.

So beef went off the menu in the Curtis cabin and the scratching got harder. Bo got himself hired for the Harvey spread, a hundred miles away, and I went in the corn patch and tended a couple of hogs we had and a few chickens and kept my eyes open for the Comanche. I've got to say, no one we knew had seen any since the war, but they did use to have the notion that they could come off the Staked Plain and roam around as if the country belonged to them, so they was always at the back of your mind, and they did burn out a feller not two hundred miles north of us, which was a mite too close for comfort.

Then, at the end of summer of '70, Ma died. She went quick. One minute she was leaning over the washtub, the next she was on the ground, and I reckon she didn't last

9

long after that. I rode the mule over to our neighbor Danny Farley and got his wife. She came and said Ma had died because her heart had stopped beating, which wasn't exactly what you might call news. But, like the preacher said at her burial, women didn't last long in Texas. They just got wore out with work and having babies and all. Anyhow, and he read it out right there and then from the Good Book, the days of men and women is as short as the grass which is winnowed and then cast in the oven, although I'll tell you, any grass that did get to grow in Clement sure didn't get thrown in no oven.

Be that as it may, with Ma gone, it left just Bo and me, him having been paid off at the Harvey spread, it not needing him after the fall roundup, and it was beginning to look like, if things went on the way they were, the Curtis clan was going to be extincted. Howsomever, whatever Ma hadn't done, she'd whipped McGuffey's reader into me so's I could read and write, and do figuring, come to that—up to the Rule of Three, almost, so I wrote to Flo. We didn't have no proper address, and, like Bo said, if she had got roped we didn't even know her name, but I wrote just the same, figuring there wouldn't be too many Florimellas floating around Brownsville, and I sent the letter to the town marshal with "Bereevment" writ big on the cover and hoped for the best.

I wrote in hope and that was about all Bo and me had to live on for the next few weeks. We bought flour and beans and coffee, killed our last hog, chopped down the last post oak by the creek for firewood, and settled in to living on flapjacks, salt pork, and beans, and there wasn't no point hoping for nothing different because the only creatures you could eat which hadn't long since been trapped out or shot off had more than four legs. In fact, there were only two things going for us. The neighbors were real kind and the winter kept the Comanche at home, so we could hit the hay without wondering whether we was going to wake up and find the cabin burning around our ears.

Mrs. Farley was truly good to us and gave us a pecan pie at Christmas and Danny helped fix our stove when it bust, but the truth was, we weren't living too well. I don't just mean bad grub and being cold because most everyone we knew lived so, but we were letting things slide, staying up later and later playing cards and checkers, and getting up later and later, too, and we were getting dirtier and so was the cabin, dust everyplace, and we slowed down on washing the dishes until the grease was so thick on them a mule would have gotten mired down in it.

We should have known better, I guess, but then Bo was only seventeen and I wasn't but thirteen, and like I say, we was living in hope, although if you was to ask me hope for what, we didn't rightly know, saving that maybe spring would bring something with it, maybe a letter from Flo saying she was coming back to look after the cabin and bake pies and all, or telling us to get to Brownsville and live with her. Something like that, anyways.

But we plugged along, except I got an awful bad toothache and the tooth splintered when Bo yanked on it with the pincers and he had to dig some bits out with a knife, which was a night I'd sooner forget, and the folks around us were real good, although they got less good, if you follow me. We got pies, sure enough, and if we went to a cabin on our old mule, we got a welcome and a meal, but as that winter wore on, we didn't get that same warm welcome. Truth to tell, the fare-thee-wells were warmer than the howdy-dos.

Bo observed this one night when we were heading back from the Farleys' place, and I can see him now, in the cold white moonlight, with a northerly ruffling the brim of his old hat.

"Fact is, Ben," he said, "them Farleys have got enough

11

kids of their own to look after and feed and they ain't got no more money than we have."

I said that wasn't so—not the stuff about Farleys having plenty of kids, because they surely did—but about them not wanting us around.

"Sides," I said, "we'll work it off come spring, make it up to them and all."

Bo shook his head. "Spring's spring and now's now. Anyhow, there ain't a thing we can do for them that they can't do for themselves. I'll tell you, Ben, come spring, we got to do something. We can't go on living like this." And like it was agreeing, the old mule blew down its nose and switched its tail.

I felt real scary, but I said, "It's going to be all right, Bo. Things are going to work out just fine."

And I don't know but that Bo heard that scaredness in my voice because he grinned, his teeth all shining. "Trouble with you, Ben," he said, "you like them pies too much."

He laughed, but it was true enough. I did like pies. I used to dream of them, and I didn't like the thought that I wouldn't get no more, so I was real gloomy for a while.

Then we got a letter from Flo. Ed Payne brought it in after he'd been down to Sweetwater, our nearest town, for some stores. It had been lying around there for a month, but now it was in our cabin and me and Bo looked at it as if it was some kind of magic spell, and I guess neither of us wanted to break it, the spell I mean, and let the magic go, but then Bo said, "Open it up."

I slit the paper open and took a peek, just a little one, because I wanted to prolong the pleasure, as you might say, but Bo told me to quit fooling around and read it, which I had to do, because, although Bo was a mighty good rider, he was like a wild mustang on a rope when it came to the ABCs. So I spread out the letter, put my finger on the writing, coughed, like I'd seen the preacher do when he read from the Good Book, and began, and I've got to say it didn't take long because there wasn't much *to* read. But this is what it said:

Boys Im sory ma is dead but she alwas was sikly I ges you can look afer yur selfs any way there no room hear I got married. And have a baby my husband ant bad. and only drinks wisky twic a week if you sell the plase a third is ritly mine. Send the cash to the post oficce here at brownsville yure loving sister Flo. My weded name is schultz.

Well, any notions I had of eating Flo's pies went flying clean through the window, and Bo sure looked blue.

"Is that all?" he asked.

"That's all," I said.

"Well, Sam Hill!" He grabbed the letter and stared at it, although that writing didn't mean beans to him. "What did it say at the end?"

"Your loving sister, Flo."

"Loving sister!" Bo spat on the stove. "There ain't much loving in that letter."

I had to go along with that. There was as much loving in it as there was in a turkey buzzard eyeing a new-thrown calf.

"And what's her new moniker? Schultz? A goddamn Dutchman."

"Yeah," I said. "Or German."

"Dutchman, German, they're all the same, ain't they?" Bo picked up the letter again. "A third of this place is rightly hers, did she say? If we ever did sell it, a third wouldn't pay the mailage!"

He glowered at me like *I'd* written the blamed letter, but

13

I felt as bad as he did, worser even, because I sure had put some faith in Flo. Then, just like Bo, I took another peek at the letter, but it didn't say nothing different from the first reading, so I chucked it away and hit the hay.

The coyotes did a power of yipping that night, and I ain't sure there wasn't a wolf out there howling at the moon, although they couldn't have been more dolesome than I was, and the blanket was smelling as rank as the mule. For, ever since that night when Bo had said the neighbors wasn't going to go on being neighborly forever, I'd been scared that he'd do what our brother Keeler had done, just light out to where the grass was greener and leave me on my own.

■ TWO ■

But even that winter ended, and it didn't end none too soon neither, because we was on the last of the flour, the coffee had run out, and we was so low on the hog there wasn't much left except the tail. However, spring edged in, the bluebonnets and the wild mustard opened and they were sure pretty, saving they would have looked nicer if you could have eaten them, although there was no way of doing that, unless you were a goat. They were a sight for sore eyes, though, and them and a touch of sun on my back made me feel better. Still, I began to keep an eye on Bo in case he got spring fever and decided to skip.

If he was thinking of going on the lam, he never showed no sign of it. And then one day when the sky was blue and the meadowlarks was making sweetheart talk to each other and Bo was making sinister sounds, like maybe we should go to the creek and have ourselves a bath, a feller came riding in.

Bo saw him coming first, because he had mighty keen eyes. He stood on the stoop, his hand over his forehead, and I was going to get out the Spencer because you never knew who was drifting around Texas in them days—these days, too, come to that—then Bo relaxed.

"It's the preacher," he said.

That preacher was called Mr. Tyler and I hadn't seen him since Ma's burial when he'd told us that fool nonsense about throwing grass into the oven. He was a lanky feller, good with the Word and mighty sharp with a dollar—too sharp for a preacher, some folks said—and his missus had sent us over some molasses after Ma died, although she'd mixed it with sulfur against the fever and the stuff had tasted downright horrible.

Still, there he was, swinging a long leg over the saddle and saying, "Howdy, boys, is the Lord with you?"

If the Lord being with us meant us having pies and cookies, he surely wasn't, but we didn't say so. We just sort of mumbled "Howdy" and asked him in and Bo offered him coffee.

"T'ain't real coffee," Bo said. "Acorn."

Tyler sat down and slapped dust off himself in a big cloud that went all over the cabin, not that it made any difference. "Never take stimulants," he said. "Water, which is the gift of the Lord, is good enough for me."

I gave him the pannikin and he took a swig, spat out a few flies, and stared at us. "You boys ain't looking too good," he said.

It wasn't the most genteel way to start a visit, but it was true at that, we weren't looking so good. In fact, we looked more like two saddle bums than like two free landowning Texans.

Bo shuffled his feet. "We was just going to have a spring

clean-out," he said, which was news to me. "The dishes and all."

Tyler rubbed his beaky nose. "I'm mighty glad to hear it," he said, as if he didn't believe a word. "Cleanliness is next to Godliness. You boys bear that in mind."

Bo mumbled that we would and that we'd look into the Godliness stuff, too, as soon as we got the time.

"Time!" Tyler was sharp. "Seems to me, time is what you boys have got plenty of."

"That ain't so," Bo said. "We got lots to do, the cooking and . . . and . . ."

I knew Bo was going to say "and the housework" but couldn't bring himself to, not the way the cabin was, and one thing you could say for Bo, he was honest as the day is long.

Tyler sniffed. "That's as may be. But I've been thinking about you boys all the winter through. Yes, sir. And I've been thinking you ain't the kind to rely on your neighbors, which is as poor as you, forever. No, independent, that's what you are."

I liked the sound of that, but Bo didn't look like he'd found a ten-dollar bill. "Just what might you be driving at?" he asked.

Tyler leaned forward, sort of poking his beak at Bo. "What I'm driving at is that you boys need cash. Dollars."

My eyes popped when I heard Tyler, and I thought he was going to get out his poke and start lashing out the greenbacks there and then, and I guess Bo felt the same because he said, "Why, that's mighty big of you, Mr. Tyler. We sure do need some cash, and as soon as I start riding again, I'll pay you off."

When Bo said that, Tyler jumped so much he sent another big cloud of dust over the place. "Now, just hold on there," he spluttered. "I didn't come here to loan you no money. No, sir! I don't hold with it. I've seen too many

16

good men led astray by borrowing. It puts off till tomorrow the evils of today, it corrupts the soul, it's the easy path to drinking and gambling, to smoking, to hellfire and brimstone, to—"

Bo waved his hand. "Cut out the sermonizing, Mr. Tyler. If you ain't come to loan us money, just what have you come for?"

Tyler grimaced, not caring for being pulled up in full gallop, because he was a powerful man for the Word. Why, I'd heard him give out a hellfire sermon for three hours non-stop at a camp meeting when the Holy Spirit had him by the collar.

"All right, then," he said, real sour. "Let's get down to it." He clacked his teeth and took a piece of paper out of his hat. "Aargh," he kind of gargled. "What do you aim to do about this?"

Bo gave me the paper and I looked it over. Some of the words were a sight too hard even for me, but I caught the drift, and when I'd finished, I was green around the gills, and when I told Bo what was in that there paper, *he* went green, too, because under that fancy language, what that note said was that Ma owed Tyler fifty dollars cash.

"Fifty bucks!" Bo said—well, he more like exploded. "What in tarnation did Ma borrow that for?"

"Now, I don't know that," Tyler said. "It wasn't for me to ask when I loaned your ma that money out of the goodness of my heart, but what I do want to know is what you aim to do about it."

"Do!" Bo glared. "Hey, you ain't suggesting that note's got anything to do with us, are you?"

"I did have that notion," Tyler said.

"Then get yourself another." Bo sure was hopping mad. "We ain't got fifty dollars. In fact, we ain't got fifty cents. Anyhow, Ma borrowed that money and she's dead and buried, so we don't owe you a dime."

17

"Now, that's true," Tyler allowed. "You don't. But that there note, which is a *legal* note, Bo, says that if your poor ma didn't pay back that money inside of twelve months, then *I* own this land."

"What?" Bo couldn't believe his ears, and I couldn't believe mine, neither. "Are you saying Ma sold you this land for fifty bucks? Mr. Tyler, you've been chewing locoweed. Just loco is what you are."

"I would be if that was what I was saying." Tyler was soothing, like he was talking to a dog that was showing its teeth. "But I ain't. All I'm saying is that your ma put this land down as security. That was her idea, Bo. She said as how she wouldn't be beholden to no one. Not even a man of God."

"Like you," Bo said, all sarcastical.

"Like me." Tyler nodded.

"And you think you're going to get this land for fifty bucks?"

Tyler did that teeth clacking again. "Did I say that? What do you take me for? This land is worth more than that, and I know it. All I want to know is what you aim to do about this here fifty-five dollars."

"You said fifty," Bo flashed.

"Ten months' interest at five percent." Tyler looked up like he did at a prayer meeting when he was moved by the Spirit.

Bo half laughed, except it wasn't really a laugh. He strode to the door and stared out and I could tell he was ready to bust something—or someone—because, although Bo was a truly good, kindhearted feller, he did have a mean streak in him when he was riled. But when he turned around he didn't look mad, not much madder than a lobo wolf, anyhow.

"I told you we got no cash money," he said, "but if you

18

try to foreclose this land, I'll blast your head off, and by God I mean it."

Tyler blew through his nose, just exactly like the mule. "That's just foolish talk, Bo, and you know it. Now, if you'll just sit down for a minute and stop fizzing around like a firecracker, I'll tell you what I've got in mind."

Bo hesitated, like he didn't know whether to sit or bust Tyler on the beak, but then he did sit, as if the weight of that debt was pressing him down.

"That's better," Tyler said. "Now, let's look at this like sensible, grownup men. I ain't a hard man; in fact, my missus goes on at me for being too softhearted. So what I'm aiming to do is *give* you fifty dollars and then take over this place. That amounts to $105, Bo, and that ain't too bad a price for something which ain't worth much anyhow and which you can't afford to live on, and which I could take iffen I wanted to. And don't go saying you're going to blow my head off, because you ain't, and if I thought you would, do you reckon I'd be fool enough to take over myself? I'd just sell that note to someone who might come along and blow *your* head offen *you*. So just simmer down and take the cash."

"And then what?" Bo said. "Go panning for gold?"

That didn't seem like a bad idea to me. We could head out someplace, strike it rich, buy all the pies we wanted— but Tyler put the Indian sign on that.

"Don't talk so, Bo. You ain't no prospector. You want to use that fifty dollars I'm giving you and use it to make *more* money, doing what you know. That's the right way, and it's the Lord's way, too. And where in this great country of ours is the hard cash?"

Bo gave that laugh again which wasn't a laugh. "It sure ain't in Clement County."

Tyler frowned, like it was wrong to laugh at money, but

19

he agreed. "Sure, but I'll tell you where the money is, boys. It's up North, is where."

Bo blinked. "You mean on the Red River?"

"No!" Tyler was irritated. "I mean the real North. *The* North."

Bo looked at Tyler like the preacher had grown another head. "You ain't saying we should go up there, are you?"

"That's it exactly," Tyler said.

Then Bo did get mad, Jupiter, didn't he just! He jumped up and stomped about and cussed. "Go there? Go and mingle with them murdering blue-belly Yankees and them niggers? I'd sooner bed down with a rattlesnake!"

"Calm down, Bo," Tyler said. "Just calm down. No one said you've got to like it. All I'm saying is you two go up there and predate on them like they're doing to the poor Southland, which they is predating on like locusts."

Bo shook his head. "That seems plain crazy to me. How are we going to get there?"

"I've got that figured." Tyler hitched forward. "Didn't I tell you I've been thinking of you boys all the winter through? I know a feller by the name of Sam Clark. He's a trail boss in Coryell County and he's taking a herd to Kansas. Now, the way I see it, you go and see Sam and show him a letter I'll give you and he'll take you on as riders, because he owes me a favor, and you go with that fifty dollars I'm going to give you, and Sam will pay you a dollar a day, and you'll end up in Kansas with a wad."

"Yeah?" Bo said. "And then what?"

"What?" Tyler waggled a finger in his ear. "You come back, buy some beeves of your own, take them North, make more money, get more beeves, and before you know it, you'll be ranchers yourselves!"

He leaned back, hands on his knees, nodding his head, while I thought that the Curtis boys were getting on in the world, what with being real ranchers with a registered brand of our own and all.

But Bo didn't have no stars in his eyes. "If it's that easy," he said, "why ain't you in the business?"

Old Tyler, he rubbed his hands together and looked at them, like he was reading his fortune. "Maybe I am," he said, all sly, "and maybe I ain't. Anyhow, that's the deal, take it or leave it. What do you say?"

"I don't know," Bo said. "It's kind of a big thing we're talking about here. Anyhow"—he sort of burst out—"how do I know that there note is legal?"

I said Bo had a mean streak in him, but so did Tyler. He strode over to Bo, and I guess because he was a preacher I'd never realized how big he was, but I did then. He was a head taller than Bo, and as broad as a barn door, and there was a kind of bulge under his coattail which didn't look like no Bible book to me.

"That there note is all legal," he said. "Legal, signed, and witnessed. You doubting my word?"

Bo was somewhat startled, I guess. "I ain't doing that, Mr. Tyler. If you say it's legal, that's jake with me. But leaving . . . I guess we'd just like to think about it, is all."

"Hmm . . ." Tyler snorted and gargled and clacked for a while, like he was trying to make up his mind, and then nodded. "There ain't nothing to think about, and Sam Clark ain't going to wait for you, but you can have a few days. But make up your minds pretty quick. Fifty-five dollars or the land."

He took a good peek around the cabin and then stalked out, us kind of shambling after him, and climbed on his horse. "How do you boys reckon to feed yourselves on a place like this?" he said.

Bo shrugged. "We'll manage."

Tyler stared down at us. "You boys ever hear tell of Haman?"

21

Bo frowned. "Haman? Never did. He from Clement?"

Tyler shook his head, ruing our ignorance, and I guess we was just two ignorant country boys at that. "You boys should study the Holy Book," he said. "Read the Old Testament. Haman there, he was hanged from the highest tree in the land of Persia, yes, siree. Hanged till he was dead."

Bo looked at me but I'd got nothing to say, so he said to Tyler, "I don't get it."

"No," Tyler said, his long legs dangling free from his stirrups. "You know enough to draw two cards to three jacks, but you don't know the words of the Lord God. Well, let me tell you, a couple of boys was hanged over in Lorenzo a month back for rustling. Rustling, which, apart from the law of this great state of ours, breaks the Tenth Commandment of the Law of Moses: Thou shalt not covet thy neighbor's ox. Heed that Commandment, and all the others, and figure out that good deal I've offered you. And while you're doing it, just bear in mind that the vengers of them there Commandments might be roaming around Clement the next few days, which is what time you've got to redeem that legal note."

Then he stuck his feet in his stirrups, hit the horse with his spurs, and rode away, all hunched up and black, with his head down, like a crow on a fence.

▪ THREE ▪

We stood and watched old Tyler ride away until we lost him among the straggly cottonwoods down by the creek. Then Bo really blew up. "Goddamn," he cursed. "What the hell was Ma doing making a deal like that?"

I couldn't answer that, and I couldn't ask Ma, so I kept my mouth shut. Back in the cabin, Bo opened his, and his language was so hot, if I wrote it down it would scorch the paper, but when he finished, I asked him what he was aiming to do.

He shook his head and sighed. "I don't know. Seems we raise fifty-five bucks or lose the land, and we've as much chance of getting that cash as jumping over the moon."

He did some more cursing, brooded awhile, then said, "We need some advice here. Saddle the mule and we'll go over and ask Danny Farley."

I put the old saddle on the old mule and swung up behind Bo and we plodded across to the Farley place. The kids were glad to see us, but Mrs. Farley was somewhat cool, and so was Danny, but when Bo said we'd come for advice, the atmosphere got less frosty, I guess because advice don't cost nothing. Anyhow, Bo told the tale, and when he finished, there was what you might call a solemn silence, like in a church.

"Well, now," Danny said at last. "I guess that calls for a drink."

Mrs. Farley got out a jug of corn whiskey and Danny poured himself and Bo a slug.

"That's some tale, Bo," he said. "You saw that note?"

"Plain and clear," Bo said, "And Ben read it through."

Mrs. Farley tutted. "What was your poor mother doing, signing away the land like that?"

"I wish I knew, ma'am," Bo said. "But we was having a hard time then, so maybe she was buying stores and seed and what have you, and I guess she figured she was doing things for the best."

"Well, I'm sure she did," Mrs. Farley said, but there was something in her voice that made you wonder—and I remembered how Ma had got herself a new dress for Thanksgiving.

But Bo was talking again and I paid attention, as much as I could while half a dozen kids was crawling over me and licking the back of my neck.

"So what do you reckon, Danny?" Bo was saying. "What should we do?"

Danny sucked his teeth, took a shot of whiskey, then said, "Bo, if that there note is legal, and knowing Tyler I guess it is, then it's pay up or get out."

"Which would be a crying shame," Mrs. Farley said.

"Surely so," Danny said, "but it don't alter the facts none."

"No," Mrs. Farley agreed. "But why does he want that land so bad. T'ain't as if it's worth much. Sorry, Bo, I shouldn't have said that."

"It's okay, ma'am." Bo half grinned. "It ain't worth much, at that."

"Maybe there's gold under us," I said.

It was Danny's turn to grin. "Sure wish there was, but there ain't nothing under Texas but rock and dirt—and we got the rock. No, I figure Tyler wants your land because of that creek. It runs when his goes dry, so that water is gold enough for him. But anyhow, Bo, the only other way out for you is to get yourself a lawyer and fight the case."

"A lawyer!" Bo shook his head. "Nearest one is fifty miles off, and sides, he'd cost more than the land's worth."

"True enough," Danny said. "Keep away from them vultures if you can. They'll pick you clean to the bone. Anyhow"—he scratched his chin—"you know, maybe there's something in it at that, going North. Maybe you'll make some money, and you'll see something of the world while you're still young. What do you think, Ma?"

Mrs. Farley shook her head. "I don't, Dan . . . but it seems like there ain't anything else for it, 'cepting they can raise the money."

"No chance of that," Bo said. "So it's leaving. Kind of hard at that, letting the land go."

"And your folks here for three generations," Mrs. Farley said. "That's a long time."

"Sure is," Danny said. "It surely is."

We sat around in kind of a morbid silence, then we headed home, and I've had better rides in my life, believe me.

Since there wasn't nothing else we could do, we took Danny's advice. We told Tyler we were ready to go and Bo gave all our stuff to Mrs. Farley because that didn't go with no legal note. The folks around us gave a fare-thee-well and most everyone came, except Tyler and his missus. It was a real nice gathering, with pies and cookies, and everyone saying how sorry they was that we was going but that they thought we was doing the right thing at that, and if *they* was twenty years younger they'd do the same thing because there wasn't anything for two sparks like us in Clement, and there was some truth in that. They'd rustled up some presents, too, which was really fine of them because not many folks there had two dollars to rub against each other, but we got a checkered shirt each, and a bandana, too.

Bo mumbled some sort of speech which no one could hear, but he got clapped just the same, and then we said "So long" to everyone, we'd see them again for sure, and rode home for the last time.

It was a sad and weary journey, with whippoorwills calling, and a scritch owl following us, and coyotes howling at the moon. The cabin looked deserted already, white and ghostly in the moonlight, and I guessed it wouldn't be long before the pack rats moved in.

I said that to Bo as we bedded down. He lay on his back for a while, then said, "Ben, there's a rat moving in tomorrow. But I tell you, if I had that fifty bucks in my hand I'd burn the place down, so help me. Now turn in, we've a tough day ahead of us."

He rolled over and I snuggled into my blanket, but it was hard getting to sleep. Every corner of that cabin had a memory for me, and it was full of ghosts that night: Pa telling us all to be good kids before he went to the war; Keeler playing his mouth organ; Flo, when she almost died of scarlet fever . . . But then I just plain snuffled and when I did get to sleep I dreamed that Ma was wandering about the place in a real fancy dress, all moaning and crying and saying she'd spent all them fifty dollars.

But the next morning the ghosts had gone to wherever they go to and me and Bo ate up everything we could shove down us and waited for Tyler to come with the dollars.

It was around noon when he did show, and he had a feller with him who sure didn't seem fit company for a preacher. He had mean eyes, a rifle, and a six-shooter that didn't seem like no ornament. He stayed in the yard on his pony while Tyler came into the cabin—and when the preacher saw the inside, he near had a fit.

"Just what is this?" he shouted. "Where's the fittings— and where's the—the stove!"

Bo grinned and said the prairie dogs had wandered off with the stuff, but Tyler wasn't amused. No, sir. He said that the cabin and all *pertaining thereto* was rightly his. "And, by golly," he barked, "you ain't getting no fifty dollars out of me."

"What?" Bo scowled. "What are you talking about? That stuff was ours, every stick of it, and never mind that pertaining thereto, whatever the hell that means."

"Don't you blaspheme at me," Tyler said. "You remember I'm a preacher of the Gospel, boy. I've got a man moving in today. Where do you think he's going to sleep?"

"Let him bunk on the ground," Bo said. "Like we're going to do the next three months."

Tyler stomped and hollered for a while, saying as how he'd have to buy fittings and have them hauled in and how much that would cost, but in the end he calmed down and said he'd only knock ten dollars off the fifty and we could thank the Lord we were dealing with a merciful man, so we had to settle for that because there wasn't much else we could do, not with that gun-slinging hombre out there in the yard.

Tyler gave us the letter to the driver Sam Clark, and the forty dollars, which Bo signed for. Then Bo burned the legal note, and we went out and climbed on the mule with our bedrolls and the old Spencer.

Bo looked down at Tyler. "You're a preacher," he said, "like you keep telling us. Well, if I was you, I'd kind of concentrate my mind on the world to come, because you might find yourself heading there when we get back."

And then we left. Left the land we were born on, and the land our folks had worked and died on, and headed out, to whatever the future might bring us.

■ **FOUR** ■

Tyler had told us to meet Clark at a town called Lookout, north of us, so we headed there, sometimes doubling up on the mule, and, more often than not, me walking.

It wasn't much short of a week's journey, and wearisome days they was, going through desolate country, a lot of it just badlands, Bo and me sleeping out, not even making a fire in case it brought company, and thinking every crackle in the sage was maybe wild Comanches, because that's when they came down off the Plains, when the grass was fresh and they could feed their ponies. But the only rider we saw on the whole trip was a feller and we rode well clear of him, and he rode well clear of us, maybe because Bo pulled out the Spencer, casual-like. Apart from him, the only other folks we saw was a family in a cabin who were the poorest white folks I ever did see, but they gave us sowbelly and corn bread and wouldn't take a dime for their trouble.

Course, the first thing we'd done when we left home was open Tyler's letter because, like Bo said, knowing him, it might say "Shoot on sight," but it was okay, saying we was two good, hardworking Texas boys and Clark should take us on, so that wasn't too bad.

For the first couple of days we plodded along in a gloomy silence, but as we moved on I got to feeling better. In fact, I was excited about going to new places and meeting new people and being a real rider and all. Not that Bo was full of the joys of spring about riding. He said that watching cowboys was a sight better than being one. But I didn't pay no heed. I was looking forward to getting new duds, a genuine hat and riding boots, and a six-shooter, too. But Bo just sniffed and told me not to count my chickens before they was hatched.

That was our last night out and we were sitting hunched up in our blankets. I asked Bo what he meant about them chickens, but he just grunted and turned in. I lay awake, though, wondering about them chickens and trying to figure out what Bo had in mind, and I didn't like what I figured because I got a sneaky notion that he didn't intend for me to go North with him! And no matter how much I told myself that was plumb nonsense, still and all, I spent most of that night counting the stars, so I was bleary-eyed the next day when we rode through good grazing land and hit Lookout.

It beat Sweetwater all out, but it still wasn't much of a burg, a real one-horse town with a couple of stores, a livery stable, an eating house, a marshal's office, a few people who looked like they wished they lived someplace else, and a saloon called the Long Horn, which, like Bo said, must have made it about the thousandth saloon in Texas carrying that name.

That was where Tyler had told us to ask for Clark, so we moseyed in, and that was the first time I'd been in a saloon in my born days, and it wasn't nothing to write home about, at that. Just a bar with some bottles behind it, a few chairs and tables, and a big picture which I thought was a storm on the prairies until I got close and saw it was called *Davy Crockett at the Alamo!*

The place was empty, unless you counted the millions of flies buzzing around, but when Bo yelled, a feller came from the back. Bo ordered two beers, saying I might as well try the stuff, and it did cut the dust but it tasted awful and I couldn't see the sense in paying ten cents for it when water did the same thing for free.

Still, I felt kind of swagger, leaning up against the bar— well, to be honest, I could just about get my chin over it— and drinking beer, and I did wonder how long it would be before I could get into cussing.

The barman swatted a few flies with a towel, lit a cigar, and studied us for a while. "That your mule out there?" he asked.

"Sure is," Bo said.

The barman chewed on his stogie. "I got feed. Cheaper than the livery stable."

Bo said he'd bear that in mind. Then I guess he figured

29

the courtesies had been observed, as Ma used to say, because he went on. "We're looking for a drover, name of Sam Clark. You got any idea where he might be?"

"I could make a guess," the barman said. "But guessing makes me kind of dry."

Bo muttered something under his breath and slammed a dime down.

"That's kind of you," the barman said. He pulled a beer—"Here's to you, pilgrims"—and he took a drink.

"So where is he?" Bo asked.

"Where's who?" the barman said.

"Goddamn," Bo snapped. "Sam Clark."

"Oh, him!" The barman laughed and slid the dime back. "I ain't charging for information—yet." And he winked at me. "So, Sam . . . well . . ." He counted on his fingers. "I guess he's near enough to the Red River by now."

"What!" Bo yelled. "What's that you say?"

"The Red," the barman said. "He took his herd out a week ago."

I thought Bo had gone plain loco. He threw his hat down and kicked it clean across the room and his language wasn't fit for no prayer meeting, believe you me.

The barman looked at Bo over his stogie. "You're mighty hot under the collar, son. I don't aim to interfere, but what's your problem?"

Bo finished cussing and kicking and told the story and the barman shook his head. "You just got here too late, is all."

"But lightning," Bo said. "Down in Clement County they ain't even begun the spring roundup yet."

"Is that a fact?" The barman raised his eyebrows. "Up here it's all over and done with, and Sam lit out as soon as he could. Looks like you've had a ride for nothing, boys."

"You can say that again," Bo muttered. The barman didn't, because a couple of fellers came in who gave us a good stare and he went to serve them, but not before Bo got himself another beer.

We sat in a corner and Bo cussed again. "Jehoshaphat!" He spat, and he spat it again, hissing away like a snake, but as that didn't seem to be doing much for us, I asked him what we was going to do next.

"I know what I'd like to do," Bo said. "I'd like to ride back to Clement and plug that goddamn Tyler right between the eyes." He cussed some more, but when he'd cooled down somewhat, he said, "I don't know, kid. We're in kind of a fix here."

"I don't see that," I said. "There's got to be other herds going through."

Bo shook his head. "It don't work the way you're thinking. Herds coming up from the South already have a gang, and if there was a herd from around here, well, the boss takes the boys who've done the roundup. And anyhow . . ." His voice trailed away and he looked down, like he didn't want to meet my eyes.

"Anyhow what, Bo?" I asked, and when he didn't answer, I asked him again, and again, until he was worn down and exhausted, like a colt being broken in, because he sighed.

"Okay. Okay. Just stop saying that, will you?" He took a swig of beer and sighed again. "It's like this. We had that letter for Sam Clark, so I figured we'd be singing, but the thing is . . . Well, I could probably get hired . . . But I just don't know about you."

"Don't know what about me, Bo?" I asked. "What is it you don't know?" And even though I asked him twice, I didn't want to know the answer.

Bo didn't want to say it, neither, but he did. Like I've said, he was as honest as the day is long. "The thing is, Ben, you're just a kid, and there ain't much of you at that, and I don't know that any trail boss is going to want to take you on."

And that's what I knew he was going to say, and had known all along, and what I didn't want to hear noway, and all them fears I got about being left alone came bubbling up, and I was all shaky as I said, "That ain't so. I can ride, you know I can. And I'm mighty strong, too. I can hold my own." And then it poured out like a freshet after a storm. "Bo, you ain't going to leave me, are you? You ain't going to leave me on my lonesome out here? Tell me, Bo, you got to. Don't leave me here with just half them dollars." And I began to cry! It's true. There I was in a real saloon and I was snuffling like a baby.

Bo stared at me like chaparral was sprouting out of my ears. "Cut out this weeping," he said. "You hear me? You'll get us thrown out. They don't let no crybabies in saloons."

I got mad then. If all Bo cared about was being thrown out of a saloon while his own kin was heartbroken, then he could go to—to the Bad Place. But when I looked up to tell him so, he was grinning, like he used to when he was teasing me in the old days.

"You sure take after Ma," he said. "Your head's just stuffed full of ideas. You think I'd leave you? We're brothers, Ben, and we're going to look out for each other." He smiled, and he sure did have a nice smile, too, but he spoiled the effect by sticking in: "And just where the heck did you get that notion that you'd have half of the dollars?"

Still, I quit snuffling, wiped my nose, and asked again what we were going to do.

Bo stuck his hat on. "One thing we're sure going to do is get ourselves a square meal. Come on, I might even spring you a piece of that pie you've been hungering after."

We fixed up with the barman about the mule and then went over to the eating house and had a beefsteak each with eggs and greens and browned hash and a big slice of melon pie—in fact, I had two slices—and about six cups

32

of coffee. It surely was some meal. In fact, it was the first good meal we'd had for about six months and I felt real fine after it, and I told Bo that.

"Yeah," he said. "And so you should after near a dollar's worth of grub. Beats all, don't it?"

I reckoned it did, and it was near two dollars, seeing as how we'd both had a meal, and I started doing a little figuring. Eating out like that and our forty bucks wasn't going to last long, and Bo was on the same trail because he said we'd be going back on beans, and when the woman who ran the joint came over, he asked about work in the neighborhood.

She seemed a nice old lady, like you see in picture books about the West, with a gingham dress and a checkered apron, and kind eyes, sort of like the ma you wished you'd had, you know? She sat down and smoothed out her apron. "Well, now," she said. "What sort of work was you boys thinking of?"

"Most anything for a while, ma'am," Bo said.

"We could do with a good shoemaker in town," the old lady said.

Bo went red because his riding boots was busting out at the heels and toes, and I was wearing cowhide boots which would have fitten easy on a mule. "That ain't exactly our line, ma'am," he said. "But we know about farming, and I've done plenty of riding."

The old lady shook her head. "Not much of either around here. I guess there is some rough work, but there's some nigger families and they do most of that, and you wouldn't want to work for nigger wages, would you?"

Bo allowed that we wouldn't, kind of rueful at that, and the old lady peeked at us. "Just what are you boys doing here?" she asked.

No man would have asked us that direct because the

33

answer might be the Texas Rangers was after us, which would have been embarrassing all around, but it was all right coming from an old lady, so Bo told her.

When he finished, the lady looked real dolesome. "That's a sad and sorry tale," she said. "Two homeless orphan boys roaming the land. Why, it's just like after the war, them soldier boys wandering about who'd lost . . . their families and their homes—all they had. Land's sakes . . ." Her eyes went wet, and mine was watering, too. It sure seemed sad, like something out of a story, although, truth to tell, I didn't give two hoots for them soldier boys. It was me and Bo I was sad for.

The lady rocked awhile, then asked if we'd anyplace to stay. Bo said we hadn't yet, and the lady did some more rocking. "There's a rooming house, but you boys need to watch what money you might have, hmmm . . ."

She brooded, like she was trying to make up her mind about something, and I got a hopeful feeling that maybe she was going to adopt us and look after us, doing the washing and giving us beefsteaks and cookies and pies and all, but all she said was, "There's a shed out back and you can sleep there free tonight, if you want. Now I've got to clear this table."

She jumped up mighty quick for an old woman and just brushed us out. But at the door Bo turned and thanked her, and nudged me to do the same.

"That's all right," she said. "I'd give a stray dog shelter! Say, why don't you hunt up the preacher? He might know of some work, and the marshal, he knows everyone, seeing as how he's the barber as well. Tell him I sent you. Widow Hatton."

She almost shoved us through the door, then called out, "You could have beans tonight, only fifteen cents!"

We moseyed down the street. Bo was looking thoughtful, and so was I, because I didn't take too kindly to that there remark about stray dogs. Bo said we'd go see the marshal because he was just plain sick of preachers, but when we got to the marshal's office, it was shut up, with a sign on the door saying "Out for lunch."

"Well, I swan," Bo said. "This just ain't our day, Ben."

He could say that again. It wasn't our day, and it wasn't our year, neither. It was like that Fate had marked us down as I heard a feller say once, although why it should have picked on us beat me.

There was a boardwalk outside the office, so we hunkered down and looked at what there was of Lookout, and you could see why it got its name, because it looked right back at us. A storekeeper across the street came out pretending to sweep up, but giving us the eye; the blacksmith must have thought we was more interesting than the horse he was shoeing; a feller in a buggy drove past, then came back again, staring; and a woman passing with two kids ran her glims over us and sniffed. And I guess we cut a strange pair, Bo looking a regular rider, or maybe, the state he was in, a bank robber giving himself up, and me, a raw country boy with everything I was wearing either too big, too little, or too old.

We squatted there, Bo with one leg stretched out, real cowboy-style. I tried it, too, but fell over, so I just sat. Time passed, the sun beat down, a dog, which was a real Lookout dog, came and gave us a good staring at, and then I asked Bo what he was thinking.

"Nothing much," he said.

"Still," I said, "we got ourselves somewhere to sleep tonight."

Bo spat into the street. "Yeah, in a woodshed, and beans for supper."

I didn't like to hear Bo talk like that. I wanted him to be cheerful so's he would cheer me up, too, so I prodded him that way.

35

"That widow woman is a real nice old lady," I said.

"Maybe." Bo spat again. "She ain't running no charity, though."

"Come on, Bo," I said. "She ain't charging us none for that shed."

"I heard her," Bo said. "And I saw a big heap of cordwood next to it. I reckon we'll be doing some sawing today."

I sighed. "Bo, I wish we was back in Clement right now."

"No good wishing," Bo said. "Wouldn't make no difference, anyhow. We ain't got no home there neither."

I didn't like that. I didn't like that one bit. No home! No kin to turn to, neither. Like the Widow Hatton had said, it was like something out of a storybook.

"Still," Bo went on. "We ain't got no ace in the hole here, but maybe we got dealt a queen at that."

"What're you talking about poker for?" I said, somewhat irritable.

Bo looked sideways at me. "You never heard about widow women?"

"Sure," I said. "What do you take me for? They're women who've lost their men, is what."

Bo grinned. "Kid, even if you weren't my born brother, I guess I'd take you along just to cheer me up when I get blue. Don't you know widow women can be kind of frisky?"

It took a while for that to sink in, but when it did, I felt like I'd been hit with a rock. "Bo!" I said. "Hey . . . you don't mean . . . you mean you aim to spark with her! Bo, she's an old woman!"

Bo laughed out loud, all spluttering and coughing. "You've got some catching up to do in life, Ben. I'll stake my wad she ain't a day over thirty-five."

He started laughing all over again, and he was still at it when I heard footsteps on the boardwalk, looked up, and saw a man staring down on us.

He wasn't a big man, but he wasn't small neither, sort

36

of bulging in the shoulders, and he didn't carry no hand-gun, but on his vest he had a marshal's star.

He gave us the glim, the way I've seen lawmen do every-place I've roamed, like they're fixing you in their minds, and maybe matching you to a wanted poster, and you can be pure as the driven snow but it makes you feel guilty as all get-out, at that.

"You boys want something?" he asked, and his voice wasn't exactly overflowing with the milk of human kindness.

We jumped up and swiped the dust off our pants and Bo said the Widow Hatton had told us to call.

"Yeah?" The marshal waved us into his office. It had a rolltop desk, a stove with a battered coffeepot, some wanted posters, a couple rifles chained in a cupboard, a few beat-up chairs, a barber's chair, a mirror and washbasin, and a pokey at the back I didn't like the look of.

"Relax," the marshal said. "You ain't going in there un-less you've broken the law. You ain't, have you?"

I said I surely hadn't, and he said that was okay then and sat in the barber chair, bit a plug of tobacco, rolled it around his cheek, then spat neatly into a spittoon. "So what's on your mind?" he asked.

Bo sort of groaned and I knew just how he felt. It was the third time he'd had to tell the tale in Lookout and we'd not been there but three hours. But he hauled his way through it and said, "That's it."

The marshal spat again and he didn't look at us with pity, like we was poor orphans in the storm. In fact, his eyes were all fishy and cold. "Let me see that letter," he said. "And the cash."

Bo didn't take kindly to that, but he turned around and got the stuff out of a secret pocket he had in his pants and handed it over. The marshal looked at them, then gave them back.

"Don't flash them bills around," he said. "This is an honest town, but it ain't that honest." He brooded for a while, swiveling in the chair. "Well, boys," he said at last, "my advice is that you move on."

"Move on just where?" Bo asked.

"That's entirely up to you," the marshal said. "But you might want to head for Waco."

"Waco," Bo said.

"That's the place." The marshal spat again. "It's slap-bang on the Chisholm Trail, a real cow town. But it's up to you. It's a free country."

"Free," Bo said.

"So they tell me." Tobacco juice went *zing*. "But I reckon you've got the message."

"We got it," Bo said. "We got it loud and clear."

"I'm glad to know it. So long now."

We said so long, or at least I did, and we headed out, but then the marshal asked if we was aiming to stay overnight, and when Bo said we was, he asked if we'd got any weapons.

"A Spencer," Bo said. "And a Colt handgun."

"That's reasonable," the marshal said. "Park them here, pronto. And close the door when you leave—keeps out the flies."

Bo closed the door right enough. In fact, he closed it so hard it near fell off its hinges. Then he stalked down the street so fast I almost had to run to keep up with him, and he stalked right into the Long Horn and swung them batwing doors so hard they almost knocked my teeth out.

"Back again, boys?" The barman was still swatting flies. "How do you like Lookout?"

Bo glared at him, grabbed a beer, sat in that corner, and glared at me.

"What are you so burned up for?" I asked.

He looked at me like I was a real half-wit. "Joshua! That marshal, you did notice him, didn't you?"

"Come on, Bo," I said. "Sure I did. He was kind of nice." I laughed. "And he's a barber!"

"I'd like to barber your mind, if you've got one," Bo said. "You heard him, didn't you? Like, you actually *heard* him?"

"Sure," I said—well, actually I whispered this. "He told you to watch out for them dollars."

"Ben." Bo spoke slow, again, like he was dealing with an idiot. "What he told us was to move on, and keep moving. He dolled it up fancy, but that's what he meant. We're getting shoved on like a couple of saddle bums."

"But why?" I asked. "We ain't doing no harm—and we've got money. He saw it."

"And if he hadn't, we'd be out of town now," Bo said. "The thing is, a burg like this don't want two kids on the loose hanging around. They're probably scared we'll rob the poor box."

"Oh," I said. I chewed that over, and then I got a thought, a real bad one. "But, Bo, that means . . . well . . . I mean, we could be wandering forever!"

"You said it."

Bo finished his beer, we collected our bedrolls, parked the hardware at the marshal's, got a receipt, and went back to the Widow Hatton's, and just as Bo had said, there was the woodpile, and next to the shed, like it might be a co-incidence, a bow saw and an ax, and the widow, who said she figured that two fine Texan boys would be too proud to accept charity, meaning you know what.

We sawed and chopped until dusk, when the widow hollered that the beans were ready. Bo put on his new shirt and bandana, which did make him look pretty sharp, and I thought if a widow woman wanted to spark with anyone, then she could do worse than him. But I thought wrong, because when we went in for supper there was a species of human gorilla in a fancy vest chomping away at a beef-steak, and he made it kind of clear that if there was any sparking going to take place, he'd be doing it. So, when we bedded down in the shed, I was beginning to think I wouldn't mind moving out of Lookout one little bit. No, sir, not one little bit at all.

▪ FIVE ▪

Bo must have been thinking the same thing because, come dawn, he told me we were bidding adieu to the fair town of Lookout. He said it was because we might as well do what the marshal had said and try our luck at Waco, but I had a sneaky suspicion it was because of that there gorilla—but I didn't say so.

Bo sprung fifty cents on ham and eggs and all the trim-mings for breakfast, saying it could be a long while before we got another good meal, but it was soured somewhat by the sight of the gorilla gnawing another beefsteak and being fussed over by the Widow Hatton.

She fussed over us, too, telling us how sorry she was. But she took the fifty cents, and like Bo said, when we went to collect the shooting irons, she wasn't sorry enough to ask us to stay. "Because we'd finished off the wood," he said.

The marshal wasn't in, but a feller waiting for a shave gave us the guns and then we hoofed it to the saloon, got the mule from out the back, and the barman told us how to hit the trail to Waco, saying it was a long trail and a hard one, which surely did dampen me down, and then he asked if we'd seen the marshal.

"No, we ain't," Bo said. "Why? Do you need a pass to get out of this town?"

"Nothing like that," the barman said. "Only he looked for you in here last night."

"Yeah?" Bo got hold of the mule's bridle. "Well, tell him from the Curtis boys that he'll look till kingdom come before he sees us again."

"Just passing the message," the barman said.

"Sure. Let it pass." Bo heaved on the bridle. "Come on, Ben."

We walked to the end of the main street, watched by most everyone in town, the which was about ten people. Then Bo climbed on the mule and we headed out.

"Why do you think the marshal wanted us, Bo?" I asked.

"Knowing that town, he probably wanted to charge us rent for holding the guns," he said. "Now quit talking and get going."

We moved on and it was pretty fine country at that, good grass, streams, trees, the birds whooping it up, and it should have been a pleasure passing through it on a fine spring morning, but I didn't feel like no meadowlark and that's for sure. Apart from the long haul ahead, I was worried about the marshal, thinking maybe there was a wanted poster with a dead-or-alive reward for two pilgrims our age and that the marshal had got the idea we'd fit the bill as well as any, so as I plodded along I kept looking over my shoulder, you know? And then I *really* looked.

"What the heck are you doing now?" Bo asked.

"Well," I said, "you know that kingdom come you was talking about back there?"

"What of it?" Bo asked, all testy.

"Why, nothing," I said. "But I guess it's the Day of Jubilee, because it looks like that marshal is right on our tail."

Bo near fell off the mule turning around, and it was true

41

enough. The marshal was coming after us at a good lick, waving his hand, and when he reached us he was madder than a steer with a branding iron on it.

"You boys," he shouted. "You knew I'd been looking for you. Why didn't you come and see me?"

"We called in," Bo said.

"Yeah, but that tomfool Mike Gray didn't hold you."

"Hold us for what?" Bo was real defiant. "We ain't done nothing wrong, saving breathing the air for free is an offense in Lookout."

"Now, don't you get sniffy with me," the marshal said. "I've ridden six miles to find you."

"Well, now you have," Bo said. "Just what can we do for you? And we don't need no haircuts today."

The marshal got red in the face. "It was what I could do for you," he said. "But I reckon a smarty-pants like you don't need no favors doing, which is fine by me."

He started to pull his pony away, but I stuck my spur in then. "Marshal," I said, all meek and mild. "Marshal, we'd be mighty grateful for *any* favor, and Bo's sorry he spoke like that. It's just he's all wore out with worry—ain't you, Bo?" And I gave him a good bang on the knee so's he'd get the message.

He did at that, because he changed his tune. "Yeah," he said. "We would, Marshal."

"Okay." The marshal was somewhat mollified. "Okay. It so happens that there's a herd moving through not far from here. The trail boss was in town last night. One of his riders broke a leg and he's looking for another man. It's maybe worth a try."

Bo pushed his hat back. "Why, that's mighty fine of you, Marshal. It surely is and we truly thank you."

"That's all right." The marshal was gruff. "You cut across the prairie there and you come to a creek. Follow that upstream and you'll find the herd. Ask for Joe Dutton. I ain't promising nothing, mind."

"No promises necessary," Bo said. "But it's a good deed you've done."

"Nothing to it." The marshal spat out a stream of tobacco juice. "You cut along now, and good luck to you."

"Good luck to you," we chimed and waved our hats as he turned and headed back for town.

"Well, I'll be." Bo shook his head. "Who would have thought that? It just goes to show, there is some good folks in the world. So"—he whacked his hat back on—"what are we waiting for! Mount up!"

I didn't need asking twice. I climbed on behind Bo and we prodded the mule across the prairie and, sure enough, there was a creek, and after an hour or so we knew that we were near the herd because we could hear them lowing, and we could smell them, too, and if you've never smelled a thousand head of cattle, you've something to learn in life.

We couldn't actually see the herd, but on a bluff by some cottonwoods there was a chuck wagon, and a fire, and a cook. Bo told me slide off the mule.

"Might look better," he said, and I got the notion. Bo was the real rider and it wasn't going to hurt none to make a good impression, although I did wonder whether arriving on a mule was the best way to do that, and I wasn't far wrong neither, because when the cook saw us he cackled and said, "Where's the plow, boys?"

I was a mite leery hearing that, Bo having such a quick temper, but he just laughed, easy as may be, said we'd lost it in a poker game, and swung off the mule, and to tell the truth, he looked more the part off it than he had on it.

The cook gave us the eye, but I guess we measured up because he said to help ourselves to coffee, and I was feeling more joyful by the minute. After all that roaming around on our own, and then lashing out cash in Lookout, and sawing wood for Widow Hatton, it was just fine being with our own kind, as you might say, and getting coffee for free. Nowadays it's like dog eat dog, but that wasn't the way on the old open range. I never saw no one who looked halfway decent ever turned away from a campfire, nor a cabin, come to that, even if all you got was flapjacks, and it wasn't no handout neither. After all, you never knew when it might be your turn to have an empty belly and no cash.

That coffee was good, too, black as sin and bitter, and while we drank, the cook stirred his pot. "Antelope stew," he said, "with real carrots. If you want to stick around, you're welcome."

"Much obliged," Bo said. "And we sure would like some, it smelling so good"—which he stuck in to be what they call diplomatic, because the stew didn't smell so good at that. "But right now we're looking for Joe Dutton."

The cook, who was called Charlie McCann, lit a stogie with a stick from the fire, and I noticed he wasn't particular where the ash went, like in the pot. "Here he comes," he said. He pointed with the stick and we could see three riders coming in. "And he's like that coffee you're drinking. Strong and bitter."

I moaned, and the cook grinned. "It's okay, kid. Joe is just fine—if you're ready to work your back off twenty-four hours a day."

"Right now I'm ready to work twenty-five," Bo said as the riders came in and climbed off their ponies.

"Mr. Dutton?" Bo stepped forward.

"That's me." Dutton was a tall jasper with a big mustache and big eyebrows kind of balancing it, and wearing a swell hat. He just turned his back on us. "Get them remounts, Tom. Jack, get me some coffee."

Bo tried again. "Mr. Dutton." But Dutton turned away

again. "Tom," he yelled, "make sure the wrangler looks at that roan's off hind leg. Now"—he finally took real heed of us—"what do you two want?"

Bo opened his mouth but closed it again while that feller Jack, who was a hard-looking bozo, handed Dutton his coffee. Dutton swigged some, then said, "What was that you was saying?"

Bo gulped, like he was controlling his temper, but he went through the tale again and handed over Tyler's letter.

Dutton read it and looked at Bo, up and down and side to side, like he might be buying a horse. In fact, I thought he was going to look at Bo's teeth. Then he flicked the letter with his finger.

"You seem a might saintly according to this."

Bo flushed. "I ain't no saint," he said.

"Don't really matter what you are," Dutton observed. "Thing is, can you ride?"

"Sure can," Bo said. "I've been around cattle three years, on and off. Worked roundups, too."

"But you never trailed a herd before, did you?" Dutton said.

"No, I ain't," Bo admitted. "But there was a time when you never did neither."

"That's the truth," Dutton said. "Well, maybe . . ." He chewed his mustache awhile, and my heart was pounding because I surely wanted us to get a job—and then Dutton nodded. "Okay. A dollar a day and your grub. You got all your kit?"

"We need a few things," Bo said. "But we can get them in Lookout."

"We?" Dutton said.

"Me and my kid brother here." Bo jabbed his thumb at me.

Dutton looked at me and his eyebrows near climbed into his hat. "Him!"

Dutton's eyebrows were near enough in his hat, but my heart was near enough in my boots. It was just exactly like Bo had said. No trail boss was going to want me along, and although he had sworn never to leave me, that was in a saloon drinking beer, and this was when he was being offered a job. But he stood firm, did Bo.

"Ben's okay," he said. "I know he don't look much—"

"You can say that again," Dutton said.

"I know," Bo agreed, and I'll tell you, I was beginning to feel mad the way they was talking about me as if I was some kind of runt that couldn't stand the heat of day, but Bo went on. "He's wiry, you know, and he can ride, and anyhow, he's my brother and I ain't going to leave him. Come on, Mr. Dutton, that herd is only going to move ten, twelve miles a day."

"Yeah?" Dutton frowned. "That means ten, twelve hours in the saddle, *and* night herd, and it's every day for the next two months, Sundays included. You think he can take that?"

I didn't know what Bo was thinking, but the more Dutton went on, the less enthusiastic I got. In fact, I was thinking I'd be better off sawing wood for the widow woman, but Bo said sure I could do it, and Dutton rubbed his chin, looked at me like he didn't believe it, then said, "Okay, he can come along."

I guessed that fixed it, and I was glad at that, but Bo pushed again! "What does that mean," he said. "Come along?"

"What it says." Dutton was sharp. "He comes along and gets his grub, is all."

"But what about pay?" Bo was indignant, but not more than I was, believe me. "If he's going to do a man's work, he's entitled to a man's pay."

Too right, I thought, but thinking, too, that if it got down to the grain we'd be better off with Bo getting paid than both of us on the loose again, which I thought we was going to be, that Dutton being a tough cookie.

But instead of telling us to beat it, he said, "Sure, and if he does a day's work, he'll get his pay. Until then, take it or leave it. This herd can manage without you."

"We'll take it," Bo said, real quick, and I liked that "we" there, Bo being on a dollar a day and me on nothing, and him and Dutton shook hands, but no one shook hands with me. Me being a kid and not counting, see.

"Right," Dutton said. "Take a couple of ponies and get your kit. See Fred Withers in Lookout and tell him I sent you. He'll give you a square deal. And be back by nightfall or maybe I'll come looking for you, get me?"

"I got you, boss," Bo said, and I did, too, Dutton seeming the kind of feller who'd be handy with a rope where horse thieves were concerned.

"And get rid of that old mule," Dutton said, and strode off.

"Will do." Bo got hold of the mule, and that feller Jack who'd got the coffee for Dutton spoke up. He was a mean-looking bird, hard, you know? And he wasn't going to melt in no April shower, that was for sure.

"Mind if I look at that handgun of yours?" he asked, mild enough.

"Sure." Bo handed it over and Jack glanced at it, spun the cylinder, broke it open and squinted down the barrel, and pulled the trigger a couple of times. "Throw that in the creek," he said, "unless you want to get your hand blown off." Then he sauntered off after Dutton.

"Well, I'll be damned." Bo looked at the cook. "Who is that guy?"

"Jack Shears?" The cook grinned. "Son, I don't know no more about him than you do. But if he told me about guns, I'd listen."

"Like that, hey?" Bo said.

"Just exactly like that. He's got that look, ain't he? Have some of the five-dollar special, boys."

He ladled out some stew, and that antelope must have been a hundred years old, the meat being so stringy, and while we was getting it down, the other rider, Tom, rode over, leading a couple of ponies. We finished the grub and Bo climbed on one, riding bareback, and I got on the mule with the other pony on tow, and we headed back to Lookout, and it was just amazing the difference. Instead of being two kids on the loose, why, we were genuine riders with regular jobs and money coming in, instead of going out and free-grubbing, and I was half thinking that maybe Ma had done us a favor at that, making the place over to Tyler.

Anyways, we got into town and found Fred Withers's store, and it was some treat for me because it was the first time in my life I'd ever bought store clothes. I got a hat, a vest, Levi's, a real good pair of riding boots, and Texan spurs with big rowels. I'd never liked them, nor them savage bits the riders stuck in ponies' mouths, because raking a pony's sides and tearing its tongue went clean across the grain with me, but Bo said for me to just wait until I was on the range on a spooky pony and I'd be glad of them. Then we picked ourselves a couple of handguns.

Sounds sinister, don't it, but you'd have the wrong idea entirely if you thought so. In dime novels you read about cowboys blasting away like Deadwood Dick, but it wasn't like that at all. Most cowboys couldn't hit a barn door at ten paces, and the real riders, they didn't go shooting at each other, any difference of opinion got settled in a genteel fashion, like them beating each other senseless. But them six-shooters came in handy, which I found out later.

That Withers, though, he was some kind of salesman. He tried to sell us fancy engraved Colts, saying they was the best and only the best riders used them and more such nonsense, but Bo said as long as we had handguns that went bang and didn't blow up they would do us, so we settled for a couple of used .32s, trading in Bo's Colt and the Spencer, and Bo made Withers go out back behind the store and loose off a couple of slugs himself to make sure they was safe.

But we hadn't finished, at that. We went to the saddler's and that's where Bo really got to work. There was a kind of dummy horse in there and Bo made me try every saddle in the place, him fussing away adjusting the stirrups and getting me to sit against the crupper because we was using a McClellan saddle, not at all like the saddles you might see at the racetrack. No, sir, they was real working saddles, built as solid and secure as an armchair, and when they got broke in, as comfortable, and they needed to be because you could be sitting in one from dawn till dusk. There used to be an old cowboy song, "A twenty-dollar saddle on a five-dollar horse," and there was truth in that, and sense, which is why I've seen riders bet every last stitch they had on in a card game, but draw the line at their saddles.

And that was the truth about all of a cowboy's rig. None of it was for show. Them big hats kept off the rain and the sun and, more important, hail, and out on the prairies you could get hailstones as big as your fist. Them bandanas around your mouth kept you from choking with dust. And high heels on your boots kept you locked in the stirrups, and if you've ever ridden through thorn brush, you'll know why you needed chaps. We had to get me a lariat, too, and you might think, well, okay, a rope's a rope, but Bo was particular over that, too, although, seeing as how we weren't going on no roundup, I couldn't see the sense in it. But that's the way Bo was. He liked getting right, and he got me a quirt, sort of a short whip most riders favored.

Then all that was left was chaps, which was a problem because all them in the store was too big for me, but the saddler cut a pair down, and I was all fixed. I felt mighty proud, too, standing there all rigged out like a real genuine Texas rider. Then Bo burst out laughing!

"What's so darn funny?" I asked.

Bo laughed again, fit to burst. "Nothing," he said. "Nothing"—hawing away. "It's just you look like a kind of midget cowboy!"

I sure didn't see nothing funny about that, and said so, but when I stepped to the door my gun belt slipped clear down my legs and I tripped right over it.

Bo and the saddler was laughing like jackasses, and I might have plugged them both if I could have reached my handgun, but Bo slapped me on the back and said not to mind some joshing because I'd just have to get used to it. The saddler poked another hole in my belt so it fitted, although Bo said it hardly mattered because I wasn't actually going to wear it much, and when we went out I saw what he meant, since walking around with a couple of pounds of steel dangling from your waist ain't exactly the most comfortable way of proceeding—not if you were my height and weight, anyhow.

So that left just one piece of business to do, which I wasn't looking forward to, which was getting rid of the mule. They ain't the most lovable animals God ever made, but ours had been around near as long as I'd been, and it was the last link with home. But there was nothing for it, so we went to the livery stable and offered it for sale, and blame me if the liveryman didn't burst out laughing!

It sure was a day for comicalness in Lookout, but Bo just grinned and said some nigger family could get a couple of years' work out of it, and in the end we got two bucks.

"And I know what we're going to do with them," Bo said. "We'll get ourselves another feed, because that widow woman might not know much about charity but she sure can cook."

I didn't want to, because that spending had made a dent

in our cash, but Bo said what the hell, he was going to eat, so I joined him, and after that he had a couple of beers, saying they would be the last till the Lord knew when, and we called on the marshal and thanked him, and he said there was nothing to it and he'd see us on the way back.

And that was that. We mounted up, and despite all that laughing, I surely did feel like someone and something, on a real cow pony, leaning back in the saddle, looking down on the world for a change, instead of up from the dirt.

But there was one thing bothering me, nagging away there at the back of my mind, and I said it. "Bo," I said, "that rider with Dutton, not the hombre who told you about the gun, the other one."

"Yeah?" Bo said, somewhat tight-lipped.

"Well . . ." I said. "Bo, he's a nigger!"

"I saw him," Bo said.

"But, Bo—" I looked sideways at him. "Bo, I just hates niggers."

Bo slapped his pony's neck. "They ain't my favorite breed neither. But you get them riding herd, plenty of them. Greasers—that is, Mexicans—too. And the thing is, I wouldn't bunk with one nohow, but out here . . . That's the way it is, and I reckon we'll just have to rub along with it. Swallow it, is all."

That didn't make me feel no better, but if Bo said that was the way of it, that was the way, so I clammed up and just enjoyed the ride across that sweet land in the purple gloaming, with the whippoorwills calling and the moon rising, calm and steady, until we saw the glow of the camp-fire like a signal saying, Come on home, boys.

SIX

We hailed the camp, which was the polite way of approaching, like knocking on a door, as you might say, got a holler back, and rode in.

Dutton was there with some fellers, sitting around the fire. "Get yourselves some coffee," he said, which was an agreeable start to the proceedings.

"These here are Bo Curtis and the little shrimpy kid is his brother, Ben. You'll get to know each other."

We got our coffee, and I was somewhat sore about that shrimpy bit but remembered about the joshing Bo had mentioned, so didn't say nothing.

"Okay." Dutton stood by the fire with the light flickering on his face and he looked a boss right enough, and what he said showed him to be so.

"The boys here know the score, but I'll spell it out for you two so there's no misunderstanding. First off, no drinking, so if you've got a bottle stashed away, get rid of it—and I don't mean down your gullet. Second, no fighting. You get a grudge, settle it when you're paid off. Third, you ride where I tell you, and no goddamn arguments. Four, depending on how we get along, you might get a break someplace, but don't depend on it, we already lost a day, and if we go straight through, that's it. Five, don't think you're going to sit around the campfire all night yarning. Lights out are when I say so. Six, no gambling."

We said "Yole," although I can't say we was jumping over the moon, but Dutton hadn't finished. "Them's the six commandments, but there's maybe one more. Don't complain about the grub. Right, Charlie?"

"You said it." The cook banged the coffeepot with the

ladle like he was ready and willing to rattle your brains with it.

The boys laughed dutifully, as if they'd heard it before, but still it was some kind of joke.

"Right," Dutton said. "Any questions?"

I shrugged, but Bo said, "Just one, boss. I'd kind of like to know where we're going."

"Oh, that. Sure." Dutton pointed to a star in the sky. "See that?"

"Reckon so," Bo said. "The folks up there don't eat beef, do they?"

"Might at that if they've got any sense," Dutton said. "No. That's the North Star, son, and we're going to follow it, all the way to Abilene, Kansas. So, another half hour, boys, and we'll call it a draw. I'll go take a peek at the herd, and when I come back, it's bedtime."

He strode off, and the boys relaxed and got themselves more coffee and gave us the glad hand, although I didn't catch their names right then. But they seemed a decent bunch. I got some more of that antelope stew—and the cook sure could have done with a lesson from Widow Hatton—and leaned back against my saddle, listening to the boys talk to Bo.

That herd was from a hundred miles south. Some ranchers had got their three-year-old steers together and Dutton was their agent, as it were, on pay and commission. The steers had all been branded with a trail brand as well as their own, and the boys around the fire had been on the roundup, so they knew each other well enough. Jack Shears, who'd told Bo about the handgun, was a stranger like us, but he was out on first-night herd with the nigger, which suited me. The other thing I gathered was that we was heading northeast, to hit the Chisholm Trail. That was all I learned that night because Dutton came back and the

53

rest of us turned in, saving me, because Dutton said I needn't take my turn on herd that night. He said it like he was giving me fifty bucks, and then kind of took it back by saying I had to wash the dishes, which I thought was a heck of a way to start being a wild and woolly cowboy.

But I did the chores and snugged down next to Bo and lay looking at the sky and I surely felt good. The stars was as bright as a girl's eyes, the wind was murmuring in the cottonwoods, the fire was glowing, and I was plumb full of free grub. It was comforting, at that. Not like when me and Bo was out on the prairie on our own, eating cold beans and jumping at every sound. Yes, sir, I was one happy cowboy for sure, and I slept like a baby.

I wasn't woken like one, though. Someone booted my feet and Bo hauled me up by the scruff of the neck, and before I could rub the sleep from my eyes, I had a plate of beans inside me and a mug of coffee which tasted like it had been made by someone who didn't like the human race too much.

Dutton was striding around sounding mighty sharp. "Come on, you buckaroos," he was shouting. "Jump to it. Goddamn, we'll still be here at noon, the way you're moving."

Well, the way we was moving, *I* reckoned we'd be half-way to Abilene by then, but Dutton wasn't kidding. He emptied the coffeepot on the fire so there wouldn't be no lingering.

When the boys went for their ponies, he turned to me. "Help Charlie get fixed up," he barked. "Then grab a pony and come over to the herd. And don't be all day over it."

Dutton was rough, and Charlie McCann wasn't any eas-ier. He rode me so that I'd done the dishes, got firewood in the wagon, and watered and harnessed the mules before he'd finished his first stogie. I'll tell you, I'd done a dollar's worth of chores before I went to the remuda to get a pony.

You hear a lot of guff these days about the cowboy and his faithful steed, as if them ponies was pets, but it wasn't that way. The thing was, on them drives there was a remuda, it being more like a herd of mounts in itself. The wrangler looked after them, and when you needed a mount, and you might switch ponies five, six times a day, he cut it out for you. After a while, you did tend to get a string of ponies kind of reserved for you, and the top riders got the best mounts. It was mighty confusing for me that first morning, looking at near a hundred ponies, but the wrangler, who was an old geezer called Amos Day, solved that, or rather Bo had, because he'd chosen one for me.

Amos saddled up and I mounted and headed out for the herd, and that was some sight. I hadn't never seen so many cattle before, over a thousand head— 1,237, Dutton told me later, and at about forty bucks a head, them figures was important—all spread out over a square mile of prairie, being roused by the boys who was riding around them, whistling and calling and cracking their quirts.

I spotted Bo, and since no one had told me different, I rode over and joined him.

"You stick close to me," he shouted, "and don't go trying nothing foolish."

I didn't need Bo to tell me that. Them longhorns was rightly named. They wasn't no dairy cattle, they was wild creatures, looking as big as houses and their horns spread out six feet and more. And there was another thing. Bo had told Dutton I could ride, and I could, if that meant I could stay on a horse if it wasn't moving too fast, but a cow pony, Jupiter! It was like being on a cat, the way it jumped and twisted and turned, darting around them steers, see, like knowing more than I did, so I was just concentrating on holding the reins, clamping my legs around the barrel, and hoping for the best—and I began to see the sense in them cruel Texan bits and spurs, too.

Well, it ain't no fool's game, rousing a thousand head of cattle and getting them in order, but them boys could handle it. Slowly they got them steers moving, not too close together, but not too strung out, neither. And I had to admit, although I sure didn't want to, and although Bo was pretty good riding there, that nigger, Tom Carney was his moniker, he looked as if he'd been born on a pony.

Anyhow, we got that herd lined up and then Dutton came riding up on a real good horse. "Drag," he shouted to Bo, "with Johnny Merill." And then to me, like I wasn't of much account: "Kid, you get down there with your brother."

I rode down the herd with Bo and he didn't look none too pleased. But I didn't pay no heed. I was a real cowboy. Earning my corn. Someone. That's what I was thinking just after sunup that fine morning. What I was thinking at sundown was another matter entirely.

When you got down to it, herding was mostly just a job of work, about as romantic as driving a streetcar, which I found out that first morning. There were usually eight riders in a trail gang, not counting the boss, the cook, and the wrangler. The riders was spread out around the herd. There was two at the front, called point; then there was two on either side, called flank and swing; and then two on drag, at the back. The best riders usually rode point, and the worst, drag, and there were better places to be on this fair earth. If you've ever seen a cow, you'll know that what goes in one end comes out the other. Multiply that a thousand times and you'll know what me, Bo, and Johnny Merill was riding through, and brother, every fly and bluebottle in Texas had joined up.

There was dust, too. Sam Clark's herd had passed that way and cut up the ground, and our herd was doing the same thing, and the dust hovered there, so we was riding through it the whole day long, which is when you blessed your bandana because without that tied around your face you would have just choked to death on dust and flies, and I began to see what Bo had meant when he said that looking at cowboys was a sight better than being one—especially on a drive.

Well, I say drive, but that's the wrong word entirely. No one in their right senses *drove* cattle. They was walked, slow and easy, keeping what fat they had on them, and that was no cinch. Them cows had to get used to the idea that they was leaving home, so you had to coax them beasts along, and coaxing a longhorn is about as easy as coaxing a grizzly bear.

But the boys knew what they was doing, point keeping the head of the herd moving the right way, swing and flank seeing no animals wandered off or stopped to graze, and Bo, Johnny, and me making sure that there wasn't no lagging and that any steers that felt homesick didn't hightail it back home, although, what with the dust and flies and smell, I kind of felt that way myself. And it didn't make me feel no better, knowing that nigger was up there riding point.

The sun got up and I was thirsty and was swigging water from my canteen when a rider came out of the dust. He was Joe Collins, who was the top hand, in charge when Dutton was away, which was every day, him and McCann taking the chuck wagon ahead after breakfast to find a good place for the noon break—that break being for the herd's benefit, not ours—and then going on again for the night camp.

"How's that pony?" Collins asked, although he didn't ask none about me.

"He ain't as frisky as he was," I said, which was so. Them Texas ponies was quick and sure-footed, but being grass-fed, they didn't win no prizes for stamina, which was why we had all them remounts in the remuda, that being a trick we'd picked up from the Comanche, who'd ride with six or seven ponies to a brave, changing every hour.

Collins ran his eyes over my pony. "Yeah," he said. "If he starts blowing too hard, you get a remount."

"Sure will," I said, and Collins reached for my canteen. He got hold of it and shook it.

"That's near empty," he said.

"Yeah," I agreed. "It's kind of dusty back here."

Collins gave me a hard look and handed the canteen back. "Better go easy on that water."

I grinned, innocent, you know? "I ain't no camel."

"No, you're a goddamn fool," Collins yelled. "What you aim to do when you're out of water?"

"Reckon I'll get some from the wagon," I said.

"Well, reckon again," Collins said. "The wagon's five miles ahead of us and you won't see it till noon, so you'd better start training to be a camel."

He cantered off and I rode over to Bo, but I didn't get no loving welcome there. "What the hell are you doing?" He shouted. "Get back over there."

"Now listen, Bo," I said, and told him about the water.

He glared at me over his bandana like he was some kind of murdering outlaw. "So you're in for a thirsty morning, ain't you. Now get back to work. This ain't no goddamn church outing."

Sure, I thought, and you can say that again, a church outing it ain't, although there was a mean-looking steer that had a resemblance to old Tyler. Still, there was nothing for it but to stick it out, and a thirsty morning it was and old Moses himself wasn't more glad to see the Promised Land than I was when we came across the wagon parked by a creek, McCann cooking and Dutton smoking a real big stogie.

Collins and the nigger had thrown the head of the herd

off the trail and we drove the rest of the steers over to them so's they could have their noon grazing, which was the routine every day. The steers ate and we ate, and although it was just flapjacks, beans, and coffee, it tasted like Widow Hatton's best to me. We had time to eat it, too, although that wasn't from no loving concern by Dutton. Them steers had to eat their fill, and if they could have done that in five minutes, we'd have been back on our ponies by then.

That nooning gave me a chance to look at the rest of the boys. I knew the cook, Charlie McCann; Joe Collins; the nigger, Tom Carney; that hard case, Jack Shears; and Johnny Merill, who rode drag with us; but I hadn't hardly passed a word with the other three: Bob Bowker, Hank Vale, and Gus King. They seemed fine boys, though, about Bo's age, free, easy, and cheerful, and with Bo they made up a kind of gang within a gang, joshing and kidding each other, while the others took it easy. As for the wrangler, Amos Day, no one paid much heed to him. I guess that seems strange, him being in charge of the ponies, but wranglers was always somewhat despised, maybe because at the end of the line they was just our servants.

So, while we was nooning, the boys joshed and gabbed, no one paying heed to me, but I kept a sharp eye out, you bet, and when I saw Dutton on the move, I was at the remuda, got me a pony, had it saddled, and was out on the range before the boys had finished their last mug of coffee, because there wasn't no way I was going to do them dishes again.

But, apart from that, I was kind of curious to see how that herd was handled and when Dutton would decide to get them moving again, and the answer to that was simple. It was when they started to lie down! They'd grazed enough, see, and ain't that just like what happens to human beings? Just when you want to relax, that's when you get prodded to get up and go.

And, like it or not, that's what happened to them steers. Just when they'd finished lunch and felt like some shut-eye, along came the boys and got them going. But them afternoon drives was always easier than the morning ones. The herd was getting thirsty by then and eager to reach water, so there wasn't much coaxing to do. In fact, as the afternoon wore on, we had to move in on the steers and ride them down, squeezing them close like, so that when we got to the campsite we had a compact herd which wouldn't start running.

So the afternoon was easier than the morning, especially as I watched my drinking, and we got to the next camp well before dusk. Dutton was waiting and we split the herd into bunches and watered them, and when that was done, and the steers had grazed and begun to chew the cud, we moved them in a circle, and Dutton liked them in a *real* circle.

"Wind 'em up," he called. "Wind 'em up," and that's what we did, and it's something to see, getting a thousand half-wild steers wound up just so, and it was something to see the boys at work, too, knowing just when to lunge at a steer and whop it, and when to lie back and ease one in. And, I had to admit again, Tom Carney was the best, ready to go right into the herd to turn a balky steer, and there weren't that many fellers keen to do that. But they all knew their jobs—saving me.

It was near full dark when we'd got the herd settled because Dutton was a hard man to please. Round and round he cantered, saying, "Wind 'em up tighter," but finally he was as satisfied as might be. "We'll do it better when they're more used to it," he said. "I've known men to disagree, but I like to see a herd wound up tighter than an eight-day clock. Don't stampede so easy."

He told six of us to get some grub, that antelope stew

again, and watched us while we ate, then told me I wasn't doing no night watch again.

"Why, thanks, boss," I said. "That's real swell of you."

"Never mind no thanks," Dutton said. "I just don't want no ignoramus out there. Stay here and help Charlie."

Well, that was better than the saddle, so I got to it, and them mules didn't know what hit them. I had them fed and watered and picketed before they knew the day's work was over, and I was quick with the dishes, too, figuring no one was going to notice a little leftover grease and gravy.

When I was done, I sat on the tailboard of the wagon next to Charlie, who was smoking a stogie, and he let me make myself comfortable before telling me to get him some coffee, which is just typical of cooks.

"And get some yourself if you want," he said. "It goes with the job. Give the boys some, too."

I got the coffeepot and poured out willingly enough, but one of them hands holding out a mug was black. I kind of halted there because, although I didn't mind too much waiting on the other fellers, serving a nigger sure went against the grain. There wasn't much I could do but pour out, and I don't know but what Carney knew what was in my mind, the stare he gave me. But he just nodded, like a thank-you nod, and said, "How you doing?"

"Getting along," I said, sounding as tough as I could, and I could have sworn there was a half smile on Carney's face.

"That's the way," he said, and lit a cigarette he'd been rolling one-handed, the way the boys learned to do.

I gave McCann his coffee, too, and got back on the tailboard.

"So you're getting along?" he said.

"Yeah," I said. "A mite sore, though."

"It'll wear off," McCann said. And I don't know whether

we was talking about the same thing there. "You'll be all right by the time we hit Indian Territory."

"Yeah," Hank Vale said. "It won't be your backside you'll worry about then, it'll be your hair."

The boys laughed, but McCann said, all serious, "That's the truth, kid, just over the Red River, that's where they'll be waiting, smacking their lips and waiting to lift your hair. You ask Tom there. He's been. Course, them Indians don't bother him none on account of him having crinkly hair. But you, with them long yellow tresses, I reckon a brave would think it mighty pretty hanging in his tepee."

"That's surely true," Hank said. "They'll be goddamn lining up for it. If I was you, I'd get Charlie to hack it off."

"Charlie!" Johnny Merill let out a howl. "Last time he cut my hair, it was *worse* than being scalped."

McCann gave a creaky sort of laugh. "You've still got both your ears, ain't you? Anyhow, it ain't you I'm worried about, it's the kid here." He looked at me sideways, like he fancied my hair, and I pulled my hat down so far I could hardly see.

Across the fire, Carney chuckled. "Don't take no heed. There's more cowboys been killed by lightning than ever were by Indians."

"And stampedes," Johnny said.

"*And* drowning," Hank added.

There was a sudden hush then, like the boys didn't want to hear no more, especially about that topic, and it was a fact that cowboys sure got the horrors, thinking about a watery end. Maybe because hardly any of them could swim. Then Dutton came in from the herd and told us all to hit the sack, so we snug down, and it didn't take me long to lose the stars that night, even though my head was all itchy.

I was rousted out that next morning, and many a weary morning after that, but life got easier as we moved on. I got used to being in the saddle all day and them raw patches inside my thighs got healed up. All of us, steers and riders alike, got used to the routine, stringing the steers out, walking them ten, fifteen miles a day, watering them, grazing them, winding them up, headed by our lead steer, a huge walleyed creature that didn't like no one or no thing near him. And maybe the most important thing of all, least-ways as far as I was concerned, I learned when to let my pony decide what to do, and when I should make the decision, although I've got to admit the pony was usually in the right of it.

I went on night guard, too, and on the middle watch at that, which meant a broken night, but saved me from doing the dishes. And, to tell the truth, I kind of liked that night herd. The way it worked was that there was two of you out there, walking your ponies around in opposite directions, keeping an eye open for any creatures like coyotes or prairie wolves which might sneak up, spook a steer, and start a stampede.

Round and round you walked the pony, singing to the steers, which everyone said soothed them, although I some-times wondered whether the real reason was to let the boss know you was awake on the job, because one thing I did notice, if any of the boys *did* stop, Dutton woke up!

But it truly was something to be out with the herd at night with the moon shining on them longhorns, which looked like a whole forest of rocking chairs, and the steers peaceful as all get-out, chewing the cud and blowing, and maybe coyotes yipping way off in the night, and listening to the other rider singing, his voice drifting across the herd. It was peaceful, you know, and kind of caring, although them boys surely did go for mournful songs, and I heard enough about poor dying cowboys to last me the rest of my days. But I remember that time, and a sound no rider ever forgot, the tinkling of them jinglebobs, which was little bells the boys liked to tie on their stirrups.

But in the daytime it was back to riding drag, for me, that is. Joe Collins swopped the boys around from time to time, although him and Carney always stayed at point, and I always stayed at drag, eating dust and swallowing flies, and looking forward to the evening, when the boys would sit around for a while, telling tall stories and gabbing about ranching life, and girls, and what have you, maybe even having a hand or two of poker, for matchsticks, seeing as how Dutton wouldn't allow no cash gambling. But as we moved along, every day getting closer to the Red River, the boys began to talk more and more about water crossings.

"What's the deal?" I asked one night. "Them steers swim, don't they, and the ponies?"

McCann shook his head, pitying-like. "They don't fly over, kid."

"Yeah, it's a shame the Lord didn't put wings on cattle," Bob Bowker said. "Thing is, kid, you get a bad river and the steers can go plumb loco and start breaking downstream, and you're in the water with them, and if you get tangled up with a longhorn, it's adios, amigos."

"Amen," Johnny said. "I crossed the Brazos once and we lost a rider. It sure is a sorry way to go to glory."

"They got a bridge there now," McCann said. "Over the Brazos. That right, Tom?"

"That's so," Carney allowed. "A feller has built what they call a *sus*pension bridge, hanging down from ropes. You pay a toll and walk the herd over, saving some bosses is so mean they still swim the steers across."

"Amazing, ain't it," Johnny said. "Save a few bucks and risk maybe a human life. Still, I reckon I'll build me a bridge someplace. Just sit back and watch the dollars roll in."

The boys sighed, like they was having a vision of dollars drifting on their heads like leaves in the fall, but that dream was broke as Dutton made us call it a day.

It was sultry, so I just draped my bedroll over me and drifted off, thinking about that bridge, which I would have liked to have seen, never having clapped my peepers on a real bridge, and I was half dreaming of the steers going over it one by one, led by old Noah, when I felt my foot being shook.

It was Dutton, which was strange because it was usually Carney or Collins who woke the men. "Get up," he whispered. "And don't make a goddamn sound."

I pulled on my boots and the entire crew was doing the same.

"Okay," Dutton said, his voice as low as could be. "Not one sound. Anyone with jinglebobs take them off. Now get your ponies and follow me."

The night ponies was picketed by the wagon and we got them and moved out behind Dutton, Indian-style. I didn't have a notion what was going on, but it was exciting at that, more like I'd thought a cowboy's life would be, and then, well out from the herd, we met Carney and stopped—and Hank whispered "Glory be!" because out there, on the horizon, the sky flashed white.

It was lightning. There was a distant rumble of thunder and then the sky flashed again and the thunder really cracked this time, and then there was another flash, blinding and going flash, flash, flash, and glowing in the middle of the flash. Then the thunder rolled toward us and it was echoed by the herd. You could hear them beginning to low, and an eerie sound it was, too, not real bawling and mooing, but like as if them steers was starting to talk to each other, anxious-like.

The sky lit up again in a huge glare, only it was south of us this time, being what they call a walking storm, now here, now there, sometimes jumping a hundred miles, and getting ready to jump right on top of us, and I remembered Carney saying more cowboys was killed by lightning than Indians! But I had to hand it to him—while the rest of us was watching the sky, he was looking at the herd, and he said, "Boss, there's some steers up."

There was some, too. In the next flash you could see animals getting off their knees, and that lowing was getting louder, and it was like it wouldn't be too long before some steer said, "Fellers, let's beat it," and then we were in trouble.

Dutton knew that, okay. "Boys," he said, "that herd is going to run. We've got to cut them off from the creek, so spread out. Quiet, now."

The lightning flared again as we pulled away, nearer this time, and it wasn't the pleasantest thought to have in your head that you were going to be on a pony with your back to a creek with a thousand crazy longhorns coming at you in the dark. I was scared as all get-out, and I was looking for Bo, when I got grabbed by the arm. I jumped, you know, and cursed, especially when I saw it was Carney.

"Kid," he muttered, "you get the hell out of here."

"What?" I couldn't have been more amazed if one of them steers had spoken to me.

"This ain't no place for you," Carney said. "Beat it, and—" He stopped. "Lord, it's raining."

It was at that. Just a few drops at first, but then a regular downpour, and I was drenched to the skin in minutes. So was Carney, of course, but he wasn't complaining.

"This'll maybe damp them down," he said.

Well, that rain did damp them steers down and the storm wandered away, and although Dutton kept us out there another hour, it was jake with us, anything rather than a stampede. And when we got back to camp, there was hot coffee and beans waiting, which is just one of the reasons why, for all the grumbles, a cook was a prized child of Creation on a cattle drive.

But although we'd been out most of the night, it didn't stop us being rousted at dawn, same as usual. Heading out, I asked Joe Collins what was that stuff about the rain and the steers, and he said, "Well, kid, not everyone agrees. I've known fellers say rain makes a herd jumpy. But if you was feeling frisky and someone threw a bucket of cold water over you, it would cool you down, wouldn't it?"

I mulled that over as we got the herd moving and we dried off in the sun, and it made some kind of sense. Steers lie down when it's going to rain, so I guessed they wouldn't get up if it was. I mulled over Carney, too. I was burned up about the way he'd grabbed me and ordered me about. I wasn't going to have no nigger handling me and telling me what to do, no, sir. Which was the most stupid, ignorant thought I ever had in my life, and I've had plenty. But, by the end of the day, I was in a sweat about it, and idiot enough to reckon I could tell Carney to remember I was a white man. But when we got into camp, first I was just too hungry, second I was too thirsty, and third . . . well, he was mighty strong-looking at that, and kind of a pet of Dutton's, too.

I did have half a mind to tell Bo about it, but we weren't getting that much time together. He was riding swing and we was on different night watches. So in the end I kept my

67

mouth shut about Carney, and I was glad I did. Not just because it would have been a graceless thing to do, but for something which happened a couple of nights later when Dutton and Collins were out of the camp, and Johnny and Bob were on watch.

The boys was taking it easy, when we heard a holler and two fellers came riding in.

They got off their ponies and came to the fire and the temperature dropped, you might say, because they wasn't the most appetizing customers you ever saw. They was ragged and dirty and unshaved, but it wasn't that what cooled the welcome because we were more or less in the same condition ourselves. No, it was that them bozos had a swaggery way with them that made you think you wouldn't want them calling in on you if you were on your lonesome out on the prairie.

But, like I've said, no one got turned away from a camp-fire, so they got coffee and gunpowder stew—that name meaning don't ask what was in it or the cook blew up—and they wolfed it down like they needed it.

One of them, who was a fat and greasy hombre, wiped his mouth on his sleeve and belched. "Why," he said, "that was almost worth the journey. Yes, siree, you've got your-selves a mighty good cook." He peeked around, and he looked mighty sly to me, and pulled out a deck of cards. "Anyone here like a friendly game, faro or poker? Ten cents a card . . . ?"

He wasn't taken up on the offer, not only on account of Dutton's commandment, but because he didn't look like the kind of feller who knew what friendly meant. Playing with him would have been like having lunch with a vulture, with you as the lunch.

"Okay, boys," the bozo said. "No offense." He stuck the cards away and pulled out a half bottle of whiskey.

Charlie growled. "No drinking, mister. This is a dry camp. The boss don't allow drinking."

The bozo bit the cork out of the bottle. "Seems more like a goddamn church outing. Still, that's jake with me, but seeing as how I'm not riding for your boss, whoever the hell he is, I reckon the rules don't apply to Sam Coles. That's me, and this is my sidekick, Bill Smith." He laughed in a senseless way and held up the bottle. "So here's to the good old Southland, and goddamn all Yankees whatsoever."

Being good Southern boys ourselves, none of us were going to say no to that, but there wasn't many "Yoles" neither. Maybe it was the way he said it, kind of taunting, and he didn't sound like no Southerner, neither. Not that it bothered Coles. He swigged some whiskey and handed the bottle over to Smith, if so be that was his name.

Then Charlie, who was fuming somewhat, spoke up. "Where might you be heading?"

"Now," Coles said, "I don't know if it's any of your business, but we're going to visit my gray-haired old ma, haw-haw"—laughing in a jeery way.

"Is that a fact?" Charlie said. "You got no pack mule with you, I see."

He had a point there. Out in that wilderness you needed a pack mount for your provisions and what have you.

"Seems strange, don't it," Coles said.

"Yeah." Charlie had an edge to his voice, like he didn't care for them bozos drinking in camp, nor for that jeer about gray-haired old mas. "Can happen, though. Why, I knew of a couple of saddle bums once before who was roaming across a wilderness without a mule. They was out on the Staked Plain—running for their lives."

"Hey." Hank spoke up, maybe trying to ease the tension. "The Staked Plain. Was the Kiowa after them?"

"No," Charlie said. "It was a posse."

Them words dropped just like stones in a well. You know, first you hear nothing, then you hear a splash, and then you hear an echo, and Coles did the echoing.

"A posse, was it?" He swigged on the bottle like a calf on a teat. "Well, there ain't no posse after us." He tried the bottle again and cursed because it was empty. "Hey, you, boy," he said. "There's another bottle in my saddle-bag. Get it."

I thought he was talking to me and was just about ready to tell him to go to hell, when I realized he was talking to Carney.

"You," he said. "Nigger. You deaf?"

The boys murmured, like in protest, and Charlie slid off the tailboard, spoiling for trouble, because Carney was a nigger, right enough, but it was like he was *our* nigger, and it wasn't for two bums to come ordering him about, but Carney just stood up and said, "Yes, sir, boss. Which horse might that be?"

"No need to run errands, Tom," Charlie said, but Carney just said it was okay, and when Coles said the horse was the roan, he went off and came back a minute later.

"You got two bottles, boss," he said.

Coles belched again. "Yeah, and them's all we do have, so you be careful with them, boy."

"All you have." Carney shook his head, sad-like, and turned them upside down and poured out that booze!

Coles's eyes bulged, just exactly like a bullfrog. Then he cursed and jumped forward, tugging at his gun, but before he had it halfway out, Carney cracked him on the jaw, and before Coles hit the ground he'd hit him about four more times.

That Smith cursed, too, going for his gun, but Jack Shears just said, "Hold it there," and he had his shooter out, and I guess Smith heard that *click clack* as Jack cocked it, because once you've heard that sound you just never forget it, and you hear it over all other sounds there might be going on whatever.

Smith held it, all right. He stood there. He stood there still as a statue. "So that's the way of it, is it?" he said.

"That's the way," Jack said, and he sounded as if he could plug Smith right between the eyes and not think twice about it.

Coles lay on the ground, retching away, as Smith looked around at the rest of us, but he didn't see no sympathy—and Charlie had the shotgun out. Then Dutton and Collins came in.

"Get me some coffee," Dutton snapped—and stopped dead. "What the hell is going on here?" he bellowed.

Charlie told him the tale and Dutton looked blue murder. "What were you doing, letting two bums come in here and start boozing."

"It was my fault, boss," Carney said.

"The hell it was." Dutton turned to Smith. "Get out of here, and take your partner with you."

Smith scowled. "I thought this was a white man's country."

"Maybe it is," Dutton said. "But do you count yourself a man?"

Smith mumbled something, but not loud enough for anyone to hear, and got hold of Coles, who was on his hands and knees, moaning and groaning. "This man's hurt bad," Smith said.

"He'll be hurt a lot worse if you don't get him out of here," Dutton said. "And so will you. Now beat it."

Smith dragged Coles up and they staggered away, but at the edge of the firelight Smith turned. "I'll get even with you, nigger," he said.

"You can try that now," Carney said. "Any way you want it."

Smith didn't take up the offer, and him and Coles moved off into the night, and after a while we heard their ponies on the way.

Dutton listened, then said, "Jack?"

"Sure." Jack stood up. "I'll see them off the premises." He walked to the picket line and surely did look sinister. Not his dress or anything, nor no foolish swaggering, just that air he had, like he was 110 percent certain he could handle anything, or anyone, that came his way.

Then Dutton turned on us, and didn't he just. He cursed us up and down, Carney, too, but finally he cooled off, although he took Carney to one side and did some muttering to him. Well, Dutton had changed the trick on the night herd, so me and Bo was on second, and we rode out together.

I was mighty excited. I'd never seen a gun pulled on a man before, and Carney—if anyone had ever told me I'd see a nigger beating up a white man without him ending with his head in a noose, I'd have called him a straight liar. But there it was, Carney had done it, in style.

Bo didn't say nothing, and when I did try to speak to him, he told me to shut up, but when we took over from Johnny and Bob, we did some talking. Usually, when you changed guard, you just said, "Howdy" and "Good night," but not this time. Bo opened up and told the boys about the goings-on.

Bob whistled. "Jumping Joshua," he said. "I sure would have liked to have seen that. Tom really busted that drifter?"

"Sure did," Bo said. "I've seen some fistfights, but I never saw anyone get hit so hard."

"Why," Johnny said, "didn't you know? Carney used to be a prizefighter. He used to take on all comers."

"Well, I'll be," Bo said. "I'll bet he never did hit no white man before, though. He'd have done the rope dance quick enough. He would in Clement County, anyhow."

"Maybe," Johnny said. "But he's been with Dutton since he was a kid, I hear. Maybe he beat up some folks for him."

"That's possible," Bob said. "And Jack, he really pulled his gun?"

"Yeah," Bo said. "And he was ready to use it. If that bum had even blinked, Jack would have sent him to kingdom come."

"I've wondered about Jack," Bob said. "What you reckon, the law is after him?"

"I don't know," Bo said. "But I'll tell you one thing, I surely ain't going to ask him!"

The boys laughed, quiet-like, and headed for camp, and me and Bo sat for a while. Everything was peaceful, the moon like pure silver and the steers lying down like they hadn't a care in the world, but I had something on my mind and I wanted to talk about it.

"Bo," I said, "that Carney . . ."

Bo pushed back his hat. "I know what's on your mind. Yeah. A nigger beating up a white man. It seems against all nature." He stroked his pony's neck. "I don't know, kid. Carney there, it seems like out here he's one of us. I'll tell you something." He turned and looked at me full in the face. "Back there, I was ready to back him up myself."

"You were!" I said.

"Keep your fool voice down," Bo said. "You want to spook the herd? But I mean it. I'd have jumped that bozo with the gun if Jack hadn't gotten in first." He sighed. "Ben, we're moving into new territory here, and I don't just mean Kansas. We've got some figuring out to do, yes, sir. Now you move along and keep your ears open in case them bozos sneak back and try to spook the herd, out of meanness."

He went one way around the herd and me the other,

listening to Bo singing one of them dolesome songs. I did some singing myself, too, a hymn it was, "Shall We Gather at the River," but it was more for my sake than the steers' because I was scared that them bums would shake Jack off and come back for their vengeance. In fact, I was so scared I took my handgun out of the holster which I always carried on my saddle horn, but I put it back because I was more scared of it going off by accident and shooting myself in the leg.

But no one came. Smith and Coles didn't come whooping out of the brush blazing away with six-shooters. Even the coyotes were quiet as I rode my guard, thinking of what Bo had said and trying to make sense of it all, until the Big Dipper, wheeling around the North Star, told me our two hours was up.

And I surely was glad I hadn't told Carney no nigger was going to give me no orders, the more so since, and it's just too ridiculous for words, he was the first black man I'd ever spoken to.

▪ E I G H T ▪

Well, that meeting with them hombres gave us something to talk about as we moved on, that Red River coming closer all the while, and I got to do more thinking about Carney.

It's true I didn't have much sense, being just an ignorant backcountry Texas boy, but I did have the sense to start to see that Carney was something of a man. First into the saddle and last out of it, and cheerful with it, a kind of cheerfulness that came out of something real steady inside him. In fact, I started to forget he *was* a nigger, and anyhow, what with us being plastered with dust and masked with bandanas and our hats pulled over our eyes, we all looked the same, anyhow. And without even noticing it, like Bo, I started calling him Tom, just like the rest of the boys.

But I was riding on loose reins by then. At home on a pony, at home with the herd, and at home with the boys, eating dust with the rest—and the best—of them, and, truth to tell, counting my blessings I was a rider. Tedious though it might be most of the time, it sure was better than sitting in Clement, half starved and wholly bored, listening to the same old yarns year in, year out, which weren't worth the listening to in the first place, unless you thought Danny Farley's mule biting his dog was of interest.

And then, after a couple of days traveling through broken country, where it took some work to keep the herd in order, we got to the Red.

We got there at noon. Dutton was on a bluff, and even through the dust I could see him waving his hat, using that sign language which was another trick we'd picked up from the Indians. I thought we was going to throw the herd off the trail, but Joe Collins came racing down to us.

"Keep them moving," he roared. "Keep them going. We're crossing."

We'd crossed creeks in plenty, but never a real river, and I was excited and scared at the same time. I expected to see a roaring torrent, but old Dutton knew his river and he'd hit just exactly the right place because the bottom was firm and when we got to the river them steers was just ambling across. Course, they needed some prodding, but that was no problem at all, us being good at that.

It was what they call a letdown after all I'd heard, but that sure suited me, not wanting to meet no watery grave, so I whistled and yelled and cracked away with my quirt, and got to the far bank with no more than my boots wet.

Bo was on the bank, keeping the herd from fanning out, which they was always inclined to do, and he shouted something I didn't catch then. A little later, though, when we'd got the herd well away from the river, I cantered over to him and asked what he'd said.

"Why," he said, grinning all over his face, "we're out of Texas, kid! Now get back to your place before Collins comes along and gives you hell."

I got back in two jumps of my pony, because I didn't want Joe climbing over me, but as we plugged along, it dawned on me what Bo meant. Out of Texas, out of the Lone Star State. Well, if you got down to it, it didn't actually mean much. The country we were in looked just the same, broken with hickory and cottonwoods and what have you, but there was something in it—leaving Texas, I mean.

Crossing the Red was more than just getting over a river. It was passing a divide, from one way of living to another, getting into new territory, like Bo had said, with all that meant, new ways of living, and new ways of thinking. In fact, I was so roped up with that thought I forgot all about them Indians that was supposed to be raving around, and then I stopped thinking altogether because it began to rain.

You know what rain is, don't you? That water that comes down and gets you wet. Right. That's rain, but it ain't like the rain we got. It came down for three straight days and nights, cold as a millionaire's heart, and sometimes so cold it was hail, big lumps of ice thudding on your hat like there was some lunatic up there trying to knock your brains out. It was so wet Charlie could hardly get the fire started, and one night he couldn't, so we had cold beans and no coffee, and my slicker bust at the seams, so I was soaking. Bo wanted to let me have his slicker, but I wouldn't take it. Besides, being wet was the least of the problem.

The thing was, them steers didn't like that rain and hail no more than we did. It took us all our time, keeping them headed into it, and plenty of them had other opinions, and to be riding along, your head down to keep from being blinded, and suddenly see six feet of horn lunging at you made your hair stand on end so stiff it came near to knocking your hat off. And Jupiter, did you bless your pony then, them spotting danger before you did. We had double night guard, too, four men on at a time, because we got some lightning with that rain and Dutton wasn't going to risk getting caught out if the herd spooked.

All the time, we was edging across country, and one morning it stopped raining, the sky cleared, the sun came out, and didn't we just bless it, and there was the Chisholm Trail, right before our eyes.

It was some trail, too. A half-Indian called Jesse Chisholm had broken it out in the first place, but now it was half a mile wide and sunk deep because of all the millions of cattle that had gone up it, and even if it wasn't marked as clear as Fifth Avenue in New York City, you could have found your way easy, just following the empty cans, tomatoes and peaches mostly, which had been chucked aside. Like the boys said, the can opener did more to win the West than all the six-guns ever made. Well, that's what they said.

Be that as it may, we were on the Trail, and it was somewhat comforting to know there was herds ahead and behind, just in case them Indians decided to jump us. But there were different ideas about that. One night we was gabbing and Amos the wrangler said he didn't like to see herds too close.

"Can lead to trouble," he said. "You can get hustled along by the feller behind you, and then you start pushing the feller ahead, and steers get mixed up and there's goddamn arguments about the trail brands, whose steers is whose. I've seen guns pulled over that."

"That's a fact," Charlie opined in his genteel way, which

meant if he said it, that *was* a fact. "I was on the old Sedalia Trail once with Fred Cage. He was halfway crazy then on whiskey and he was running that herd like we was in some goddamn horse race. We kept prodding the herd ahead of us, and one day its boss came visiting with three Mexicans. Jesus, they was tough hombres, half wolf, half rattlesnake, and half cactus."

"That makes one and a half, Charlie," Hank said.

We laughed, but Charlie gave Hank a look that said he wouldn't be getting full plates of stew from then on. "So what?" he barked. "I'm telling you they was tough."

"Sure, Charlie," Hank said, soothing. "You is just being poetic."

"Yeah?" Charlie sounded like he didn't know whether that was a compliment or another joke, but settled for the compliment. "Anyhow, Fred went for the shotgun and one of them greasers shot him clean through the shoulder. Yes, sir."

"Didn't you back him up, that Cage?" Bob asked.

"The hell we did." Charlie chewed on his stogie. "Not when Cage was in the wrong. But, all the same, it ain't bad to have some company if you get Indians or rustlers moseying around."

"Yeah," I butted in. "But where is them Indians? I thought they was around here."

"They is, kid," Charlie said. "They is all around. Just arguing which of them is going to get your hair!" Which I guessed was his idea of a joke. He opened that Dutch oven, which was like an iron box for cooking. "Right," he said. "Grub's ready—if anyone wants it"—that being another joke.

I ate, slept some, went on guard, and, young and foolish as I was, I hoped that somewhere along the Trail we'd run into some trouble, greasers or Indians or what have you, and I'd get the chance to join in a real gunfight. Me and Jack Shears being the heroes!

But nothing out of the way happened as we shoved along, and it was real easy going and pleasant country, rolling prairie with plenty of clear streams and timber—why, there was all a feller could desire, blackjack oak, cottonwoods, willows, and shaking aspen. It was country a man could have settled in, you know?

Anyhows, on we went, fifteen miles to Beaver Creek, another fifteen to Stinking Creek and Monument Rock, where about a million riders had carved their initials, which I'd have like to have done as well, but Dutton shoved us along, up the east fork of Stinking Creek, then a long haul to Rush Creek, where Dutton broke out the shotgun and went hunting, coming back with enough quail to feed a pack of wolves.

We was getting on at that, sixty miles from the Red, and when we'd crossed the Little Washita, we was only four miles from the Washita itself, which the boys said was a real easy crossing and nothing to worry about, which it was, for everyone but me.

We'd got the herd over without no real problems. Some of the steers balked at the south bank, maybe because it was a mite sticky, red clay, which they didn't like for some reason, but there was a good rock bottom, so once we got them in the water they strolled it, and we had the entire herd on the north bank, when one of them steers took it into his head to do some exploring all on his own. I went after him, but he stretched his legs, and the closer I got, the faster he went, and them longhorns could really run, so I was near enough at a hard gallop when my pony stepped into a gopher hole, or some such burrow, and we both went down.

I flew over the pony's shoulder like a bird and landed

with a crash that knocked what sense I did have clear out of me, and I didn't recall nothing else until I came around and found Tom leaning over me. I was real dazed and my leg and shoulder hurt awful bad, and it was like some terrible weight was crushing me.

I tried to say, "Help me," but couldn't get the words out. I managed a sort of moan, because Tom stared down at me for a moment, then pulled out his handgun! Jeepers, I thought, he's going to shoot me. Like paying back for slavery and all, and then that pistol banged and I passed out again.

When I came to, I was lying by the wagon, the thing having been that my pony had broken its back and was half lying on me, so Tom had shot it, hauled it off me, stuck me over his saddle, and carried me to the camp.

Charlie, who passed for a doctor, would you believe, looked me over, said I didn't have nothing broken but I was badly sprained and wouldn't be fit to ride for a while.

"That's all," he said. "No real problem, kid."

Well, it wasn't no problem for Charlie, but it was for me, because I reckoned Dutton would be mad as all get-out, but he wasn't, much.

Course, he cursed and grumbled, but that was like for the sake of it, because ponies did go down and riders did get hurt, but as long as nothing foolish had been done, it was just taken as part of the hazard of the job. So Dutton said I could ride in the wagon, although he had a look in his eye which made me wonder if I was going to get my dollar a day while I was doing so—assuming I was going to get it anyhow.

Tom beat it back to the herd, and Charlie looked at me somewhat thoughtful. "I figured you for a halfway decent kid," he said.

"Why," I said, "I hope I am—in fact, more than halfway. What's biting you?"

"Didn't it occur to you to thank Tom, is all."

"Hey," I said. "I'm all shook up here, and—"

"And Tom's a nigger." Charlie got himself some coffee, and he didn't offer me none. "Don't try and fool me, sonny, I've been around too long. If it wasn't for Tom, you could have been crushed to death. He's the one who followed you and he heaved that pony off you." He spat. "Maybe you don't like niggers, and maybe I don't neither, but times you've got to look through the color at the man. Bear that in mind."

"Come on, Charlie," I said. "I've been real friendly to Tom these past weeks."

"Jesus H. Christ!" Charlie was real disgusted. "You've been friendly to him. What you think, you're doing him a favor? Listen, me, Dutton, and Tom go back a long time together, and you grow up to be half the men they is and you'll be doing well. And I don't mean getting a few more inches on that runty frame of yours."

He stalked off and began chucking them navy beans in the pot and doing the chores, until the herd rolled up and the boys came in for their grub. I got joshed a lot, you know, the boys saying I was faking and all, but it was only kidding, although it was strange, Bo was mad at me! Like I'd let him down! But kin can be like that. One thing I did do, though, was to thank Tom. He just shrugged and said nothing to it. Well, actually it wasn't exactly like that. What he said was, "Nothing to it, kid," which was the first time he ever spoke to me like that—sort of friendly. And I'll tell you, life sure is mixed up at times, because I felt good after.

Anyhow, come the next day, I was hoisted onto the wagon and lay back against a sack of flour as we went ahead, following Dutton, who was on his big bay, which was his day horse. It was surely nice, too, lying back after weeks in the saddle, watching the world go by instead of the tails of a thousand steers. There was plenty to look at, too, if you knew what you were looking for, hawks and buzzards soaring, jackrabbits and coyotes beating it out of the way, and some pronghorn antelope, which would have gone down well in a stew, and bobolinks and red-winged black-birds singing at us.

And I don't know but that Charlie had heard me thanking Tom. He didn't seem sore at me being with him, although maybe that was because he'd got a listener for his tall stories. Jupiter, to hear him, he'd spent his entire life fighting it out with gunslingers and wrestling bears and shooting half the Northern army back in the war.

At around ten, Dutton found a good strip of grazing for the herd, so we pulled up. It was a mighty fine place, too, under a big tree the name of which I didn't know, but green and shady, with little birds hopping in the branches, and I've done worse things in my life than lying there in the shade while Charlie got the fixings ready for lunch. We got coffee, too, and it was better than usual, and I got the notion that when he was away from us Charlie lived somewhat higher on the hog than the rest of us.

So it was swell sitting with Charlie and the boss, and he was saying maybe he'd go and see if he couldn't get some game, when I looked up.

"Boss," I said, and pointed, because out there was three riders.

They weren't moving, just sitting on their ponies, and them not moving was sinister, you know? At any rate, they seemed so to me, and I guess they did to Dutton, because he took one look and said, "Kid, reach around you and break out the shotgun and that Winchester. Don't wave them about. Just lay them by you."

"Who are they, boss?" I whispered, my mouth all dry.

"We'll find out soon enough," Dutton said. "Now do what I told you."

I reached behind me, feeling in the locker, and when I turned back, one of them riders was walking his pony toward us, like he'd made up his mind about something or other.

He came forward slow and easy, as if he had all the time in the world, and as he got nearer I could see he was a cowboy, wearing a regular hat and chaps, but when he got closer still, I saw that he was wearing a buckskin shirt and he had a couple of feathers in his hatband, and long braided hair coming out from under it, and it didn't take no genius from Clement County, Texas, to know that, put together, that spelled out Indian.

You know, all my life I'd been brought up fearing Indians, and the tales I'd been told, I'd got reason to, at that. In fact, Danny Farley's pa had been killed by Apache when all he'd been doing was staking out a lawful claim to some land. But I hadn't never actually seen an Indian myself, and I hadn't never even heard of one getting all dressed up like a white man, the which I guessed was some real cunning trick, so my hair was really prickling. But Dutton didn't seem fazed.

"Wondered when," he said, sipping his coffee. "Just act natural, kid."

Well, if I had acted like my natural instinct told me, then, bad leg and bruising and all, I'd have been on my feet and hightailing it out of there like streaked lightning, but, that not being an option, I stayed where I was, trying to whistle, like folks do when they is scared out of their wits, and keeping a hand on that shotgun as that Indian reached us.

He was a hard-looking hombre at that, big, with high cheekbones and a flattened nose, like someone had given it a good poke sometime, someone like Tom, that is. He stared at us and we stared at him, and I was wondering why in Sam Hill he wasn't like he was supposed to be, near mother-naked and splashed with war paint, when Dutton spoke.

"Howdy, Chief," he said. "Like some coffee?"

Jeepers, I thought, next thing Dutton would be asking him to join in a Bible reading, but that Indian just nodded, swung off his pony, took a mug of Charlie's hell brew, tasted it, pulled a face, and made a stirring motion with his finger.

"Pass the molasses, Charlie," Dutton said, us not carrying sugar, and poured it right into the mug. "That okay?" he asked.

The Indian nodded and sat down. I was beginning to think the next thing was we were going to start talking about Grandpa's rheumatics and smoke the peace pipe, but the feller pulled out a hand sack of Bull Durham Special, which was better than our boys smoked, rolled a cigarette, puffed out a stream of smoke, and said, "Cherokee!"

"Is that so?" Dutton said.

The Indian grunted and held out his mug for more coffee.

"Kind of out of your territory, ain't you?" Dutton said. "You live far east"—pointing that way.

The Indian gave a grim smile, if it was a smile. "We're moving around some," he said in real American, just like Dutton was speaking!

I was so amazed I swallowed my coffee down the wrong way, but when I'd finished coughing, I was even more amazed because that Indian, he was asking Dutton how many cattle we had. I'll tell you, that was like going up to a perfect stranger and asking how much money he'd got, but Dutton didn't seem enraged or nothing. He just shrugged.

"Don't see what business it is of yours," he said evenly.

That Indian, he kept that smile on his face. "Tax collector," he said. "For the Cherokee Nation!" And he pulled out a kind of letter and handed it over.

I figured I was dreaming, you know, but Dutton just glanced at the letter and handed it back.

"Okay," he said. "So you're a tax collector. But this ain't your range and you ain't going to get no tax off me. I could maybe let you have some flour and molasses, maybe even a steer. But that's all."

Dutton sounded as tough as old beef, but that Indian didn't bat an eyelash. He rolled another cigarette and lit up, looking at the sky like he had all the time in the world, which maybe he had, and said, "We reckon you've got a thousand head. Ten cents apiece, that's a hundred dollars."

It was all like a dream to me, especially when Dutton said he didn't carry that much cash. "Anyhow," he went on, "this here is Osage territory."

The Indian waved his hand, like brushing flies away, and he did the same when Dutton said we'd got plenty of friends on the trail.

"Plenty," Dutton said. "There's herds strung right along the trail."

Actually, the Indian looked pleased when Dutton said that, like it was more money rolling in, and anyhow he jabbed his thumb over his shoulder.

"I've got friends, too," he said.

We looked where he was jabbing, and them two riders up there had been joined by some more—and it might have been the light, but they didn't look what you might call civilized, same as our Indian halfway looked.

"Okay," Dutton said. "I don't want no trouble, but you ain't going to goddamn screw me out of no hundred bucks. I'll give you twenty-five. Take it or get your goddamn tomahawks out."

The Indian laughed then! Right out loud like it was real good joke, then said, "Fifty," and jeepers if they didn't sit there bargaining like two storekeepers, and finally they settled at thirty-five dollars and some molasses and tobacco and stuff.

Dutton pulled out his billfold and handed over the cash, looking like he was having his teeth pulled out, and Charlie handed over the stores and that Indian gave Dutton a stick, notched, which was the tally, and he gave that smile and cantered off with his buddies.

We watched him go, then Dutton said a real bad word and kicked the wagon! "Goddamn!" He spat. "Goddamn!"

"Tough luck, boss," Charlie said.

"Luck!" Dutton cursed some more. "What in hell are the Cherokee doing this far west?"

"Don't know," Charlie said.

"Don't know?" Dutton glared at us like it was all our fault. "The hell you don't"—which was somewhat senseless, but I guess relieved his feelings. "I'm going back to the herd." He glared at us again, then mounted and rode off.

"Lightning!" I said. "What in Sam Hill was that about?"

"You saw it, didn't you?" Charlie said. "You've got eyes in your head"—being sarcastical.

I allowed I had seen it, and Charlie grunted. "In the thirties, old Andrew Jackson moved them Cherokee across the Mississippi. Should have moved them clear across the Rockies and into that goddamn Pacific Ocean, if you ask me."

"But I thought—" I began but as usual got cut off.

"I know what you think," Charlie said, like he was some sort of mind reader. "You listened to that joshing from the boys and figured them Indians would be all dressed up in war bonnets and whooping and all and waving tomahawks like them Comanche and Kiowa. But them Cherokee ain't like that. They're what them Indian lovers back East call one of the *civilized* nations. Jesus H. Christ, civilized!" He spat, like that word had a bad taste. "They got their own

86

writing and schools and churches and all, and 'they're pretty good at cattle raising. See the way that buck wouldn't take no steers? That's because their cattle is better than what we're trailing. They claim that toll because they say it's their grass our steers are grazing on. Theirs! Goddamn, they got it all figured out. You saw that tally stick? Dutton can show that to anyone and he won't get charged none again. It sure took Dutton by surprise, though, seeing a Cherokee here. They used to swarm all over the place on the old Sedalia Trail, but here—" He cackled suddenly. "I wonder if that buck wasn't trying it on for size!"

"How do you mean?" I asked.

"Maybe they was just bluffing. Just a few of them wandering around and they figured they might as well see if they could skin the boss. I sure ain't never seen no Cherokee this far west."

"Yeah?" I said. "But why did Dutton pay?"

"Ah." Charlie waved his hand, like he was disgusted at my ignorance. "You want them sneaking after us, spooking the herd and all?" He laughed again. "Did you see the look on Dutton's face when he handed over the cash?"

"Sure," I said. "Like he was in pain. But, Charlie, them Indians—"

"Them?" Charlie stopped laughing. "There's only one thing to do with that red scum. Wipe 'em off the face of the earth."

He got to work making flapjacks and they was just about ready when the herd got in around noon. There was plenty of talk about them Cherokee, you bet, which was just like Charlie had been saying—wipe them out, and the sooner, the better.

In fact, the boys seemed to get excited at the prospect, like it would be going out for a night on the town! They were all smacking their lips, except for Tom and Jack

Shears. Even Johnny Merill, who was as kindhearted a rider as you could ever meet, was glowering like them Cherokee was his personal enemies, and Joe Collins was plumb murderous, cussing them for hogging good land that rightly belonged to white men. The way he talked, you'd have thought he wanted to start homesteading there and then, and the boys howled about them thirty-five dollars like it had come out of their own pockets!

I tried to stick in my ten cents' worth, mentioning them houses and churches, but got told to keep my mouth shut because I was a kid and what the hell did I know about anything. So I did keep my mouth shut, but that didn't stop me thinking, and one of the things I thought was that I'd like to know a little more about them Indians, and the whole wide country, come to that.

▪ N I N E ▪

So, with Dutton thirty-five bucks lighter, we moved on, making sixteen miles to Walnut Creek, which was pushing the herd some, and that creek was kind of a bad crossing. Nothing terrible, but bad enough to make you wonder if you'd be playing a harp by the time it was over. It was deep and what they call turbulent, and the steers didn't like it one little bit, trying to break downstream. But we got them over without losing any, and then Dutton took it easy, sort of ambling to the South Canadian, which was another bad crossing. Dutton said there must have been real heavy rain in the Rockies. Bob Bowker got near hooked out of his saddle, and a couple of steers broke downstream, so they had to be got back.

Still, we got over and there was a real dandy campsite on the north bank, and it was one more river behind us at that. I got turned off the wagon, which made me gloomy, because I was still real sore and bruised, but I got back in the saddle without moaning. Not to mention, I was counting up dollars in my head.

After the North Canadian, we was on high rolling prairie where the grass rippled in the wind like a girl's hair. And that ain't no crazy fantasy, like there are girls with green hair, because that grass was tawny, red almost, till the fall, when it cured on the stalk and made the best hay on God's earth.

It was getting hotter, too, the sun beginning to beat down like it was muscling up, getting ready to try you out, seeing how much you could take, and away from the creeks the land was dry as a bone. Looking back, I could see a cloud of dust where another herd was following us. There was probably a cloud of dust ahead, too, but being I was riding drag, I couldn't see that far.

But the going was easy and there was no rustlers, no bandits, no more Indians, and no stampedes. Like the boys said, Dutton must have got a spell on the herd, because no one had ever heard of a drive that didn't have a stampede. In fact, there were herds that got the habit and did nothing but. So, all in all, we was getting along, all of us sick of beans and Charlie's stews and hankering for real grub, but with no one hurt bad and not a steer lost, splashing through the creeks, Deer, Kingfisher, and the Cimarron, too, which was said to be a real killer of a river, and once over it, Dutton laid us off after the noon break. It was to give the herd a rest, but it wasn't no big holiday for me because I had to go along the river and get firewood.

I sure did some cussing, like why always me? But I did it, and when I got back, there was a stranger sitting at the fire.

It seemed he was a geezer called Old Hobs, that's all, Old Hobs. He was an ancient geezer, all gnarled and dry, and was shacked up with an Indian woman way out in the wilds. He'd spoken to Sam Clark, heard we was coming up the Trail, and knowing Charlie from way back, had come visiting to mingle with Christian men, and get some Christian tobacco and coffee, too.

He was old, but tough-old like some fellers get, and amiable enough, leaning back with his stogie.

"And you paid them Cherokee?" he was saying to Dutton, incredulous as might be. "They saw you coming. If any Indians got a claim on this land, it's the Osage"—making Dutton look blue—"but you saved yourselves some harassment. There is a lot of moving about with the tribes right now. They're getting shoved, you know, edged west all the time."

"Edge them into hell for me," Collins said.

"It's a point of view," Old Hobs allowed. "But push a man too hard and he's liable to push back."

"Ain't no redskin going to ever push me none," Bob said.

"No?" Old Hobs was somewhat disbelieving, and I thought how the Texan border had been pushed back a hundred miles during the war by the Indians. Old Hobs let it pass. "They'll go, anyhow."

"Go where?" Bo said.

"Just go." Old Hobs made a gesture, rippling his fingers. "Pass away. When the farmers get here."

The boys just burst out laughing. "Farmers?" Bob said. "Did I hear you right? Jupiter, you'd need a million of them just to scratch this here land. Where in hell you think they're coming from?"

"They'll come," Old Hobs said. "They'll follow the railroad. East Kansas is filling up rapid now. It's free land, near enough, and folks'll come a long ways for that. All the way from that Europe."

"I ain't buying that," Bob said. "There's that goddamn Atlantic Ocean between us and them. How are they going to cross that?"

"Sonny," Old Hobs said, "you never hear of ships?"

Charlie spat and cursed. "More foreigners!"

"We was oncet," Old Hobs said, mild-mannered. "Anyhow, don't take things so hard, boys. At least that dough got handed out to a friend."

"Friend?" Bo said.

"Surely." Old Hobs lit another of Charlie's stogies. "You was allies in the war."

"Hey?" Bo leaned forward, and some of the others did, too, sharp-like. "What was that?" He sounded mean, because the War between the States was a sore point with us Southern boys and you had to watch your words when you mentioned it. "You saying the Confederate States of America was fighting alongside a tribe of redskins?"

Bo was mean, but Old Hobs wasn't fazed one little bit. "Sure am," he said. "Didn't you know that? You're still wet behind the ears, sonny. There was Indians joined up with the Union and there was lots of tribes joined up with Dixieland. Cavalry, they was. They'd been hustled so long by the Yankees, they figured they'd do some hustling back."

"But—" Bo and us couldn't hardly believe our ears. "Hell, they is colored!"

"Hee-hee!" Old Hobs gave a creaky laugh. "Sure they is, but it ain't the way they see it. Sides, they figured they'd a lot in common with you boys."

"How in Sam Hill do you figure that out?" Gus King spoke, real surly.

"Why"—Old Hobs didn't sound like he cared two hoots whether Gus was surly or not. Like I say, he was a tough old rooster. "Why, they got slaves and they sure like the wide-open spaces. Just like you cowboys." He halted for a moment, his little sharp eyes peeking out of his gnarly face and whiskers like an old porcupine's. "Picked the wrong side, though, didn't they."

"What's that?" Gus pushed in again and he was more than surly, and so was the rest of us. "You saying the Southland was wrong back there?"

"Why, no, boys," Old Hobs said. "It's just a notion some folks have that you lost the war, is all. That's what they think up where you're going, anyhow. But it don't mean beans to me, boys. So long as me and my old woman can live out our time in peace, I don't give a damn for all the wars that ever was fought. Right, Charlie?"

"You said it," Charlie agreed, and him and Old Hobs cackled together like it was the comicalest joke ever made.

It was my turn out with the herd then anyways, so I rode out with Gus, who was sharing watches with me. "I don't get it, Gus," I said. "That bird back there. He's living with a squaw, but he sits around with us white men and no one said a word about it. I'll tell you, back in Clement, if a feller lived with a nigger woman, he'd get tarred and feathered."

"Yeah," Gus said. "But it ain't like that out here."

"Why ain't it?" I asked.

"Because—" Johnny hesitated, and I'm not sure he knew why himself, but he plowed on. "Them old hunters roaming around out here, if they didn't hitch up with Indians, they could lose their scalps."

"Sure," I said. "But why—"

Gus groaned. "Kid," he said, real exasperated, "will you stop asking tomfool questions. Why? Why? Why? You'd wear a body down to dust. Just shut up and ride your guard."

He moved off, and I heard him say to Hank Vale and Bob Bowker, who we was relieving, "That kid and his questions." But I didn't mind. I rode quiet around the herd, humming at them. It sure seemed a crazy mixed-up world to me.

The next morning we said "So long" to Old Hobs, and I'd bet five bucks him and Charlie had spent the night with a couple of bottles of red-eye. We headed for Turkey Creek, and jeepers, there was a prairie-dog town there about five miles long. You never saw so many creatures, and there was rattlers around too, which kind of liked the taste of them prairie dogs, and they'd like the taste of you as well, so you had to give the campsite a good beating out before you settled down. There was skunks, too, and Charlie and Collins and Dutton was more scared of them than rattlers, would you believe? Them creatures could creep up to you in the night and start chewing away at you, the which might not have been so bad in itself, but they all had that rabies, the wolves, too, and what I heard of that disease, it was the most terrible thing that could ever happen to you. In fact, Dutton said he'd known a feller got bit and started having the symptoms, and that hombre had shot himself! And Dutton wasn't a feller for stretching a tale, neither, so there was more amusing things to brood about as we slogged along to Hackberry Creek, which was a favorite campground for them Osage Indians, Dutton said, but there weren't none around then, and to Skeleton Creek. A whole band of Osage had died up there, back in the sixties when the cholera swept across the West. Me and some of the boys rode up to take a look at the bones and, Indians or not, it was a sad and sorry sight, the bones shining in the dusk—skulls, arms, legs, little ones, too, which was kids, and some of them bones gnawed at and cracked, and all unburied.

We got back to camp in a somber mood, but Charlie told us to think of the poor cowboys who'd died of cholera, and a lot more things, which made us feel gloomier. But we cheered up plenty when we had a real good feed of wild turkey, Dutton having gone out with the shotgun. Charlie sure made us laugh, too, telling us about a creek on the old Shawnee Trail. He said some settlers heading for California in '45 had tried to take a piano but had to dump it there when their oxen died.

"Yes, sir," Charlie said. "That piano was by that creek for many a year and the Indians used to go there when they was getting ready to go on the warpath, sitting and playing it and whooping and hollering"—which I guess *was* stretching it, and so did the others, because Hank said, dry-like, "What was they playing, Charlie? 'Jingle Bells'?"

And then we got to Salt Fork. It was a branch of the Arkansas River, with flash floods and quicksands and real miry banks, so the steers had trouble getting out of the water. And that's where our luck started to run out.

Dutton had us throw the herd off the trail while he and Collins and Tom went to take a good look at the river, and though Dutton wasn't none too pleased about it, the rest of us went and took a look as well, and none of us liked it one little bit. That river looked a mile wide, there sure was some current, that water hurtling along, all muddy and sinister, and it started to rain as well. Dutton, Joe, and Tom spent a goodly time together, then Joe cantered off one way and Tom another.

"Looking for another crossing," Charlie said while we was having our grub.

"And, Jupiter," Amos said, "don't I just hope they find one. I surely don't fancy getting the ponies across there, leave alone the steers."

But hoping didn't help, because after a while Tom and Joe came in, shaking their heads, all gloomy, but they wasn't more gloomy than we was when Dutton said we was crossing.

We stood around in our slickers, the rain pouring off us,

sour, you know, but no one said a thing, until Jack Shears stepped forward and spoke, and it was a surprise because he hadn't hardly said ten words the entire trip.

"What's the rush," he asked, in that quiet voice of his.

Dutton glared at Jack. "There ain't no rush," he said. "I've never rushed a herd in my life."

"I ain't saying you have," Jack said. "But we've made good time on this trip. We could wait over a day or so, let that river fall."

"Listen, mister," Dutton said—growled, more like. "That water there is coming maybe a thousand miles, and I'm telling you it ain't going to get no easier than it is. We wait, we could be stuck here for weeks, getting tangled up with every goddamn herd from Texas. We're crossing and we're crossing now. Anyone don't fancy it can get the hell back to Texas. On foot."

"Yeah?" Jack just stood there, but there was something about the way he was standing that made the hair stir on the back of your neck, and I noticed Collins and Carney edge out from Dutton, only they wasn't running away, if you get me, like if Jack made a move it was three to one there—four, really, since Charlie had moved over to the chuck wagon, and he hadn't gone there for more beans.

Well, Jack was one tough hombre, but he wasn't that tough, and seeing it was a choice of crossing the river or hoofing it five hundred miles, there wasn't much in it, so he shrugged and said, "If that's the way it is . . ."

"That's exactly it," Dutton said. "Now let's get moving."

So we did, and it was a crossing to have bad dreams about. We fixed the wagon, lashing barrels to the outside, and got it to the bank, but the mules balked, and I didn't blame them. In fact, it was a sorry sight to see them, rolling their eyes and trying to turn as Charlie and the boys whipped at them with their quirts, merciless they was, and them mules slipping and sliding in the mud, and when they was in the water, Tom rode downstream of them, slashing them across the muzzles with his quirt to keep them straight.

And then, Lord! it was the steers' turn to play up. They was half crazy and the boys earned their corn that day, fighting to keep their ponies facing the right way, leave alone the steers. But the real trouble came when a big brute, which was one of the meanest animals in the entire herd, went totally loco. I don't know but he'd found some sort of footing because he turned and was hooking at the rest of the steers and threatening to break up the whole file, and, holy Moses, if Tom didn't get out of his saddle and heave the steer around and *rode* it to the bank, and why he did that when they weren't even his steers, I couldn't figure.

Come to that, they weren't my steers, neither, but I had to go into that river, too, once we'd brought the drag up, and that wasn't no picnic, neither. I guess the steers could hear the bellowing and shouting ahead and sensed what was waiting, because plenty of them decided it wasn't bath time and turned around, heading at us.

We lashed at them and blazed across their noses with our handguns because *that's* what they was mainly for, and I say we, but it was really Johnny Merill because I didn't keep but more than one shell in my .32, being scared it would go off and plug me, but I lashed away and yelled but in the end Joe and Gus had to come back and give us a hand, and then it was into the river, into that jumble of crazy animals and huge horns, and the murky water roaring down on you. Jeepers, I truly never thought I'd make it—like I figured, there I wasn't crossing the Salt Fork, it was Jordan I was going over.

We got them steers across in the end, but it was like a nightmare, and after maybe six hours, and us soaked to the skin and cold to the marrow, we got the herd bedded and had time for coffee, which Charlie had ready, hot as Hades and black as sin, and didn't we need it just! But before we got more than a sniff of it, Dutton asked where Tom was.

It was like a bomb going off. Everyone was talking at once, saying they'd seen him wrestle that huge steer, or that he'd been on the north bank shoving the steers onto the prairie, or that he'd gone back into the river, but Dutton shut us all up.

"Jumping Jesus!" he roared. "I ain't asking when you saw him, I'm asking where he is now."

None of us could rightly answer that, but we all sure thought we knew the answer. He was downstream, all tangled up with a dead and drownded steer, and dead and drownded himself.

Dutton opened his mouth, but there was no need for him to say nothing because every man jack of us, worn and weary though we were, was ready to climb on our ponies and go looking for him. But Dutton put the slows on that, and he was right. There wasn't no point in the whole crew galloping about, so Joe, Jack, and Bo mounted and rode out.

The rest of us stood around the fire feeling blue, and looking it, too, with the cold, but Dutton hadn't finished. "Johnny," he yelled, "you and the kid get out to the herd."

Johnny looked as mad as Jack had, and I thought he was going to tell Dutton to go to you know where, but Charlie said, in a reasonable way, "If that herd ain't watched now, it's sure going to spread, and that's just more work later."

Well, reason won, which it don't always, because if we didn't keep that herd wound up, we could spend the whole night getting them unspread, and maybe the next day, too, so we got our ponies and went out, and there sure wasn't no singing.

We did our turn, then Gus and Bob came out, shaking

their heads, and we went and got some grub. There was no sign of the others and it looked like Tom had got himself drownded at that, and it was bad news, too. Black or not, he was some man and some rider.

I sloshed some stew down me and asked Charlie if he really thought Tom had gone.

"If he is," Charlie said, "I sure hope he ain't washed up on the other bank."

"What the hell does that mean?" Johnny said, real sharp, like it was some kind of bad joke.

Charlie didn't usually let anyone speak to him like that, but this time he let it pass, saying, "You don't want to cross the river again, do you?"

Johnny frowned. "Cross again?"

"That's what I said." Charlie threw more coffee into the pot. "You don't think we'd leave his body over there unburied, do you?"

Johnny didn't answer but looked even bluer, which was how I was feeling. We couldn't leave Tom's body lying there, but I had a real bad thought about facing the river again—which was blown away just then because there was a hailing and in came Bo, Collins, Jack, Tom, and a half-dozen steers.

It surely was a relief to see the boys, although you wouldn't have thought so from the way Dutton carried on.

"You goddamn black jackass," he roared. "Where in hell have you been?"

"Them steers broke downstream out of the drag," Tom said. "So I went after them."

"Steer!" Dutton was really worked up. "You risked your life for them?"

"They're worth maybe two-fifty bucks in Abilene," Tom said.

"Two-fifty!" Dutton spat. "That ain't worth the price of a human being."

I was just staggered when I heard that. After the way Dutton had driven us across the river! He'd risked all our lives to get the herd across and now he was cursing Tom for doing his best! But, I figured, maybe all of us crossing was just part of the job, whereas Tom going downstream was more than could be asked in reason. But then I was more staggered, because Tom stood there in the rain and said, "It's what your pa paid for my ma!"

For a moment there I thought Dutton would kill Tom, just pull out his gun and blow him away. His face was all tormented and his hands was twitching, but he just turned on his heel and walked off to the remuda.

Tom got himself coffee and handed some to Jack. They lit cigarettes, and then Jack, who I reckon was the only feller on the drive with the nerve to ask the question, said, "That why you did it?"

"Did what?" Tom asked.

"You know what I mean," Jack said. "That about your ma. You clearing something off?"

"What's it to you?" Tom said, and if Jack was the only man on the drive who could ask that question, Tom was the only man who could have answered him the way he did.

Jack shrugged. "I guess it ain't nothing," he said, meek and mild. "I just wondered, is all."

"Yeah?" Tom brooded for a while and, Jupiter, he sure did look a tough son of a gun, and I wondered if he was going to slug Jack, and if he could do it before Jack got his pistol out, but he just said, "Maybe a feller like me's got to push it."

"Maybe," Jack said. "Maybe you have to, at that. Yeah."

TEN

The drive went sour after Salt Fork. The boys was sullen because of the way Dutton had rushed us, and we'd lost nine steers, so Dutton was in the meanest temper, and it looked like any bonus we might have had was just vanishing like a dream.

Them drenching rains came down again, and when they cleared, it was like riding through a furnace, the bugs getting worser, too, so's we all was near bitten alive, mosquitoes mainly, but Gus had got a blowfly sting and there was eggs in his skin, so's he had to have them cut out, and although we wasn't too worried about Gus, it was another thing to get under *our* skin.

We met some more Indians, too. That was by Pond Creek, only three miles on from Salt Fork. We crossed Black Dog Trail, an old Indian warpath where there was some mounds, like they was old Indian burial places. The Indians was Osage. Dutton showed them that Cherokee tally stick, but it didn't mean beans to them. They said what the Cherokee did was their business, and kind of hinted Dutton was some kind of fool, paying up, because the Cherokee was off their territory.

Them Osage was tame, at that. One of them tried bluffing, scowling and looking fierce, but you could see at a glance there was nothing to him, and if they'd got any rifles, they was hidden away. In any case, Dutton wasn't in no mood to bargain with a handful of savages, and we was so mean we was ready to gun the whole pack of them down, so they didn't get even a steer, although, as a kind of peace offering, Dutton gave them tobacco.

One of them bucks, he was wearing a U.S. Cavalry jacket, and if we'd been convinced it was from a white man he'd killed, he'd have gone to the happy hunting grounds before his time. But when Charlie, who reckoned he knew some Osagian, spoke to him, that buck just said "Scout," so he could have been one for the Army at that. In any case, it wasn't worth bumping him off on the evidence. That feller, he wanted to do some racing with us for ponies, but Dutton wasn't having that, neither, so that buck jibed at us, and him and another feller did some trick riding around us, and they surely could ride, but it was taunting, them making fun of us, so we got even sourer after that.

And I don't know but what it was that sourness that kind of forced Dutton into doing something amazing. He gave us another lie-over! A whole half day off. And he did something even more amazing. We was up at Polecat Creek, where there was millions more prairie dogs, and he went up the creek hunting, and when he came back, he was all excited and got out the Winchester. Jupiter, I thought, *more* Indians, but he said any of us free could go with him, the which we did, and up that creek there was some buffalo! It was mighty interesting seeing them, a bull and some cows, I guess. I'd never seen one, so it was a real sight, them huge creatures, massive heads, and high in the shoulders, covered with crinkly black hair like Tom's, which was why Indians called nigger soldiers in the U.S. Cavalry buffalo soldiers.

I liked seeing them, just browsing and blowing, but Dutton got out the rifle and blasted away and killed one, and although we had a buffalo hump steak that night, which was mighty good eating, it did seem a terrible waste to leave half a ton of meat rotting.

I did mention that but, like usual, got howled down. Some of the boys said what the hell, there was millions of them, although Charlie said that wasn't so, not where we was, anyhow, they having near enough all been shot off, and that them millions was way out West.

But that shooting put Dutton in a better frame of mind, and things eased up some, so the boys started joshing again and telling tall tales, although they was less about the past than the future, because we were almost through Indian Territory and nearing Kansas, which is to say Abilene, which was to say saloons and dance halls and girls, and the way the boys spoke of them, you'd have thought that burg was bursting at the seams with female angels.

We still had to get there, moving the herd, the country kind of heaving up, getting higher, you know? Higher and flatter, and sort of bare, and then we splashed across Bluff Creek and Fall Creek, and we was in Kansas, and back in the United States. And I say *back* in, because Indian Territory wasn't part of the U.S., and, in fact, none of us figured Texas was, neither. No, sir, we reckoned Texas was part of nothing. Even during the war, we'd reckoned that the Confederacy was part of *us*.

Still, there we was in Kansas, and didn't the boys curse the soil they was on. They hated it more than New England even, because they reckoned the war had started right there, them Abolitioners from the North pushing in settlers so's it would be voted a free state and not a slave state, and many a poor farmer from the Southland had been murdered in his sleep by anti-slave preachers like John Brown and his sons. Course, no one mentioned fellers like Quantrill and his gang, who'd gone around murdering abolishers in *their* sleep, but that was only natural, us being Southern ourselves.

I did wonder, though, what Tom made of that talk, him being a nigger and his ma and pa slaves, but he kept clammed up about it, like the boys wasn't talking about him, which had some truth in it at that. As for me, I just bore in mind what old Preacher Tyler had told us, "Go and predate on the North," and I was just itching to do that, predate like all get-out!

We was on the high prairie land then, walking the steers and letting that Plains land slide by, and, brother, there sure was plenty of it. I've heard some folks say they don't like the Plains, saying they're tedious, all the same whichever way you look, but I had a feel for them, especially in the evening. They had a kind of haunting, the grass rippling, and the sense you got of the land rolling and dipping away, like it might be forever, all the way to the end of the earth, and over it all the huge sky, sometimes with rainbows a hundred miles across. I could half imagine then how them Indians must have felt roaming free and unfettered over the whole wide country, yeah, and how they got the notion that the earth was their ma and the sky their pa, and all being part of some bigger god, although, whoever he was, he surely was partial to wind, because didn't it blow! Jeepers, it was like there was some giant out there with a bellows shoving hot air onto us.

One blessing, we wasn't hurrying now. Short drives and plenty of loafing, because old Dutton, he sure knew his business, and he was letting the steers get some fat back on them before hitting the market. So we was merely ambling, crossing the Arkansas River, which was just no problem at all, and the last we had to cross, which was a good day's work at that and just all downhill to Abilene, so we was all in a good humor that night. Only Dutton and Tom was somewhat distracted, moving away from the campfire, snuffing the air, and muttering together. Hank asked what was the matter, and Dutton shook his head.

"You boys reckon it's getting hotter?" he asked.

It had been hot as Hades all day, and you expected it to cool off some in the evening, but, now Dutton had mentioned it, cool it wasn't, and the air felt different somehow, although just how would be hard to say.

Dutton rubbed his chin. "Could be a storm coming."

We all looked at the sky, but it was as clear as glass,

stars shining and all, so Dutton sort of let it go, which was a relief, us thinking he was going to order double watch. "But keep alert out there," he said. "Just keep goddamn alert."

We said we would, and didn't we just mean it, and turned in, and turned out, too, the watch having been shifted again, me and Bo taking over from Tom and Jack, who always rode night herd together.

They was kind of serious, and before they moved off, Tom got hold of me. "Remember what I told you once," he said. "Keep clear of trouble."

Not being as ignorant as I had been, I didn't feel no resentment, just saying "Surely," and took my turn around the herd. It was a strange night, hot and stuffy, with little puffs of wind, which was even hotter, the sort of night to make a feller feel restless, and it made the steers so, too. They wasn't exactly doing anything, but you could sense a kind of *mood*. They just didn't seem contented, so I kept my distance, aiming to give myself room in case they did run.

As our watch wore away, the weather turned cooler, and I relaxed somewhat, leaning back in my saddle, letting my legs hang free, and singing about some poor cowboy. And, you know, I didn't have no timepiece, but you got a feel for the time out there, so, just to make sure, I looked up at the Big Dipper, and it wasn't there, and while I blinked, because it sure had been the last time I looked, the sky just opened like it had been split by an ax, a flash of lightning blinded me and a gigantic crack of thunder deafened me, and, almost as quick as that lightning, the whole herd was on its feet and heading right at me.

I was that confused I didn't know where I was at, but my pony did. He was out of the way in two jumps, but he hadn't jumped far enough because the herd had split and half of it was heading right at me with what seemed like the sole intention of putting an end to my brief existence, so I did exactly what Tom had advised. I lit out of there as fast and as far as I could, and I must have gone a mile before I pulled up. Way over to my left I could hear them steers bawling and the hammering of their hooves, and the banging of six-shooters, so it was more like a battle raging away than anything else.

But I figured them steers was heading in the right direction—away from me, that is—so I turned and headed back, whooping and hollering like the best. I even blasted off the round out of my handgun, just to let the boys know I was on the job. Not that I need have bothered, because no one was concerned about me that night. It was the herd that mattered, and it was heading south like it had an urgent appointment in Texas—and between them and it was the Arkansas River.

I'd got over my worst scare by then, but it still wasn't no fun galloping across the prairie in the dark, not to mention that occasionally I'd find a steer coming at me out of the darkness, and if you want to taste that experience, try standing in front of an express train sometime. But me and the pony was of one mind that night. Anything we saw move, we moved too, faster and in the opposite direction.

One time we moved wrong, though. A shape loomed up and we was ready to get going, but it was Collins, spitting with rage and fury worser than a mountain lion. I was truly sorry to see him, knowing he'd be heading where the going was roughest and I'd have to follow him, which he did and I did, so I found myself right up against the main herd, and sparks! wasn't they going some. I could see them white horns tossing up and down and the flashes of the six-shooters as the rider shot across the noses of the steers at point, trying to turn them. It looked just like a wild sense-less scramble, but as I followed Collins, I saw that most of the boys was on our side of the herd, leaning on it, as you might say, trying to get it turned and milling, which would bring them to a halt sooner instead of later, and together at that.

I did the best I could, like whooping and shouting, and it was the scariest night I'd ever spent, because there was always the chance of being thrown and breaking your neck or getting hooked and trampled to death. One blessing was that we was on a prairie, so there wasn't thrashing through mesquite or chaparral or thickets. On the other hand, them steers had a clear run with nothing between them and the river, and if they hit that, the whole herd could have been lost.

As it worked out, we did lose steers in the river, but we got most of the herd turned, although we didn't get them to mill, so when dawn broke, the herd was spread out over miles of prairie, just miles and miles, and we had a wearisome time that morning rounding them up. In fact, what with that and getting steers out of the river, it was near dusk when we'd finished, and every last man of us was fit to drop, including Tom. But it was double watch that night all the same, and to make that watch even more wearisome, Gus said, "And that's surely the end of the bonus"—which it was at that, us having lost ten, twelve steers, and them left being ten pounds lighter. Figure it out, ten pounds of beef of a thousand steers. Which is a powerful lot of beef.

So, although, funnily enough, Dutton was what they call philosophical about it, just saying herds did stampede, it didn't make our last haul sweeter, over that Kansas plain where the sun beat down like it wanted to get at what brains you had and frazzle them up. Days of it, your nose and mouth clogged with dust, your tongue like a block of wood, and your eyes like the two of diamonds. Jeepers, I thought of Old Hobs saying how them sodbusters was going to come out and farm there and figured him living with them Indians had driven him loco. Any sane man would

106

have sooner lived in hell, where he'd at least have had plenty of company. And we run out of most all of the grub, and Dutton wouldn't break to go into a nearby town, so I got to thinking we was going to end up like that old king in the Bible that went loco himself and ended up living on grass.

Then one nooning we got to the chuck wagon, which was by a muddy creek that wasn't no more than that. Charlie was scowling and Dutton had a grim look.

"Sam Hill," Johnny croaked, "what's wrong now?"

Not being mind readers, we couldn't say, but we threw the herd off the trail all subdued, and having the last of the beans, we was more so when Dutton spoke to us, looking even grimmer.

"Right, you buckaroos," he said. "You think you've had a hard time. One bad river crossing and one stampede! Moses, I've been on drives when *every* crossing was bad, we had a stampede every night, and was fighting off wolves and Indians and Jayhawkers and farmers and the Lord knows what else. But then you ain't cowboys, you're just a bunch of greenhorns. I've seen women better in the saddle! Well, now you're really going to earn your corn. You see there?"

He pointed across that apology of a creek to where the prairie kind of rolled up.

"We see it," Jack said, real tough, like he didn't much care for being told off like some schoolkid. "What of it?"

"That's what you're going to find out," Dutton said. "You all tooled up?"

We looked at each other, the boys patted their holsters, and there was some coughings and licking of lips, wasn't there just, all nervous, you know?

Then Jack spoke up again. "If there's something over that brow that means using a gun, I want to know what it is before I get there."

"Yeah." Dutton waved the Winchester he was carrying. "Well, I'll tell you. There's something over there we can't escape from, and if you want to eat, we've got to face it. Take my word for it."

Put like that, there wasn't no use in arguing, so we got back on our ponies and followed Dutton up the swell, nervous as all get-out. Then we got there and looked, and Dutton, Joe, and Tom burst out laughing fit to bust, because there, after all them wearisome miles, snaking away across the plain, shining in the sun, all black like two snakes, was the track of the Kansas Pacific Railroad, and miles down that track, a smudge really, but just recognizable as buildings of some sort, was a town.

"And that's it, boys," Dutton said. "That's Abilene."

MAKING IT

▪ ELEVEN ▪

So that was it, the end of the trail, not counting them few miles down to Abilene, which was no more than a saunter. I figured that, before the day was over, we'd be down there, frisking with the girls and drinking—well, I'd be drinking lemonade, but it would be real strong lemonade—and going to the theater, laughing at comics and all, and generally whooping it up. But wouldn't you just believe it, that ain't the way it worked out.

The way the cattle business was handled, the herds were kept out on the prairie until the boss found a buyer, and weren't we blue when Collins said sometimes herds were kept out there for months, maybe because the boss was holding out for a good price, or just fattening the steers up on the grazing. So the drive wasn't over until them steers went into the stockyards and someone else took the strain.

Be that as it may, we had to move the herd on again because Dutton wanted them bedded near better water, which we did, our faces as long as the steers, and they was even longer when we had got them bedded down and found there was no Dutton, and no chuck wagon. Just Charlie and the coffeepot! Wasn't there some cussing! Not much, there wasn't, only enough to start a prairie fire is all, but we cooled down when Charlie said Dutton had gone into town to get supplies and would be back that night.

It wasn't exactly dusk then, and normally I'd have been

glad to just lie back early, but I had something else on my mind, so I had a quiet word with Bo and he had a word with Tom and he had a word with Joe.

"I don't know." Joe pushed his hat back, shaking his head, but Tom, who was grinning, said, "Come on, Joe. It can't hurt."

"Well . . ." Joe hesitated. "If someone will ride herd . . ."

Jack spat in the fire and said he didn't mind staying, and Amos said he'd go out on herd, too, so Joe said okay, he'd take care of the camp with Charlie, and the rest of us mounted up, rode over the prairie for a couple of miles, reined in, and looked down.

"So that's it," Johnny said.

"That's it," Tom said. "That's the Kansas Pacific Railroad."

Course I'd heard of railroads, but I'd never seen one, and now here I was, gazing at a 100 percent genuine track, and I've got to say, it wasn't much to look at, just them two rails snaking away on them ties, and Jehoshaphat, wasn't there some of them! Just millions is all, propping up them rails, and every one brought from the Lord knew where, because there wasn't enough timber on them prairies to pick your teeth with.

But there it was, splitting the prairie, and I thought of what Old Hobs had said, way back in Indian Territory, about railroads meaning the end of the free West, and figured he was even crazier about that than them farmers. Why, a gopher could have picked up them rails and carried them off. Still, we all stared solemnly down, and I guess we was feeling somewhat stupid because once you'd seen one bit you'd seen all there was *to* see.

Then Bo looked around. "And that's the telegraph line?"

We stared solemnly at that, too, and felt just as stupid because that wasn't much more than a lot of poles sticking up with wire slung between them.

"Yeah," Tom said. "You listen and you can hear them messages."

We listened and it was true, leastways we thought it was, you could hear the wires humming, you know, and it was a strange thought that you could just stick up them stumps and wire and get a message as far as that stuff went.

"There's another thing you can hear," Tom said. "You put your head on them rails and you can hear the train coming."

"Come on now," Bo said, scornful.

"It's the truth," Tom said. "So help me. You try it."

Bo looked at Tom, and at the rail, and then, you couldn't help but notice it, both ways along the track, swung down, swallowed, and stuck his ear to the rail. "There ain't a sound," he said.

"Then there ain't no train coming," Tom said. He turned to the rest of the boys. "Go ahead, you try it."

Somewhat pale under their tans, they did, too, and then it was my turn, but there wasn't no way in tarnation I was going to lie there with my head across a railroad track, and I didn't mind being thought a chicken, because I intended staying a chicken with its head on.

We did some more staring at the track and listening to the telegraph, until Tom said we ought to be getting back. We mounted and was just pulling away when Tom held up his hand.

"You hear that?" he said.

We all strained our ears, but to tell the truth we didn't know what we was listening for, but then I caught a kind of weird *shuh-shuh-shuhing* somewhat like a snake, and then a chugging, and then it came—a real train! Yes, sir, a real train coming along, smoke pluming out, getting bigger and bigger as it headed at us—and didn't our ponies buck! They'd never seen nothing like that, and neither had we, but the boys weren't fazed.

113

"Jupiter," Bo said. "I thought them things went twenty miles an hour. I'll give that mossyback a race."

That train got to us, all smoking and sizzling and swaying and bucking like it was going to jump the rails any minute, smelling something terrible. Sparks was flying out of the stovepipe. The engineers leaned out of their cab and waved at us, and the boys lit out, waving their hats and hollering, racing that train down the line.

At first they *did* race it. It surely was a sight, them Texans riding free as birds right along that train and at first beating it, because it wasn't going fast at all, but the train kept on going, if you get me, and I reckon it kept on going at the same pace all the way to Kansas City. The ponies couldn't keep up the pace, and I don't think a corn-fed horse could have, neither. After a quarter mile or so, the boys' ponies were blown out and they had to pull up while that train chugged away, the engineers giving the thumbs-down sign. And they must have had some kind of blower or whatever, because the train gave a big whistle, like saying, "Fare-thee-well, suckers!"

And that was the end of our trip to the railroad. We walked the ponies back real slow, letting them get their wind back, because Dutton would have blasted us to kingdom come did he know we'd been racing them. And that amble back sure was nice. The stars peeking out, one by one, like they was shy kids in a cabin when a stranger calls, all of us real buddies, and to hell with Tom being a nigger. And miles and miles away, the train making that mournful whistle, which I surely grew to love, because sometimes out there on the Plains, with maybe the nearest human being forty miles away, you'd hear it—and if them engineers saw a light out there they'd sound it—and you'd sleep better for it, and I guess millions of Americans have felt the same, too.

And there was something else which kind of moved me.

We were crossing one of them rolling swells, with the prairie dark and somber, and that darned wind had fallen for once so that all was still, so you could have heard a leaf fall a mile away—if there'd been any trees, that is—and far away across them tracks there was a light shining, a yellow speck, like it might be a settler's cabin, and it made me think of home and get somewhat weepy, and I guess millions of Americans have thought of *that*, too, no matter where they've roamed.

Then we was over the swell, and down below was the glow of our campfire, and the herd, and the boss, and the chuck wagon.

And, jeepers, what a meal we had that night. Dutton did us proud. We had steak and fresh hens' eggs and greens, and a can of peaches apiece, which was the most delicious things I'd ever tasted. Lord, as that juice ran down my throat, I reckoned I wouldn't never live on nothing else so long as I lived. Yes, sir, that meal set us up, and we was in high spirits when Dutton hushed us up because he had something to say.

He stood against the chuck wagon, a mug of coffee in his hand. "Okay, boys," he said. "I reckon you know the job ain't done until the herd is in the stockyards. I want that to happen as soon as you do, and I've been into Abilene checking out prices, and I ain't selling yet."

We all groaned, and Dutton got sharp again. "I said I ain't selling yet, and I ain't going to sell until I get the right price. I've a responsibility to the owners of these steers, so quit that groaning. Anyhow, you'll be having it easy *and* getting paid."

Well, that wasn't so bad, and Dutton hadn't finished. "I ain't a hard man," he went on, which was news to us. "And I know you're all itching to get into town, so I've no objection to you taking it turn about, and advance you some pay. How's that?"

He didn't need to ask, because it was just fine, fine and dandy, although Gus asked why we needed anyone in camp at all at night, saying the herd wasn't going noplace and, left alone, they'd just settle down. "Then we can all go into town together," he opined. "Same way as we got here."

But Dutton wasn't wearing that. "There's other herds coming up," he said. "And I don't want the steers getting mixed up. Anyhow, Abilene's got a night herd law."

Charlie cackled and got a glare from Dutton. "All right," he said. "That law is to stop the herds trampling on crops, and there ain't hardly any farms this side of the Smoky Hill River, but it's the law and I'm sticking by it. Now decide among yourselves who's going in and who ain't, and it's night herd as usual until tomorrow."

Us boys gabbed for a while and decided we'd take turns to go in groups of three apiece, and we drew sticks—well, I didn't, because it was taken for granted I'd be going with Bo, and it turned out him and Jack Shears won. So, come the morn, we were going to have a holiday, and didn't we relish that? Not much more than a dog relishes a bone, we didn't.

At dawn we was up and raring to go, but Dutton had a word with us while he was advancing us ten bucks each.

"Don't you boys go thinking you can go charging about that town whooping like redskins. They got laws, and they got law enforcers, a feller called Hickok, Wild Bill, they calls him, he's the town marshal, and he's got six policemen who ain't no blushing rosebuds. And you ain't allowed to carry handguns, so park your shooters with the marshal."

"Not carry a gun!" Bo blew out his cheeks. "This ain't no Sunday School outing. I hear there's some tough hombres in that town."

"Which is why I'm telling you to hand in your guns," Dutton said. "If you run into trouble, go to the lawmen.

116

And steer clear of crooked card games, bad whiskey, and worse women. But I guess that's baying at the moon."

It sure was, since them things was what the boys was longing for and aimed to get, too, but I reckon Dutton had to say it. He shrugged and said that was okay then, and we was getting ready to mount up when Gus said, "What the blazes is this here?" And coming into camp was a horse and a kind of square wagon driven by a feller in a stovepipe hat, who was a picture man, wanting to take a tintype of us. Course we all wanted a picture taken, but we wanted it in new duds and us cleaned up and all, but Dutton said we might not get another chance with us all together, so we had it done. The feller said it would be ready in a couple of days. Then we mounted and Jack said, "Well, boys, let's go and see the elephant," which was a phrase fellers used a lot in them days when going to see something new or special, it coming from a giant elephant which was being shown back East.

"Why, sure." Bo grinned and winked at me. "Come on, kid, let's do that thing. Let's go see the elephant."

I sure was excited. Riding through a couple of herds and splashing across the Smoky Hill, where Dutton split from us, saying if we needed him he'd be at the Drovers Cottage, a swank hotel by the stockyards where the dealers hung out, and leaving us to go to where the real action was.

And didn't that look like some town to us Curtis boys! We'd come in from the east, right onto Texas Street, and I hadn't seen nothing like that in my life. Them saloons and stores and offices and the street choked with wagons. It sure was something to see, but I got hustled into a barbershop, where we got a hot bath and a haircut. Then, about twenty pounds lighter, and feeling all strange at that, we went to the Great Western Store and got new cowboy duds on credit Dutton had fixed for us, then went and hit the town.

First off, we went to the Alamo, which was just about the most famous saloon there was, with a bar a mile long, all shiny woodwork, looking glasses big as doors, and pictures of ladies with no clothes on! They sure looked funny, too, but Bo told me not to look, although he spent some time staring at them, when he wasn't admiring himself in one of them looking glasses. Then we settled down in real luxurious chairs like I guess millionaires can sit in anytime they want, stretching out our legs and smoking big cigars, and I reckon no one, however rich, felt better than we did—well, better than Bo and Jack, because after a couple of puffs on my cigar I felt real sick, so I chucked it away.

It was something at that, laying back and seeing all them folks, the like of which I hadn't ever seen before, drovers and dealers and traveling men and riders, all dressed up flash as anything, all drinking and yelling and playing cards.

I could have sat there all day, but Bo said we should maybe look around and check in our handguns, although no one had complained.

We went out and Jack said he'd mosey around on his own for a while and maybe meet up with us later. I asked Bo where he'd gone, but Bo said to mind my own business, which I got to doing, and anyhow there was too much to look at without bothering about Jack.

I was dazed, you know? Them sights, and the noise! We'd been weeks and weeks hearing nothing but what you might call *natural* sounds, steers lowing, birds, the wind. And here there was this amazing racket. Jeepers, there was some noise, bands in saloons, pianos crashing away, banjos twanging, and wagon drivers cursing—and just the din of fellers talking and shouting, because there was a mass of folks wandering up and down that street, hundreds of Texan riders, real Southern boys, high, wide, and handsome, and greasers and niggers and bullyboys, too, hanging

118

around the saloons shouting "Come in, boys, come right in, gals and whiskey and a straight game. Come on, faro, keno, poker."

But we didn't play no games then, Bo saying he'd get into a game later, so we checked our handguns at the marshal's office, handing them in to a policeman who, like Dutton had said, didn't look like no blushing rosebud. Bo asked him where that Wild Bill Hickok might be, curious to see him, you know, but the feller just grunted and said he didn't get around till later. So we left and had a slap-up meal and went to the Novelty Theater and that *was* something, with a juggler, an acrobat, a singer, and the most comicalist feller you ever did see, and I laughed till the tears was rolling down my cheeks.

It sure was turning out to be some day, one I reckoned I wouldn't never forget, and I kind of wrote it in my head, the 13th day of June 1871, just so's it would stick there.

And that day hadn't hardly even begun for us, because we went into a saloon called the Bull's Head and Bo got himself a drink and we got into a keno game. It was one of the best games I'd ever played at that, maybe fifty riders with their cards, listening to the numbers being called and hoping you'd get a line-up and shout *Keno!* and get a wad of dollars. I nearly did get a line, too, but then Bo said he'd like something with a little more action and he got himself another drink, did some talking to a barman, nodded, then waved me to follow him outside into that heat and racket, and headed off Texas Street, down to the South Side.

Sounds innocent, don't it, the South Side? Like it's just another district, it standing to reason every town's got a north and a south, but that South Side was across the railroad from Texas Street, and it was the wrong side of them tracks. The way of it being, them Western towns had what you might call a respectable side, and one which wasn't, and the South Side wasn't, for sure. Course the law operated down there, them policemen roamed around, but so long as there wasn't no shooting, why, they was ready to turn a blind eye to what was going on, although that day I didn't really have a notion as to what *was* going on.

But as we crossed the tracks, I knew that I didn't like it any too much. It was shabby, there weren't no stores or plush saloons, just a shantytown full of low dives kind of pretending to be saloons, daubed with a bit of gaudy paint, real cheap-looking and kind of an insult, as if the fellers who ran them didn't really give two hoots what you thought, knowing they was going to get you in the end. And I didn't like the barkers outside them dives, neither. They was tough hombres, like you'd expect, but tough the wrong way, greasy and not shaved, and if you didn't go in, they shouted after you, taunting as may be. It sure didn't look like no place to be, and I told Bo that, but he just grinned.

"Kid," he said, "I feel like having me a dance! You'd like that, wouldn't you?"

Well, I didn't mind, because I'd been to a couple of barn dances back in Clement, so I said okay, and Bo steered me into a kind of shed and there was a dance going on in there, but it sure wasn't like no barn dance.

There was a band—well, it was a fiddler and a feller playing the banjo—and you paid a quarter, went in, picked yourself a girl, and hopped around, hat on and spurs, and wasn't there some hopping going on! The boys was hopping around, jumping and banging into each other, most of them drunk, and jumping so's you'd have thought the floor would bust. Bo urged me to have a dance, but I hung back. Why, I'd have got trampled to death, and besides, girls wasn't the right name for them partners. They was older than the Widow Hatton, most of them, and all plastered with white powder which smelled terrible sickly and kept flaking off so's it was like being in a blizzard in there.

It wasn't my idea of fun. In fact, it seemed plain crazy doing that when we could have been in the Alamo, or playing keno, but Bo kept at it, dancing and drinking, until finally he came over to me, all flushed and laughing.

"That's got some of the jumps out of me," he said. "Some, haw-haw!" Laughing, although why beat me. "But now, kid, I'm going to do a little depredating."

"De-what?" I asked, because it sounded something awful.

Bo grinned. "You remember old Tyler, when he said go North and depredate on the North like they'd done to us? Well, that's what I'm aiming to do right now, because I feel lucky tonight. Real lucky."

When he said that, I had a bad feeling, low as it might be. "Bo," I said, "just what you aiming to do?"

"Kid," Bo said, "I'm going to sit in on a poker game."

That's what I thought he'd meant, and it made me feel even lower. "Bo"—I had to shout over that noise in there— "Bo, I don't think that's what Tyler meant."

"No?" Bo had a big drink of whiskey in his hand, and he drank it right back. "I don't give a goddamn what that old buzzard meant. I was just talking to a feller at the bar and he says next door there's a real good straight game, and that's where we're going."

He gave a whoop and rolled his eyes and so there wasn't nothing for it but for me to follow him into Coogan's, a sort of drinking den next door, and the minute I went in, that low feeling went right down to my boots. I didn't like the smell of that place one little bit, and I don't just mean the stink of sour beer and bad whiskey. It was badly lit, only a couple of hurricane lamps flaring away, and although there was a couple of riders in there, they was dead drunk, and the other fellers looked more like them saddle tramps we'd met on the trail. A woman who looked old enough to be our grandma, with more paint on her face than a Comanche on the warpath, came over, smiling and showing rotten teeth and saying "Howdy," and what a fine-looking boy Bo was, and had I come along for the ride or what. In fact, although I hadn't been in any saloons saving back in Lookout and them swell places on Texas Street, it looked like the sort of place where *we* was going to be depredated on.

I tugged at Bo's sleeve because it seemed plain crazy to me to be in a joint like that when we could be someplace else, but a bozo in a frock coat and a dirty green cravat with a big stickpin came over, too, and started giving Bo the glad hand and free booze. What with Bo getting drunker and that old woman putting her arm around his neck, I was getting just disgusted. And then, and I've never been more glad to see anyone in my life, a door at the back opened and Jack Shears came in, buttoning up his vest.

Well, Jack wasn't the kind of feller to show much expression, but his eyes widened when he saw us in there—at least they did when he saw me—but he joined us, and that feller and the woman eased away.

Bo shoved a drink on Jack, which he took, and they talked for a while about the town, Bo saying what a dandy time we'd been having, and then he said he was going to play poker.

"Poker, huh?" Jack nodded in that cold way he had. "Where?"

"Right here," Bo said. "There's a game going on."

Jack looked at a corner where a game was being played. "Why here?" he said, keeping his voice down.

Bo grinned and he looked real foolish, too, not like Bo at all. "Because it's close to them home comforts," he said and burst out laughing. "Which I reckon you've tasted!"

I thought maybe there was an eating place through that back door and thought maybe some more grub wouldn't hurt at that, but I was going to say I'd sooner eat someplace else, when Jack spoke again. "You played much poker?"

"Sure have," Bo said, drinking more whiskey. "When I rode for the Harvey spread, we played all the time come night, and I was mighty good."

"Yeah." Jack took a drink as well. "That's one thing."

"Course it's one thing." Bo did that foolish laugh again. Someone half drunk bumped into Jack and he gave that bozo that look he had, and half drunk though he was, the feller got the message and eased away.

Then Jack turned back to Bo. "It's none of my affair," he said. "And if you want to lose your wad, that's up to you. But playing in here ain't like a game in a bunkhouse."

"Hell"—Bo started to look mad—"you saying I can't hold my own?"

Jack glanced around that terrible barroom, then shrugged. "Okay," he said. "It's your business"—and he kind of faded into a corner.

"It sure is"—Bo was almost shouting.

Well, like I say, I didn't know much about saloons, and I knew less about gambling, but I knew enough to listen to Jack when he gave the word, so I got hold of Bo's arm and said, "Listen to Jack, won't you?"

I reckon I made a mistake there. Bo was drunk but no fool, and though he might have been swayed by Jack, he wasn't going to be told nothing by me. He shook me off, saying he didn't need no advice from a calf that hadn't hardly learned to suck, and found himself a space at that poker game. And the company wasn't nothing to write home to Ma about.

There was a couple of riders peering at their cards like they was seeing ten cards in their hands, a regular gambling man, dolled up fancy but filthy underneath it, a bozo who might have been anything but who was mighty tough-looking, and next to Bo on his right, a tight-faced hombre wearing a dust coat and a sneer, who seemed as drunk as the riders.

"Deal me in," Bo shouted. "And have a drink on a Texan who knows an ace from a deuce and learned to wink at a one-eyed jack when he was in his cradle"—and such-like foolishness.

The other fellers haw-hawed, took the drinks, slapped him on the shoulder, saying what a fine feller he was, and that gambling man bought Bo a drink, telling him he looked a mighty sharp player and they'd all have to watch out, and then they settled down to rob Bo blind.

Course, I didn't know it then, although I sure do now. It wasn't the riders, they was nearly out of the game anyhow, but the other three, who was just pretending to be drunk. First they let him win some, then made him lose some, then win, then lose, and as the hands got dealt, Bo started losing more than he was winning, but with a lucky hand every now and then just to keep him simmering, and then they gave him a real hand, like a real one, a hand you'd bet your life on anytime.

Bo stared at that hand and laid it face down, brooded for a while, not looking like the Bo I knew at all, then put every cent he'd got on the table, and I mean he put down them bucks from Tyler, too—and he got cleaned out.

That feller in the dust coat it was, he laid four aces, taking his time doing it, one by one, and when Bo saw the last one, his face went red and then white, which is a terrible warning sign in a man, and like I've said, Bo sure had a temper when he was riled. But it wasn't just the losing that riled him, nor being cheated, neither, I guess, because many a man's had that happen to him and just swallowed it like medicine and learned his lesson. No, it was the way them bozos behaved, because all at once they wasn't drunk no more and sat leering at Bo, as if it wasn't enough to rob a poor cowboy but they had to rub it in as well.

And that got Bo. "Why," he said, "you goddamn four-flushing sideswindlers," and jumped to his feet, but that's as far as he did get because one of them bruisers got him in an armlock and another came over with a billy club and he was swinging it back when Jack moved in.

He didn't carry no gun so far as I could see, and either of them bruisers could have made two of him, but they eased off just the same.

"No need for that," Jack said. "He'll come quiet."

The bruiser with the club hesitated and took a good long peek at Jack, then jerked his head at the door. "Get him out of here—and see he don't come back."

"That's the notion," Jack said, and grabbed hold of Bo and started to walk him out. That, I guess, would have been that, but those fellers around the table started whistling Dixie, taunting-like, and when we got to the door, they was laughing like them hyenas you read about in Africa, which they sure resembled.

Hearing that, Jack stiffened some, but he kept on walking and steered us back onto Texas Street and into the Bull's Head, where he got us seats, which wasn't that easy, the time being what it was, and told us to hold tight while he got us some drinks.

Bo surely did look mean and sore, but not more than I felt. All that money gone! All gone up in smoke, just like that!

I told Bo, too, told him how sore and hopping mad *I* was, and he really rounded on me.

"Shut your goddamn mouth," he said. "You hear, now? Shut it or I'll shut it for you. Goddamn money's all you ever think of. I'll *give* you your share out of my pay. But shut up."

He leaned back, and I never saw him look so mean. It was like it wasn't Bo at all but a total stranger there, glaring at the drinks Jack brought and muttering to himself.

Jack tried to ease things off somewhat. He said he'd been taken himself the same way, but it was like paying for a lesson, and in a while it wouldn't mean beans.

"Anyway," he said, "the night's still young and I've got a stake left. We'll have another drink here, then maybe go see the Drovers Cottage. You been there? It's a mighty fine place"—saying more than he'd done the whole trip through, but although Bo was sort of nodding and muttering yeah, I could see he wasn't listening, and I wasn't listening much myself neither.

Finally Jack gave up the attempt and we sat for a while, then Bo said we would go to the Drovers but he was going to the back first.

He left and we waited, listening to a nigger minstrel who was bellowing over the din in there, until Jack got impatient.

"Go get him," he said. "The way he was, he's probably out cold."

I got up and was trying to push my way through the mob around the bar when I heard roaring and shouting at the door, like there was a fight starting. The fellers around me was yelling what was it, and a big hulk shouted, "It's a cowboy. Killed outside Coogan's place!"

I knew who it was, knew it without thinking, and I was right at that, because when I ran down there, with a big crowd of riders coming out of every blasted saloon like they was off to a free show, there was Bo, lying outside that filthy, dirty bar, face down in the filthy, dirty street.

Things was kind of confused after that. There was a lot of noise and men and lights, but the next thing I really remember was sitting in a jail, with Jack talking to a feller with long yellow hair who was Marshal Hickok. Then Dut-

126

ton came and there was a lot more talking, until Dutton hauled me off to the Drovers Cottage. I recall struggling a lot, saying I wanted to be with Bo, but they wouldn't let me, and when I got to the Drovers, I was given some kind of medicine, which was for sleeping, and I just collapsed on a real bed, which was the first I'd ever slept in, but it didn't mean a thing.

The next day we found out what had happened, or what was said had happened. Bo had gone out of the Bull's Head and down to Coogan's to face up to them bullyboys. Them fellers there said the feller in the dust coat, whose name was Dutch Kessel, had gone out to calm Bo down, but Bo had pulled a gun, so Kessel shot him in self-defense. They handed over a pistol they said Bo had tried to use, but the whole thing was a pack of lies. Bo wasn't no gunslinger, and he didn't have a handgun anyway, and where would he have got one from?

No, we figured that Bo had gone around, seen he was up against real killers, and left, only to get shot down anyhow, which was plain murder. But the only witnesses was them bozos in the bar, and Kessel had run out of town, so there wasn't much anyone could do.

Not that they didn't try. Like all cattlemen, Dutton carried weight in Abilene and he used it, making sure there was a proper investigation, an inquest and all, although I ain't saying he needed to lean hard. In a town like Abilene, with a council and regular lawmen, a killing wasn't taken lightly, especially a rider, since that town lived on the cattle trade, and the businessmen who ran it didn't want it getting a bad reputation. And Marshal Hickok did the best he could, sending policemen out to look for Kessel and sending telegraphs to Kansas City about him, and although the marshal sure wasn't brokenhearted about it, he was decent enough to me, saying how he was sorry, especially since they hadn't had a murder in town in twelve months.

Anyways, they had the inquest, the verdict of which was open, meaning the jury couldn't make up their minds. And although there was some sizzling in town, all the riders being burned up about that killing, especially since, like a lot of gunmen, that Kessel was from some big city, New York, I heard, it fizzled out like rage and wrath tend to when it ain't your kin involved.

Then we buried Bo, and that was a sad and sorry day for me, even though it was some swell funeral, with a regular hearse and horses with black feathers on them. There was a regular preacher, the mayor, Marshal Hickok, businessmen and their wives, and most every rider in town, all hushed and respectful. The cattlemen and dealers paid for it all, and a marker, but it left a kind of bitter taste, Bo there having more money spent on him dead than he'd ever made in all those years of hard work.

I was fussed over some, and there was talk of a fund for me, but that didn't come to nothing, neither. Not that it mattered to me then, because all I could think of was Bo dead and another Curtis gone, and how I'd never see him again this side of Jordan, and how good he'd been to me when we was alone, like saying back in Lookout how we was brothers and was going to care for each other all the days of our lives, and now he'd been snuffed out by a feller worser than a rattlesnake.

And right there, when that coffin was lowered and the dirt shoveled on it, with all them riders singing "Rock of Ages, cleft for me, let me hide myself in Thee," when I really did know that I'd never ever again see Bo, I made me a vow! I vowed I'd get Kessel and do to him what he'd done to Bo. Yes, sir, Bo had gone to see the elephant, sure enough, and I was going to make sure Kessel went to see it, too.

■ TWELVE ■

After the burial, I went back to the herd and stayed there, because I couldn't stand the sight of Abilene no more. The boys was real kind, trying to comfort me, looking all gloomy and solemn and saying how they'd string Kessel up if they got their hands on him. But after a day or so, they got less gloomy and solemn. Not that I blamed them for it, Bo wasn't their brother, but it got to hurt, them joshing each other like nothing had happened. And although when I was around they tried to look sad, I could see it was a strain, so I took to riding double watches, day and night, riding around the steers, which had never done no harm to anyone, which was soothing, but then I'd get to thinking that they was just going off to be slaughtered, and I'd start to cry, remembering Bo. And, would you believe, that tintype hadn't come out, so's I didn't even have no picture to remind me of him.

Then, after a couple of weeks, Dutton said he'd sold the herd and we'd be moving it into the stockyards the next day, which we did, driving them into those huge corrals, getting the tally right, weighing them on that gigantic weighing machine, prodding them into the cattle cars, and that was the real end of the trail.

We went back to the chuck wagon for the payout. It was dusk and Charlie had lit the hurricane lamp and we stood around in its glow while Dutton got out his tally book.

"Right, boys," he said. "Payday!"

The boys whooped, and Dutton went on. "I was hoping to spring you a bonus, in spite of losing them steers coming up, but the price wasn't what I reckoned on, so there ain't going to be one."

129

That stopped the whooping, didn't it just! The boys looked as dolesome as I did, which irritated Dutton.

"It ain't *my* money," he said. "I'm just the drover, is all. When we get back to Texas, I'll try and spring a few more bucks from the owners. But you're getting what's due you, so stop pulling them faces like you is a lot of babies. Okay, I'll call out your names and you come and sign or make your mark."

One by one he called them forward, and they got their pay in hard cash, and then, last of all, he called me.

"Kid," he said, "you know how badly we all feel about Bo, but . . . well . . ." He coughed. "Anyhow, I said when I hired you that if you did a man's work you'd get a man's pay and you have. So here it is. Fifty days, a dollar a day, less"—he peered into his book—"less ten bucks' advance. Right?"

I said it was and signed the book, and there were some crosses there, but I noticed Tom had written his name in real fancy writing, and Dutton gave me forty bucks.

"Okay." Dutton slapped the book shut. "I reckon that wraps it up, boys. You can go and get lit up to your hearts' content."

Then a quiet, edgy voice come out of the gloom. "Ain't you forgetting something?" Jack Shears said.

Dutton frowned. "Forgetting what?"

"The kid's brother. He came up the trail with us."

"I know that," Dutton said.

"So where's his pay?"

Dutton shoved his head forward. "What are you driving at? I can't pay a dead man, can I? Saving your presence, kid."

"No, you can't," Jack said. "But you can give it to the kid. He's lawful next of kin, ain't he?"

"Now, you just hold on there," Dutton said, but Jack

130

butted in, "That money was rightly earned, so you hand it over—and I ain't arguing about it."

"Are you trying to intimidate me?" Dutton growled. "If you are, you've picked the wrong man." And that was true, him not being the kind of feller to back down from anyone.

"I ain't aiming to intimidate no one, whatever the hell that means," Jack said. "But I *am* aiming to make sure that kid gets a square deal."

He stepped forward and he had his pistol strapped on, which made him look even tougher than he usually did.

Dutton scowled. "You on the prod?"

"No, I ain't," Jack said. "Although, if Charlie there has any notion about reaching for that shotgun, he'd better forget it."

I don't know whether Charlie did have such a notion, although the way Jack spoke, if I'd have been him I'd have forgotten it, but in any case, and it surprised me as much as Dutton, Charlie said, "Pay the kid."

Dutton glared around. "What the hell is this, a goddamn debating society?"

"Nothing like that," Charlie said. "But it ain't going to sound good in Texas, you not paying the kid."

Maybe Dutton wouldn't have backed off from Jack, because, like I say, he was one hard hombre, and he would sure have had Tom on his side, but I guess it was the thought of folks talking back home that made him change his mind. At any rate, he paid up, and I got Bo's forty bucks, too, which meant I'd got eighty dollars in my poke.

That night, the boys went into town, and although they invited me along, I didn't go and stayed with Charlie by the fire. Course I thanked Charlie for speaking up for me, but he just told me to shut up and let him get down to some serious drinking in peace and quiet, his idea of a peaceful drink being howling at the moon and cussing the

131

rest of Creation. But that suited me because I was doing some thinking, and by the time the Big Dipper had swung halfway around the sky, I'd figured out what I was going to do and how, and hit the hay feeling better than I'd done for a long time.

We spent a few more days out there, just me and Charlie, with the boys coming in to sleep, which they did more during the day than the night, and then one evening Dutton rode in from town with all the boys.

"Okay," he said. "I've got all my business done and sold off the remuda, so, come tomorrow, me and Charlie is heading home. Tom's coming, too, definite, and Amos. The rest of you, it's your deal. Come or stay."

The boys yoled, and I guess it was time for them to go, being all spent up. Then Bob asked where Jack was.

"He ain't coming." Dutton sounded sour, like he was still burned up about that pay. "Anyhow, I'm spending the night in town, but I'll be back at dawn, and when I'm back, we move, pronto, and anyone ain't ready can walk home."

With that, he mounted and rode off, Tom following him, which he usually did, like he was a shadow, and the boys settled down for a good last drink, there being a few bottles handy, and to talk about what good times they'd had in Abilene, some of which wasn't exactly fitting for mixed company. Then Gus mentioned Jack, and where he was, and who he was.

"Hell"—Charlie spat in the fire—"a feller like him can find work to do anyplace out here. He could be scouting for the Army or riding guard on the railroad, buffalo hunting, or just plain honest bank robbing!"

That raised a laugh, being as no one in their right mind cared about a bank being robbed, so long as the robbers burned the debt notes, which all halfway decent robbers did.

"Anyhow," Charlie said, "one thing's for sure, he ain't gone farming."

That got another laugh, and Bob said it covered all the possibilities.

"The hell it does!" Charlie flared up like he did when he thought he was being contradicted—and when he wasn't, come to that. "He could be a lawman somewheres."

"A lawman!" Bob guffawed. "Charlie, that Jack was on the run *from* the law."

"You don't know that." Joe Collins spoke up, and he was somewhat wrathful.

"Not to actually know it," Bob admitted. "But—"

"But nothing," Collins shoved in. "You learn not to spout your mouth off. Anyhow, suppose he has got a tag on him. What of it? Maybe all he did was stick up a stagecoach to raise a grub stake. Goddamn, half the wanted men in the West is just poor soldier boys who got out of the Army to find the pickings gone to them who'd stayed home while they was fighting the goddamn Yankees."

Collins sounded more than sore, and I wondered whether he done some law-breaking himself, but Bob was mollifying. "Hell," he said. "I didn't mean nothing against banditting. *I* ain't got nothing to get banditted from me, anyhow."

"All right," Joe grunted. "Only don't go shooting your mouth off about a man's past, or you might find someone else shooting it off for you."

"We get you," Gus said, and handed over the whiskey bottle as a peace offering, and peaceable it was, really, sitting around the fire, as the night wore away, and the whiskey, until there was just one drink left, and Joe poured it out, then said, "Well, boys, it's fare-thee-well to the North and back home for us. But here's to Bo Curtis, who was as good a rider as I ever did see. And here's hoping that murdering dog who shot him gets what's coming to him."

133

The boys raised their cans and Amened that and we turned in. The others was soon asleep, but I lay awake, looking at the stars and listening to the wind, and it was nice and reminded me of the first night we'd joined the drive and how glad I'd been, but I didn't start no weeping. No, sir, it's a sad thing to say, but the iron had got into my soul, right into it.

Dutton had meant it when he'd said he'd be back at dawn, because the sun was hardly up when he rode in with Tom. He'd brought back some prime steak, which we had for breakfast with eggs, then we got cleaned up and the boys got their ponies, but I just stood by the wagon.

Dutton gave me a sour look. "Come on, kid," he said. "We ain't lingering."

"No, sir," I said. "But the thing is, well, I ain't going back."

"What!" Dutton stared at me. "What the hell does that mean? You can't stay here."

I shrugged. "It's what I'm doing, though."

Dutton muttered something under his breath, then got down from his horse and walked over to me. "Kid," he said, and he sounded halfway human. "This ain't got nothing to do with Bo's pay, has it? That was just business, and maybe I was wrong at that."

"No," I said. "It ain't that."

Dutton gave me a long look and rubbed his chin. "You wouldn't be figuring on staying around to get that Kessel, are you?"

"No." I looked him straight in the eye. "It's just I ain't got no folks left in Texas, and no home neither, so I'm going to stick up here and see something of the country."

"This ain't no country for you to be roaming around loose. You get on your pony. Hell, I'll fix you up with a job."

"I thank you," I said. "I truly appreciate that. But I'm staying."

"What the hell!" Dutton was exasperated. "You boys," he shouted, "come and talk some sense into this jackass."

The boys gathered around me, arguing and persuading and even threatening, like when Charlie said why the hell bother talking. "Tie him to the wagon," he said, but that was just bluster, and we all knew it. There wasn't a thing they could do and they knew it, so in the end they had to drop it, especially when Charlie said he didn't give a damn whether I stayed or not but he was lighting out.

So they gave in. They shook hands with me, said they'd see me sometime, and mounted, all except Tom.

"Kid," he said, "if you do run up against that Kessel, steer clear of him. Those handguns you've got won't be no use to you. In fact, I'd take them now if I didn't know you could get another anytime."

"I ain't looking for Kessel," I said.

"Sure," Tom said, all disbelieving. "Sure. Well, all the best."

He held out his hand and I took it, which was the first time I'd ever shaken hands with a nigger, but I was glad to do it. Then he mounted and they rode off, leaving me.

I stood there on the prairie in all that blazing heat, feeling proud and noble, like you do when you imagine you're dead and everyone is standing around your grave, weeping and saying how sorry they are for all the bad things they've done to you. That's how I felt, instead of feeling what I really was, which was a plain, stupid, ignorant, goddamned idiotic fool.

But that feeling sure began to creep in when I looked at what I'd got in front of me, two saddles and bedrolls and guns and all, and wondered how in Sam Hill I was going to get them to Abilene, because them saddles each weighed as much as I did. But I wasn't going to leave the stuff out there. It was worth cash and I was going to need it because I lied myself blue in the face to the boys. I was staying in Abilene to get Kessel. I'd figured it out that a dog like him would come back sooner or later, cowboys being his natural prey, like a coyote slinking after a herd. I knew it was wicked and wrong to lie, and the Almighty would pay you out for it, but I was kind of hoping by the time I got around to meeting Him it would have slipped His mind.

Anyhow, I stood there in that blistering heat, beginning to feel like that withered-up grass Tyler had told us about being thrown into an oven, when something like a bug came crawling over the prairie, which turned out to be that photograph feller, who picked me up, took me into town, and dropped me off at Texas and Cedar Streets, where there was a saddler's.

"Sorry about your brother," he said.

I thanked him and went into the store and the storekeeper said he was sorry, too, because all the town knew who I was and Bo's murder was what you call a talking point. In fact, I heard riders used to crowd into Coogan's bar to see where the killing had happened, which was disgusting, because Coogan made more money out of Bo's death than he ever had before.

Anyhow, although the storekeeper said he was sorry, it didn't make him openhanded because I didn't get more than a few dollars for Bo's stuff, him saying a used saddle and what have you weren't worth much, which was true at that, but was I burned up when a day later I looked in and saw it all laid out with a big sign saying: SAD AND SORRY RELICS OF BEAUREGARD CURTIS. SHOT DEAD IN TOWN. Which was what you might call a religious way of getting customers in the store so's they'd buy goods.

After selling Bo's gear, I went for a room. When I'd been in town before, I'd seen a rooming house which looked like the cockroaches weren't carrying it away, so I checked in there, although I near fainted when I heard the price. Since there wasn't much sense in sitting in the room all day, I went out and got some grub, and that cost a wad, too, and it grieved me, having to pay for it after eating for free on the trail, then I did a real vague thing. I headed down toward the South Side. I don't know, but I'd got a hazy notion I'd get some news about Kessel, maybe hear some bullyboy talking. I walked down Texas Street, dodging through them hordes of riders out on the spree, but I hadn't gone but a few yards when a feller hailed me. He wasn't no rider, a townsman more-like.

"Hey," he said. "Ain't you the Curtis boy?"

Jupiter, I thought, the news is spreading fast, and it was thrilling, like something in a dime novel, *The Curtis Kid in Town!* I felt real tough and braced myself and hooked my thumbs in my belt and sneered. "What if I am?" I said.

Looking back, it's so ridiculous that I wonder why that feller didn't turn me upside down and tan my backside, but he just said Marshal Hickok wanted to see me. "He's in the Alamo," he said.

"Yeah?" I don't know, but the sun had got to my head, because I sneered again. "If he wants to see me, I'll be around!"

The feller looked amazed. "Sonny," he said, "if the marshal says he wants to see you, I'd jump to it." Then he walked off, shaking his head and laughing.

I guess it was him laughing that took the sand out of my craw, and I thought, well, if the marshal was keen on my company, it would only be polite to call on him. In fact, the more I thought about it, the more convinced I was, so I turned around and moseyed up to the Alamo, and there was Marshal Hickok sure enough, playing poker with some buddies, and if you think that's a strange way for a marshal to run a town, all I can say is that's the way he did, like he let his policemen do the patrolling and he sat drinking and card playing as if the very name Hickok would strike fear and terror into the hearts of evildoers, and there was something in that. He had a name, you know, although he didn't look like no wild man because he was a real fancy dresser, in a frock coat and vest with embroidery on it and a cravat and long yellow hair that a woman would have been proud of.

I waited until the hand was finished, which Hickok won, and didn't he rake in some chips, then said, "Marshal?"

Hickok studied me for a while, like he was sizing up a poker hand, lit a huge cigar, and ran his glims over me again, and they was cold glims, too, blue and icy, although, would you believe, that iciness was because he was short-sighted! Amazing, ain't it. The most feared lawman in the West and he couldn't hardly see!

"What are you doing in town?" he said. "Dutton's moved out."

Well, dumb I might have been, but I had that figured out, which I'd done on the prairie, remembering that marshal back in Lookout.

"Marshal," I said in a dolesome voice, "I'm an orphan and Bo was all the kin I had"—leaving out Flo—"and it just doesn't seem fitting to go and leave his lonely grave without no one to care for it and all." Which last bit I recalled Ma reading to me out of a book she had and which always made her and Flo weep. But it didn't make Hickok weep none.

"And just what are you aiming to do, apart from tending your brother's lonely grave," he said, all cold.

"Well, sir," I said, "I reckon I can get me a job. I'm willing to do most anything. I can do the three Rs, Marshal."

"Yeah?" Hickok didn't sound like that was earthshaking news to him. "You got a handgun?"

"No, sir!" I lied. "I sold it. And I got some money, Marshal."

Hickok blew out a huge smoke ring and looked at me through it, like staring through a hangman's noose. "You ever hear of a white affidavit?"

"Yes, sir," I said, them white affidavits being what lawmen might stick on someone they didn't want around, which meant they'd shoot them on sight, and which was against the law, but they did it!

"Okay." Hickok took another big puff on his cigar. "You can stay, but if you go to the South Side or in a saloon, I'll put a white affidavit on you. Got that?"

I got it, but Hickok hadn't finished.

"If you've any notion of revenge, get it right out of your head. There's only one law in this town, and I'm it. You got that as well?"

I said I surely had, and that I didn't believe in venging anyhow, it being for the Lord—sticking that in to soothe the marshal.

"Right." Hickok waved me away, but he had a last word at that. "If you ain't got a regular respectable job in a week, you're with the next team back to Texas."

The Alamo had a big sign outside saying *Palatial Splendors*, meaning it was like some king's palace, and I guess it was, but I left them splendors with mixed feelings. One way of looking at it, I'd talked Hickok into letting me stay. The other way, all them restrictions made it downright impossible for me to find out about Kessel, and they meant I was in for a real dreary time in Abilene. The small towns is dreary enough now, but in them days, if you didn't go into saloons you didn't go anyplace saving the church, and I sure didn't want to go there.

So I was feeling blue, standing there watching all the boys reel about, and I might have found me some boys going back to Texas and beat it with them, but a hand grabbed me by the elbow. I jumped and turned, and holding me was one of them fellers from the marshal's poker game.

"Son," he said, "I heard you in there. Was you telling the truth?"

I didn't know what business it was of his, but I figured it wouldn't do no harm to do some more lying, so I said I was.

"Well, now," the feller said. "If you can read and write and figure, you go down the street to the *Chronicle* office and turn right. You'll see a Chink eating house and then a store, run by a feller named Besser. Jacob Besser. You got that? Right. You tell him you're looking for a job and tell him Dave Heaney sent you. I hear he maybe needs some help."

He slapped me on the back and beat it back in the saloon before I could thank him, so I moseyed down to the newspaper office, found the Chink's joint, and sure enough, next to it, off Texas Street, there was a store with *Jacob Besser, General Merchant* painted over a small window. I peered in and it didn't seem much of a place at that, dark and all higgledy-piggledy, but I went in and it had that smell of a real country store, made up of kerosene and flour and seed, musty-like, and after all them weeks living in the open air it downright depressed me.

I said, "Anyone to home?" and near jumped out of my skin when a voice right behind me said, "Yah."

"I'm looking for Jake Besser," I said.

"*Jacob* Besser," the voice said. "Jacob Besser. What you want with him?"

Well, actually he said, "Vot you vant mit im?" so I reckoned I was dealing with some foreigner, and I thought Judas Priest, why don't you learn to speak American, but

I wasn't there to give no lessons in speaking, so I let it pass and said, "I reckon I'll tell Besser when I meet him."

"I'm Besser," the feller said.

"Oh," I said, peering at him. My eyes was more used to the gloom, so I could see what he looked like, which was an average child of Creation, saving he was going bald, wore specs, and had a big beard. "Okay, Mr. Besser. Dave Heaney sent me. Said you might give me a job."

"Give you a job?" Besser sounded somewhat baffled, and I guess he had reason to be, seeing a kid in riding boots and spurs and all pop up out of nowhere and ask for work. "What can you do for me? I got no cattle."

"Heck," I said. "Don't let that faze you. I can do anything you want, I reckon. I can read and write and figure, and"— I had one of them brain waves you read about—"and I can do weights. Sixteen ounces, that's a pound, ain't it?" And I stood back for some admiring from him.

He didn't seem to get it, though. "I don't understand," he said. "You're a cowboy, why do you want to work in a store?"

I pitched in there, all the stuff about Bo's lonely grave and what have you, but when I finished he looked more baffled than when I started. Sam Hill, I thought, if this just ain't my luck, I get a helping hand off an American and end up with a dumb foreigner. "Listen," I said. "All I want is a job. A *job*"—sticking it to him again to make sure he got the message. And I was going to say it again, but he held up his mitt.

"You got one!" he said.

I tell you, I near fainted on the spot. "I have?"

"Yah," Besser said. "I need some help, and if Mr. Heaney says you're okay I'll try you."

"Jeepers," I said. "I'm obliged, and you won't be sorry nohow."

"Right." Besser nodded. "A dollar a week!"

I near fainted again! A dollar! "Why," I said, yelled more-like, "that won't get me a room for a night, and Joshua, I was getting that for a day on the trail."

Besser shrugged and said he ran a store, not cattle, but he did say I could sleep in a little room at the back where he kept seed and stuff, and have free grub, and he'd do me a deal on new duds, seeing as how I couldn't go clanking around the store in spurs.

It was getting dark then and Besser lit a lamp about as bright as a glowworm and kind of hinted that I could start earning my dollar right there and then, but I figured I'd done enough for one day. In fact, I was so tired I near fell down on the way back to that rooming house. But I had some grub at the Chink's, and although it made Charlie's seem like the manna old Moses lived on, it made me feel somewhat better, and the coffee did, too, so I was at least halfway alive when I got to my room, but didn't I simmer when I found a feller sharing it!

He was a rider from a herd which had come in that day, a regular Texan, who cheered me somewhat by making it clear his one ambition was to get out of that room and whoop it up, and then cast me down by saying his two buddies were going to share the room with us! He was a decent feller, though. He said I could go out with him and live wild, but I said I'd just stay in and have a quiet night, at which he burst out laughing and left.

I hitched a chair up to the window, looking down on the street, seeing all the boys parade, and listening to some piano music from a barroom, which for once wasn't "Dixie." In fact, I remember that tune now. I guess a real music lover would call it plumb rubbish, and maybe it was, but it was like music you hear that sort of plays on your heartstrings because of when you heard it and what state you were in.

And I was in some sort of state, too, sitting side-straddle on the old chair, thinking of Bo moldering in his grave, not a quarter mile away, and I made another vow to care for that grave proper, and I did feel somewhat weepy, but I pulled myself up on a tight rein and counted my blessings, thinking, Lightning, only that morning I'd been on my lonesome out on the prairie, wondering what was going to happen to me, and now here I was, with a job, so's I wouldn't have to go forking out money like it grew on trees.

Wondering what old Besser was going to be like to work for, and yawning so wide I near split my face in half, I rolled into bed that tired I didn't even notice them Texans coming back, and anyone who doesn't notice three drunk Texans just has to be tired.

And the next morning I started work in the store.

▪ THIRTEEN ▪

Like I'd figured, old Besser was a foreigner, sure enough. Once he showed me on a map where he hailed from, right there in the middle of Europe. The way he talked, it was a mighty fine place, plenty of grass and water, and dirt so good you could plant a wooden leg and it came up a tree. In fact, he made it sound so fine I wanted to ask him why he lit out, but I figured he had a wanted poster on him. Either that or he was a plain straight liar.

Those first weeks I was too hassled to care about where he came from, or why. You know, he had me dusting! Dusting and feathering, with an apron hitched around my neck. I felt the biggest fool in all Creation but stuck it out because if I did that work which was only fitting for women, it showed how noble I was, making that sacrifice so I could keep my bounden word and vow to venge poor Bo.

But it was pure misery, being indoors all day, in the gloom and dark, with all them sickly smells getting at me, and the ceiling pressing down, and I sure got big pangs if any riders sashayed past, all rigged out in new duds, spurs flashing in the sun, and as carefree as jaybirds. And the work was plumb *wearing*. Not body wearing but brain wearing. Besser, he didn't cuss or holler like Joe Collins, but he pressed me all the time, remorseless, pressing on me, saying, "Where's the pickled eggs? How many? How many cans of tomatoes we got? How much denim? How much molasses?" It was sheer misery, and I couldn't even cuss, because iffen Besser wasn't crowding me, his missus was.

She was even more foreign than Besser, with yellow hair, and blue eyes bulging out. Mostly she sat at the back of the store with her daughter, Goblinka or whatever her name was. It beat me, at that. Like a feller might come, just looking around, and you'd have thought Mrs. Besser would have swanned over and given him the eye like them girls in the dance halls, because she wasn't a bad looker if you didn't mind two hundred pounds of beef on the hoof, but did she ever? No, sir, she was like her old man, forever fussing over them sodbusters who came in and lurked at the back of the store.

Having been brought up on what you might call a farm if you wanted to be sarcastical, I knew them fellers and their womenfolk, didn't I just. A woman about thirty looking ninety, with a brood of barefoot kids hanging on her skirts, and her feller with no teeth, trudging behind a mule, getting frazzled by the sun or froze by the winter, and then seeing what pitiful crop they raised, which was a miracle if it happened, getting all munched up by grasshoppers, and looking like he'd been struck by lightning.

But them months on a pony had got me despising anyone who plodded about, and them farmers there *did* plod, clumping about the store, mumbling about the weather and all, and watching every cent as if the government was going to stop making money. Why, they'd buy a pint of vinegar and expect the jar thrown in for free!

Old Besser fussed over them, and his missus fussed over the women, jabbering away over them mail-order catalogues which showed what women was wearing in New York, or in London, England, or Paris, France, and which was the most foolish, senseless stuff you ever did see. Mrs. Besser kept them magazines corralled mostly, but I got a peek at them now and then, looking at the back pages, where they showed what women wore under their dresses and which was downright amazing and would have been pure cruelty to put on a mule, leave alone a female woman.

And them nights was tedious, too, wasn't they just! We'd have supper, like some sort of bean cake which took a ten-pound hammer to crack and the jaws of a wolf to get down, then I'd go back in the store with Besser, who'd sit staring at a barrel of flour, and if I tried to chew the fat with him, he'd just grunt, more like an Indian than a human being. In fact, them nights was so tedious I used to go walk around the North Side after work, seeing as how Marshal Hickok hadn't said I couldn't go for a nice quiet stroll there.

Not that there was much to stroll about, if you get me. There were streets—well, there were pegs where streets might be one day if enough suckers came out and bought the vacant lots—and a few frame houses, sort of scattered around at random, and then there was the prairie.

I used to stand there looking at it, thousands of miles of it rolling away into the darkness, with that Kansas wind blowing—all empty, I was going to say, saving when you got down to it, them Plains were just packed with herds and riders and buffalo hunters and soldier boys, not to mention coyotes and wolves and rattlesnakes and Indians and such-like.

Still and all, it looked lonesome, and it felt lonesome. I used to look at the Big Dipper hanging up there in the sky and think how often I cussed it for taking it easy, swinging around the North Star when I was on night watch, and then I sort of pictured the boys having an easy ride home, sitting around the chuck wagon, joshing and tormenting Charlie, and come near to handing in my time to old Besser and tagging on to an outfit heading south, which I could have done any time, easy.

But then I'd remember my vow and head back to the store and my room, being in which made me feel like that Daniel in the Bible that got chewed up by lions in the fiery furnace and which I wouldn't have slept in but that Besser wouldn't let me bed down outside. I'd lie there, sweating and batting insects, thinking of Bo and Kessel, and how I was going to get him, and think of him sprawled in the dust, same as Bo had been, which might not have been a Christian way of ending a day but which sure suited me.

But, like a feller said to me once when we was riding the rods in New Mexico, you can get used to anything, and he ought to have known, seeing as how he'd done ten years in Leavenworth state penitentiary for blowing up his boss's house during a strike, and for which he was truly sorry, sorry the boss was out and that he'd been caught, that is. There's a lot of truth in that saying, and I sure got used to plenty of things in my time compared to which old Besser's joint was like paradise.

Things did brighten up one day when a couple of riders called in. Besser was at the back of the store, haggling with some millionaire sodbuster who'd got fifty cents cash to blow, and he waved me over to the riders.

I was somewhat amazed because I hadn't never been allowed to serve, I mean what you call *serve*, anyone before, but I moseyed over and asked the boys what I could do for them.

Well, them boys were more amazed than I was. They looked me over like a calf with six legs. "You Texan?" they asked.

I said I surely was, and a poor orphan child, too, and told them the whole shoot about Bo, and by the time I'd finished, they was sobbing on each other's shoulders, and I sold them a fancy belt, a skinning knife, a big box of candy, and a pound of Bull Durham, and they'd only come in for a hand sack of that!

They headed out, swearing they loved me more than ten brothers stuck into one, and I handed the cash over to Besser.

He took a mighty long look at the dough. "That was a good sale," he said.

"Yes, sir," I said, and to rub it in, I told him the boys had only dropped in to ask the time.

Besser didn't say no more, but after that, I got some freedom, serving any riders who called, and even sodbusters, so be it they spoke American. And if any traveling men dropped in, I got to helping Besser order, telling him what the boys liked, such as jinglebobs and fancy scarves, and trinkets they could take home for their sweethearts. Some of that stuff Besser would get in, but some he wouldn't, saying they cost too much to carry, like having too many stock on a range.

He showed me how that worked in his tally book. You put the profits in black and the losses in red, and old Besser, he looked like he didn't know why the chicken crossed the road—in fact, he looked like he didn't know they came out of eggs—but there wasn't much red in that book. And I've got to admit, even though it was for someone else, making money had its own interest.

So, working in the store had something going for it, and

I had a free room and grub, even if it was terrible, and if I wasn't exactly predating on the North like old Tyler had told us to, I was breaking even, and I still had that eighty in my socks—and my gun.

I tried my hand with that, getting ready for Kessel, because that was a worry. Like I'd think as how maybe he'd got back into town and was holed up somewhere, disguised in false whiskers, and that he'd heard about my vow and decided to plug me before I plugged him. And although I was truly grieved about Bo lying in his lonely grave and all, I wasn't in no hurry to keep him company. Not that I'd any fool notion of shooting it out with Kessel in a duel, which is merely a notion dreamed up by them writer fellers, all of who is plain loco anyhow, sitting around all day pretending they is someone else. No, sir, I was going to shoot him in the back like he'd done to Bo, and if you think that ain't exactly a genteel way of proceeding, then you've something to learn about the Old West.

But Sunday afternoons, which I got off, instead of Sunday morning, which Besser would have let me have to go to church, I used to plod way out on the prairie with the handgun, some shells, and old cans, and practice, and for all the good it did me, I might as well have stayed in the store counting beans. Half the time, them guns misfired, some shells didn't even go off at all, and the times the gun did shoot, I missed them cans by miles. In fact, I missed from three feet! But that's the way it was with them pistols, misfiring and jumping and bucking in your hand, and smoke pouring out, making you cough and near enough blinding you.

But it seemed ridiculous, too. A kid blasting and blazing away at empty cans on a prairie about a million miles across, just plain ridiculous, and them shells cost money as well, so I quit practicing, wrapped that handgun up, and headed back to being respectable—for a time, anyhow.

And that respectability was a powerful force in Abilene! There were lots of folks, and not just preachers, who was all out for reform. I guess there was near as many reformers as barmen, but they didn't all want the same kind of reform. Some reformers just wanted the riders to act nice and quiet like they was in church. Some wanted to close the saloons, and some didn't, because the town got money from taxes off them. Others wanted to close the dance halls, because of the girls, you know? Them reformers was all tangled up, too, because a lot of what side you was on depended on whether you made money out of the cattle trade. And there was some crazy folks who wanted to close near enough everything, saving the church and the banks.

It was amazing, really. On the South Side you had thousands of lit-up riders milling around with them saloon-keepers, and gambling men predating on them like all get-out, and the policemen prowling about with six-guns and billy sticks, and what went on down there ain't fitting to tell in a nice family story like this one. But on the North Side you had them reformers, and *temperance* meetings!

No kidding, I went to one once. Francher Washbourne, the schoolteacher, roped me in, and I went out of plain boredom, but I'd have been better off watching the grass grow. It was run by some reformers called the Order of Good Templars, which was anti-liquor businessmen and church folks, and they'd brought in a feller all the way from Akron, Ohio, to talk against the Demon Drink, and I declare, he could talk. Moses, he went on for hours about water! Plain ordinary water, how it got made and how it got up, and how it got down again, which was like some kind of joke in a Kansas summer, and how pure and good for you it was, the Lord having made it special for us all. And then we sat around drinking the blamed stuff! It would have driven Charlie McCann clear crazy.

But them temperance reformers was strong in Kansas.

In fact, they was out to stop the liquor trade entirely! It sounded laughable at the time, but they meant it, sure enough. Although I couldn't believe my ears the first time I heard that.

Besser was out and I was checking some medicine which had come and which was guaranteed to CURE ALL KNOWN DISEASES, when Mrs. Christopher, who was the wife of one of the Reverends in town, came in.

I said, "Howdy, ma'am," and she said, "Good morning," but not with what you might call overflowing warmth, because she used to get at me to go to church and was somewhat cool because I didn't. She went to the back of the joint, where Mrs. Besser was sitting with Goblinka.

I got on checking, thinking as how I'd try that medicine myself, and Mrs. Christopher started off talking, low— whispering, as it might be.

Well, lady, I thought, you're playing a busted flush trying that, because Mrs. Besser, she didn't half understand American anyhow. It was comical, really. I could tell Mrs. Christopher didn't want me to hear what she was saying, but there was no way on God's earth you could have gotten Mrs. Besser out of that store while her old man was away, so Mrs. Christopher just had to speak loud and clear, and that was comical, too.

The thing was, two gambling men by the name of Thompson and Coe ran that saloon called the Bull's Head, and they'd got a big sign, which was a picture of a bull painted across the front, which the respectable ladies of the town didn't like, thinking it was rude, and that's what Mrs. Christopher was talking about.

"You see," she said, trying to keep her voice down, "some of us from the Ladies Church Society have been to the Town Council about it and, really, they should make Marshal Hickok *force* those awful men to paint out that . . . picture. But nothing is happening, simply *nothing* at all, and why we pay the marshal all that money every month from our taxes is beyond me, so we ladies are signing this petition and we want you to sign it as well."

I peeked over my shoulder and could see Mrs. Besser goggling away with them big bulging eyes. "What is?" she said. "Petition?"

Mrs. Christopher tutted. "Why, it's . . . it's like a big letter."

"But why I write big letter?" Mrs. Besser said in that God-awful mumble she thought was American.

"Not *write* the letter," Mrs. Christopher said. "*I've* written it. All you have to do is sign it."

"Sign?" Mrs. Besser waved her arms, like she thought Mrs. Christopher was asking her to do that Indian sign language. "What sign?"

Mrs. Christopher sort of groaned. "Your *name*," she said. "You just put your name here. *Sign*, about the sign—I mean, the painting."

"What painting?" Mrs. Besser looked around like she thought Mrs. Christopher was saying the store could do with a lick of paint, and I just burst out laughing. I tried to make it sound like coughing and dashed out and hee-hawed like a jackass until a feller walking past gave me a bang on the back that near knocked me into Indian Territory.

I sobered up some and went back, making out I was still coughing, and Mrs. Christopher, she gave me a look like she'd enjoy sticking a tomahawk in my head.

"Young man," she said, "haven't you anything to do in the yard?"

"No, ma'am," I said, because there was no way I was going to miss that scene. "I've got to finish off these shelves. Mr. Besser told me most particular."

Mrs. Christopher gave me that look again, it was like she wouldn't mind sticking *two* tomahawks in me. But there wasn't nothing she could do, so—and you had to hand it to her, like she had that pioneer spirit—she got back to Mrs. Besser.

"We want to make this town nice," she said. "Nice. Fit for decent people. Just think, if your daughter here . . . er . . . ?"

"Goblinka," Mrs. Besser said.

"Of course, Goblinka—"

"She fine big girls!" Mrs. Besser said, and I nearly stuck in that she could say that again.

"Yes." Mrs. Christopher gave Goblinka the glim. "Yes, she certainly is."

"She get good husband!" Mrs. Besser said.

Well, I ducked under the counter, chewing my hand to stop from guffawing. And it got worser!

Mrs. Christopher said she was sure Goblinka would get a good husband, but went on, "You don't want her to walk down Texas Street and see that picture, do you?"

"Goblinka never go down that street," Mrs. Besser squawked. "Why she go there?" And blame if she didn't start jabbering to Goblinka and Goblinka jabbered back, and you didn't need to speak foreign to know what she was saying, and I was right at that, because Mrs. Besser rounded on Mrs. Christopher, her face all red.

"Why you say Goblinka go down that bad street. She never go there!"

At that, Mrs. Christopher did give up, just plain exhausted. She gave a big sigh. "Mrs. Besser, I certainly did *not* say Goblinka *went* there. All I'm saying is we want that sign painted out and the town made decent for respectable people, and *close the saloons!* But I'll speak to Mr. Besser about it." Then she walked out, redder in the face than Mrs. Besser.

Gee whillikers, lady, I thought, you've been chewing locoweed. Close the saloons! A thousand thirsty Texans wandering around and you want to stop them drinking! It was the craziest notion I'd ever heard of, but I put it down to women's foolishness, which just goes to show I'd a lot to learn about women. But I didn't have time to bother my head about that right then because Mrs. Besser came over to me, and was she fuming!

"Why she call Goblinka bad girl?" she said. "Why she say she go down that bad street?"

I'd kind of got the hang of foreign lingo by then, so I soothed her down. "She no say Goblinka bad girl," I said. "She say Texas Street badski"—which I figured was good of me, because Mrs. Christopher, when I wouldn't go to church, stopped giving me lemonade when I delivered stuff at her place, so that showed I *was* a Christian body all the same, because I sure was tempted to say Mrs. Christopher had said Goblinka was bad.

▪ FOURTEEN ▪

It was a hoot at that and something to cheer life up in that blamed store, the high spot of the week in there being when the farmers, which is being sarcastical, came in on Saturday and bought coffee and stuff, the amounts of which was so small you'd need a magnifier to see. Then they'd sit around, littering the place, mumbling about the herds coming and trampling their land and bringing Texas fever, and then getting around to cussing the Railroad Company, although they did have a point there. That company had tempted them out, offering cheap land and slapping up handbills all over the East, and that Europe place, too, saying as how Kansas was like some kind of paradise right here on earth, and then squeezing them dry with freight charges.

But I didn't give a darn for them so-called farmers, nor them reformers neither, seeing as how when I got Kessel I was going into the cattle trade. I used to dream of it, you know? Like I'd buy some steers and make money and end up a real big shot like Mayor McCoy or Shanghai Pierce. And weren't they big shots just!

They used to hang out at the Drovers Cottage, all dressed up like a million dollars, lounging in them big armchairs, and drinking drinks with real ice in them which was hauled down from the Republican River. I used to take a peek in there and then go back to the store and look at them sod-busters and it was pathetic, just plain pathetic, hearing them talking about *stopping* the cattle trade, would you believe, which brought the dollars into town, and it was truly disgusting listening to them.

But Saturday was a brilliant day for me because, although I had to put up with them farmers, who had even less teeth than they had dimes, that was when I went out for my Saturday-night treat!

Yeah, after them farmers had beat it and I'd got the store cleaned out, I got a couple of hours free, and maybe you'll think, well, I snuck into the Novelty Theater and watched a burlesque show, or crept around the South Side, listening out for news of Kessel, but you'd be as far out as Alaska there, because my Saturday-night treat was going to the Chink's and having supper out!

Yes, sir, I was the original Bronco Billy, going there and springing a quarter on a plate of chipped beef—leastways, that's what the Chink called it, although I'd got a feeling that, maybe a couple of days before, it had got long ears and been hopping about on the prairie, but it was meat, and it sure made a change, feeding without being goggled at.

There was another reason I went in there, it being I'd got to know a feller who ate there sometimes. His name was Henry, Henry Schneider. He was a foreigner, too, although he spoke American near as good as I did, and which he needed to, seeing as how he was the printer on the mighty *Abilene Chronicle*.

That was the town paper, and it was something else, believe me. It was run by a feller called Vear Porter Wilson, who'd brought out a bunch of farmers who'd settled up at Buckeye Creek. They was all in old Wilson's own church, the Universal Church of America, which I'd never even heard of before, and except for them sodbusters of his, no one else had neither. But, come Sunday, he'd be up there in his pulpit, hollering about salvation and honesty and whatever. Then, come Monday, he'd be in his office, writing the most amazing lies you ever did read, like how Abilene was a great and glorious city, with the honestest businessmen in the world and the fairest maidens and the purest water and best dirt and all. To read his stuff, you'd have thought the burg was full of marble palaces and museums and parks with shade trees, although there wasn't no timber higher than a grasshopper's knee within sight, instead of what it was, a bunch of shacks any self-respecting cyclone could have blown away without thinking about it. But that's what he wrote and there were plenty of clucks back East who read them lies and came out because of it, which is why he wrote the stuff, because he had a hand in the land racket, and the more folks came out, the better the price he got for town lots. Which was the reason all them Western papers existed.

Anyhow, that's the paper Henry worked for. I'd got to know him just by saying "Howdy," then waving at him through the door of the *Chronicle*, then sitting next to him, taking it for granted he'd be glad of my company, although I guess there were plenty of times he cussed under his breath when he saw me coming. But he was a real kindly old geezer. He told me he'd set up the type for the story when Bo was killed, and he looked sad at that, too, like he knew what it was to lose kinfolk, and he understood about us losing our land, saying it was a sorry thing to have to leave the place you'd been born in, which, him being a foreigner, I guess he did. And seeing as how he was a foreignist, I thought maybe he'd be a buddy of Besser, but he said he came from Germany, which was a different place entirely. In fact, he was somewhat sneery about Besser's old stamping ground—Besser, too, come to that.

Well, that Saturday night after Mrs. Christopher had been in, I thought I'd give him a laugh, so I told him about that sign and the petition. "Ain't that something?" I said, wiping my eyes.

Henry there didn't exactly split his breeches laughing, but he gave a faint smile, polite, as you might say. "Hmm," he hmmed, and pulled out a huge big pipe he had, stuffed it with about half a pound of tobacco, lit it, and puffed out smoke like he was some kind of human locomotive.

I coughed and batted the smoke away. "What do you mean, hmm? The boys ride a thousand miles to get here and they sure ain't looking forward to no temperance meeting. Gosh, I've been to one, and it was the most awful evening I ever spent."

Henry grinned. "You'll spend worse."

"I truly hope not," I said, and I truly meant it. "But they close the saloons and dance halls and the herds will just go someplace else. Why, the railroad is building a branch line to Wichita right now."

"Maybe," Henry admitted, and lit his pipe again, which them pipe smokers is always doing and which must cost them a powerful lot in matches.

"There ain't no maybe about it," I said. "Who spends the dollars here? It's the riders, is who."

"That's true," Henry said. "Course, they don't pay no taxes, do they?"

Jupiter, I thought, old Henry wasn't as smart as I'd figured. "Course they don't pay no taxes. They don't live here, is why. You've got to live in a place to pay the taxes—in America"—saying that because Henry might not know, him being foreign. "Anyhow, there ain't nothing to pay taxes *for* in this joint."

"There's the judge," Henry said, "and the town clerk, and the schoolteacher, and Marshal Hickok and the policemen, and the land registry . . ."

I sighed. "Henry, them ain't got nothing to do with us riders, and don't tell me about the law. It didn't save our land. In fact, it helped take it away. And it didn't do nothing for Bo, neither. Anyways, them lawmen make money for the town."

"You reckon?" Henry said.

"Sure," I said. "They buffalo some poor rider that ain't doing nothing but having a good time and throw him in the pokey and fine him, and what happens to that fine? Them lawmen get half, and the rest goes to the town."

"Yes," Henry agreed with that, like he had to, it being the truth. He stuck his finger in the bowl of his pipe, and why it didn't burn him beat me. "Course, the way the taxpayers look at it, if there weren't any cowboys, there wouldn't be any need for the lawmen."

I'd given up telling people cowboys was riders, so I just sighed. "Henry, there ain't no need for them policemen, anyhow."

Henry squinted at me through the smoke like he didn't swallow that one.

"Well," I admitted, "maybe the boys do whoop it up, but they don't mean no harm. Them respectable ladies like Mrs. Christopher, did you ever see a rider act bad to them?" Which didn't need saying, because the boys were as polite

157

as may be, it being the dance-hall girls that jeered at them ladies. "I ain't saying a boy might not get lit up and shoot up a sign going out of town, but they sure don't go around murdering. It's coyotes like Kessel that does that."

"Sure," Henry said. "But if there weren't any cowboys here, there wouldn't *be* any Kessels, would there?"

Sakes alive, I thought, you sure are a wrangling cuss. I took a deep breath, which I regretted because I took in enough smoke to choke a steer. "Henry, you can talk till you're blue in the face, but them reformers ain't going to stop the cattle trade."

"No," Henry said. "But the farmers will. They've got votes, and as soon as they get organized—"

"Organized!" I yelped. "Did you say organized? Henry, I see them fellers and they couldn't agree which way the sun comes up, leave alone stop the herds. Anyways, this is free range. Free!" And it was kind of crazy at that, although I didn't have a steer to my name, and was working in a store, I got all worked up! But it wasn't just the cattle. It *was* free land. A country for riding, riding along free as a bird, looking at a horizon that never ended, because when you got there, the land just rolled away to another horizon, and all you needed was a good pony, a rifle, and a bedroll and the whole blamed world was yours. And then them farmers came crowding in from the Lord knew where, busting up the land, and for what? So's the wind could blow it away, is all. And I don't know but I was feeling real mean there. I guess it was because I was all penned in the store and the North Side while Kessel roamed free that I got this rage, which wanting to do something and not being able to gets you, and I was just pouring that rage out on the sodbusters.

"They is just nobodies, is all," I said.

"Nobodies . . . ?"

"That's the word," I said. "And they ain't never going to be anybodies."

Henry didn't say anything to that, just gave me a thoughtful look, took a peek at a watch the size of a watermelon, waved the Chink over, and paid him. He tried to pay for me, too, like always, which I wouldn't allow him to, seeing as how he had steak and eggs and greens and stuff, so I couldn't afford to return the compliment. So I paid my own check and we eased out.

He headed down to Texas Street, and like I usually did, I tagged along until we hit the corner, where he stopped, knowing as how I wasn't allowed no farther and which he agreed with, saying the marshal was right, the South Side was no place for me, which was fine and dandy for *him* to say, seeing as how he was going there.

He leaned against the wall of the *Chronicle* and lit his pipe again. The match flared, and on the street, and down on the South Side, the lights were flaring, too, making the sky all red and yellow, and you could hear music, pianos and bands and banjos, and whooping and hollering, like it was one of them burgs in the Bible that got burned down and turned into salt because the folks there whooped it up *too* much. Plain wickedness and sin, that's what did for them, and it's what the Reverend Christopher and the reformers said would do for Abilene as well, but I wouldn't have minded joining in the fun before it happened.

Henry got his pipe going and leaned against the wall. "Nobodies," he said. "Well, Ben, there's nobodies all over the world just lining up to get here, and when they do, all that"—he pointed with his pipe to the South Side—"all that will go."

"Okay," I said. "Then we'll move someplace else. There's plenty of land."

"Yes," Henry said. "That's America, plenty of land. You

don't like it here—move on. Plenty of forest, cut it down. Plenty of game and buffalo, just keep killing them. Move on, find someplace better, then move on again."

Jeepers, I thought, what's he going on about? I mean, he sounded real mad about something, and I nearly said it wasn't *his* land, it was ours and we could do what the Sam Hill we wanted with it, but I just said, "What's wrong with that? Moving on."

"What's—" He looked down on me, then shook his head. "Nothing, I guess. Forget I said it. Just what happens when the land runs out? So, good night, Ben, you'd better get indoors. Been nice talking to you."

I said it had been mighty nice talking to him, too, and I don't know but there was something in my voice, wistfulness as might be, because he hesitated.

"You haven't got many friends here, have you?" he asked.

"Nope," I said, which was the truth, me not having any. Everyone in Abilene was too young for me, or too old, and them that was near enough my age, I was too old for them. Too old by a million years.

"Hmm . . ." Henry lit his pipe up again. "You play checkers?"

I said I sure did, when I could get someone to play against.

"Come and have a game with me sometime," Henry said. "At my place."

I said I was mighty obliged for the offer, which I was at that, and that I would get time off and call around the next night, but Henry just grinned and said some other time was more like what he had in mind.

"I'll let you know," he said. "My landlady makes mighty nice cookies."

Then he moseyed off, down to the bright lights and all the fun, and I moseyed off, too, back to Besser and the flour barrels.

FIFTEEN

Well, a game of checkers was something to look forward to, although it says something for that exciting life I was leading that checkers with an old geezer was a whoop-up, don't it?

It was them nights that did it. During the day wasn't too bad, especially when Besser sent me out delivering, not that there was anywhere much to deliver to, seeing as how you could have walked around the whole blamed town in ten minutes. But when I'd done that delivering, like it might be some eggs for a lady too refined to be seen carrying the stuff herself, I'd take time off and go down to the depot, which I truly liked, seeing the cattle dealers, and the locomotive coming in, all hissing and panting, with its bell clanging to warn off any pooches or drunks that might be snoozing across the track, with the engineers looking down from the cab like they was God Almighty, which they thought they was, too. And that hustle of folks getting on and off the train, all kinds of folks, traveling men and gamblers, prairie politicians, preachers out to save a few souls—and make a few bucks while they was at it—and soldier boys getting a drink before they went for a haircut, a Sioux haircut, that is, up in the Black Hills.

I used to ask around there about Kessel, like had anybody heard of him, but nobody had, and I got to figuring they never would, neither. Still, I reckoned I'd keep my vow, until October anyhow, which was when the cattle season ended, then head for Texas or someplace.

But then dusk would creep in and I'd stand yawning in the store and looking at Goblinka, wondering whether she wore that harness under her dress. In fact, one night, when by a kind of miracle both her folks was in the back room,

I even tried sparking with her! I bore in mind what Bo had told me once about girls. "Just say nice things about them," he'd said, the trouble being, when you got down to it, Goblinka didn't have all that much going for her. In fact, apart from being a girl, there was only one thing she did have, so I horned in on that, and in foreign, too.

"Goblinka," I said, "you sure do eato goodo."

She just stared at me with them huge goggly eyes, which was like two giant blueberries stuck in a flapjack, so I tried again.

"Mucho," I said. "Gustamento bueno. Plentiski." But she still didn't say nothing, so I thought, what the heck, if you're too dumb to understand your own language, you can find someone else to spark with. And I got back to the amazingly interesting chore of picking flies out of a barrel of lard we'd got in.

And then something happened which made life altogether more interesting. A traveling man called in. Well, that wasn't interesting in itself, because there was millions of them roaming the West, selling anything from garters to Gospel books, and believe me, you got as much as one family stuck out there on the prairie and sooner or later one of them fellers would come knocking on their door.

This feller was typical of the breed, a real glad-hander and full of smooth talk, saying what a dandy store Besser had and what a pretty girl Goblinka was, would you believe! He was a real city slicker at that, with a line of fancy goods from a new outfit in Chicago, which he went through with us, saying how that stuff was the best ever made in the entire world and at the lowest prices, which is how them fellers talked, their motto being: The hog that squealed the loudest got the most swill. But while he was sounding off, I had a good look at his catalogue, and there was a line of rider's hats that was worth looking at twice.

162

The feller finished his hollering, Besser grunted that he'd think about it, the feller said that was fine, just fine, he'd call back, thanked Besser for his time, which I first got to hear in Abilene and which I couldn't believe my ears, like as if time cost something, and beat it. Then Besser looked at me and said maybe he'd try some of them goods.

"Maybe," I said. "They ain't bad, and them hats . . ."

"Nah." Besser didn't have much neck, so when he shook his head, he had to roll it, like a buffalo. "We don't make no sales."

"But if we did," I said, "we'd make a mighty fine profit. And even if we didn't, why, we could sell them easy at the price we paid, so we wouldn't lose nothing."

"Nah! Nah!" Besser did the buffalo roll again, but, and I don't know why, because it didn't mean beans to me, I horned in again, maybe thinking if enough cash flew around, some of it might stick to me.

"It's worth springing a few bucks on," I said, pressing him. "You've got to spend money to make it, ain't you?"

"Yah," Besser agreed, seeing as how it was him who'd told me that. He brooded for a while, scratching inside his beard. "You got any money?"

That wasn't a question you got asked out there, saving it was by a gent waving a six-shooter under your nose, but I just sort of mumbled that I'd maybe got a couple of bucks.

Old Besser gave me a look, and I got a feeling that he'd took a peek inside my socks, which is where I kept my wad, although how he could have done that beat me, seeing as how I didn't hardly ever take them off. "Maybe *you* buy them hats," he said.

Jeepers! Me buy them! Next thing, he'd be asking me to pay him for working in the joint. "Come on, Mr. Besser," I said. "It's your store."

"Yah," Besser agreed, which he had to, but gave me a

squinty look, did some more beard scratching, then said, "But you buy those hats, put them in the store, and we go fifty-fifty on the profits."

I couldn't hardly believe my ears. "You mean like partners!"

Besser nodded, meaning he leaned his whole body forward. "But only on the hats."

"Gee," I said, "I don't know about that."

"Right. We forget it." He handed me a paper. "Now tend to these orders."

I went in the storeroom and began making them orders up, little bags of peas and coffee and sugar, and I was shaking! It was crazy, but every time I stuck that scoop into a sack, I thought of the profit I might make. Then I stuck it in again and thought of how much I might lose! I hadn't put down a blamed cent, but I was all churned up, sick right down to my stomach. I kept saying to myself it was ridiculous even thinking of buying them hats, but I just couldn't shake off the notion, like, it having been stuck there, it was staying stuck, and by the time I'd finished them orders, I was wishing that traveling man had never called in, and that I'd kept my fool mouth shut, too.

But it got to noon and the notion was still there, and it was like someone was talking in my head, saying, "Ben Curtis, here's a chance to make some easy money. Ben Curtis, you can make some easy money!" Yes, it was there, the chance to get around to that predating which I sure pined to do, so, sweating like I had a fever, I asked Besser for some time off, which he made a thing of, as if he was trying to calculate how much to knock off my pay—which I got so little of, it would have taken a genius to work out. But in the end he said okay, so I shucked off that fool apron and went out, down to the Great Western Store.

The Great Western was owned entirely by a fellow called Karatofsky, another foreigner, would you believe, and it was some store at that. In fact, it was more like what you'd call an emporium, and a body could have spent all day in there, dreaming of what to buy—if he had his own private gold mine, that is. But I didn't, and I didn't have all day, neither, so I headed for the hat counter, and, my, didn't they just have some hats there! Plug hats, straw hats, stovepipe hats, narrow brims, wide brims, sombreros for the greaser trade, even hats for mules and horses! And hats for riders.

I took a real good gander at them, checking the prices and the quality as best as I could, and trying some on. In fact, I got somewhat absorbed in that, putting on the different styles and seeing how I looked in the mirror—which was truly comical—until a clerk chucked me out.

I stood on the street with all the boys sashaying past, and the dance girls parading, and wagons and carts getting all mixed up with mule skinners and bullwhippers cursing fit to make the air blue, but I wasn't paying no heed to them. No, I was thinking of them hats and money. I wasn't even looking out for Kessel, which I always did if I went out, and then I said to myself, "Ben, what you need here is advice, and the feller to ask about making money is one who is." And the man I knew who was doing just that was that Dave Heaney, the land agent, who'd steered me into Besser's in the first place, so I sort of combed my hair with my fingers and headed for his office.

It was a real Western office, four walls trying to keep each other from falling down, maps on them showing the county with land marked out with farmers' claims, what they called plats, and a big safe and a rolltop desk.

Heaney was there having some lunch, which was eggs and green stuff, and drinking water, him being one of them Good Templars and a reformer and all—which didn't stop him going into saloons, because, like a lot of them businessmen, he had a finger in cattle, too.

I said to excuse me but would he give me some time, it being as I wanted some advice.

He looked at me all cold. "You in some kind of trouble?"

"No, sir!" I said. "I certainly ain't. The thing is, I'm thinking of going into business for myself and I figured I'd ask you first, seeing as how everyone in town says how smart you are"—sticking that in to make him feel good.

Heaney smirked. "I didn't know that," he said. "But I reckon I do know a thing or two. Yes, business . . ." He dropped his voice, all low and reverent, like it was a sacred word, which it was to them fellers. Then he pushed that grub aside, stood up, and grabbed hold of the lapels of his coat, and when you see a feller do that, you know you're going to get your ears pounded as long as that feller has breath in his body.

"Let me tell you about business, son," he said. "Business is the heartbeat of this great land and this fair state of Kansas. Business made America great and it will keep it great, and why? Why? Why?"

I wanted to say I didn't know why, why, why, and I didn't give a cuss neither, because all I wanted to know was should I buy them hats. But you don't stop an American businessman easy once he's in his stride, and I've got to admit, old Heaney could spout better than a preacher, saying how business was noble and thrilling, which I sure did like, and then saying how the frontiersmen and pioneers had dared and tamed the wilderness, although he allowed how there was some taming left over, which he needed to, seeing as how most of it was still being roamed over by millions of wild Indians.

Still, I was feeling pretty good, and then he said, "And *why* is the American businessman the true descendant of those brave explorers, and is in fact more daring than them? Son, it's because they may have risked their lives, but the modern American businessman dares risk his capital!"

It took a moment for that to sink in, but when it did, I was ready to leave that office like a bat out of hell, because I sure liked being called a noble darer and all, but I didn't want to hear about maybe losing money! No, sir, I wanted to hear about making it, and I was just ready to thank him kindly and scram when he sat down, looked at me like a feller who knew what he was talking about, and said, "Now, son, what's on your mind?"

I told him, and he nodded, then said, "Just how much money have you got?"

Holy smoke! It seemed like every jasper in town wanted to know that, but Heaney said it wouldn't go no further, so I told him, more or less, meaning less rather than more, if you get me, and Heaney waggled his eyebrows.

"You're off to a flying start," he said. "Why, there's millionaires in this country didn't have that many cents at your age. Yes . . ." He fiddled with his fork for a moment. "Now, I'll tell you what you do. You invest half of what you've got in them hats and tell Besser you'll go seventy-thirty on the profits—only don't tell him I said that." He gave me a shrewd look. "You might have a financial future at that."

"That's what worries me," I said. "I mean, what if Karatofsky hears about them hats and starts selling cheaper than me?"

"Huh-huh." Heaney did some more fiddling with his fork. "Well, that's what I meant about being daring. But I wouldn't worry too much about old Karatofsky undercutting you."

"You wouldn't?" I said, thinking Heaney wasn't me.

"No." Heaney waved his hand. "You just take your chance. Fifty cents."

"Fifty cents?" I asked.

"That's it," Heaney said. "Seeing as how you're just starting out, I'm halving my rate for advice. Good luck to you."

Good luck! Jeepers, I was going to need all the luck going in Kansas. I hadn't even started being a businessman and I was fifty cents down. And just for talking! I figured that when I got going in business *I'd* start lashing out advice, although I'd maybe charge only a quarter to begin with.

Then something happened which knocked any thoughts of nickels and cents clean out of my head. I was heading back to the store, still figuring out what to do, when a whole raft of fellers rushed past me like a stampede. They was yelling and excited, running to the Bull's Head, where there was another big crowd of riders and dance girls and all, and they was all excited, too.

Like I've said, the Bull's Head was run by Thompson and Coe, who was two shady customers at that, and they said Thompson had killed a couple of fellers down in Louisiana. There was bad blood between them and Hickok, and not just because of that. Some said it was through Coe running a crooked faro game, others that it was woman trouble, but whatever it was, they hated each other like poison.

Anyways, I stood on the boardwalk opposite the saloon, jammed in with the crowd, and across the street was the marshal.

It was a surprise to see him at all, his idea of early rising being getting up at 4 p.m. But there he was, duded up real swell, a sort of cape over his flash vest, and that yellow hair flowing out from under the stovepipe hat he wore, and facing him was Frank Blaine, and peering over the batwing doors of the saloon was Thompson and Coe.

Blaine was a bouncer in the Bull's Head and as ugly a bullyboy as ever beat up a poor rider—and he had a pistol in his mitt. He was howling and whooping like a wolf, but when he stopped for breath, Hickok said, all cold and sinister, "Throw down that gun!"

"Who says so?" Blaine yelled, which was foolish, because it was plain as daylight it was the marshal.

"It's against the town ordinances," Hickok said, which wasn't exactly the most sinister thing to say, and which sure didn't sinistrate Blaine because he told Hickok what he could do with them ordinances, and I was glad Mrs. Christopher wasn't there to hear what he did suggest.

"All right," Hickok said. "Then I'm coming for you, and you know what that means."

"It don't mean beans to me," Blaine roared. "I've eaten better men than you before breakfast. In fact, I've eaten them *for* breakfast."

And that raised a laugh! It was crazy. There was a drunk waving a handgun, and them things went off by accident all the time, and there was the deadly Wild Bill Hickok, and we was laughing like they was two comics in the Novelty Theater! There's just no telling what foolishness folks will get up to. Not that I was any different. It took some hard times to knock horse sense into me. Hard times, and some killings, too.

But we all stared at the marshal, waiting for him to make his move, which he did. "Blaine," he said. "You've been warned loud and clear." And he stepped forward, and he was holding a handgun, too.

And that was the thing. Hickok was a lawful, swore-in, paid marshal, vowed by a regular judge, wearing a star, and having the right to carry that six-gun, and to use it, whereas Blaine, or anyone else, come to that, if they used a deadly weapon it could lead to them having a hearty breakfast for free—although they wouldn't be needing no more lunches. And that gave the lawman the edge. Hit or miss, even if he didn't win, you sure lost.

Then Hickok began to walk forward, slow, and that *did*

look sinister, and you could see Blaine was having second thoughts, his face all gray and sweaty, whereas Hickok looked cool as a mountain spring. He had sand at that, which is what it really took to be a lawman, that and the ability to shoot a man dead, then go and have a drink and supper and tell jokes.

"Drop it," Hickok said, taking another step. "Drop it." And just for a second it looked like Blaine wouldn't. His arm twitched and he looked at it like it belonged to someone else, and his shoulder moved up and down, but then Hickok was on top of him, crowding him, and he gave a moany groan and let the gun drop.

And would you believe, the crowd groaned, too, like they was disappointed! That was because it was a story to tell the rest of your days, how Hickok and Blaine shot it out on the streets of Abilene at noon.

But the action wasn't over, because, as Blaine stood there, greasy and dripping with sweat as the booze poured out of him, and actually pointing to the gun like saying, "See, I done what you told me," Hickok buffaloed him, smashing him on the side of the head with that big Colt, dropping him like a shot buffalo, which all them lawmen did, showing who ruled the town. And you know, them riders watching, they didn't mind Blaine getting a beating because he'd handed it out in his time, but they hissed and catcalled because they didn't like that buffaloing, seeing as it could happen to them, and they didn't like lawmen, neither.

Hickok glared at us, his fallen foe at his feet, if you want to be poetical, looking like it wouldn't be too much of a chore for him to cross over and start buffaloing us, and in case you think that was maybe too heroicalist, a couple of his policemen had moved in with shotguns and billy sticks.

"Break it up," they growled. "Move along. Come on, beat it"—which we did, seeing as how none of us wanted to pay five bucks for a big lump on the head and a night in the pokey. And I've seen lawmen order a man to take his hat off before he got buffaloed, just to make sure that lump was a big one.

We broke up, everyone gabbling and excited, and I was heading back to the store, trying to get out of the way of Hickok, and darn me, someone trod on my heel and I went sprawling, and when I got myself picked up, Hickok was staring right down at me. He glowered at me like he was ready to blast the life out of anyone and anything. "You," he said. "Ain't you that Texan kid?"

"Yes, sir," I said. "I'm him right enough, and I—"

"Yeah"—Hickok cut me off—"didn't I tell . . . didn't I tell you to keep away from saloons?"

"Yes, sir," I said. "And I do. I truly do. But I've got to walk down this street sometimes . . . doing chores and all . . . just in the day . . ."

"Day?" Hickok's eyes didn't look right, and he was swaying, standing there swaying with that gun in his hand, and I thought, jeepers, he's drunk! And that did scare me, because there's no knowing what a drunk will do. "Day," he said again. "Weren't you going to stay here and tend your brother's lonesome grave?"

"That's right, Marshal," I said, hoping he wasn't getting notions.

Hickok's eyes seemed to clear and he stopped that awful swaying. "Ain't been no tending I can notice."

"No, sir," I said. "Sorry, Marshal. I've been going into business, is why. Hats . . ."

But I didn't get to say no more, because Hickok batted me away like I was a fly and roared at Coe and Thompson, who had stuck their heads out of the saloon again. "Get that goddamn sign painted out or I'll come for the both of you!" Then he headed off with them policemen, who was dragging Blaine off by the heels.

And would you believe, just then a wagon came up from the depot with a whole horde of new settlers on it with all their stuff, and did they look full of the joys of spring! Brother, what with the marshal there waving a pistol and them policemen tooled up with shotguns, and Blaine's head being bumped in the dust, it sure wasn't like one of them posters of the Kansas Pacific Railroad and they looked as if they'd wished they'd taken a return ticket to wherever the Sam Hill they'd come from.

I headed back to the store, my head all itchy, and Besser was itchy too, grumbling about how long I'd been, as if me not being there meant less customers had called, like I was some kind of human magnet. But he calmed down when I said I was getting them hats, although he wouldn't go for the seventy-thirty split, settling for sixty-forty, which made me feel pretty smart at that, and not feeling too bad about that fifty cents I'd paid out.

But I felt jumpy all afternoon, waiting for that traveling man to call back, still worrying whether I should get them, thinking I'd got time to change my mind, and nearly doing it, too, but when he did call in, smelling like he'd tried to drink every saloon in town dry, I handed over the dollars and signed on the dotted line—and then I felt better!

Yes, it was like I'd done something, really done something. All of my life I'd been doing what I was told, always someone else being boss, and now I'd struck out on my own. In fact, it hadn't been more than a couple of months since I'd been a barefoot kid down on the farm without a dime to my name, and saving I went out banditting, there wasn't no way I'd ever have more than two bucks to rub together, and now—Jupiter, I was an American businessman!

Yes, sir, I was an American businessman, noble and daring and all, but tell the truth, I didn't *feel* like a noble darer. In fact, I felt worser than when old Tyler showed us that note. It was worry, worry whether I could sell them hats when they arrived, because it's one thing saying and another doing entirely, especially when it's your bucks riding on the horse. It got so's I dreamed about them hats, ridiculous dreams like there was jackrabbits jumping all around town wearing them!

They was sweating days for me, sweating days and sweating nights, feeling sick most of the time and having them crazy dreams, when I could get to sleep. And, ain't it strange, doing that waiting, it was like every day dragged like they was a year each, but October, which was when the cattle season ended, so's there wouldn't be no call for the hats, it just seemed to be *rushing* at me!

Every day me or Besser would trudge down to the depot, and every day we'd trudge back with no hats, and the town just boiling with riders, all with money to burn, and me with nothing to sell them! I'll tell you, life can seem awful raw at times. Why, when I did what the marshal had told me, tending Bo's grave, for which I got a pickle jar off old Besser—and he charged me a nickel for it!—and swiped some flowers from a garden, so-called, and sticking them on the grave, that jar got stolen! Beats all, don't it. I was surely glad I hadn't got a big jar, which would have cost me ten cents.

But, and it's a terrible thing, I wasn't that caring about Bo, nor Kessel, neither. I didn't care nothing about anything except the chance that I might lose my money. In fact, I'll tell you something you won't hardly believe.

A circus came to town, and even that didn't cheer me up. I sat with all the riders, who laughed themselves silly at the clown, and cheered a tightrope walker, although they didn't reckon much to the bareback rider, saying as how he couldn't do them fancy tricks on a cow pony. And there was a lion, too, a dangerous, man-eating lion, BROUGHT AT GREAT EXPENSE BY THE MANAGEMENT ALL THE WAY FROM AFRICA, the posters said, but it looked as dangerous as a gopher. All its hair was falling out, its teeth too, I reckon, and that lady lion tamer who ran the circus, she was so ugly it would have been more exciting if the lion had stuck *its* head in *her* mouth.

But ain't that something, not being excited by a circus? Jupiter, it wasn't that long since seeing one would have been some kind of miracle, and now I wasn't hardly interested.

And them blues I had got worse when I read in the *Chronicle* that the last herds was over the Red River. I got on to Besser to write to that Chicago firm to get the hats to us quick, but he just said you had to give firms some time to deliver.

"Sure," I said, "that's fine for you. Your stuff is for them farmers, and they'll be here all winter. My stuff is for the riders, who won't be. And what happens if we get stuck with them hats?"

Besser stared at me and gave his buffalo grunt. "What you mean, *we* get stuck. *You* get stuck."

Well, ride on, brother, I thought. Father Christmas you ain't, and I wished I'd kept my mouth shut.

Nothing cheered me up. I stopped looking at Goblinka, and didn't go to the Chink's no more, so's I could save a quarter, which meant I didn't see Henry, and he didn't call on me neither, even though he only worked a couple of doors away.

Holy smoke, I won't forget them days in a hurry, standing in the store swatting flies, waiting for Besser to get back from the depot, him doing the buffalo roll and me knowing I'd got to wait for the next train, which was like a million years, thinking that salesman had made a sucker out of me, and cursing myself for being the biggest fool this side of the Red River.

Saving my investment, nothing interested me. Not even them sodbusting farmers, so-called, who was getting up a Farmers Protection Association to stop the cattle trade, nor the reformers, who was blasting away at the saloons and dance girls. Even when there was more trouble between the marshal and Thompson and Coe, I didn't care.

Jim Edwards, who hauled ice around town, told me about it when I was sweeping the boardwalk—which was the most senseless thing you could do in Abilene, since every time you swept that dust away, it got blown right back—when he stopped his wagon right next to me.

"They're painting out that sign on the Bull's Head," he called.

Well, for me they could paint the entire saloon and the whole of Abilene pink and purple if they wanted to, and I said so.

"Yeah?" Jim said. "Well, you go take a look. They're painting it out with turpentine, but you can still see that picture as plain as ever. Ain't it a hoot?"

Maybe it was comical, but it didn't comicalize me none, and I didn't feel more like laughing when old Besser rolled up from the depot looking like his ma had just died and giving me a beady glim, like saying what was I doing, actually talking to someone and wasting enormously valuable time.

Edwards beat it and I went inside, checking out some kerosene cans we had which was leaking and smelling something terrible, while Besser did some paperwork, bills and such-like, for a while. Then he looked up and fixed me with his beady eyes, frowning, so's I thought he was going to tear a strip off me, and I was just going to say I'd been trying to get Jim Edwards to buy something, when he said, "Hats!"

Yes, they'd come, and I near jumped through the window to get down to the depot to collect them, and didn't I feel swell, looking at them boxes and signing the delivery note, and feeling real important, like all them giant business brains back East had been working overtime just for me!

Back in the store, me and Besser opened the boxes, and I've got to say, there seemed a powerful lot of hats, like that store was overflowing with them, but they was mine, and saving my duds and saddle and handgun, they was the only property I'd ever owned in my entire life. In fact, I doted on them so much, I didn't hardly want to sell them!

Course that feeling wore off in about five minutes, so I stuck one in the window and stood back, admiring it, you know. Then I got a notion, like one of them brain waves waved over me. I got a piece of card and wrote in big letters, HATS. But that didn't seem enough, so I put CHEEP HATS, which didn't seem right somehow, so I got another card and wrote: THE BEST AND CHEEPEST HATS IN—I was going to put Abilene but thought why hide them hats under a bush, so I put KANSAS and the price. In fact, I was going to say the United States, then figured that might be stretching it too far.

I was as proud as all get-out. Every ten seconds I ducked out with the broom, making I was going to sweep the boardwalk, but it was just to look at the sign, and every ten seconds I expected a heap of riders to sashay along and throw cash at me.

No one did, though. When Dave Knights, who was a clerk

at the First National Bank of Kansas, called in for some tobacco and I tried the selling on him, saying, "Care to see this new line of hats, just in from Chicago, best value this side of the Missouri," he said he wasn't interested *and*, would you believe, tried to sell me a necktie he'd got no use for. The nerve of some folks!

The thing was, I hadn't reckoned on selling all of the hats the first day, but I had figured on selling some—well, at least one. But that day wore off and I hadn't even had anybody try one out, so I got to feeling blue again. I lit the lamp, which had the smallest wick I ever did see, and went outside again, standing in the dusk and looking for a last customer.

That was a time of day I kind of liked, as a rule. It was a mite cooler and folks were lighting their lamps, the light spilling out of windows and seeming comforting, you know, homely as might be, but I didn't feel no comfort just then, not with that hat grinning at me from the window like a skull, and I was cursing myself again for being the worst sort of fool, when Dave Heaney came along.

I didn't rate too highly in the social register of Abilene, so not many businessmen ever spoke to me, saving to pester me to go to church, but Heaney did, which was only right and proper, seeing as how I was a client of his.

"How's the hat trade, son?" he asked. "They come yet?"

Gee whillikers, I thought, if you can't see that there sign, you ought to spring a few bucks on a pair of specs, but I just said they'd come that noon. "And I ain't sold one"— being sort of accusing.

Old Heaney grinned, although what was funny about it beat me. Then I showed him the sign and he stopped grinning.

"Son," he said. "You've got the right notion. But I'll give you a tip. Knock a cent off that price. Never sell things at round numbers. Folks will buy something for ninety-nine cents which they wouldn't for a dollar. And don't wait for customers. Go out and get them, you hear me? Be American, *get up and go!*" And he gave me a bang on the back, which everyone did all the time out there and which sure was aggravating.

But getting that advice, and for free, drove some of the blues away, and before I hit the hay, I did another sign, knocking a cent off the price, which did make them hats seem amazingly more cheaper—and I got the spelling right this time—and went to sleep feeling altogether better and more American, because the next morning I was really going to do that getting up and going. Yes, sir.

And I did. I had that store beat out before that notion of a breakfast Mrs. Besser had, which I wolfed down, and was at the door ready to drum up trade. That store wasn't in a good location for the cattle trade, so not many riders passed. Any that did, I was at them like greased lightning. None of them was interested, though. In fact, and it was truly aggravating, most of them just laughed at me, like I was joshing them! So when that day ended I felt worser than the night before, because, as well as being blue, I was just plain wore out with all that getting up and going, and I hadn't sold a single hat, and I had a terrible feeling that I wasn't never going to, neither.

That was bad enough, and the next few days was even worser than that, which I wouldn't have believed possible. There'd seemed a powerful lot of hats when they'd arrived, but, as time passed, it was like there was more of them, like they was breeding overnight! It was crazy at that, I'd been tortured when them hats hadn't come, and I was being tortured even more now they had! In fact, when Henry moseyed in one day, saying he hadn't seen me around and would I care to have that checkers game the next Saturday night, I didn't know whether to say yes or no, because it would mean me being out of the store and maybe losing a sale! But he just said he'd leave it up to me, and that, although he thanked me kindly, no, he didn't need a hat right then.

That was Tuesday, and come Saturday I still hadn't sold a hat, and that Saturday was plumb terrible. The sodbusters come rolling in, all mumbling about the cattle, and they was really talking about getting themselves organized properly in the Farmers Protection Association and going with them reformers and shutting out the herds, which if they all voted the same way they could do, especially seeing as how Abilene was inside the Kansas quarantine line but them clerks was bribed to look the other way. It was amazing, you know? There was me with all them millions of hats, the which cost more than most of them farmers was ever going to see in their whole lives, and they was talking about stopping my customers, and they had the votes to do it, and I had none at all, and they called it a democracy!

Course, they didn't only talk about cattle, they'd got other fascinating topics, such as grasshoppers, which made me even madder, like I hadn't exactly traveled all them miles to listen to talk about bugs, and it was brilliant how they could keep talking about them, hour after hour, until they beat it, heading out to their dugouts on the prairie, because there wasn't one in a hundred of them could afford lumber to build a house.

I followed them out, just to make sure they didn't do nothing reckless like going to the South Side and having a dance, and jumped on a drunk rider who'd lost his way to sell him a hat, but he just guffawed and lurched off, me giving a last shout, plaintive as might be: "Mister, all right, then, but any fellers you meet . . . tell them . . . best and most cheapest . . . and I hope you get buffaloed!'' That last bit speaking in a sort of whisper, in case he turned back and buffaloed me.

I went back inside then, into all that musty gloom, with Besser sitting by the flour barrel like a big old spider, and, hats or no blamed hats, I just couldn't spend another night in there, so I got washed, dusted myself down, and hoofed it over to Henry's place.

He roomed right past the depot with Pat Brady and his missus. Pat was the telegraph operator at the depot, and he used to let me in his shack to watch that telegraph gizmo pecking up and down, like a chicken getting its feed in quick. And it was something to see, at that. Just that little key tapping away and sending messages clear through from New York City to San Francisco—if the Sioux hadn't chopped down the telegraph poles.

I hadn't never met Mrs. Brady, but Pat was fine, and you know, there I was, going to their house to play checkers and have cookies, but I felt terrible, just terrible, and wandering across the North Side didn't make me feel no better. In fact, I felt worse. Some of them frame houses hadn't got their blinds down, so you could look in and see businessmen who'd made money instead of losing it and who were making more, sitting reading that lying *Chronicle* or getting their grub down them with womenfolk fussing, and in L. A. Burroughs's house, who was a big reformer, someone was playing one of them harmonium organ things, a hymn or something, and there was me wandering the streets. I felt locked out, as bad as when me and Bo was going to Lookout, but I'd changed since then. Like I've said, some iron had got into my soul, so I was all chewed up, mean and jealous and wanting money. I was more like a prairie wolf than a human being, slavering away and waiting to get its fangs into its prey—and right then I had my prey in mind.

SEVENTEEN

And he was waiting for me, innocent as a suckling babe, leaning on the picket fence, smoking his pipe as peaceful as all get-out, and without a notion of what was going to hit him.

We howdy'd each other and he said he'd seen my sign, which made him about the only feller in town who had.

"Yeah," I said. "I'm a businessman now."

"A businessman, that's something to be." Henry nodded, but I wasn't sure there wasn't something in his voice I didn't like, mocking as may be, which made me feel even meaner and sorer.

"It surely is," I said. "You've got to be daring. Taking risks and all."

"I reckon," Henry said. "You sold any?"

"Not exactly," I said. "But I ain't had them long. I will, though. I'll sell them all and make a big profit." And then I told the most amazing lie I ever did tell. "Then I'll buy some more and sell them! Get even more profit!"

"Profits, huh?" Henry said.

"Sure." I made myself sound real tough. "Profits is what life is all about."

Henry struck a light on the seat of his pants and lit his pipe, looking at me over the flame, and I don't know but he was looking at me like a feller who's just drawn an ace to a straight flush. "It's a point of view," he allowed. "So come inside and we'll celebrate a little."

We went inside and it was a mighty nice house, purple drapes, real paper on the walls with big pink and purple flowers on it, and a regular carpet all blue and orange. Pat was at the depot working late, but Mrs. Brady was home. She was a homely body, all dried up like women got out

West, but with a nice smile, and brother, could she cook. I had the best pie and cookies I'd ever had, and I got to wondering if she'd take in an orphan child at reduced rates. I ate till I was fit to bust, then Henry grinned and said maybe we'd play checkers and took me into his room, which I was curious to see.

Well, that room wasn't much bigger than mine, but it was about as different as a pokey is from a palace. There was a bed, but it had a fancy cover on it, and there was a little table with a white cloth, an easy chair, a lamp with a green shade, and books—jeepers, there was millions of them, all lined up on shelves, and I reckoned Henry was making money on the side selling them. There was pictures on the wall, too, a burg like something out of a storybook, all towers and stuff, another of a real pretty river, and a big one of a feller who was the ugliest, hairiest creature I ever clapped eyes on. I was minded to ask what tree he'd climbed down from but thought he might be kin to Henry and didn't want to embarrass him.

"You like this little room?" Henry asked.

"Surely," I said.

"I've lived in worse." He smiled and I thought, I bet you have, one with bars at the window.

"Take a seat." He began laying out the checkerboard. "The easy chair."

I said thanks and lowered myself into it, somewhat nervous, being in a swell room like that, but I was just hitting the saddle when something squawked and spat and a creature jumped between my legs and skedaddled under the bed. Jupiter, I was halfway to the door when Henry laughed and said for me to hold on.

"Hold on!" I said. "Just what in Sam Hill was that?"

Henry bent down and stuck his arm under the bed, which I wouldn't have done for a hundred bucks, and came out with a cat. Well, I say it was a cat, but it was more a kitten, brown and white, with green eyes and real long whiskers.

"Here." Henry handed it over, and I declare, it was the cutest little thing I ever did see, and it played with me, trying to get inside my shirt and licking my nose. It was really something, because although the West was just over-run with vermin, you didn't hardly never see a cat in the towns, on account of them blamed coyotes wandering in at night, nosing through the trash, and, I guess, figuring cat meat would be a nice addition to the menu.

"You like it?" Henry said.

"Too right." I stroked it and, blame me if it didn't just curl up on my lap and hit the hay! "And it likes me," I said. "What's its handle?"

Henry gave that faint smile of his. "Karl. You like something to drink?"

I said I would, and he went out and I settled back and it was something, it truly was. I should have felt grateful, but I didn't, because I wasn't. That envy I'd got gnawing inside of me was still there, and being in that dandy room only made it worser. So when Henry came back with my root beer, and something for himself that wasn't, and poured out the drinks in real glasses, laid out the checkerboard, and we'd settled down, me drawing white, I said, casual as may be, "How's about playing for a dime a game. It's what all the riders do."

Henry lit his huge pipe. "Ten cents . . . I don't know. You any good at this game, Ben?"

Well, wasn't I just! Me and Bo had played a zillion games back in Clement. In fact, Bo had taught me how to play, and he was only just about the best checkers player there'd ever been back home. But I didn't tell Henry that. No, sir. Bo had told me once there were times it paid to act dumb, and I reckoned this was one of them times. Sickening, ain't it? But the way I saw it, Henry had plenty and I didn't have nothing but them hats, so I aimed to do some equalizing.

"I did play some," I admitted, "but that was a long time ago. Matter of fact, I can't hardly remember the moves."

"Is that so?" Henry shook his head, but I could see he looked pleased, and I thought, ride on, you're just like the rest of us at that, especially when he said okay, he'd play for a dime.

Being in white is somewhat like riding point on a herd, guiding, as it were, and I could see right off that Henry wasn't no good, but I let him push me around for a while, did some pushing back, so's it wouldn't seem too easy, then let him win.

Henry leaned back, rubbing his hands together. "One to me," he said.

"Yeah," I nodded, frowning. "You played good there. Same stakes again?"

"Okay." Henry was eager, and I let him win again, just so's he'd think he could beat me anytime.

"Gee whillikers." I sounded exasperated. "You were lucky there, Henry. Just plain lucky."

"It wasn't luck." Henry was mighty pleased with himself. "Maybe I should give you lessons, haw-haw."

"Maybe you should." I hawed, too, but I was hawing up my sleeve, thinking, brother, have you got a surprise coming! "Tell you what, though, this dime stuff ain't very exciting. Let's make it a dollar."

"A dollar!" Henry sucked his teeth. "That's kind of high stakes, Ben. I'm not a gambling man."

"Shucks, I ain't neither," I said. "I just figure you're being lucky, is all."

"Maybe . . ." Henry hesitated, then shrugged. "All right, a dollar. But don't blame me if you lose."

"I ain't no blamer," I said. "I take the trail as I find it. Let's play."

"Right." Henry had white, seeing as how he'd won before, so he had the odds, but I stuck into him and moved him around that board, after that dollar, but not wanting to be too obvious, since I wanted some more after that, and I had him, I had him exactly where I wanted him, when he made a move the like of which I hadn't never seen before, and which was a dumb move at that, but the game just slid away from me and I lost!

I stared at that board, not able to believe my eyes. The game had been in my poke as certain as could be, but there I was, beaten again and a whole dollar down. Goddamn, it was a week's pay gone, plus twenty cents, and we hadn't been playing for more than fifteen minutes.

"That move," I said.

"Which one might that be?" Henry asked.

"That hornswoggling thing you did there." I pointed at the square.

Henry shook his head. "Can't say I remember. I just move where there's a square free. Maybe you're right, I'm just lucky." And he began to put the pieces away!

"Now, hold on," I said. "Just hold on there."

"You want more?" Henry sounded sort of surprised.

"I sure do," I said, and I meant it.

"Okay." Henry shook the pieces back out of the box. "Only this time we play for fun, hey?"

"The heck with that." I flared up, like I wasn't dumb enough to half sucker a cluck and then let him walk away with my money. "A dollar."

Henry blew out his cheeks, but he agreed, and this time I beat him. He tried that move again, but I used some special ones Bo had shown me, got him fenced in a corner, and wiped him out.

I was mighty pleased. I'd known I could beat him and I'd got my dollar back, but I hadn't *made* any money, so I said, "Henry, we're about equal, you and me, saving you've got the edge. So let's make this . . . two dollars."

"What's that?" Henry's eyebrows climbed so high they near crawled over his head down to his back collar stud. "Ben, that's too hot for me, and I reckon it's too hot for you."

I didn't like that remark one little bit. No, sir. When he was winning, he didn't mind playing for a dollar, but now he knew I could handle him, he was backing out—and saying it was too hot for me! Goldurn it, I was a daring businessman and I'd risked a heap more than two bucks on them hats. "It ain't too hot for *me*," I said.

Henry rubbed his chin and puffed on his pipe like it was the noon train coming in. Running scared, which figured, him just being a printer on the *Chronicle* and not ever having risked and dared and all. He looked up at the ceiling and down at the board, drumming the table with his fingers, all on edge, then he drank some of that hard liquor he had and said, "Ben, are you *sure* you aren't any good at this game?"

And ain't it crazy, I felt angry at him saying that, doubting my word and all! "I'm just as good as you see," I said, real surly.

"Okay, then." Henry spoke like he'd screwed up his nerve. "We play. Make it five."

"Right." I held out my hand to move and then it sank in. "Five!" I yelped. "Did you say five!"

"Sure did," Henry said. "Course, if you want to quit . . ."

"The hell with that," I said—well, snarled more-like because it burned me up, him suggesting I was a quitter. But five bucks! Snakes alive, my knees was knocking so hard they could have been heard on the South Side.

"You all right, Ben?" Henry asked, kindly as may be.

186

"All right? Sure I am," I said. "Why shouldn't I be. Let's get down to it."

"Good," Henry said and wiped me off the board without even breaking sweat.

▪ EIGHTEEN ▪

"Well, goddamn it! Goddamn it all!" I stared at that board, not able to believe it, my face all red, burning with rage. "You took me! You played me for a sucker."

Henry leaned back and had a look in that pipe bowl, like it was important it was still lit. "Reckon I did at that," he said, cool as I was burning.

I tried to speak but couldn't get a word out. I just couldn't believe it. Five bucks gone, just like that. Me thinking Henry was a dumb old Dutchman and me being taken like the greenest horn that ever thought an antelope was a pony with a chair on its head. I felt like plugging Henry, and I don't know but what if I'd been carrying a gun I might have done so. Then I screwed some words out. "You took me. You suckered me—and I thought you was my friend."

"Yes?" Henry spat out one of them little bits of tobacco them pipe smokers is always getting stuck in their mouths. "And I thought you were mine. I asked you around for a friendly game and you tried to skin me. That's kind of slim, isn't it?"

Put like that, I guess it was, but it didn't make me feel no better. "You made out you ain't a good player," I said. "But you are."

"Well, you made out you're a bad player," Henry said in a maddening reasonable voice. "But you're good. Least-

187

ways, you think you are, but I could give you three pieces and beat you blindfolded any time I pleased. Ben, I learned that game before you were born."

"Okay," I said. "Okay. You're smarter than I am, and maybe you made five bucks, but you lost yourself a friend."

I threw that kitten clear off my knees and headed for the door, and then Henry said, "What about that five dollars and twenty cents?"

I looked at him with pure loathing. "You'll get it."

"That's good." Henry picked up the kitten. "There was no call to hurt this little creature."

Well, *I'd* been hurt that night, but him saying that hurt me a lot more, sort of wounded me deep down because I'd have no more harmed that kitten than I would myself—in fact, I'd have sooner—so I mumbled that I was sorry about that, and I was, truly.

Henry stroked the kitten. "All right," he said. "Now sit down!" And there was iron in his voice, like he was used to telling men what to do, and them doing it as well, which was surprising, him seeming such a mild geezer. And I did, I sat down, although I'm not sure there wasn't a notion sneaking around the back of my mind that I could get out of paying off them dollars.

"So." Henry put his hand flat on the table. "Let's you and me talk, Ben. Let's talk about money."

"Money?" I said.

"Right." Henry turned his hand over, palm up, and under the lamp you could see that ink stuff he used. "Money. It can do funny things to people, like it did to you tonight."

I opened my mouth to speak, but he held his finger up.

"Hear me out. You came here thinking you could cheat me. You think I didn't see that? You were greedy, Ben, and I'll tell you something. Greed makes people stupid. But let me ask you something. Who was the last feller you knew got cleaned out the way you've been tonight?"

I was going to say I didn't know who in Sam Hill he was talking about, and didn't care none, neither, but then I got it, and I guess it showed, because Henry nodded.

"Yeah," he said. "You know. No one better."

I stuck my chin out. "Are you saying Bo was stupid and greedy?" And I was ready to bust him one, believe me.

"Ben!" Henry sure banged the table. "I didn't even know your brother. All I know about him is he's dead, and he got killed thinking he could make money gambling, and gambling isn't nothing but a sort of greed. It's what I'm trying to tell you. Money can get between people. We could have had a nice time tonight—maybe you could have learned to play checkers, even. But it ended up you wanting to kill *me*. I saw that. I saw it clear in your face. Think about it."

I did, and maybe there was some truth in it, at that. But, still and all, money. After what me and Bo had gone through, I figured there wasn't nothing in the wide world better than hard cash, saving maybe a Winchester when you were going to see the barber—a Comanche barber, that is. "You ain't saying a feller can live without money, are you?" I asked.

"No." Henry gave that half smile of his. "You can't live without it. But if it's *all* you live for, then your life won't be worth living."

"You reckon?" I ran my glims around that room with all them books and pictures, and Henry, he was a downy old bird, because he knew what I was thinking.

"You're looking at a lifetime," he said.

"A lifetime?" I didn't get it.

Henry waved his hand. "I've worked for a whole lifetime and this is what I've got. All of it, saving a few dollars in the bank. Not much, when you think of it."

I did a Besser buffalo grunt, because that was Henry's opinion. Back in Clement, our folks had worked three lifetimes and we'd ended up with one old mule. "Sure," I said, somewhat sarcastical.

Henry raised his eyebrows again. "All I'm saying is that people are worth more than money."

"Depends on the people," I said.

Henry sighed. "I know what you mean. There's some I'm not keen on." He did some more sighing, stroking the kitten, then, sudden-like, he said, "Ben, do you like sarsaparilla pop?"

Now, I'll tell you, I liked sarsaparilla pop more than anything. I mean, it beat root beer clear out of sight, but being as boneheaded as a Missouri mule, I said I wouldn't be drinking.

"No?" Henry leaned forward, his specs shining in the lamplight. "I got it special for you."

It was hard to resist, that old feller appealing to me, but I shook my head just the same.

"Oh, well." Henry sounded regretful, but not much, and began putting the checkers away, just dropping them in the box one by one, like he was in no hurry, but if the session came to an end, he'd got things to do if I hadn't, and the durn thing was, even though I was still burning, I didn't want the session to end. What in Sam Hill did I have to go back to? But there was something else. I'd been brought up to be plain and honest, mostly, to let a feller know just where you stood with him, and although I hadn't done it that night, I reckoned I'd get back to them principles—with Henry, that is.

"It's that money I owe you," I said. "I just can't drink with a feller I owe to."

Maybe a firecracker going off underneath him might have made Henry jump more, but I doubt it.

"What!" he yelled. "*Gott im Himmel*"—scooting off into foreign. "Isn't that just what I've been telling you? It's *exactly* what I've been saying. You're letting money get in the way again. I don't *want* the dollars. I wouldn't take them if you offered them to me now." He rumbled off into more foreign, which I guess was cursing, until he simmered down. "Ben," he said, "if I say I'm sorry and we shake hands, will you have the sarsaparilla and *stop thinking about money?*"

He stuck out his mitt and I thought what the heck, I'd save myself five dollars twenty cents *and* get that sarsaparilla, and maybe he was right at that, so I stuck out my mitt, too, and we shook on it.

"That's better," Henry said. "Now I get the drinks."

He handed over the kitten, which was doing some traveling that night, and went out. I did some playing with that little cat, rolling some paper across the floor and watching it jump after it. It was fun, and I was thinking if it was mine I'd maybe teach it some tricks, when Henry came in with the drinks and more cookies, and milk for the kitten.

The three of us set to, the kitten going at that milk like all get-out, and being a guest, I figured it was bounden on me to do some jawing, so I asked Henry about them books, not asking how much he made on them, but being more genteel, like had he read any of them.

I don't know what was funny about that, but Henry grinned and said he had and that he'd be glad to loan me some anytime, but that they was foreign. "German, mostly," he said. "Some French."

My attention wandered, hearing that, but anyways, I was more interested in them pictures he had, and I said what prime land it looked by that river and how if I lived there I'd get me a homestead and raise stock.

"Looks like a feller could live high on the hog there," I said. "No Indians whooping around?"

"No." Henry lit a different pipe, like he was changing mounts.

191

"How do you get on with cyclones and such-like?"

"Hardly any," he said.

"Grasshoppers?"

He shook his head. "None to mention."

Well, I shook *my* head, baffled. I mean, that sounded some kind of paradise they had there, so, being as we was friends again, I asked flat out: "Henry, why does them foreigners come here? I know land is near free, but the only reason for that is no one in their right minds would pay a red cent for it. Jupiter, it's worser than Clement County."

"You think?" Henry asked.

"I don't think, I *know*," I said. "Saving grass, there ain't nothing ever been growed on this land, and there ain't nothing growing on it now, and there never will be."

"Maybe." Henry puffed away for a minute, then tilted his head, which is a thing he did when he was seeming to agree with you but about to start an argument. "Maybe. I don't know much about farming. It isn't only free land, though that's a powerful pull, Ben. But there's other freedoms go with it."

"Such as?" I asked.

"Oh, being free to speak your mind, free to write what you want. You know, Ben, there are countries in the world where you can carry a firearm but you aren't allowed a printing press? Not even a broken-down one like that Army press at the *Chronicle*"—sounding somewhat rueful when he said that—"and not having someone's foot on your neck." And he sounded real fierce all of a sudden, like he'd had someone's foot on *his* neck and not been able to do much about it.

I'd like to have pushed him there, maybe found out why he'd come to America, but he pulled out that big watch of his.

"Ben," he said, "I'm happy for you to stay as long as you want, but don't you have to get back?"

192

I was sorry to have to say so but allowed that was the case, seeing as how, although old Besser stayed open late, when he did lock up, he stayed that way till dawn and wouldn't open for anyone, so I said I'd better beat it, which was a pity. But there it was, so I moved out, giving that little kitten a last tickle—and wouldn't I have liked to take it with me—thanked Mrs. Brady for the grub, and walked to the gate with Henry.

It sure was a hot night. One of them Kansas nights with lightning in the air just ready and waiting to start striking, and if you combed your hair, it crackled and stood straight up. I thought of that cool river in the picture and how it would be lying under one of them shade trees with a line out for catfish.

"Henry," I said, "I don't know about that freedom stuff, but it still beats me, them dumb foreigners leaving all that to come here."

"Hmm." Henry leaned on the gate, his pipe glowing red. "I guess all foreigners are dumb, hey, Ben?"

"Why, sure," I began, and then could have bitten my tongue off. "Gee, Henry. Not *all* foreigners"—cause, of course, he was one. "No, sir, I was thinking of them sodbusters. Say, when you get down to it, all sorts of folks is smart. Why, I knew a nigger once"—thinking of Tom Carney—"who was near as smart as a white man."

Well, I didn't know why, but I guessed it was because foreigners was peculiar, but old Henry began laughing, really laughing, haw-hawing away fit to burst, wiping his eyes and all. "Ben," he said, "you're worth knowing. You certainly are. You make sure you come again. Go on, now."

I said good night, thanked him, and moved off, but I just couldn't help myself, knowing if I didn't, I'd be thinking about it for days, so I turned. "Henry," I said, "excuse me for asking, but that gent on the wall, with all them whiskers, I was wondering whether he was kin of yours.

Maybe"—I didn't want to say Pa, figuring he'd get mad—"maybe your uncle?"

"No." Henry stopped laughing sudden. "No, he's a writer. A German writer. Name of Marx. Good night, now."

I moseyed away, turning to wave, although he couldn't have seen me, but me seeing that red pipe light glowing where Henry was, hoofed it a few more yards and turned again, and the light was gone.

And it's strange. That night with Henry, which had started out real terrible, had turned into one of the best I'd ever had, and what with him being so kind and that grub, and the kitten, all my cares and worries had just gone out of my mind. But not seeing that little red glow was like I'd been deserted, shut out of someone's life, as if Henry had just gone back inside that dandy house and clean forgot all about me, just like I was of no account at all.

It made me blue all over again. Them hats started pressing me, so's when I got back to the store, I was blue as could be, and being in that store didn't exactly make you want to praise the Lord, neither.

Old Besser was there as ever, sitting in the gloom, staring at nothing, and gosh knows what was going through his head, working out how to make money out of grasshoppers maybe. We did some grunting at each other and he got on them stumpy legs of his and was just going to lock up when a feller came in.

I took one look at him and thought, Jupiter, a holdup artist! He was all tattered and wore-out-looking, like them saddle bums we'd met on the trail, and he was carrying a handgun! I was just going to reach for the sky and say he could have the whole blamed store but would he leave my stuff, being as how I was an orphan, when he said, "I hear you got cheap hats!"

Moses, I near fainted on the spot like them ladies is always doing—well, they're always doing it in novels, although I've never seen one do it.

"Cheap hats," I croaked. "Mister, I've got the best and . . ." I tried to recall the gab that traveling man had said, but couldn't remember a word! Not that it mattered, because that hombre just said to hand him one, and he jammed it over his head, paid, and beat it, heading out like he was on the lam. But, as he got to the door, I shouted, "Hey, mister!"

He turned quick, like he was going to draw, but just said what did I want, and I asked him how come he knew about the hats.

"Feller told me in a barroom, a cowboy," he said, and went through the door.

Jehoshaphat, that was something. There was me all downcast, and then that feller just came in out of the night, and going into it as well, and where he was heading—your guess is as good as mine—but a hard case, a mystery man, and there was plenty of them wandering around, like Jack Shears, but buying a hat off me!

Like old Tyler used to opine, the Lord did His doings in the most mysterious way. But I'd done it. My first sale! I'd been daring and risking and it had paid off and I had the cash in my hand to prove it. It was like I'd found that El Dorado gold mine. Gosh almighty, it was okay old Henry saying money didn't count, but it sure counted for me that night. All them blues went clear out of me. I hit the hay feeling like a million bucks and spent most of the night working out how long it would take to make that much, which I guessed wouldn't be all that long now, and just determined that the next day, why, I was going to show Abilene some getting up and going like it had never seen before.

That feller coming in was like a sign, a sign like them old folks in the Bible saw in the sky and all, telling me that I was going to sell my hats.

Yes, sir, I felt real religious, especially as it was Sunday, although I could have done without that, the town being quiet, with the riders sleeping it off, the respectable folks at church, and them sodbusters out there in the wilds at prayer meetings, asking for rain, although it was as if the Lord was hard of hearing where that was concerned. Course, I'd got nothing against folks praying, but that holiness was getting in the way of my business. I wanted that town brisk. Brisk and lively.

There was just me and Besser in the store, because Mrs. Besser and Goblinka went to some foreign preacher who was in town, so just to while away the time I told Besser what good grub Mrs. Brady dished up, sticking it to him. "And that Henry," I said, "he's a real nice feller. *Open-handed*"—sticking it to him again.

Not that he seemed stuck. He brooded for a while, chewing on a straw. Then he said something amazing. "That Henry Schneider is a bad man!"

"Are you kidding me?" I asked.

"Nah!" Besser didn't have much range of expression, his being either plain gloomy or downright gloomy, but right then he looked ferocious. "He wants to take money off people."

"What!" I said. "You mean he's a bandit?" Jeepers, I thought, old Henry a robber! Not that it bothered me none, there being millions of them roaming around the West. Why, most of them lawmen was robbers in their spare time. But when I thought of Henry it was just ridiculous. "Mr.

Besser," I said, "I reckon we're talking about a different feller entirely."

"Nah," Besser said. "It's the same man. You ask my brother."

"You got a brother!" I got some more amazement. It was like hearing some old mossy stump saying it had kin.

"Sure," Besser said. "Brusik. He's at Dodge."

Dodge! The world was going to run out of amazements at that rate. I mean Dodge, that *was* wild and woolly. There wasn't no railroad and there wasn't no town, come to that. Just the fort and a couple of stores for the buffalo hunters. Jupiter, there was real wild Indians roaming around there, Cheyenne and Comanche and Pawnees and all. "What's he doing there?" I asked.

"He's a dealer," Besser said. "Hides and skins. He knew that Schneider in Chicago. Schneider worked on a paper for the Germans. It said business was bad for workingmen. Schneider used to speak at meetings in the Haymarket, telling them workingmen to go on strike. He said they should get more pay. That's why he had to leave."

"Leave?" I said. "Why should he leave for that?"

Besser spat out that straw. "There was folks after him."

"Yeah?" I said. "What kind of folks"—not believing a word of it.

"Plenty folks." Besser did the roll and looked grim. "Detectives!"

"Mr. Besser," I said, moving to the door, "you're just stretching it, is all. You saying lawmen is after Henry! Pull the other one."

Besser did some whisker rubbing, like his brains was in his beard and he was stirring them up. "Not regular lawmen," he said. "Private detectives. Pinkerton men. Them big firms back there, the meat packers and the railroad company, they pay them, and maybe they take Henry Schneider for a trip on Lake Michigan."

I shook my head. "What would they do that for?"

Besser did some more whisker rubbing. "They take Schneider on that trip, only maybe he don't come back."

"You mean they'd kill him!" I said—well, yelped is more like. "Just for saying fellers should get more pay!"

"He made trouble," Besser said. "Big trouble."

"Well, why don't them detectives detect him here?" I said, getting somewhat heated. "He ain't exactly hiding himself away."

Besser waved that aside. "They don't care about him being here. He don't make no trouble for them. But he makes trouble for us."

"Us?"

"*Us.*" Besser sounded real mean. "Fellers like him, they cause trouble, and Americans say all foreigners are the same, all against business, so get back where you come from. Yah. Now I say no more."

"Okay." I got the broom and went outside, really thinking. I mean, that news about Henry, it was like getting shot in the foot. Old Besser, he wasn't the sort to string you along for a joke, so what he said he meant. But detectives after Henry! And just for saying fellers should get more pay! I wouldn't have minded him asking Besser to raise mine, although I had to admit it was wrong for Henry to be against business, seeing as how I was a businessman myself. Course, that talk about him making Americans not like foreigners was plain nonsense, because they didn't need no Henry to make folks dislike them, the way they all huddled together jabbering so a decent body couldn't understand them, instead of being sociable like regular folks. Anyhow, half the blamed businessmen in town was foreign, like Karatofsky and Lebold the big land agent and no one disliked them!

But the more I thought about it, the less ridiculous it seemed. I'd seen stuff in the *Chronicle* about labor trouble back East and fellers who went around blowing places up. Anarchs, they was called, and maybe Henry was one of them, which is why he was in Abilene, joining the rest of the fellers who had the law after them. In fact, that's what the West was for, in a manner of speaking—fellers on the lam and roamers of any kind you cared to mention, just roamers drifting around like tumbleweed, same as Jack Shears, or that hombre who'd bought the hat last night. Me, too, come to that, leastways like I was before I went into business.

Anyhow, Mrs. Besser and Goblinka got back and we had lunch, and you know, most places Sunday lunch is better than other days, but at Besser's it was even worser, would you believe. Something to do with their religion, penitanting or whatever, although why they should count me in on their penancing beat me.

But I got it down and let the afternoon drift away, me swatting flies mostly, and thinking about Henry, when who should walk in but Tom McInnery.

He was in business, like me, but in boots, Lone Star riding boots, and he made a powerful lot of money out of them, too.

I said, "Afternoon," real respectful, but he made a beeline for old Besser, shaking his hand and backslapping him and giving him a cigar, which Besser took, even though he didn't smoke, figuring to sell it for a dime, I guess.

McInnery horned in at Besser, telling him what a dandy feller he was and all, and how them farmers, so-called, respected him, and maybe he should use his influence to hold back the Farmers Protection Association from bringing in them quarantine laws, saying how everyone, businessmen and farmers, made money out of the cattle trade, them riders eating lots of eggs and greens.

"Which reminds me," he said, "I was telling Mrs. Mc-Innery the other day, *why don't we get more supplies from*

Mr. Besser!" Which made me think, brother, you're kin to old Judas himself.

Besser did the buffalo grunt, which no one on earth could have told what it meant, but you had to hand it to McInnery. He said, "Now, I'm glad you agree with me. And say, some of us businessmen are having a meeting next week to discuss all this, and it just wouldn't be representative without you"—and a lot more sweet talk and lies, until he beat it.

Old Besser sat there, and I stood there, swatting my millionth fly, but it was interesting, at that. Like there was businessmen such as McInnery who made money out of the cattle trade, and there was some farmers made money that way, too, like he'd just said, selling eggs and greenstuff. But there was other businessmen, like old Heaney, who was making money out of the farmers and who was looking forward to making more. So the fellers in Abilene was splitting, some wanting to keep the herds coming, and some wanting to enforce them quarantine laws and ban the cattle, and you'd maybe not guess, would you, that them fellers who was against cattle was reformers, too? Not much, you wouldn't.

But I was itching with curiousness, too, so I said, "Going to that meeting, Mr. Besser? Be fun, meeting the fellers, and they is all big shots."

Besser didn't even grunt, so I reckoned that was the end of that amazing brilliant conversation, and I was going to clean the window out of sheer boredom, when he said, "Fun? I ain't got no time for fun"—that figuring—"but maybe I go."

"You going against them reformers and the Farmers Protection Association?" I was surprised, seeing as how he was like the sodbusters' friend, them that had two cents to rub together, that is, but glad because I wanted the cattle trade to keep going.

"Nah!" Besser did the buffalo roll. "I told you, Besser makes no money from cattle. But I go, and McInnery, he buys from me, and I make money out of him."

He made a strange creaky noise and I realized he was laughing! Yeah, laughing, which was more amazing than that Blondin lunatic tightrope walking across the Niagara Falls. And when Mrs. Besser and Goblinka came out of their room, he gabbled at them and they laughed, too, like it was the funniest thing since Grandpa caught his whiskers in the mangle.

It was disgusting, you know? Like making a buck was one thing, and McInnery had only called to make use of Besser because he normally wouldn't have given him a "Howdy." But laughing and cackling away, it was plain *sordid*, and I felt so sick I got the broom and went outside, making out I was going to sweep the boardwalk, which, if I'd done it every time I pretended to, there wouldn't have been no walk left, and leaned there, watching the fascinating sight of Joe Evert's dog scratching itself, when a rider came down the street, so I did the getting-up-and-going stuff and asked him if he wanted a hat, and he said, "Sure!"

Like I'd said, it was a day for amazements. I'd asked millions of fellers if they'd buy a hat and never got more than a laugh, and now this feller said yes, even though he was wearing one which looked okay to me. But we went inside and he got a hat and rammed it right over the one he was wearing, gave me a ten-dollar bill, and walked out without waiting for the change!

Course, he was as lit up as you can be without actually falling down, and I reckon he didn't even know he was buying a hat. But I'll tell you something, I didn't go after him with the change, and I didn't tell Besser how much I'd got, and I felt disgusted with myself.

It's a fact, I'd been disgusted with Besser, and there I

was, doing the same thing. Worser really, because Mc-Innery knew the score, but that drunk, it was like taking money off a blind man—and he was a rider, too.

But came the dawn, as they say, I was feeling somewhat different. Them dollars was mighty comforting, and I thought, what the heck, that rider would have only blown the cash in a saloon. In fact, by noon I'd got around to believing I'd done him a favor, reckoning he might have got into a crooked poker game and got killed, same as Bo.

There was another thing on my mind, though, that was real bad. There was a slump in the beef market, so the prices was low, which meant the drovers was keeping the herds out on the prairie, so the town was just crammed full of riders—but riders with hardly enough money to buy a beer, leave alone a hat. It was mighty strange, like them folks back East had decided to stop eating, but the *Chronicle* said there was a business slump and there was a lot of folks out of a job, so they couldn't afford beef.

And then something happened which blew away all my other thoughts like a cyclone.

Next day I was clearing the back yard of trash, which got piled up there. I can't say my mind was completely on that interesting chore, because it was full of stuff about hats, and Henry and detectives and all, but it got a break for a minute when I got hold of a copy of the *Chronicle* I'd missed which had a really comical piece about the alphabet, such as: "Why is the letter B like a fire? Because it makes oil boil!" and such-like, and which was really taking my mind off all the worries haunting me, when I heard the grunt and then there was old Besser scowling at me.

"Just about finished, Mr. Besser," I said. "Been looking in this paper to see if there was anything about market prices"—soothing him, you know, but he didn't look soothed. No, sir, he looked at me with a face like doom and said, "There's a policeman wants you!"

"Me?" I said. "He wants me?"

"Yah," Besser glared at me. "What you done wrong?"

Well, gee whillikers, there wasn't much I *could* do wrong in Abilene saving sparking with Goblinka, and I hadn't got far with that, but all the same I felt scared and guilty as all get-out. But I went in the store to that policeman, Elmer Moore, who had no semblance to a prairie flower whatever, and asked him what the trouble was. He didn't tell me, just grunted, like that grunting was catching, and said Marshal Hickok wanted me!

Jerusalem, that did scare me, and I was white around the gills, following Elmer down the street and into the Alamo, where Hickok was playing poker, his shooters hung on the back of his chair, all ready for action, although the truth was, he hardly needed them at all. In fact, a marshal before him, Ben Thompson—"Bear" they called him— didn't carry a gun at all, saying they only led to shootings and killings, him settling any differences of opinion with his bare fists. Course, I've got to admit he got shot dead in the end, but that was out of town and was more an accident than anything else. And one thing *is* sure, when John Wesley Hardin, who *was* a mad-dog killer, worse even than Kessel, when he hit town and swaggered about with two six-guns on his belt, which was clear against them town ordinances, Hickok didn't go up against him. No, sir, as a matter of fact, they ended up drinking together!

But be that as it may, there was Hickok, and there was me, sweating like I had a fever, wondering what I'd done wrong. And it came to me sudden—it was that rider I'd done out of his change! Jupiter, did I curse myself! I stood there vowing I wouldn't never do any more chiseling as long as I lived, and hoping like all get-out that the marshal would win the game, so's he'd be in a good temper.

As it happened, he split the pot, and made maybe twenty

dollars, too, and I leaned forward and said, all husky, "Marshal?"

Hickok leaned back and lit up a cigar that must have set him back twenty cents, and stared at me with them cold blue eyes, and it was like looking down the barrels of a shotgun at that.

"Marshal," I said, "I'm real sorry about that rider, no kidding. I looked for him to give him the change, and I'm a regular businessman and I tended my brother's grave, I truly did, only someone swiped that pickle jar, which I was going to report to you it was five cents . . ." And I sort of run down, like a bolted pony, with Hickok and them other fellers staring at me mystified, and for which I didn't blame them, because I was mystifying myself.

Hickok leaned back, took a big puff of his cigar and a big drink of whiskey, and said, "Kid, I don't know what in hell you're talking about, but you better have been going straight, because you know what'll happen to you if you don't"—giving me that icy stare like he was ready to buffalo me on the spot. "But I got some news for you about *Dutch Kessel!*"

Snakes alive! My heart near jumped clear out of my mouth. Kessel! That killer, roaming the streets someplace! It meant I had to get my handgun and go and do my venging, which I was going to do, or thought I was, which is by no means the same thing, even though it might mean leaving them hats, and I guess that vengefulness showed on my face, because Hickok gave me the glare again.

"I know what's on your mind," he said. "You're thinking you'll rustle up a gang of Texans and have a necktie party"—which just went to show how even a smart feller like Hickok could get his reins tangled, but which was an idea at that, and I was thinking how to organize that party when Hickok went on. "You can forget that notion, and forget it once and for all, because *I'm* the law in this town,

204

and because"—he took another drag on that cigar—"and because Kessel is dead!"

"Dead?" I croaked. "Dead?"

"That's it, kid." Hickok dipped the end of his cigar into his whiskey. "A cattle dealer just got in from St. Louis. Seems Kessel was over there running a crooked poker game and one of them Missouri gents took exception and plugged him. So that's it, kid. You and your brother can both rest easy. Yeah, I guess you might say justice got done in the end."

■ TWENTY ■

Jehoshaphat! Kessel dead! Course, *I* was glad, but it was like the whole town was, too. Mayor McCoy slipped me five bucks just like I'd shot Kessel myself, and real important fellers like L. A. Burroughs and T. C. Henry and Lebold shook me by the hand. The Reverend Christopher lassoed me, trying to get me to church to thank the Lord for his many-folded mercies, as if the Reverend had done that killing himself. I went and bought me a huge beefsteak with eggs and all the fixing, celebrating, and the Chink didn't charge me none for the pie and coffee, and he hissed and grinned at me, which I guess meant he was glad, although, for all I know, he might have been saying he'd like to stick a cleaver in my head.

And I sold them hats! Every last one of them. The riders came in clamoring for them as remembrances, and would you believe they got me to write my moniker in them! That was because old Vear Porter Wilson ran a story about it all in the *Chronicle*. It was on the front page in big black letters. JUSTICE DONE, it said, with a lot of stuff about how it was a pity JUSTICE had been DONE by a sordid GAMBLER instead of the LAW, and how drinking and gambling, and smoking, too, would you believe, was downright terrible and *always* led to a SHAMEFUL END, which I didn't take kindly to, it hinting that Bo had met one, and anyway it wasn't true. Jeepers, Mayor McCoy himself gambled and drank and went with dance girls, too, and he lived as high off the hog as you could get.

But how I really sold them hats was because Henry stuck in the paper I had them! It sure made old Wilson mad, it being *free* advertising, which for Wilson was like breaking all them Ten Commandments at one go. But it didn't bother Henry none. He told me Wilson wasn't going to fire him because good printers didn't exactly grow on trees west of the Missouri, and anyways, although Wilson owned the means of production, it was him who controlled them, which meant as much to me as the Chink's hissing but sure seemed to amuse old Henry.

So there it was. I was free. Really free, because all the time I'd been in Abilene, well, I'd been mighty busy in the store and being a daring businessman, and maybe I hadn't grieved over Bo as much as I ought to have done, like them folks in storybooks, but all the time that vow had been dragging at me like a dead hen tied around the neck of a hound that's been at the chickens, dragging at me day and night, and no escape from it.

And it was strange. In one way, nothing real had happened. I was still just a kid pecking for a living, but I *felt* different. I guess I was like the slaves when they was freed. They still had to go on chopping cotton and plowing, and for all the difference it made to them, old Lincoln might as well have saved his breath—down in Dixie, anyhow— but still and all, *something* had happened to them. I guess, like one of them niggers, if he didn't take to being where he was at, he could pull up stakes and head to wherever he blamed well wanted to live, if the folks there would have him—which cut down the choice considerable.

But that's how it was with me, somewhat. Bo could rest easy, I'd sold them hats, I had a pocketful of tin and was as free as a bird. But the first thing I did with that freedom was take a day off! Besser was blue about it, but I didn't give a cuss, I got out my riding gear, went down to the livery stable, and hired myself a pony.

It wasn't much of a mount at that, having been worn down on a drive. In fact, I was somewhat shamefaced about it, but it sure was something to be in the saddle again, looking down on the world for a change, instead of having to look up at everything in sight, and having the reins in *my* hands.

I headed southwest, across the Smoky Hill, what there was left of it after that blazing summer, and onto the range, through the herds that was being held out there, and, jeepers, there was some steers. It looked like a squirrel could hop on them all the way back to Texas and never touch ground. There was riders and chuck wagons out there, but I didn't stop, just drifted on until there wasn't nothing but the prairie and me, out on my own, looking at the land shimmering away, the grass yellow under that sun, and even though it was into fall it was still beating down like it had something personal against human beings.

It was crazy, I guess, but I pulled up out there, right out on the bare prairie and under that sun, slouched back against the crupper, hat pulled over my eyes, sweat pouring right down into my boots. There was a drowzy buzzing of insects, hawks swung across the sky, the sun beat down and the heat came right back out of the ground, whiles I sat there thinking—well, not real thinking, more like having vague thoughts and pictures moving across my mind, like them big slow clouds we got in Texas in the fall, vague thoughts and all, drifting, drifting, my eyelids drooping, and then it was like I was floating, floating clear up to the sky with them hawks, just as if I was someone else up there looking down at a kid on a pony, and then I seemed to be going higher, as high as an eagle, and that kid was getting smaller and smaller until he was just a dot, just a speck on them endless plains, a nothing. Nothing a breeze couldn't blow away in one puff, as if it had never existed and didn't matter none even if it had.

Some little birds cheeping under the pony woke me and I rode to the nearest chuck wagon. It was just like old times. A couple of riders stretched out in the shade and a cook who might have been Charlie McCann's brother, all irascible and full of red-eye, gave me a plate of stew and coffee. That herd had come all the way from near Corpus Christi, down on the Gulf, which made our drive seem like a stroll, and the boys was just wore out, fine-drawn and near in rags, that herd not having been sold yet, and the few bucks the boss had handed out being blown in some saloon or other, and a thousand miles from home! I said how was they, and they said how was I, but the truth was, we didn't have nothing to say to each other, so I said so long and headed back to town, following the pony's shadow.

I pulled up once, at a cabin, and asked for water. They gave it to me, a real prairie family, living in a dugout roofed with sods, a woman who looked plain crazy and a feller who was catching up with her fast, but they didn't hand over that water in no spirit of Christian charity, more like they wished it was poison. I guess because I was togged out like a rider, and when you looked at that pitiful crop they'd got, and realized a few steers wandering at night could wipe them out, you couldn't blame them, at that. But I drank that water and I was a blamed fool for asking, it being half a mile to the nearest well. Just nothing on a pony, but a long haul with a bucket.

It was getting near dusk, then, all purple and blue, like the colors was rising out of the ground. A few stars was showing their faces, and there was fireflies glowing in the juniper bushes along the Smoky Hill River. A train, eastbound for Kansas City, gave that long, mournful whistle, and when I crossed the river, I could see Abilene, and it was glowing, too.

The pony needed feed, but I reined in, looking at the lights, and the campfires sparkling, and beyond them, lamps shining where them settlers was starving to death and going insane. It was just exactly like when me and Bo arrived, and I don't know but what them Indians had got it right about sitting in the sun and having visions, but it was as if me spending them hours out there had kind of told me what to do, even though I hadn't been thinking. But I knew then, looking at the lights, and all the empty darkness beyond, just what I was going to do.

The thing was, I could go back to riding, but when you got down to it, what was that? Sure, you had your glory days, sashaying around some cow town like you was kings, but then it was back, broke, like them fellers I'd just met, waiting for another drive, and then spending three months looking at the wrong end of a steer. Or I could maybe buy me some land, but brother, I'd been that way before. I knew just exactly what farming was—busting your back six days a week; then, come Sunday, sitting on the stoop hoping and praying a face would come along you hadn't seen before; and all the while the wind blowing away your land and what brains you had.

On the other hand, there was towns like Abilene, where there was things going on, new faces all the time, a newspaper, even if it was a pack of lies, a theater, the depot . . . Like you take them riders, they'd get back to some godforsaken bunkhouse and boast about how they'd seen Abilene and all its splendors, as you might say, whereas I could just live there, all the time. I guess what I was really thinking was, it was just more plain *fun* being in a town.

So that's what I decided, riding through the dusk, with goldenrod dusting the pony's legs yellow. I was going to stick around and see what happened, because one thing was sure, it was a big country, where most anything at all could happen, such as changing an ignorant country boy like me into an all-American businessman.

But I had something to think about there. I could carry on storekeeping maybe with a big feller like Karatofsky, or take up land surveying, or pay Pat Brady to show me how to do that telegraphing. I could even go into the newspaper racket, saving that the smell of that oil and ink was just too terrible.

So that was the way of it, but it seems there's times when you can do anything and you don't do nothing, which is how it was with me. I sort of dawdled, working in the store, not doing no more investing for a while, relaxing, as you might say, dusting out and selling in the store, going to the Chink's, and going to Henry's place, too. He taught me that game of chess, which was mighty difficult, although I got the hang of it pretty quick, all saving that knight, which jumped ever which way like a good cow pony with a horsefly you know where. We used to sit in that room with the cat and pictures and them books, and I'd have given a million dollars to have asked Henry about them detectives and Chicago, but I never let out a peep. Strange, ain't it? But there was something about Henry that didn't exactly encourage you to ask questions, not them sort, anyways.

So it was come day, go day, for me, but if there was happening as far as I was concerned, there was plenty going on in the town. All that struggling between the reformers and the saloonkeepers was coming to a head. You could hear it, almost, like a kettle coming to the boil. And I was right there when the kettle boiled over.

TWENTY-ONE

The way that boiling up started, like it might be the last stick that was shoved on the fire, was what happened at the Town Council meeting in September.

The reformers had been getting stronger, howling against sin and such-like, although I don't know it was sin getting them down so much as the taxes they had to pay for the lawmen, and most of them reformers was making money out of the farmers, not the cattle trade, so it didn't mean beans to them whether the herds came to Abilene or not. In fact, although they was against wicked sinning right enough, they was against the cattle trade more, being as how they actually *wanted* more sodbusters in the county, and it was true, in them days, before that feller Glidden invented barbed wire, the cattle trade and farming, the which is being sarcastical, didn't mix.

So, at that Town Council meeting, them reformers rode clear over Mayor McCoy and got an ordinance passed saying that if they couldn't stamp out the bars, the dance halls had to be closed and them dance girls had to leave town!

McCoy and them saloonkeepers blustered, saying them girls had a right to live where they wanted, it being a free country, which I could have told them was wasting their breath, remembering how me and Bo had got moved on from Lookout. And that's all it was, bluster, because there was a million ways the Town Council could get them girls out, such as making them pay a huge poll tax or whatever. And, anyway, it was more like was they pushed or did they fall, because some of the girls was drifting off anyway, seeing as how there were less riders in town, and them that were being broke, mostly.

Still, them girls didn't like being driven out, for which

I sure didn't blame them, so when they did go, they made like a procession, crossing the tracks and marching right down Texas Street, all dolled up and painted, and weren't they cussing the reformers and respectable folks! Talk about the air being blue! And when they climbed aboard the train, all the riders and cattlemen was there to give them a send-off, with the band from the Novelty Theater playing, and when they did leave, you could hear the girls squealing halfway to Kansas City.

So that was the end of the dancing girls. The policemen who patrolled the South Side got fired, and the reformers was really crowing, like they won a mighty victory, but it was strange *not* having the girls around. The grass was growing on the streets down there across the tracks, and there was no music or whooping. It was respectable, sure enough, but dull, you know, dull as ditchwater.

And them reformers rubbed it in. They upped the fines for a feller being maybe a little rowdy, and they forced Thompson and Coe to really paint out that sign—and they put on a play!

I didn't believe that when I heard they was going to do it. Henry told me. I ran into him on the street and he said they was printing off posters for it. "The Good Templars is putting it on," he said.

I laughed out loud. "Henry," I said, "you're barking up the wrong tree. Them Templars is *against* theaters, like they is against drink"—which was true. Them Templars was even worse than the other reformers, being against *anything* whatsoever that gave you a good time.

But it was true. They did put the play on at the Novelty Theater, and it was free! Well, it was free to go in, but they had a collection, which I ducked out of. The play was called *Ten Nights in a Barroom*, which sounded a crazy play for them Templars to stick on, but after seeing it, you knew why.

First the Reverend Christopher made a speech, which was as bad as that feller from Ohio, all about the evils of liquor, and then we got that drama. It was all about a feller who was a regular God-fearing businessman, like Lebold, who started drinking in secret—although it didn't tell you *why* he started drinking—my guess being it was because he couldn't stand his missus anymore, her idea of a good time being reading the Bible aloud. And then that feller started going into barrooms, being a regular feller and whooping it up, but that drink getting to him so's he lost his business and all his money and house. He had this little girl who was cashing in her chips because she wasn't getting enough grub, her pa blowing his cash on booze, and one night he got back from the barroom and she was dying and talking about how she was going to a better world with angels and all waiting for her, and her pa said: "FORGIVE ME, MY DARLING CHILD," which she did, and then died. It was pitiful to see. Even some riders at the back who'd been guffawing was sobbing at it, and they was still sobbing away over their drinks in the Bull's Head later.

There was something else which was interesting. Like that theater, when they put on a vaudeville show, even if the acts weren't no good, the riders made up for them, laughing and joking and fooling around like they was *enjoying* themselves, whereas the folks in there that night, they was all dolesome, like they was in church, and when a feller rolled in who looked as if he'd spent *ten thousand nights* in a barroom, they was real frosty and disapproving and had the marshal arrest him, when all he did, when he saw the stage set, was think he *was* in a barroom and climb up there and ask for a shot of red-eye.

Then, would you believe, the Reverend made *another* speech, saying as how he hoped we'd all learned a most valuable moral lesson and stay clear of liquor and join the Good Templars, which was plumb ridiculous, seeing as how, apart from them few riders, there wasn't no one there who did drink.

That was the kind of respectableness that started going on in Abilene now that the reformers had got their hands on the strings. But that victory for them, it left a sour taste in them that lost, which is the same with all victories, I guess. The winners feel fine, but the losers are sore and fractious, and in fact there was more rowdyism *after* the girls had gone than before, fellers galloping down Texas Street, which was illegal, breaking windows, shooting at the placard saying *No shooting*. Nothing to speak of, but signs, as it might be. Signs of resentment.

I mentioned that to Henry. We'd been playing chess, me still biting back them questions about detectives, and although he'd beat me, the game had gone twelve moves, which was some kind of record, and we were standing at the gate, like we usually did.

"I know what you mean," Henry said. "It can be the case, though, where there isn't nothing much to do, you can get rowdyism. Course"—doing what he always did, saying one thing, then turning around and saying the complete opposite—"course, you get rowdyism where there *is* plenty to do. Yeah, it's a problem. But a lot of this here is resentment. You know what I mean?"

I reckoned I did. "It ain't a bit like the old days," I opined.

Henry grinned. "Something in that. And I reckon there won't be any new days."

"You reckon not?" I asked.

"No." Henry did some smoking. "This town is finished, Ben. Finished as a cattle town. There's going to be a vote on the quarantine laws this winter, and as sure as eggs, it'll get passed. You won't see any herds next year. In fact, the Kansas Pacific Railroad is getting ready to move the stockyards to Ellsworth."

It didn't surprise me, him saying that, because I'd heard

plenty of that talk in the store, and the *Chronicle* was full of it. "It'll be kind of solemn then," I said.

"Solemn's the word," Henry agreed. "It'll be like a grave-yard." He kind of sighed. "You ever lived in a small, quiet town, Ben?"

I laughed. "Henry, this is the *only* town I ever lived in."

Henry lit up his pipe again. "I have. I spent a winter in one once. You know what it was like? It was going out on the prairie here in the middle of summer and sitting under ten blankets. That's what it was like."

"Henry," I said, "I ain't got the faintest notion what you're talking about. One minute you're talking about win-ter, the next about sitting under blankets. Just speak plain American, can't you."

"Okay," Henry said. "Put it this way: if you *did* sit under those blankets, you'd suffocate, wouldn't you? Slowly. What's that the cowboys do with wild horses when they round them up?"

"Them's mustangs, Henry," I said. "But they brand them."

"And what's that place they put them in?"

"A corral," I said.

"And what do they do if they can't tame a mustang?"

"*Break*," I said, somewhat irritated that a clever feller like Henry didn't know them words. "You break them in. And why, if you can't, you shoot them, Henry."

"Yeah." Henry struck a match, it flaring and showing his face, and I don't know but what there wasn't something bitter showing there. "That's what they do in small towns. Corral you, brand you, and if they can't break you . . ."

"Come on, Henry," I said. "Folks don't go around shoot-ing other folks."

"No." Henry blew out that match and broke it. "Just a figure of speech. Good night now."

I said good night and started to beat it, then a thought

hit me, so I turned, but he wasn't leaning on the gate, like he mostly did. He'd gone.

I moseyed home, but being as how, with Kessel dead, the marshal had took the shackles off me, I went down Texas Street, even though it was night. There'd been a show on at the Novelty Theater, one of the last, with comics and jugglers and singers who claimed they'd performed before the CROWNED HEADS OF EUROPE, which was kings and queens, a feller told me, and which I guess was stretching it somewhat. Well, it was if it was the same show I'd seen them perform once on a free ticket. Either that or them crowned heads was plain half-wits, which they probably was, at that.

Well, I'd just got past the Novelty and there was a crowd of people coming up the street, riders mainly, having a last fling before going back home. They was making some racket, singing and shouting and cursing the North generally and them reformers and farmers in particular, giving out the old Reb yell. And leading them was Phil Coe from the Bull's Head, who was as lit up as the other fellers. And to make matters worse, there was a dog, which was the curse of them cattle towns, barking away and snapping at everything that moved, and this was no exception.

Just as the crowd got near the Alamo, that dog jumped at Coe. It was a big dog, at that, and anyhow, dog bites was serious because, like a lot of other animals out there, they carried them rabies. Coe lashed out at the dog, but it came at him again, so Coe pulled out a pistol and shot at it!

He missed, like you'd expect, and that dog ran away, but that pistol shot brought out Marshal Hickok, who'd been in the Alamo, where else.

He held back them bat-wing doors, the light spilling out, and him framed against the light all sinister, and what was even sinisterer, the piano in the Alamo stopped, and the racket in the street died down.

Hickok stood there, black against the light. "Who fired that shot?" he roared.

No one answered. Them riders just stood there, staring at the marshal, and you had to hand it to him. He was one against maybe twenty fellers, but he was going to use his star, as they say. "I said who fired!" he roared again, and sounding real mean, like as if he'd been on a winning streak at poker and was mad at having it broken. "Goddamn it, I'll blast the daylight out of the boiling lot of you."

Well, the boys was lit up, but they wasn't so lit up they didn't know when a feller meant what he said, and they began shuffling back, but not saying anything.

"Right," Hickok roared. "You asked for it."

He took a step forward, but sideways, too, showing he knew his business at that, cause he was out of the light, and then Phil Coe did a real crazy thing. He stepped forward. "I shot at a mad dog," he said, and held out his pistol.

It's a thing, you know. Maybe Hickok misheard, maybe he just wanted to get Coe anyhow, or maybe he really did think Coe was aiming at him, but whichever, he drew *his* pistols, and then, and I don't know but it was an accident, seeing as how them handguns could go off by themselves, and if it wasn't an accident then Coe was crazy, but Coe fired. He shot at Hickok, who wasn't but six feet away, and missed, and that was the second last thing he ever did do, because Hickok shot back and got him in the belly.

Coe screamed and went down to his knees, shot again, the bullet going Lord knows where, then fell on his hands, scrabbling in the dirt in the most awful way and being sick, and then, and you wouldn't really believe it, saving it was true, a man came out of the alleyway at the side of the Novelty. Hickok swung around, blasted at him, and *he* went down. And someone shouted, "Goddamn you, Hickok, you've killed Mike Williams!"

He had, too, Mike being the bouncer at the Novelty and a special policeman, who'd come out with a shotgun to give the marshal some help. And Moses, wasn't it a terrible sight, them two fellers dying there, moaning and retching, their lives leaking out of them, and all because of a dog.

It sickened me, bringing back memories of Bo and how he'd died in the street. And now there was two more fellers gone, just gone like they'd never been, and maybe that Coe wasn't much of a loss to the human race—still, he was a human being, and it didn't seem right he should be dead for a dog.

Leastways, that's what I told Henry, but he wasn't having it. "Where there's guns, people get killed," he said. "That's what guns are for. Killing people."

It made me think, at that. Think of guns and killing and fellers screaming and sobbing in the dirt, and I was sick to my stomach. In fact, I got out my handgun, aiming to throw it in the Smoky Hill River, but I didn't. I sold it to Sam Naylore instead for three dollars. Like I say, that money can get to you.

But that shooting didn't just make *me* sick. There were plenty of folks in the county who felt the same, and even some who hadn't supported the reformers started to, saying the money the cattle trade brought in wasn't worth killings and shootings, especially them that didn't get but a small piece of that money. Like L. A. Burroughs, the land agent, said, there wasn't much sense us having law if you didn't get order, and it was order brought the orders in, if you get me.

They held an inquest on the killings. Course, Hickok got away clean. Justifiable homicide, they called it, seeing as how Coe shouldn't have been carrying a handgun, so it was like I said, the lawman had the edge whichever way you looked at it.

But after that excitement blew over, I still hadn't made up my mind what to do. That stuff Henry had said about how tedious life was in a small town had got to me somewhat, although I was ready to take some of that boringness if it meant there wasn't no killing, but I wasn't looking forward with no great longings to a winter in the store, especially since, the way Henry was talking, he might beat it, so I wouldn't have no company at all, saving going to church or Good Templaring.

But then what you might call Fate took the deal, and I'm telling you, that Fate can be mighty strange at times. Like it says in a hymn someplace, God moves in a mysterious way, and it was mysterious how I got dealt a new hand, because it was an old widow woman and a cow made my life go one way, out of all trails which was laid out waiting for me.

The way of it was, I was hanging around outside the store with a broom in my hand, wondering what to do with my dollars, when there was something of a commotion started down by the *Chronicle* office, and I was going to slide down there and see what it was about, when a feller ran past, all wild-eyed, and he shouted at me, "Chicago's been burned down!"

I figured he was just lit up, or fooling, but he wasn't. It was true, Chicago *had* burned right down!

Jeepers! I mean, I hadn't never been near the burg, but I'd heard plenty about it. That *was* a city, a real one, with hundreds of thousands of folks living there. I mean, it was the sort of city old Vear Porter Wilson tried to make out Abilene was, with genuine marble palaces and whatever, and it had just gone up in smoke!

Brother, did that make for some talking. Why, folks talked about nothing else. Even the sodbusters, who usually mentioned nothing but money and grasshoppers, talked about it. And the Reverend Christopher, he had a special service, saying it was the hand of the Lord at work because of all the sinning that had gone on there, and the same could still happen to Abilene, which made me wonder, you know—Chicago sure must have done some sinning in a big way to get ahead of the Lord's vengeance before Abilene.

The Reverend, he said it was the Lord's doing, but there was lots of folks said it was them Anarchs, who was all foreigners and didn't believe in nothing, not the Word of the Lord, nor owning things, and not even getting married, which made them worser than them Popists Tyler used to holler about. In fact, they was worser than them Mormons, would you believe, because they *did* believe in getting hitched, although they liked more than one horse in the team, for which they was persecuted, which just goes to show you can't hardly win in this world. If you ain't wed to the one woman you're shacking up with, you're wrong, and if you're married to more than one, you're wrong as well. But them Anarchs was said to be worse even than that. They was worser than *Heathenists!*

Yeah, that's kind of hard to believe, but that was what they said, in fact they claimed we was descended from *monkeys*, would you believe, and which made me think about that picture on Henry's wall, and the *Chronicle* said they was everywhere, which was kind of thrilling at that, thinking about them Anarchs roaming about the country worser than Comanches—or Republicans. After what old Besser'd told me, I'd reckoned Henry was one. But I didn't say nothing because, the way folks was talking, any Anarch who was in Abilene might have found himself doing the Texas rope dance. And even when it was showed that the Chicago fire was started by that old widow woman's cow kicking over a lantern in a barn, there was folks saying,

"Well, who put that lantern there if it wasn't the Anarchs?"

So that big fire gave us a chance to talk about something different from reform and quarantine, but the real thing was, there was people in Abilene, businessmen, who lost money because of that fire. In fact, I found out that company I'd got the hats from had got burned, so it was lucky for me that fire didn't take place sooner or I'd have been out them bucks I'd handed over.

Anyways, the excitement died down, although old Vear Porter Wilson kept writing in the *Chronicle* that if citizens didn't obey the fire ordinances and clear the trash away, Abilene would go up in smoke, too—which nobody paid any heed to at all, reckoning that trouble always happens someplace else. But it don't, which was how the widow woman's cow altered my life.

Some little time after that fire, me and old Besser was in the store. He'd been acting strange, or what I reckoned was foreign-strange, like he'd got something big on his mind, which I'd guessed was a gigantic deal, like buying some new brooms, but that evening he was acting even stranger, peering at me, then looking away, and muttering to himself. It was somewhat scary, like he was going crazy, peering and muttering, and I was beginning to wish I'd got my handgun around, and then he waved me over to him. I went, but kept on the other side of the flour barrel, just in case, and asked what I could do for him.

He did some brooding, then said, "I took you in here. Yah, gave you a job, and a room, and *food!*"

Food, I thought. Gee whillikers, if that's what I've been eating, I'm a billy goat, but I didn't say nothing, just grunted back.

"Yah," Besser said. "And you made money out of me!"

Lightning! Me made money out of him! It was the other way around entirely, and I told him so.

"Yah, yah." He waved that interesting piece of information aside. "Okay, we both made money." He brooded again, his lips moving, and I was ready to jump right through the door and get the marshal when he said, "Ben"—which was truly amazing, seeing as how he usually just said "Huh" to me, so's I'd got around almost to thinking that was my name, *Huh* Curtis.

"Ben," he said, "that fire in Chicago was real bad."

"I guess so," I agreed.

"Yah." He yanked at his beard like he was trying to pull it off. Then, speaking as if his teeth was being pulled out slow, he said, "That fire was bad for me!"

"What!" I'll tell you, I near burst out laughing. "You lost out? You?"

"Yah!" He said something in foreign and I wouldn't even like to guess what it was in American, and then told me what had happened, and would you believe, him and that brother of his, Brusik, they'd owned property in Chicago which had got burned down, and the insurance company had gone up in smoke, too, so he couldn't get his cash off them.

"Well, that's tough luck, Mr. Besser," I said, trying not to laugh. "But you can't win every time."

"Nah! Nah!" he bellowed sudden. "It's . . ." And then he told me—he'd borrowed money on that property in Chicago to buy land up at Chapman Creek, and his note was being called due, so if he didn't pay the interest quick, he stood to lose everything he'd got!

"That *is* tough," I said, because I didn't want to see him come to no real harm, but figuring there was something shady going on, seeing as how that land was supposed to be reserved for genuine settlers. "But say, you can borrow more money. There's the bank, and there's plenty of rich folks in town. Ain't you thick with Tom McInnery these days?"

Old Besser, he shook his head. "It's them I owe the money

to. But see, I *got* money coming to me, from Pennsylvania and the Old Country, but it's going to come too late."

"Heck," I said. "Just tell the bank, and the fellers, they'll hold off."

Besser gave me a look, the sort of look that says, if you believe that you'll believe anything. "Ben," he said, "I don't need much cash."

Right then I began to get a real creepy feeling, like there was a scorpion creeping down my back, and I started to edge away, but Besser fixed me with them beady eyes of his. "Ben, you got some money!"

I jumped, like that scorpion had stung me where it hurts the most. "Gee," I said, "I ain't hardly got no money at all, and loaning out"—and I got one of them brain waves of mine—"my ma said I wasn't never to loan out. Never loan and never borrow. She made me promise, and I couldn't go back on that. No, sir, not never."

Besser wasn't an easy feller to read, but one dollar would have got you fifty he didn't believe a word I was saying, and he'd have been right, but he tried again, pleading as might be.

"It's just a few dollars. Just a few. Only a hundred dollars!"

I did laugh then. Not cruel-like, but rueful. "Mr. Besser," I said, "that may be a few dollars for you, but it ain't for me. And, like I told you, I don't loan out cash."

Besser's face twisted, him gnawing his lips and all, and I guess it was hard for him at that, there being not many things worser than, when you're broke, asking for a loan and getting it refused.

"Okay," he said, finally. "Then you go."

"You mean I'm fired?" I asked.

"Yah," Besser growled. "You move out. Now!"

So that was like Fate dealing the hand, sort of deciding what I should do, and I don't know that I was sorry. In a

223

way, I'd got used to Besser and the store, but it was a big country and there was plenty of things waiting out there for me, so I just shrugged and said that was okay with me and no hard feelings. I made to go and get my bedroll and stuff, but Besser said, "Wait. Wait."

Wait for what, I thought, there being nothing for me to wait for, but Besser said would I have a coffee!

Jeepers, I figured he was going crazy, first firing me, then giving me coffee, and when Goblinka brought it in, it was all sickly, with cream and sugar in it, like them foreigners drink it if they can raise the cash, getting which from Besser was like having that Champagne wine Mayor McCoy and the big cattle dealers drank. And would you believe, Goblinka brought cookies, too, which I didn't even know they ever had!

"Sit, Ben," Besser said, so I did, and we drank the coffee for a while, embarrassed you might say, then just as I was about to beat it, Besser coughed, like clearing his throat, and said, "You loan me that money and . . . and . . . and I make you a partner!"

I couldn't hardly believe he'd said that. Partners! Me owning half an entire store! Even such a dump as Besser's!

"Are you kidding me?" I said. "Partners? Regular partners?"

"Sure," Besser said.

"Well, now," I said, "That's somewhat different. Course"—I ran my eye over the joint—"course, if I *was* a partner, I'd want to make some changes to this place. Maybe get—"

"Nah! Nah!" Besser got all agitated. "Not a partner in this store! It won't keep us all. I mean, you go out and start a store with Brusik, in Dodge!"

I just laughed. "That's downright ridiculous. I don't know nothing about hides and skins."

"Brusik does," Besser said. "He knows that good. But

you open a little store there. Make plenty of money. Yah."

"Yah, yah," I said. "Why not open a store in Ellsworth? That's where they say the cattle trade is going next year."

"Brusik don't live there. He lives in Dodge," Besser said. "Look, you go there, I help you and teach you storekeeping real good. It's a good deal."

"Maybe," I said, and I was tempted at that. "Maybe. And I ain't saying no and I ain't saying yes, but before I say either, I'm going to get me some advice."

Besser didn't like that. He didn't like it one little bit. "I don't want my business talked of," he said.

"It won't be," I said. "It'll be as private as all get-out. And if you want them dollars of mine . . ."

I didn't need to finish it off. He was right over a barrel. In fact, he was so far over, I stung him for another coffee before moseying out and going down to see old Heaney.

He had a feller with him, so I kicked my heels for a while, looking at a county map he had pinned up outside his office, and it was interesting at that. Them farmers' plats was marked on there, and it was amazing how many new ones there was from the last time I'd looked at it. You could see the open range disappearing before your eyes, as they say. And that was the thing. When the riders hit town, saving you was deaf, dumb, and blind, you couldn't hardly miss them, but them sodbusters, it was like they was invisible, drifting in so's you didn't hardly notice them, but coming in just the same, and you didn't need much brains to see it wouldn't be long before the entire county was platted out.

After a few minutes, that feller came out and Heaney called me in. I told him the story, and when I'd finished, he leaned back and looked at me hard, picking his teeth, thinking.

"Son," he said. "I ain't out to sting you, but this sounds like five-dollar advice. You ready to pay that?"

225

Jehoshaphat! Five bucks! I felt as bad as I guess Besser was feeling, but there wasn't no way out of it, so I handed over the bill and it slipped into his vest pocket like it knew the way home.

He teetered back on his chair, the way folks did out West—if they had a chair to sit on, that is. "Son, where did you say you come from?"

"Clement," I said. "Clement County, Texas."

"And you came up with a herd?"

"Yes, sir," I said.

"And your brother"—he dropped his voice, all reverent, like he was talking about money—"he was murdered. That right?"

"Sure is," I said.

"And you've no kin?"

"None to speak of."

Heaney sighed. "Son, I reckon the Lord has got an eye out special for you."

"He has?" I was surprised, thinking, the way our folks had bit the dust, the Lord had forgotten all about us.

Heaney allowed that the Lord had an eye on everyone all the time, counting their whiskers and all. "But," he said, "I've a feeling He's leading you into the paths of righteousness and blessedness."

"You mean this is a good deal?" I asked.

"Now—" Heaney looked somewhat pained. "Now, that ain't the exact way I'd express myself about the doings and workings of the Lord, but you may be on to something here. The thing is, there's good money to be made in buffalo hides, and running a store along with the dealing, that ain't a bad idea at all. And Dodge, it's in what you might call virgin territory now, but when the settlers start arriving . . ." His voice died away, like he was having a vision, same as I'd had out on the prairie. "Why, then a feller with his foot in the door could make a powerful sum of money. Yes, sir!"

"Sure," I said. "But do you reckon I could handle it, everyone saying how tough that camp is and all."

"Son," he said, "you'll have this Brusik backing you, but I reckon you could handle Big Chief Red Cloud all on your own. Now, let's take a closer look at this deal, because what Besser is offering you ain't worth a dime."

He got out some special paper and scratched away, and when he'd finished, I'd got a genuine, 100 percent gold-plated contract a gorilla couldn't have wrestled out of. But, ain't it the way, just when you feel secure, there's something with a big sting waiting to jump out at you, because Heaney said, "This is the best I can do for you, son, but if Besser goes broke before that money from back East gets here, you could lose your cash. *If* he does go broke, I'll do the best I can for you, but there might be a line of creditors ahead of you. But it's a good risk, and if I'd known about it first, I might have tried to get some of the action myself."

I hesitated. "You don't think I should stick my money into cattle?" Wistful, as might be.

Heaney waved his hand. "What you've got ain't worth looking at where cows is concerned. No, you go right ahead and sign."

So I did, and Besser signed, too, although he near had a fit when he saw that legal contract, because old Heaney, he hadn't made my money out as no loan for a share on some godforsaken shack in Dodge. No, sir, he bought me into a share of Besser's store right there in Abilene, too! Real collateral, as he said. Real security.

Wasn't Besser blue! But unless he wanted to go broke the next day, there wasn't nothing he could do about it, although he insisted that there contract had to be a secret between the three of us, so there was something behind them whiskers of his, like pride or whatever. He put his moniker right there on the dotted line, with Heaney watching him like a hawk, too.

Yeah, blue Besser was, but Heaney said he was lucky to have me as a partner.

"Mark my words," he said. "That boy is going to make something of himself. Why, he's as smart as a whip!"

■ TWENTY-TWO ■

Make something of myself! That was something, and I reckoned I was going to. Jeepers, the way I was going on, I'd be President of the United States before I was twenty-one, and if I wasn't that, I'd be president of a bank, at least!

But first I got down to really learning about storekeeping, pestering Besser about what he knew and reading a book old Heaney sold me, *Store Keeping Made Simple*, which was twenty-five cents, would you believe, showing that the bozo who wrote it knew something about making money. I got my nose stuck into it, learning about profit and loss and percentages, and the Handy Hints at the back, such as being polite to customers, even if you hated the sight of them, which I tried out on ours, hauling out chairs for the womenfolk, and dusting them before they sat, and opening the door when they beat it, bowing and saying, "Thank you for your custom, madame, and we trust you will call again," which was a pure waste of time with them women, who looked at me like I was loco, but which was good practice for me.

And I started going to church! Although it was a secret,

228

me being a partner in a store, I figured I ought to mingle with them respectable folks, even though they did bore the pants off me. I'd have even been a reformer if there'd been anything left to reform, and I went to the Bible class! At first, I went because I thought there might be girls, although there wasn't none at all, but, and this will surprise you, I guess, I carried on going, the reason being, the Reverend there, he made it clear that when the Lord said if you was good and holy and all that stuff He'd favor you, He hadn't just been talking about you getting a harp and a pair of wings when you cashed your chips in. No, sir, He meant that you was going to get your share of what was going right down here on earth, while you could enjoy it, like old Laban with them sheep of his, increasing. And the fellers at that class, being businessmen like L. A. Burroughs and T. C. Henry, they talked plenty about profits and land values and interest rates, so it was as good as being at a business college. Better, really, because it was free!

Henry got the word about me going to the class, and one night, after we'd played chess and was chewing the fat, he said how he'd heard I'd got religion.

"Shucks." I wriggled in my chair. "Don't say it like that, Henry. I ain't turned into no Holy Roller. It's interesting, is all. The Bible, it don't *only* tell you of the wondrous doings of the Lord. It shows you how to make money on the way to Salvation. In fact, making money *shows* the Lord is with you—and what in Sam Hill are you grinning at?"

"Nothing," Henry said, quick. "Nothing at all. But isn't there some stuff in the Bible about it being good to be poor?"

"Henry," I said, "you've got hold of the wrong end of the cow there. That poor in the Bible don't mean being poor like them sodbusters, or us back in Clement. It means being poor in . . . in . . ."

"In spirit?"

"That's it," I said. "Like ghosts and all. Leastways, that's what the Reverend says, and he ought to know."

"Reckon so," Henry allowed. "It's a handy mixture at that. Salvation *and* making money."

"Sure is," I said. "The Reverend says that's why this here country is the greatest there ever was, because the businessmen follow the teaching of the Lord."

Henry jumped up sudden and dashed out, and I might have been wrong because he was coughing, but it sounded mighty like laughing to me. I wasn't none too pleased, neither, sitting there and trying not to look at that terrible hairy feller on the wall, which I wouldn't have had in my room if you'd paid me. But when Henry came back his face was straight, and he'd got cookies and sarsaparilla, some milk for the little cat, and hard liquor for himself. He poured out the drinks, saying over his shoulder, "You seem mighty keen on business, too, these days, Ben."

"Maybe," I said, wondering whether he was going to give me some Anarch talk, and if he did, intending to give him some real American talk right back, but kindly, just putting him on the right trail. "Nothing wrong in that, is there?"

"It's a free country," Henry said, which didn't exactly answer the question. "Only, I thought you was keen on going back to cowboying."

"*Riding*," I said, and to tell the truth, I was somewhat uncomfortable, because I sure didn't want to tell Henry no lies, but I didn't want to tell him the whole truth, neither. "Maybe," I said.

"Huh-huh." Henry didn't press me none, so we finished the grub and moseyed down to the gate.

Henry leaned on the gate and lit up his pipe as usual. "Nice night," he observed.

It was, too. A real clear night. Cool, after the summer's

blistering heat, just a mild breeze, and a sickle moon floating up there.

"Remember that first night?" Henry said. "Playing
checkers?"

I sure did, although I didn't want to, and I was glad it
was dark because my face was burning red.

"We've moved on some," Henry said.

"Sure." I was quick to agree with that, wanting to get
away from it, and anyhow, it seeming like a million years
ago. "Playing chess. Why, the way we're going on, I'll
maybe beat you soon."

Henry didn't speak for a moment, just puffing away, one
long arm dangling over the gate. Then he turned and looked
me full in the face. "Ben," he said, his voice somewhat
somber. "Ben, we won't be playing many more chess
games."

Jeepers, I thought. He's turned against me because I'm
in business and all religious, which showed how bad Anarchs was, but then he took his pipe out, looked at it, stuck
it back in, and said, "I'm leaving, Ben."

"Leaving?" I said in an even voice, kind of knowing this
was coming.

"Yes." Henry got a box of matches out. "I told you I
didn't relish a winter in a small town. Now I've got me
another job."

"In Chicago!" I blurted out.

"Oh." Henry gave me a long look. "Someone been talking, Ben? No, don't tell me, it's of no account. Anyhow, I'm
going to New York City, just as soon as Wilson gets himself
another printer. But the thing is . . ." He sparked that match
off and started sucking at the pipe till it was all glowing.
"The thing is, if you wanted to, you could come along. See
something of the country, learn printing . . ."

Well, Lord! If he'd said that before the Chicago fire, I

might have taken him up on that offer. I mean, New York City! If only half of what folks said about it was true, it was worth the trip just to see it. Lightning, they said it was bigger than Kansas City and Topeka together, with Abilene thrown in. But it was too late, and I said so.

"That sure is a mighty fine offer," I said. "It sure is, but the thing is, I'm all fixed up."

"You are? Besser's store?" Henry sounded real disappointed, and I didn't want him to be. I just didn't want him to go off thinking I wasn't nothing more than a clerk, and I thought, what the heck, it ain't much of a secret at that, so I told him.

"I'm opening a store," I said. "In Dodge."

Jupiter! I thought Henry was going to drop down dead on me! He must have got a cloud of that smoke down him the wrong way, and for a change *I* did some back-slapping until he was near enough okay.

"Dodge?" He gasped. "Did you say Dodge?"

"That's the place," I said.

"Ben." Henry coughed some more. "You got to go home right now?"

I said not really, because, seeing as how I was a partner, I'd got myself a key.

"Then you'd better come back in," Henry said, sounding real grim.

We went in and Henry called to Mrs. Brady, asking if she'd rustle up some coffee, and he sat facing me and puffed on that pipe so hard I thought it and him would catch fire, until Mrs. Brady brought the coffee in.

Then he glared at me, and I mean glared. "Did I hear you right?" he said.

"Sure." I told him the story, not about the loan to Besser, because that was secret, but making out I'd just bought my way in. "It's a big chance," I said.

"But . . ." Henry did some foreign muttering to himself,

then got back to plain American, waggling his head. "That Dodge . . . Ben, it's a wild place. Do you know what you're getting into?"

"I reckon," I said. "I got me a business advisor who says it's a good deal."

"But you're just a boy," Henry said.

I got a little mad when he said that. "I ain't a *boy*. Well, I ain't a grown man, neither, yet, but I've seen some things. I can handle myself. Sides, that Brusik is there."

"Brusik!" Henry did some more foreign mutterings. "That Dodge is no place for you."

"It's a place to make money," I said. "If I play my cards right, why, I can be a real big shot, like Joe McCoy."

"McCoy," Henry said.

"Right," I said. "Could I make big money in New York City?"

"Maybe not," Henry admitted. "But there's other things—"

"Why, sure there is," I cut in there, wanting to be agreeable. "There's having swell clothes, eating beefsteaks whenever you want, telling folks what to do, and drinking that wine stuff. I know that, Henry. But you've got to have money to *do* them things. And I wants to do them."

I'd have reckoned that was enough to satisfy anyone, but old Henry sat there shaking his head and looking dolesome. He tried a couple of times to get me to change my mind, and I don't know but that he tried too hard because I got real obstinate, and finally he said if I had my mind set on it, there wasn't nothing more to say, so he walked me back to the gate.

"It's okay," I said. "You don't have to worry. And say, before we both go, we'll maybe get more games in. What do you say?"

"I hope so." Henry stuck out his mitt. "Good night."

I shook hands and beat it back to the store and climbed

into the hay. But I lay awake pondering, wondering whether them detectives had detected Henry, so he was going on the lam. And another thought came to me, which was that Henry had said when I first met him that everyone in America was always roaming around, which, the way he said it, sounded like he thought that was wrong, and now he was doing that himself! I figured I'd take him up on that next time I saw him, but before I'd worked out what I was going to say, that old sandman came along and it was lights out for me.

It was near lights out for Abilene, too. The last herds was coming in and the last boys was paid off. The marshal, too, there not being no need for him no more. More buildings got knocked down, too, and folks moved off to Ellsworth, so, even though there hadn't been a county vote on the quarantine laws yet, you could tell how the wind was blowing. Them businessmen was smart enough to see the writing on the wall. In fact, you'd have to have been as blind as a bat not to. And there was other straws in the wind. A farmer called Tom Elliot, who was what you might call a real farmer, having good land and milking cows, and who'd made good money selling greens and what have you to the cattlemen, some of his cows died and he blamed it on the tick fever and asked for money from the compensation fund that McCoy and the big cattle dealers claimed to have set up, and he didn't get a dime, because there *wasn't no money in that fund at all!* So Elliot joined in the anti-cattle-trade crowd, and if a feller like him was against it, you could bet it was the end of the herds anyways, it meaning the county vote was sewn up. But, and it's strange at that, it cheered me up, like if Abilene was just going to be a farm town, then, like Henry, I was glad to be leaving.

There was other things, too. Pat Brady told me he was leaving and going up to Denver, the reason being the telegraph office was going to be closed down, and he told me that the businessmen in Ellsworth had offered Moses George, who owned the Drovers Cottage, four thousand bucks to move it there!

So there it was. Old Abilene was disappearing before your very eyes. In fact, with all them holes down Texas and Cedar Streets, it was beginning to look like a sodbuster's teeth, all full of gaps, and what was left, nothing to write home about.

Still and all, it wasn't my problem no more. I didn't give a hoot if the next cyclone that came along picked the whole dump up and dropped it out in the Great Lakes. What I was concentrating on was the store in Dodge. Me and Besser had our heads together, plotting what to get in. We ordered a tent, and a stove, and most of that stuff the Reverend Christopher wouldn't have approved of, like whiskey and tobacco and ammunition. And looking at them lists, I was sure hoping that Brusik out there was tough enough to handle the sort of customers it looked like we was going to get.

Well, we got the last of them orders off, and that was the moment, as they say. There wasn't no real reason to stick around Abilene no more, unless I stayed in for Thanksgiving, when the church was having a dinner I'd have liked to have gone to, them church women sure knowing how to cook, and reckoning the Reverend owed me some free grub, the way I'd gone to his church, but that was too far off. And the truth was, I didn't want to go before Henry left, so I told Besser I'd let him know soon enough, and went to the *Chronicle* office to ask Henry what was happening that way.

I peeked into the *Chronicle*, seeing old Vear Porter Wilson at his desk scribbling more lies, probably saying they was going to start pineapple farms in Kansas, and waved to Henry, who was oiling that old Army press. He came to the door, wiping his hands, and said, "Was going to call on you. How'd you like to come around tonight. I'll let you know what's happening."

I said that suited me fine, went back to the store, and passed the afternoon taking a good look at Besser's accounts and watching Goblinka, who was getting more like her ma every day, sort of swelling, you know? Then come dusk I skipped supper and went over to Henry's place.

I banged on the door, and Henry opened it, but as I made to go in, he held his hand up. "Come in," he said. "But you're in for a kind of shock."

A shock is what I got at that, because that room, like I've said, it was the dandiest you ever saw, like it was homely the way them lying magazines tell you all American homes is, but now it was as bare as could be. All them books had gone, and the pictures, so it was just a bare room with a chair and a bed. And rooms, you'd think when stuff was taken out of them they'd look bigger, but this didn't. It looked smaller, like more than just old books had been taken out, leaving it just another room in just another frame house stuck out in Kansas.

Henry spread out his arms. "Sorry, Ben," he said. "I'm all packed. But never mind. We'll play some chess, and Mrs. Brady has got special food, so we'll have a good time. Sit. Sit."

He pressed me into that best chair, the cat jumped on me, we got the chess set out and played just about the best games we'd ever had. In fact, I *drew* a game! And Henry, it was amazing, because he was real funny. He could do impersonations of folks! Jeepers, he had me laughing fit to bust, doing McCoy and Shanghai Pierce and Burroughs and all them leading citizens. Why, he could have gone on stage at the Novelty Theater any time at all, and I told him so.

"Just a party piece," he said, but looking mighty pleased. "Now, maybe I do you something else."

He went over to a chest and pulled out a squeeze box, what they call a concertina, and started playing it! Yeah, he could knock out a tune, giving a regular concert right there, playing tunes like "Swanee River" and "I'm a Girl from the Bowery," and some songs he sang in foreign, although I've got to admit, his singing wouldn't have got him no round of applause off a bunch of riders.

Yes, sir, it was some party we had there, and that special grub—it *was* special. Beefsteak and onions and a cake with sliced peaches in it, and real apple pie. Brother, I was glad I'd missed out supper, gorging away there and then sitting back, drinking sarsaparilla, until Henry called time.

I didn't want him to say that. You know how it is, you're having a good time and you don't want it to end, so I said, Gee whillikers, we could sit up late, but Henry said no, that was it—saying it like he meant it, too.

"Okay," I said, all regretful, hoping he'd change his mind at that. "But say, Henry, let's have another swell time like this before we go. I'll stick in some cash for the grub . . . no?"

"No." Henry looked solemn. "Sorry, I can't do that. The thing is, Ben. I'm . . . well, I'm leaving tomorrow!"

"Tomorrow!" I couldn't really take that in. "Leaving?"

"Yeah," Henry said. "Wilson's got another man coming. I didn't tell you because I didn't want to spoil this evening."

"You mean—" I said. "You mean this is . . . this . . . the last time?"

"Last time here." Henry looked real sad, but he wasn't no sadder than I was, because I felt emptier than that room.

"Gee," I sort of whispered, groping for words but not finding any.

"I know how you feel." Henry gave that faint smile. "But tell me, are you going to see me off?"

"I sure am," I said.

"Fine." Henry smiled again. "I'm getting the 3 p.m. east-bound. Why not meet me at noon down at the depot? We can have a meal and talk."

I said that would be fine, and it cheered me up some, pushing off parting from Henry and giving me something to look forward to. Like I say, he was a wise old bird.

I gave the cat a last stroking, thanked Mrs. Brady, and we walked to the gate, and it was hard to believe it would be the last time. But we didn't do no dawdling. Henry just said good night all abrupt and went back inside, leaving me on my own. And I'm telling you, I was a successful American businessman, and I was going to be an even more successful one, but hoofing it back to the store, I sure didn't feel that way. I just felt like a kid without no friends. With-out a real friend, that is, someone who was good to me because he was kind, and, tarnation, someone who could talk about something other than money.

There was a wind blowing again, stirring up trash and litter. It had something of an edge to it, just to let you know it wouldn't be too long before it was sharp enough to slash you to ribbons. There was a shooting star, too, falling out of the sky like it was too tired to stay up there, and I thought, Moses, even them stars can't stay in one place for long. And when I got into bed, I was more dolesome than I'd been since I couldn't hardly remember when.

But the next morning I was more cheerful, maybe be-cause seeing someone off made me feel important, so I got through the chores mighty quick and was at the depot about an hour too soon. And that depot, which next to the courthouse was the pride and joy of Abilene, was already getting to look derelict, bits fallen off and not put back, the boss's sign over his office hanging on one nail. Why, there was even some fellers knocking down part of the stockyards! I stuck my head into Pat's shack and asked him about that.

"Sure," he said. "They're going to Ellsworth, too. Just leaving a couple of cow pens here."

Then Henry came, a mite early, for which I was glad, carrying a carpetbag and a couple of parcels, which made me curse myself for not going around to Brady's to give a hand.

But Henry made nothing of that and took me into the Drovers Cottage, and there sure was a change in there, too. It was still swell, with mirrors and fancy chairs and genuine hand-painted oil pictures and all, but kind of faded and dusty. McCoy was there with a couple of fellers, but even he looked shrunked up, and although there was a gambling man at the faro table, he didn't have no customers. There was no riders, neither, nor no dance girls, nor band. Just an old darkie professor tinkling the ivories, but halfhearted about it, like a feller working out his time.

But the grub was okay, and plenty of it. And Henry was good, keeping up easy talk about the places he'd worked in, and hinting as how it wasn't too late for me to change my mind about Dodge, but as that big clock in the saloon ticked around to three, I just couldn't keep my mouth shut no longer. There was a question I just had to ask or bust.

"Henry," I said, "are you an Anarch?"

"Ah . . ." Henry had his pipe lit up and he looked at me through the smoke, real sharp, like he had the first time we'd met, then said a real surprising thing. "What if I am?"

That was kind of confusing and I didn't know what to say, truth to tell, so I just mumbled that if he was, it was kind of funny, me being a businessman and the Anarchs wanting to blow us all up and kill us, but he'd been real friendly to me.

Henry was drinking whiskey, real whiskey out of a bottle, and he took a swig and lit a big cigar he'd got, for a change. "You weren't a businessman when I first met you," he said.

"Henry!" I was hurt some. "You mean you don't like me now?"

Henry didn't exactly laugh but came near enough to it. "I guess I can overlook your business activities. Put it this way, Ben. I like to see folks get a square deal. I don't like to see kids working twelve hours a day, nor women, nor men, neither. I don't like seeing these settlers getting ripped off by the railroad, and I don't like millionaires."

"But I want to be one," I said. "One of them millionaires."

"Sure," Henry said. "Well, when that day comes, maybe I'll think of you differently. Until then . . ."

He didn't finish that sentence, because there was that whistle, the train coming in almost on time, which was a kind of miracle, them trains' movements being as mysterious as the Lord's.

"Time to get going." Henry stuck the whiskey bottle in his pocket. "Here." He handed over a piece of paper. "It's an address in New York City. If you ever change your mind about coming, write me. Write me, anyhow."

We went out and stuck the bag on the train, and I don't know but what it wouldn't have taken much of a shove to get me on it with him. Then the conductor gave that long call, "Aaaaall abooooard!"

Henry and me shook hands. "So long for now," he said. "Oh, I nearly forgot. Something for you, a keepsake"— handing over one of the parcels.

"Thanks, Henry," I said, real mad with myself for not having got him one, although what that might have been, I couldn't have rightly said, saving it was some flour or peas.

"Okay." Henry swung up onto the carriage. "Be seeing you."

"Sure," I said. "Sure will"—and then a thought hit me. "Henry, where's the little cat?"

"Karl?" The train whistled and started up, so I had to walk along the track to keep talking. "Didn't want to say, Ben. It's dead. Died this morning. Someone poisoned it."

"Poisoned!" I shouted. "Why? Why?"

"Someone didn't like Anarchs too much, I guess," Henry yelled, and then he was lost as the train picked up speed and lurched out on the haul to Kansas City, taking with it the best friend I'd ever had, and to heck with him being against business.

I dragged back to the store, and wasn't I feeling blue. I went straight into my room and just did some blubbing. Ridiculous, wasn't it? Me a noble darer and blubbing away like a crybaby. But I was, and thinking about the little cat didn't help none. Why, when I'd dried out some, I figured I'd find out who done it and poison *him*.

I surely was upset, near as bad as when Bo died. In fact, I near forgot to open the parcel Henry had given me, and when I did, I near blubbed again, because he'd given me the chess set.

I stayed in that room, sad as can be, until I couldn't stand the silence no more and went into the store. The Bessers was all there, not speaking or nothing, just sitting like three dumplings, and I couldn't stand that, either. Just the thought of being goggled at was enough to drive me crazy, so I said, "Mr. Besser, is there any reason why I should stick around any longer?"

Besser did some brooding and whisker scratching, which he'd have done if you'd have asked him if flies had wings, then said there wasn't, making that sound like he was sick of the sight of me, which I guess he was, and the sooner I blew, the better him, his missus, Goblinka, and the whole of Abilene would like it.

"Sooner you go, sooner we start making money," he allowed.

I liked that "we," but it was true at that, and I was doing

241

the right thing. Getting myself organized stopped me brooding, and I'd got plenty to do, selling my saddle, getting good warm clothes, and seeing Heaney and making him my permanent business advisor. Like, I'd send him all them dollars I was going to be making and he'd invest them greenbacks so's the interest would come rolling in like the cows at milking time.

I said "So long" to the folks I knew, like the Reverend and the fellers at the Bible class, who said, "Well, how's about that?" and "Good luck," but like they was amazed at me bothering to tell them. I even let old Vear Porter Wilson know I was heading out, because the *Chronicle* used to have notices about prominent people coming and going, but all he did was try and sell me a subscription. I'd have told the Chink, had he been around, but he'd gone, probably trying to kill off the riders in Ellsworth. In fact, the only folks who *was* nice was the Bradys, and when I did go, Pat hailed me at the depot and gave me a big parcel of grub from his missus. The other thing I did was interesting, though. I saw the foreign preacher the Bessers went to and showed him that address Henry had given me, doing which because part of it was foreign. And that preacher didn't like what he saw! If preachers was allowed to cuss, he'd have done so, he was so sore, saying it was the name of a newspaper back East that was wicked and Godless and I should be ashamed of even knowing anyone there!

That about wrapped it up, saving for one thing. I went to Bo's grave.

I've got to admit I hadn't done much tending there. You couldn't hardly see it, what with weeds and stuff growing all over the marker. And I've got to admit, as well, I don't know that I felt much, standing there. I mean, I knew I ought to sob or whatever, and I kind of tried to feel that way, but it was just like being a play actor. Bo, he'd gone, is all, vanished, and although I remembered him clear enough, his face and all, it was like looking down the wrong end of a spyglass.

Anyhow, come Tuesday, which was when the westbound train came through, I took a last look around that store. Like I've said, it was just an ordinary store, and I guess there were thousands of them across the United States just exactly the same, gloomy, small, stuffy, the storekeeper not making much more of a living than the folks he sold to, if that. Nothing to them, you know? But what had happened to me in that store had done more to change my life than anything, I guess. And leaving wasn't no more dramatic than me starting there. I said "So long," and the Bessers did some grunting back, and I might have been going out to sweep the boardwalk, for all the feeling they showed. Then I went to the depot, had me some pop in the Drovers, and at noon that old train clanked in—with a whole crowd of immigrants—and I got on board, the whistle blew, the bell clanged, and I said farewell to the great and glorious city of Abilene.

BUSTED

▪ TWENTY-THREE ▪

I was on the train as far as Hays City, where I got a ride on a bull wagon hauling supplies across the prairie. It was raining when we started and didn't stop, so it was nice and cheery, dragging toward the Santa Fe Trail with a bunch of teamsters whose idea of a good breakfast was half a bottle of red-eye, lunch the other half, and for supper a whole bottle. But it gave me plenty of time to gloat over the deal old Heaney had got me, which was, I'd got a share in Besser's store in Abilene, and me and him was going to start a store in Dodge, me getting most of the profits from it. Brusik there, he'd do the hide dealing and show me how it went, so's I could be a hide dealer as well, and I'd get me a share of them profits, too! Amazing, ain't it, getting all that just because old Besser had made some plumb foolish investment in land? He sure got bitten there, but I wasn't going to get bit the same way, no, sir! I was going to let old Heaney handle my profits, which he was going to invest for me in mighty good shares and all, making my money work for me, as you could say. Course, I was going to stash a few bucks away someplace so's I'd always have cash to hand, and what the Bessers did with their profits, why, it was up to them.

So thinking which comforting thoughts, I stuck it out until we got to Dodge. When we got there, I climbed off the wagon and that dump sure was some sight for sore eyes, har-har! There was a few tents strung out alongside a low bluff, mule trains and bull wagons piled with hides all mired in the mud, with the drivers cursing like all get-out, and drunks lurching about all tooled up with pistols!

Jupiter, I stood there in that freezing rain, staring at the worstest place I'd ever seen, where the citizens looked like they'd escaped from a cage, and slowly sinking into the mud, until I figured I'd better move or get swallowed up.

I walked along the street, saying which is pure sarcasticism, since it was like plowing through molasses, the making of a boardwalk not having occurred to the folks, looking for someone who was halfway human who wouldn't pick me up and bite my arms and legs off, so's I could ask them about Brusik. I peered into one of them tents, which was some kind of saloon, although it was more like a lunatic asylum where the lunatics was allowed all the booze they could swallow *and* to carry handguns and knives. I decided to give it a miss, and carried on slogging until I saw a feller who looked halfway civilized, like he'd had a shave during the past two weeks, and asked him where I might find Brusik.

"Brusik . . ." He looked at me kind of curious. "You keep going the way you are, you'll find him."

"Thanks, mister," I said, being grateful for a kind word.

"Mooar," the feller said. "Josh Mooar. You kin of Brusik?"

"I'm his partner," I said.

That Mooar shook his head, baffled, as it were, though he wasn't as baffled as me, and moved off one way while I went the other, struggling through the glue, and then found I was on open prairie, what you could see of it through that drenching rain.

Moses, I did some cursing, figuring that Mooar had hazed me, and I stuck him in my black book, you bet, then turned and heaved my way back until I saw a couple of fellers by the side of a tent, standing by a wagon all piled up with hides. I grabbed hold of one of them, tugging at his slicker, and when he turned, I said, real mean, "Mister, I want Brusik Besser, and I don't want no fool jokes. Just Besser, is all."

I figured I'd made that clear, but that feller clapped his hand to his head and staggered back. "Jesus H. Christ!" he shouted. "Look what we got here! General Tom Thumb, or is you just pretending to be a midget?"

The other feller came across and they started patting me on the head and saying senseless things like they didn't know Brusik had a baby boy, or was I an orphan lost in the storm, and I was just about ready to give up and find someplace nice and quiet where I could blow my brains out, when that mass of hides stirred and something came out of them, the which when I saw it I thought, jeepers, it's a buffalo they forgot to shoot! Then I saw it was something like a human being—well, it didn't have four legs and horns—and it said, "Who wants Brusik Besser?"

One look and I near said it wasn't me, but I stammered, "Ben Curtis, is who."

He goggled at me, real genuine Besser style, and I got a terrible feeling he'd never heard of me and this whole store business was just a way of getting rid of me, and I was thinking of going back to Abilene and sending old Besser for a trip to where them little fellers with hayforks jump around a big fire, when that buffalo's face cleared.

"Oh, yah," he said. "Be right with you," and dived back into them hides while I stood in the rain, shivering with cold and wet and hungry as a wolf, until Brusik finished whatever the Sam Hill he was doing, fixed up some kind of deal with them fellers, then got to me.

"We go inside," he said.

"Sure," I said. "Maybe you'd kindly tell me where that might be, exactly." Because there wasn't nothing I could see that you could get inside of, if you see what I mean.

"Just here." Brusik heaved around to the other side of the wagon and went into what looked like a giant gopher hole! I wondered if he was doing some gold mining on the side, but he shouted at me to get in after him, and when I did, I couldn't hardly believe my eyes.

There was a rough bunk in there, an old packing case, a battered stove with its pipe sticking up through some bits of wood which was the ceiling, and a floor, which was just plain liquid mud.

"What the heck is this?" I asked. "I mean, just what is it?"

Brusik shrugged, spraying me with water. "It's where I live."

I took a big gulp of what passed for air in that joint. "You mean you *live* here?"

"Sure," Brusik said. "Where do you think?"

"Hell, I don't know," I said. "Ain't you got a shack?"

"There ain't no shacks here," Brusik said. "Lumber's too expensive."

I got a real creepy feeling then. I peered around and said, "You mean *I've* got to live here, too?"

Brusik nodded. "Unless you want to dig one yourself."

"Dig . . ." I started, then got another terrible creepy feeling. "Where is the blamed store?"

"Ain't come yet," Brusik said.

"Ain't come!" I was madder than a swarm of hornets. "What do you mean? Mc and Besser placed that order a while ago."

Brusik creased his forehead, like wondering what the fuss was about. "You come early. When the tent comes, we open the store."

"Jehoshaphat," I groaned. "You saying there ain't *nothing* come yet?"

"Not yet." Brusik was real unconcerned, and I thought

sure and ride on, brother, it ain't your dollars laid out. But I was just too wore out to go into it all right then.

"I want some grub," I said. "Where's the best place?"

"There ain't one," Brusik said. "Just Hoover's and it's terrible." And he laughed! But I don't know but what that laughing was good for me. In fact, I grinned, which a moment before I'd thought I'd never do again in my life.

"I take you," Brusik said. "I want some feed, too."

We sloshed down the street and went into that tent I'd peeked at which was full of fellers drinking and gambling and raising hell, sat at a table, which was a strip of buffalo hide dried out stiff as a board, and waited till a feller with a huge stogie in his mouth and greased up thicker than a skillet came over and asked what we wanted. Well, he didn't so much ask as tell. "Hump or tongue?" he said.

We ordered buffalo hump and I said to get me some spuds with it and plenty of coffee, and Brusik got a small whiskey, about a quart, and began banging it down him, which sure made him different from his brother, and I sat back and looked around. That was some place. The Reverend Christopher would have dropped down dead had he seen it, what you could see through the smoke. I was sure glad old Brusik was there right beside me, him not looking the sort of feller you'd want to tangle with if you could help it.

The feller came back and we stuck into the grub and it was like there was a contest going on in Kansas as to who'd do the worst cooking, the Chink or this bozo, and him winning by a mile. But it was hot and I needed it, and as long as Brusik was going to sit knocking back the red-eye, I figured I'd have me some dessert, getting tinned peaches, which was delicious, and when I finished, I was feeling about one million times better than I'd done an hour before, until I got the bill, when I felt a million times worser.

"What's this?" I said. "I ain't aiming to buy the joint."

"Ain't for sale right now," the feller said. "But that's fifty cents for the coffee, a dollar for them peaches, three bucks for the spuds, and twenty cents for the hump. We don't charge none for the elegant surroundings."

There wasn't nothing for it but to stump up, but I was bitter, you know? When we got back, I asked Brusik why he hadn't told me how much grub cost.

"Yah," he said. "That grub costs plenty here. It's all got to be hauled in. Buffalo meat, that's cheap. You got to eat plenty of that liver, though, or you get scurvy. All your teeth fall out! Hah-hah-hah!" He burst out laughing, although what was funny about that beat me. Then, without another word, he fell on his bunk and began snoring!

Since there wasn't nothing else I could do, I wrapped myself up as best I could and lay down, right there in that mud, listening to that awful snoring and snorting, cursing myself for buying them spuds and peaches, and for being in Dodge at all, and just hoping there wasn't going to be no snakes or skunks come wriggling in and making a cheap supper out of me.

That was some night. Next to when Bo got killed, it was the worstest of my life, stuck there with a feller who drank whiskey like it was cooling water, no store, no goods, and all that cash I'd got laid out! And that place! It made old Vear Porter Wilson's lies about Abilene seem true. Even Besser's store was like a dream of home, sweet home. And there was Henry! I could have been in New York City right there and then, instead of sleeping in a hole in the ground, feeling like goddamn beetles were crawling over me.

"Ben," I said to myself. "You're the biggest fool in all Creation. But come tomorrow you're getting on the first wagon out of here, even if you have to write them dollars off. Yes, sir, that's where you're going—out!"

But, came the dawn, I began to think of all them dollars I'd laid out, and having a feeling if I did beat it, the stuff I'd ordered would be homeless, I figured I'd stick it out until the goods came and make sure they was taken in by their rightful pa, Ben Curtis. Then I'd sell out and go where the grass was greener, which, as far as I could make out, meant anyplace else in the entire United States.

So I stuck it out, trying to make that dugout as comfortable as could be, knocking up a rough bunk—and did that timber cost!—and hanging up an old slicker to stop the water pouring in on me, and then got down to making money out of buffalo.

Buffalo. That's what we was there for, and it's what that camp was for, too, there being nothing else but the Indian Reservation, and Fort Dodge, five miles off, and a few settlers scattered around who must have lost their way or they sure wouldn't have ended up there.

But if you were going to start a business out in the wilds, Dodge wasn't a bad place to start. It was near where the Santa Fe Trail crossed the Arkansas River, so there was wagon trains passing through going to Colorado, and it was where the Atchison, Topeka and Santa Fe Railroad Company was going to cross, too, one day, and south of the river was buffalo.

There was buffalo north, too, clear through to Canada, but that range south of the Arkansas was kind of handy, you know? There was the camp for supplies, you got yourself a wagon, a team of bulls or mules, hired a couple of skinners, bought a Sharps .50, and keno! you was in a bank with no safe!

Course, white hunters wasn't supposed to go hunting

across the Arkansas. That had got forbid by a treaty made by General Sherman and the Comanche and Kiowa and them other savages down at Medicine Lodge back in 1867, but there wasn't no treaty ever signed on God's earth that was going to stand in the way of a feller making money—not if that treaty was between a white man and a red man.

But me and Brusik didn't break no treaty, because we didn't go hunting, is why. We just stayed in camp and the hunters would haul in them hides and sell to us, or maybe another dealer, because there was a couple in town, and another used to come to Dodge now and then, and that didn't make no difference to us because there was plenty of hides, there being millions of buffalo roaming around, and that ain't stretching it, neither. One of them hunters, Sam Dawson, said to me once, "Kid, if you ever want to learn buffalo hunting, you come along with me and I'll learn you and you'll have a job for life."

I thanked him kindly, that not costing nothing, but turned him down, seeing as how winter out there on the range wasn't exactly my notion of a good time. The thing being that in the summer, with the buffalo molting, their hides was all scraggy and not worth a dime, but come winter, when the hides—robes, they was rightly known as—was in prime condition, that was the time to hunt and make the dollars, and if you risked losing your hands or feet with frostbite—and maybe your life, too—that was the chance them hunters took.

Anyhow, our stuff had finally come, so me and Brusik really got started up in the storekeeping line. Leastways, that's what we called it, but it wouldn't be like nothing you've maybe got in mind, and it wasn't what I'd had, neither.

What we had was a tent. It was about seven feet high at the ridge, fifteen feet long, and ten wide, with a stove in the middle and our dugout at the back. It wasn't no palace, but it was just right for us because them hunters, they needed grub and ammunition and all, but they liked a drop of warming liquid, too, so although we had our stock of goods as respectable as get-out, pride of place went to a great big barrel of red-eye. Them hunters would sit by our stove, warm as could be, and drink our whiskey for free. Leastways, they thought it was, because by the time they woke up next morning, they wasn't in no state to remember nothing, saving we bought hides at a fair price!

In fact, we got a regular crowd. Fellers who wanted a nice quiet drink before going down to George Hoover's real liquor tent to have a nice loud drink, with some brawling thrown in for free. Them boys would call in and sit snug, belting it back with Brusik, and what with the rain drumming on the roof and the stove glowing red, it wasn't a bad way to pass the time.

And them fellers could be real interesting. I mean, there were bad hombres in camp, the type who'd slit your throat for your boots and figure they was doing you a favor by not cutting your ears off as well. But our crowd, they was men out to earn a living, is all, and they knew a thing or two. Why, Sam Fuller, he'd been to China, and if he got a few slugs of red-eye down him, he could spout poetry by the yard. One night he recited a speech from that Hamlet play, which was an old geezer giving advice to his son who was lighting out, and like Josh Mooar said, the feller who wrote that had some savvy.

"That's it," he said. "Don't loan and don't borrow. Don't shoot your mouth off, but if a feller tries to stick it to you, stick it back hard. You bear that in mind, kid."

I said I sure would, especially that stuff about not loaning out, and it was something to bear in mind in camp, because them hard cases, they'd try it on, asking for credit.

Course, when you got down to it, credit was what we lived by, but you had to know who you was allowing it to.

255

Know them and trust them, which was fine with the regular fellers, but them scalawags who hung around doing nothing so far as you could see but drink and gamble, they was something else again, so I didn't need no advice to keep clear of them.

Anyhow, I spent most of my time in the tent because the days was getting bitter cold and the nights more so, with snow now and then, and the wind had started up again, battering at the tent and howling, like saying, "Har! Har! Old Man Winter is waking up and he's coming for to get you. You hear me? Get you!"

Brother, I was glad not to be out hunting then, holed up in some draw maybe, with them huge buffalo wolves howling around, fancying some human beings, to vary the menu. It was dying time at that, but it was the time to be out hunting, and it was a dying time in camp, too. Them bad hats boozing night and day, why, a feller might say a wrong word, or draw a wrong card, and out would come a knife or maybe a six-shooter, and there were fellers about who didn't give a plugged nickel about blowing out another man's candle. And I saw one blown out.

I was going to see Moses Cagney, who had a team of mules, about getting us some stores. I was passing Hoover's tent when a feller staggered out, holding his stomach. I paid no heed, thinking it was just another drunk, when he belched, a real huge one, opened his hands, and the blood poured out of his belly. Not just a few drops neither, more like someone had poured out a whole bucket of red paint on the snow.

They got the doctor from the fort but there wasn't nothing to be done, and he died, is all, and for why? For some foolish argument about whether mules was better than bulls at hauling. The most senseless, foolish, sickening nonsense you could imagine, and a man dead. And the decent fellers, they just shrugged and said that bozo was no loss to the human race, which had some truth in it, at that. But he was dead, dead and hauled off to some draw and stuck in the ground, that being before they started burying on that bluff behind the camp, Boot Hill, as they got to calling it later, in the cow-town days, seeing as how many a feller was said to be planted there with his boots on, although if you asks me, it was because they was buried with their boots off, boots costing, you know?

But there was nothing done about that killing, nothing at all. And when I said it was somewhat pitiful, that hombre not even having had a prayer said over his grave, Josh Mooar, who was in, cocked an eyebrow at me and said there wasn't nothing to stop me doing the right thing.

"Which I would," I said. "I've studied the Bible some. But I don't know where he's buried at."

"Don't let that bother you, kid," said Ray Huntley, who was a sort of part-time hunter, doing some work as well for anyone who'd hire him. "Just go out and say a prayer. If that hombre ain't under you, sure as hell there'll be someone else!"

The fellers grinned and laughed, and ain't that something? Like our crowd was decent fellers, but they weren't turning a hair about that killing.

"But, Sam Hill," I said, "what about the law?"

"Hell." Ray spat on the stove. "You think that sheriff at Hays City going to ride a hundred miles because some muleskinner got what was coming to him?"

"Maybe not," I admitted. "But what about the Army? There's a whole squadron of cavalry not five miles off."

Jupiter! That was like setting off a firecracker! I was howled right down, and Sam Dawson gave me a real scowl.

"The hell with the Army," he said. "This here is a democracy and I sure ain't going to have no goddamn soldiers telling *me* what to do."

"But—" I began, only to get shut up again.

"Don't give me your goddamn buts," Sam shouted. "We had that goddamn British Army stamping on us till we blew them out, and I was in the goddamn U.S. Army for three goddamn years in the goddamn war and I got enough goddamn orders to last me the rest of my goddamn life! We're civilians and we'll attend to our own affairs and let the goddamn soldiers attend to theirs."

"But what *is* their affairs?" I asked, getting it in quick.

"Getting rid of the goddamn Indians," Ray Huntley said. "Instead of being their goddamn nurserymaids."

"Nurserymaids!" Moses Cagney laughed. "The Army has been hacking them down since the war."

"There's plenty left, ain't there?" Ray said. "Jesus, they dish out free grub to them at the fort."

Well, Ray had a point there. Like there was a tribe of Osage Indians who'd got moved out of eastern Kansas to make room for the sodbusters and been given some God-awful reservation land north of us, and now and then the Army gave out beef and blankets—part of the deal, so-called, although I'll sure bet Dave B. Heaney would have got them a better one. But they was tame, blanket Indians they was called, whereas you got farther west, there was wild Indians roaming free as the buffalo and who just plain wouldn't go on no reservations and attacked white men, same as the Comanche did in Texas, and the U.S. Army out there in the real wilds, why, they just shot them, is all—when they could catch them, that is.

"Anyhow." Ray took a swig of comfort. "This is a democracy, and like Sam says, we can take care of our own." He went and peered out of the tent. "Weather's changing, I guess. Maybe get out hunting the next few days."

He was right on both counts. The feller who'd done that stabbing, he got blasted out by someone with a shotgun one dark night, and the weather cleared, so a lot of fellers went out after buffalo, which was a time we sold more supplies than whiskey, although that was a supply, come to mention it.

We loaded up them big wagons and watched them roll out of town across the river and creak over that iron-hard prairie, and jeepers, wasn't it cold! The Arkansas froze clear to the bottom, and if you was fool enough to touch metal with your bare hands, it would tear lumps out of your flesh. And it was silent, like even sound had been frozen. And wasn't them dawns and sunsets something! You'd get the sun all fiery-red, the sky shading to Union blue, and underneath was that pure white prairie stretching away forever. You could let them sights and that pure air go to your head and get poetical if you wasn't careful. But although I did slide into it sometimes, most of the time I didn't poeticize much. In fact, I was doing more studying, getting to grips with *Store Keeping Made Simple*, and doing some figuring out, too.

The thing was, we was making money, and making it easy, but them profits wasn't nothing to write home about, and I was hoping we'd make a lot more when the railroad came, and them settlers and all, but Josh Mooar poured cold water over that notion.

"That Santa Fe's in trouble," he said. "Running out of money, I hear, so the Lord knows when it's going to get here, if ever. And when it does come, and I mean *if* it comes, there's a lot of Kansas between here and Abilene to fill up. In fact"—and he said it real cool—"in fact, I don't reckon there'll ever be any settlers to speak of. It just ain't farmland."

Well, it was fine, him being cool, but I was hot under the collar. "Jupiter," I said, "that ain't what my business advisor told me."

"Kid," Josh said, "I don't give a hoot what your advisor told you. I'm just saying what I know."

That sure gave me something to chew on. I'd figured that

when the railroad came the camp would be like Abilene before them reformers ruined it, full of saloons and dance halls, and with a theater and all, and no one to stop me going in them, neither. But years of . . . well, of nothing really didn't grab me none. No, I didn't aim to spend the rest of my days in a camp, most of which was like a human zoo, and where there wasn't hardly anything doing in summer, anyhow. So I thought about it and then wrote me a letter to old Heaney, asking him what about them golden opportunities he'd spouted about. It was a dandy letter, too, full of ten-dollar words, showing how all them nights I'd spent studying the Bible in that class hadn't been wasted—and I didn't stick no fee in it, neither.

I was going to hand over that letter to the next team going to Great Bend, but the weather broke. That icy clearness went as blizzards came howling down, and wasn't they blizzards just! Moses, there was days you was daring if you even went outside, because that snow came down so thick you could choke to death on it, so there wasn't no way a team was going to make it through to the post office up there.

And that blizzard blew on right through Christmas, when them officers up at the fort had a party. Not that most of us was invited, for which I didn't blame them, but we had a party all of our own, like getting blind drunk and brawling and stabbing and singing hymns, the which is sarcastical, and carrying that party clear through to the New Year, so there wouldn't be no tedious break in the proceedings.

And I guess you know how it is. Come New Year and you think spring is around the corner, although the worst of the winter is waiting to hit you, and jeepers, that weather got worser and worser, so I couldn't get my letter off, and then something happened which changed the picture entirely.

Some of us was in the tent, cursing the weather and the Army and the Indians, while I walked around poking at the roof of the tent to keep the snow off, when who should walk in but Eugene LeCompt.

Eugene was an agent for a hide dealer called Lobenstein in Leavenworth, and a mighty big dealer, too. Course, we was real surprised to see Eugene, but he said he'd come in on the tail of that blizzard and there'd been nothing to it. He joshed away, saying the fellers ought to be out hunting or old Lobenstein would starve and we wouldn't want that, him being such a good straight feller, which he was, for sure. "And I see you're having a shot of Brusik's red-eye," he said. "Well, boys, you can have one on me, if you ain't too proud."

Sam Fuller there, he grinned and said, "Why, we'll take a drink off you. In fact, we'll take as many as you want to hand out, not being mealy-mouthed temperance sons of bitches. But just so's there's no misunderstanding, I've got a regular deal with Brusik and the kid."

"That's okay," Eugene said. "There's enough business to go around. You can still have a drink on me. In fact, you can have two. *In fact*, you can drink that barrel dry, and I'll pay to the last drop!"

He grinned all over his face, and the boys looked at him thoughtful.

"What's the catch?" Sam said.

"No catch," Eugene said. "Fill them up, kid."

I filled them up, then again, with Eugene grinning away, until finally Sam said, "Eugene, I know your heart's in the right place, and you're kind to widows and orphans and all, but would you mind telling us exactly why you're grinning like an idiot? Have you struck it rich? Is there a goddamn gold mine around here we ain't heard of?"

"Well, now"—Eugene grinned away—"just maybe there is! Maybe I was digging at the back of old Brusik's dugout

261

and found me a great big nugget, haw! haw!" Laughing, because Brusik near jumped out of his skin, and so did I, thinking there maybe *was* a gold mine there.

"Haw! haw!" Eugene went. "But, boys, maybe we have got a gold mine!"

"Okay, okay," Sam said. "So we've got a gold mine. Now quit joshing and tell us what's going on."

Eugene smiled, a secret, maddening smile. "Why, the thing is, I've brought you some reading matter. You like that, don't you? Newspapers and stuff?"

"You know damn well we do," Sam said. "But is them funny papers, being as how you're so goddamn comical?"

"I'll put it this way," Eugene said. "It's a laugh, but it ain't comical. Take a peek."

He handed over a newspaper, and Sam, who could read pretty good, ran his finger over a bit of a page which was marked out. "So," he said. "Some goddamn British firm's bought some hides. What am I supposed to do, cut my whiskers off?"

"Just read on, Sam," Eugene said. "Just read on."

Sam did. He put his finger back on the page and read on, and when he finished, he threw that paper in the air and let out a yell that could have wakened every feller lying under six feet of Kansas dirt.

"Goddamn!" he yelled. "*Goddamn!* It *is* a gold mine. Sweet Jesus H. Christ, we've struck it rich!"

"And no goddamn shoveling," Eugene said.

TWENTY-FIVE

Struck it rich, and no shoveling! I'll tell you, the whole of camp went on the spree and didn't stop for a week, and there wasn't even one stabbing, which was some kind of miracle, I guess.

And what was that celebrating about? I didn't know myself at first. When the boys rushed out to whoop it up, I took a look at the newspaper, read the bit LeCompt had marked, and said I didn't get it.

Old Brusik, who was moving out to join the festivities, gave me a pitying look. "Rawhides," he said. *"Rawhides."*

I shrugged. "So?"

"Ygrumglishky," Brusik muttered, or some such word, which I took to mean was foreign for how dumb can you get. "What kind of hides we get now? Them's *robes*. Hides with wool on, right?"

"Right," I said.

"And them hides is *winter* hides, right? Because that's when the wool is thick. Them summer hides is no good because they is all scraggy, right?"

"Right," I said again.

"Yah." Brusik got a gigantic swallow of red-eye down him. "Now, this Englisher firm, they say they buy rawhide. All the rawhide they can get."

That seemed to take us back where we started from. "Okay," I said. "So what?"

"Gashkristushovsky!" Brusik was getting real mad. "So, rawhide. It don't matter what the wool is like..They just want the skins. We got a market for *rawhide*. Them hunters can shoot winter *and* summer. All the time!"

And he was right, at that. Them Britishers, they'd figured out a way to use buffalo skins. Thing was, we sold them robes for coats and blankets and such-like, but they wasn't no good for leather, being all spongy and what they called porous, the which is a ten-dollar word for letting water in. But the Britishers had found this way of tanning them, which is turning them into leather so's it could be used for all sorts of things. Not so much soles, they was too soft for that, but coverings, riding boots, facings for soldiers' coats, and I don't know what all. *And* some German had figured out how to cure the hides quick, the thing there being our fellers did it the Indian way, which took almost forever, but this new way, with chemicals, why, it didn't take hardly no time at all!

So LeCompt was right. We'd struck it rich, and there was another thing. LeCompt, he told us that railroad company, that old AT and SF, had started laying track again and was really flying, because if they didn't get to the Colorado state border by the end of 1872, they'd lose all that government money they was swindling the public out of.

Well, them two things got me to thinking hard. There was plenty of money to be made out of hides, and now that we could do it all the year around, it was a temptation to stay, and the railroad coming was going to make a difference for sure, so I tore up that sarcastical letter to Heaney and sat back, waiting for the slaughter time to begin.

And it did, but it didn't start off with no big explosion. The way of it was that, come spring, the real hunters, instead of pulling up stakes and going gold mining up in the Dakotas, or stagecoach robbing, or whatever, they stuck around and carried on hunting the buffalo, and you might say them shots echoed clear across the West, and there were plenty of fellers who got the message, which was, "Pilgrims, head for Dodge and make yourselves some easy money."

And they did head in and, brother, you wondered just where in Sam Hill they'd come from. The camp sure hadn't been no bed of roses before, with angels tripping around, but the fellers had been hunters, real hunters, with a trade in their fingers, or regular teamsters, and you knew them, who they was and who they worked for. But these new bozos who came drifting in, jeepers, they could give you nightmares while you was awake! It was hard to put them down as human beings, saving only they had two legs. And it was with some of them I pointed a gun at a feller for the first time in my life.

The way of it was, there'd been fever in camp, real bad fever, killing people. Typhus, someone said it was, the saying which seemed to cheer folks up, like naming it was the same as curing it! Old Brusik went down sick, I guess with the same thing, though not dying sick, and lying wrapped up in the dugout. So come one day, and it wasn't a bad one, neither, the sun shining and birds cheeping, Brusik was in the back sweating away and I was minding the store and reading *Store Keeping Made Simple*, and thinking I'd be getting me a harder book before long, and two fellers came in and said they'd got some hides for sale.

They was two terrible-looking hombres, and their rig— they had two ponies and a broken-down wagon pulled by three mules that had been treated something awful, whipped and gouged, and one with its eye hanging out. And the hides they'd got, they was perforated as you might say, it being clear them fellers couldn't put a buffalo down save they shot it a hundred times, and the hides hadn't even been cured right.

I'd got to know quite a bit about hides by then, so I went out and gave them hides a look and said I wasn't interested. "LeCompt's around," I said. "He might make a deal"— hoping they'd beat it.

But them bozos glared at me, and one of them who'd got big boils loomed over me, breathing whiskey in my face and sort of toying with a skinning knife. "We ain't asking no goddamn Lee Compt for no deal. We're asking you, get it?"

"I get it," I said, and like a real tomfool, I backed to the tent, and them bozos was on my toes, and they backed me *into* the tent, which is exactly where I didn't want to be.

"Okay," the feller with boils said. "We got thirty hides out there. We'll take two dollars fifty apiece, *and* a bill of sale."

"Mister," I said, "there ain't no one on God's earth would pay two-fifty for them."

"Saving you," the boily man said.

"Saving me," I agreed. "But we don't carry that much cash. You'll have to take a credit note."

"Credit, huh?" The boily man got himself a big slug of red-eye, stuck it down, and said, "We don't deal with credit. Cash on the barrel. And let's get on with it"—waving that skinning knife about an inch from my nose.

"Okay," I said. "Okay. I'll make out the bill of sale." And I went behind the counter we had, reached down, and came up with the shotgun!

Sounds real romantic, don't it? But it didn't feel romantic. I was so scared I could hardly stand up. My legs was shaking, my voice was shaking, and every part of me that could shake was shaking. The trouble was, them bozos wasn't! In fact, the boily feller laughed!

"You ain't thinking of using that, is you?" he said, sneery as may be.

"I ain't thinking," I croaked. "Get out of here or I'll blow you apart!"

"Yeah?" That boily man bared what teeth he had like a mad dog. "You son of a bitch—"

He yanked at his six-gun and came for me. I closed my eyes, and would you believe, I pulled both triggers and that gun went off like a cannon. I went flying backwards, there was a huge banging, a cloud of black smoke, something like an elephant trampled over me, there was cussing and screaming, and I got to my feet and, Jupiter, the tent was half down, the stovepipe was busted, and wrestling under the canvas was Brusik!

Moses, that was some scene in there. What had happened, I'd blown the stove up, Brusik had heard the racket, like you'd have needed to be dead not to, had a miracle cure, and come tearing in with an ax, so it was like some earthquake had taken place in there, which in a way it had, Brusik being a sort of human earthquake when he got going.

I struggled through the mess to get at Brusik, who was laid out, but while I was pawing at him, a big hand got hold of my collar and yanked me clear, it being Charlie Rath, one of our customers, who'd turned up with some other fellers.

They got most of the mess cleared away, wrapped Brusik in a buffalo robe, and stuck him back in the dugout, then asked me what in Sam Hill was going on.

I was shook up, real shook up, so it took some time for them to get the story out of me. The boys listened, serious, and they was right to be so, because robbing a store was something new, even for the camp.

"They had ponies?" Frank Finlay asked, and when I said they had, he said he'd seen two fellers hightailing it down to the Arkansas.

"Too dark to go looking for them," he said. "Well, you'll be okay for the night, anyhow. We'll be keeping an eye open for you tonight and see you in the morning. But keep that blaster with you, loaded."

The boys moseyed off, all talking and jabbering, and I got in my bunk with the shotgun next to me. I was scared. Scared and shaken, but what I was thinking most of all was whether, when I blasted off the gun, I hadn't kind of deliberately missed that saddle bum, not being able to face killing a man. Sometimes I thought I had, and sometimes I thought I hadn't, but lying there with Brusik moaning and groaning, I'll tell you, I surely hoped I'd never need to try again.

But that hope got dimmed the next day. I was getting the store to rights, and giving old Brusik healing soups, by the which I mean whiskey and beans, when Finlay called in.

He looked around the tent, which was black as night from all that soot, and peppered with holes as well, and grinned. "You did all right, kid. How's Brusik?"

I said he was doing okay, and Frank laughed. "Nothing like dollars and cents to work a cure. Better than any medicines. Pity he didn't kill them sons of bitches." He poured himself a slug of red-eye and pondered for a moment. "Still, we'll get them next time."

"Next time!" I near jumped out of my boots. "You ain't saying they'll be coming back, is you?"

"Why not?" Frank asked. "When you get down to it, they didn't actually do nothing wrong. Just asked for a price on them hides."

"Frank," I said, real exasperated. "Them fellers was going to rob us, certain, and let the daylight into us if needs be."

"Sure," Frank said. "Nothing a court of law would pay heed to, though."

I got even more exasperated. "We ain't got no courts of law."

"That's right," Frank agreed. "Lucky for us at that, because there won't be no fooling around when we get them bozos."

"You reckon we will?" I asked. "They're probably half-way to El Paso by now."

"I don't reckon so." Frank shook his head. "They left something behind."

"Something—" I didn't get it for a minute, then it clicked. "The rig and the mules."

"That's it, kid." Frank spat a stream of tobacco juice out. "But don't worry, next time we'll be ready for them. Now let's get old Brusik out of that dugout and get him some air."

We did that, laying Brusik on a robe, with plenty of healing soups to hand. Then Frank moseyed off, and I got down to doing some thinking. Well, I say thinking, but that's putting it kind of handsome. What I *was* doing was being terrified! I mean, if them bozos did come back they wasn't exactly going to walk in and say, "Excuse us for that little dust-up, can we have our rig back and, oh, by the way, here's five bucks for your trouble." No, sir, what they was going to do was come sneaking back in the middle of the night, slit our throats, rob us blind, and *then* take the outfit.

It sure was some pleasant prospect—what you might call nerve-racking—and helped wreck my nerves all right. It was hard to concentrate, you know? I'd be trying to do the hard sums at the back of *Store Keeping Made Simple*, and all the time I'd be thinking of them bozos, waiting for them to arrive, and for all I knew, them lying up there on the bluff spying on us. In fact, I told Frank that if he was so keen on catching them scalawags, *he* could look after the rig, but he wouldn't go for that, saying it was better I had it, being as how I was just a kid, so them fellers would be more likely to try their luck with me! Moses, I used to lie awake at night, thinking every sound was them murderers coming to get me, and to tell the truth, I hoped they *would* come and steal them away. And didn't I wish old Marshal Hickok and his policemen was on hand! Not more than a dog likes bones, I didn't!

But one thing I did do. I got me some pickle jars and stuck a heap of dollars in them, which was my share of cash money we took in, and when Brusik was lying out in the sun, I dug a hole under my bunk and buried them, which eased my mind somewhat.

And it eased off more as a couple of days went by and no one come for the rig, and then a week, and some more days. Brusik was getting better and I was glad of it, having him around being comforting, and I was getting around to thinking, to blazes with Frank. I'd just sell that outfit, there being fellers drifting in who'd have been glad to have it cheap, when right in the middle of the day, when Brusik was doing some getting better in Hoover's liquor tent, a feller came in I hadn't never seen before.

He was just an ordinary, regular type of citizen—that is, he needed a haircut, a shave, a bath, and his clothes had big holes all over. Nothing remarkable, you know, and he spoke civil, saying "Howdy," and buying a drink and sitting down all relaxed.

I asked what I could do for him, and he said, "Get me another drink, son, and maybe we can do some trading here."

"Sure," I said. "That's what we're in business for. What sort of trading did you have in mind. Hides?"

"Yeah," he said. "Hides. And horse trading."

"Sorry, mister." I shook my head. "We don't trade none in horses."

"No, but you do in mules, don't you?" he said.

Something happened to my throat right then, like someone had jammed a hunk of wood down it. "Mules?" I croaked.

"Sure." The feller was cool and unconcerned. "You've got a rig outside, ain't you?"

"Yeah," I said. "There is, but they ain't mine." And then I said, "You got to talk to my partn—I mean, my boss—about them. I don't know nothing about that rig. I just work here!"

Cowardly, wasn't it? Sneaky as all get-out, but then, it wasn't you sitting on your own, facing that feller.

"Yes, sir," I babbled. "Just work here. Old Brusik—I mean Mr. Besser, you'll have to talk to him"—wondering whether I could leap through the roof of the tent and get away.

But that feller, he just stuck a stogie in his mouth, lit it, blew out some smoke, and said, cool as may be, "Okay, let's have a word with him."

"You mean I can go?" I said, real incredulous.

"Sure." The feller was incredulous back. "Why in hell not? Go get him."

I didn't need telling twice, believe me. I was out of the store like greased lightning, and five minutes later I was back with Brusik and Frank and the other fellers, who was all tooled up like they was going to start Civil War number 2, and was that feller surprised when we burst in and he found himself looking down the muzzles of half a dozen fare-thee-wells. But he kept his cool at that.

"What the hell is this, boys," he said. "The Fourth of July already?"

"Never no mind the wisecracks," Frank said. "You asking about that outfit?"

"Sure," the feller said. "Why not? It's mine!"

"Yours!" Frank was staggered, and so was the rest of us. "You saying it's yours?"

"That's the word," the feller said. "I came out of Texas, and them two skinners of mine took off with the rig and most everything else I had. I figured they'd head for here, so I've come, too, and now I want that rig back, and the mules, and them hides. Well, it ain't so much as I want them back, more I want to sell them."

"Well, now . . ." Frank was somewhat uncertain, and he'd reason to be, that thieving not being what you'd call

271

rare—skinners, who was mostly real bad hats, doing it when the spirit moved them.

"You got a bill of sale for that rig?" Charlie asked.

"No, I ain't," the feller said. "Didn't I just tell you I was robbed?"

"And why didn't they plug you while they was doing it?" Charlie said.

"Because I was out on the range, is why, and when I got back, they'd beat it."

"Yeah?" A hunter called Elmer Skite leaned forward. "Then where's your rifle?"

Well, that was a mighty shrewd question. Because if that feller had been out hunting when them bozos stole the rig, they couldn't have taken that, too. The boys started staring hard at that feller, but he didn't seem fazed at all.

"Ran into some Indians, Shoshone," he said. "They made me hand my rifle over."

"You gave a buffalo rifle to a goddamn Shoshone?" Charlie said, and he was really blazing, for which he had reason to be.

"You think I wanted to?" The feller snorted. "It was that or my hair. What would you have done?" He glared at us, and you had to hand it to him, he wasn't the sort of feller to be intimidated. "Now, if this court of inquiry is over, I'd be obliged if you'd all go to hell and let me get on with my affairs."

"This inquiry is over when we say so," Frank said. "We're going to have a talk about this." He headed out, the rest of us following, and said over his shoulder, "You sit tight, mister, and have yourself another whiskey!" Which was mighty good of him, seeing as how that was ours.

Well, we all stood in a group away from the tent, and I guess the truth was, no one really knew what they thought. Like Frank said, that story held together, but Elmer wasn't having it.

"Hell," he said. "I could swallow that skinner yarn, but that Shoshone stuff—Christ Almighty, they'd have taken his gun *and* his hair. The way he tells it, it's like some goddamn tea party they was having out there."

"There's something in that," Frank said. "So what do we do?"

"I know just exactly what we do," Elmer said. "We ask him one more question. Good old Texan style."

And that's what they did, and which was the first time I'd seen that Texan-style question, which was as simple as the ABC, because all you needed was a pony, a rope, and a tree, although not having no trees in Dodge, the boys made do with the ridgepole in Hoover's big tent, putting one end of the rope around there, the feller backwards on a pony, and his neck being connected to the ridgepole by the other end of the rope.

"And now," Elmer said, "asking you politely, and for the last time, what happened?"

Moses, it was something awful to see. That jasper on the pony, sweating and white-faced, and his bowels had gone loose, too, so there was a terrible stench.

"I've told you the truth," he moaned. "It's the truth. I'm Jack Wilson from Selma, is all. Jesus Christ Almighty, what are you doing?"—and so on, until Elmer stepped forward, a quirt in his hand. "Okay, Mr. Jack Wilson from Selma," he said. "You tell us where them skinners is hiding out and you go free. That's my word on it."

The feller twisted his neck in the noose, all bulgy eyes and moaning "Help, help." Then Elmer, real grim-faced, raised the quirt and the man screamed, which I'd never heard a man do before.

"All right," he shrieked. "All right. I'll tell you, I'll tell you."

He did, too, the story being him and the other two bozos had been skinners for an amateur hunter out of Selma, and they'd murdered him, although he swore he hadn't done no killing. But he told us where them other two bums was hiding out, and the fellers went to find them, which they did, although they didn't come back with them, and that Wilson, so-called, he was let go, although it didn't do him no good, because he met up with two fellers on the prairie who did unto him as he'd done unto others, only them doing it first, in spades.

■ TWENTY-SIX ■

All three of them bozos got what was coming to them, and I ain't denying it. You could say it was like Kessel—justice had been done, but it made me uneasy. I mean, supposing that feller had been telling the truth? He'd have swung just the same. So maybe it was justice, but it was rough justice, and a mite too rough for me.

Be that as it may, things on the murdering and killing front quieted down, for a while anyhow. Course, there was plenty going on in the brawling and knifing line, and out on the prairie there were fellers who didn't do no more waking up, but that near-hanging had done the trick, and compared to what it had been, the camp was like a Sunday School and the excitement moved to what them college professors call a higher level, which was making money and waiting for the railroad to come, when we was going to make even more money.

That railroad sure was luring folks to camp. A feller called Henry Sitler built a real house out of sod, sort of as if he was there to stay, a new booze tent opened, and then two fellers called Brown and Stewart hauled lumber in from Russell, Kansas, and built a one-floor saloon, selling whiskey at twenty-five cents a shot.

That did us a power of good with our hunters, us giving them drinks near for nothing, so they kept bringing us their hides, and didn't they bring them just! Out they went, "Boom, boom" went them Sharps, and in came the hides, even calves, which prompted me to ask a question of Charlie Rath, who really knew about buffalo hunting.

Charlie listened, then laughed and slapped me on the back, that irritating habit having spread West.

"Don't you worry none," he said. "If you got out and saw them buffalo, why, a goddamn army wouldn't make no impression on them. Them animals will last forever. So don't pay no heed to them damn fools in Topeka."

That cleared my mind, because I'd been getting worried that maybe the buffalo was going to get wiped out, which was why Charlie had mentioned Topeka, the thing there being back in east Kansas, and in the East generally, there was folks worried about just that and trying to enforce the laws passed to stop *all* buffalo hunting.

That was a real sore point in camp. You'd have some fellers having a quiet drink and you mentioned them conservers, it was like an Anarch bomb going off. In fact, I did it deliberate once, just to have a laugh.

"I know about them goddamn idiots," Moses Cagney said. "City folks! Jesus, they wouldn't know a buffalo if it jumped through their goddamn window."

The boys bayed agreement, sounding like a regular pack of wolves.

"Trying to take a feller's living off him," Charlie butted in. "And what is them fellers—"

"And women," Sam Fuller stuck in.

"Right, and *women*." Charlie spat that word out like it

275

was poison. "Jesus, they're worser than the men. And they is all nigger lovers, and if it hadn't been for them, there wouldn't have been no war, and they is—"

"Indian lovers, too," Sam said.

"*Yes!*" Charlie roared. "*Goddamn Indian lovers!* And if for Christ's sake you'd let me finish a sentence—"

"You'd say they was out to stop liquor," Sam said, real straight-faced, while we all burst out laughing, it being so comical, although I don't know Charlie saw the joke.

Them conservers was a sore point, sure enough, but like Charlie said, it was them who was Indian lovers, too, which really made the fellers mad. Lordy, the way they talked, you'd have thought the Indians was all living like millionaires on our taxes, not that anyone in camp actually paid any, as far as I knew. And as for them living rich, well, them I saw didn't. Course, they was only blanket Indians on the reservation who hung out around the fort waiting for handouts and who was the most miserable creatures you ever laid eyes on and not up to hurting a fly. But when I mentioned that to the boys, I got shouted down—what else!

"Them ain't real Indians," Charlie growled. "You ever seen a horse Indian?"

"I've seen Osage, Cherokee too," I said. "On the Chisholm Trail."

"Hell, they're halfway civilized," Charlie said. "Just you wait till you see a real wild one, a Comanche or Kiowa."

"Okay," I said. "What is they like?"

Charlie chewed some tobacco for a while, then spat. "Kid, I'll put it this way. If you ever do see one, you won't need telling."

Well, the buffalo and Indian lovers was two burning topics, as you might say, but the real talk was about the railroad, which had got started again, and the way we heard it, them track layers was really throwing the rails down,

276

but they'd stopped outside six shacks some optimist called Hutchinson City, because a ship bringing rails from England had sunk out there in the Atlantic Ocean. But it was coming, no doubt about it, which was mighty exciting. And I got excitements all of my own. I got a letter! A real letter, from Henry! Sent all the way from New York City and reaching me way out West!

It was a kind of dry letter, like Henry himself, saying he was working on that German paper, he'd got a new cat, he hadn't blown up anything for a while, he hoped I hadn't got scalped, and saying any time I wanted to see a big city I should go stay with him. And he ended: "Come when you've made your million—and even if you don't make it, you'll still be welcome."

It was real swell, getting that personal letter. Like I had a friend still. A real friend. One who didn't want nothing from me and who would go to the trouble of writing that letter and sending it halfway across the United States. And I decided I would go to New York City—when I'd made my pile.

And I *was* making money. In fact, it was hard not to. More and more fellers was going out hunting, and the money we was all making was drawing businesses in with it. Why, come July, we'd got a blacksmith's shop, a general merchandiser, a grocery store, and we'd even got a barbershop, and that barber must have cut enough whiskers in his first week to stuff a million armchairs. There was even talk of a restaurant being opened, and a dance hall! In fact, two dance girls came, Nell Saintclair and Nell Pool, sort of before the dance hall. Testing the water, as you might say.

Yes, sir, there was big times coming, and there was something that came I hadn't dreamed off, because in July, in real shriveling heat, into our tent, rubbing his hands together and beaming away, came old Heaney!

We got him settled in our best chair, the one with four legs, and Brusik offered him a slug of red-eye, at which he shuddered and turned it down—and I could have made ten cents a head in camp showing him doing that—but he said he'd appreciate a refreshing glass of lemonade. I explained that we didn't go in none for that particular type of refreshment, so he settled for coffee, and we gabbed for a while. He told me how things were back East. There wasn't nothing doing in Abilene but land business, and he was going to open another office in Newton soon, the settlers having gotten on to enforcing the quarantine laws in Ellsworth already, would you believe. "And Goblinka's getting married!" he said.

I was somewhat fascinated by that, wondering who'd be dumb enough to get hitched to her, but Heaney said it was another foreigner, which figured, and then the social affairs being attended to, he hinted to Brusik that we'd appreciate a little privacy. Brusik not up to handling genteel language, I just told him to beat it, which he did, and we got down to it.

Heaney had brought a lot of papers and certificates from the bank, showing how I was doing, and an account book from Besser, showing what I was making there. So what with this and that, and some cash I was stashing away in those pickle jars under my bunk, I was getting to be worth quite a wad. In fact, I was predating on the North like all get-out. But I figured Heaney hadn't come all the way to show me stuff he could have mailed, and I was right, because he gave me that holy look of his.

"Ben," he said, "I've been advising you right, ain't I?"

I said he had and that I'd got two ears which was ready to listen to any more advice.

Heaney did some hand rubbing. "Now," he said, "I'm going to give you a little inside information. *Inside information*, the which, Ben, is worth more than gold!"

More than gold! Gee whillikers, I thought, tell me more, and Heaney didn't need no prompting.

"Ben," he said. "You know if a railroad gets someplace and builds a depot, that's the place to be?"

"Sure thing," I said. No depot, no town. No town, no trading. No trading, no money. No money, no town. It was kind of the history of the West, which was why you got folks fighting like cat and dog to get a depot.

"Okay." Heaney looked over his shoulder and dropped his voice. "Now, I happen to know that the Santa Fe is thinking of making a depot right here. It's a natural place. Water from the river, the fort, and all that free land for when the settlers come."

"Them," I said. "They ain't coming till doomsday, the way I hear it."

"Oh, they'll come," Heaney said. "Maybe not for a while, but they'll get here. In fact, before then, this might be a big cow town. Them cattle trails keep getting pushed west, so this would be a mighty fine place for the herds, as soon as the buffalo is shot off. But don't you worry about that, Ben. The thing is"—he leaned forward, real confidential—"Colonel Dodge, there at the fort, he's going to organize a syndicate to found a town!"

"Jeepers!" I said. "You mean a regular one? With a council and all?"

"I certainly do," Heaney said. "You know how founding a town works?"

Well, I did, in a hazy kind of way, but old Heaney spelled it out for me. You got a state, like Kansas there, which was half empty. Some of that land was Indian reservations, but most of it belonged to the U.S. government, saving them millions of acres they gave to the railroad for building the track, and the government, it was ready to sell its land dirt cheap to settlers, and if so be you could get six hundred folks living in an area, that area became a county of the state it was in, and once you got a county organized, you could form a township company and buy the land from the government and build a town, meaning you could raise town taxes and hire regular lawmen—just like Abilene, in fact—and if you was lucky, you could get that town made into the county capital and then really make money in land and trading.

"Well," Heaney said, "that's what the colonel and his buddies are going to do, and with that big depot coming, this town is going to boom, so I think we ought to get into the action. What do you think?"

I was thinking it was a goddamn fairy story, that's what I was thinking, because there wasn't nowhere near six hundred people around Dodge, unless you counted them underground, but I let that pass. "There's something you've overlooked," I said. "I ain't old enough to buy land."

"Now, that's so," Heaney allowed. "But I am." And he kind of smirked. "Thing is, Ben, I buy them shares in my name but you put up some of the cash—hold on—" saying that because I was just going to kindly inform him that if he thought I was going to agree to that, he was as crazy as a jackrabbit in spring, and I was going to change my business advisor pronto.

"Hold on," Heaney said again. "You'll be what us businessmen call a *sleeping* partner. I'll have proper legal papers made out, so's I can't swindle you—not that I ever would, Ben. Now, we get shares in the Township Company, we get first choice of the lots, prime lots, because the more shares we buy, the more lots we can have. We'll buy the land you're on now and you can put up another store on one of the lots—and there ain't no law says you can't run two stores—pay me rent, which goes into our little partnership, and when the railroad gets here, we can maybe develop them other lots, or sell them for a real good profit."

"Or lose every last cent," I said.

"Ben!" Heaney looked real pained. "Ain't I told you that you've got to take a little risk if you want to make real money? And have I ever steered you wrong? Well, this is a chance to make real money, and Ben . . ." He peeked at me sort of humorous. "Ben, you've got enough money now to take a gamble. But if you ain't interested, why, no hard feelings, I'll get me another partner." But he'd said enough. I could feel the crinkle of ten-dollar bills right there and then, so I told Heaney he could just wander off and get as many shares as he could, like maybe one million.

He beat it, and I wandered around the store, excited, you know, and I was more excited when he got back all smiling, by which I knew the Lord was smiling on *us*, and I was right, because the colonel and them other fellers who was organizing the company had said we could go right in with them!

That night we got rid of Brusik and put our heads together and Heaney told me the plans for the Township Company. They was going to sell six hundred shares at ten bucks each, then buy in 320 acres, selling the lots at fifty bucks each. A. A. Robinson, who was the chief engineer of the Santa Fe Railroad, was going to survey it, so everything would be hunky-dory. Me and Heaney had a hatful of shares and was guaranteed at least one prime site, right along the tracks, when they got there.

Buffalo City it was going to be called, and Heaney had a rough plan of it. There was Front Street, where the store would be, and Spruce Street, and Maple and Walnut and Cedar, real pretty names, and some lots reserved for a school and a church—like them reformers casting a shadow there. But I had a real good feeling, looking at that map. Being in on the development made me feel noble, real noble, helping to build a whole new town out of nothing— and making money doing it! And like I said to Heaney, all we needed was a lying newspaper, like the *Abilene Chron-*

icle, which could let the world know what a dandy town we was going to have.

But there was one thing bothering me, and I let it out the next morning when I was seeing Heaney off on a wagon.

"It's Brusik," I said. "Ain't we letting him in on the deal?"

Heaney got a kind of dreamy look on his face. "Look at it this way, Ben. We cut Brusik in, it means cutting old Jake Besser in, too. Now, if—"

But I cut him off, that being something I was getting around to, having dollars, see, and them giving you them cutting powers. "Mr. Heaney," I said, "as long as old Besser keeps making money for me in Abilene, I don't give two hoots of a scritch owl for him."

"Why"—Heaney smiled—"I figure that's a right smart businesslike way of looking at things. And if they ain't smart enough to have a business advisor, that's up to them, ain't it? Sides"—he climbed up on the wagon, and mighty limber for an old geezer, and looked down—"they didn't tell you about Goblinka getting hitched, did they? Maybe they got other little secrets, huh? No, let's just keep this to ourselves. All cozy. So long."

There was something in that, for sure, so I said okay and shook hands and watched that wagon crash out to Hutchinson City, then turned and walked back to the store, looking at the camp, and, brother, it was some sight, a few frame houses and tents blistering away under that broiling sun, and I thought of that plan: Chestnut Street! Walnut! Spruce!—and not a goddamn tree within a hundred miles. It was like there was a crowd of lunatics sitting around making up them crazy names. What they ought to have called them was Whiskey Street or Stabbing Row. I had to laugh, but as long as them names brought in suckers to buy the lots, it was jake with me. In fact, they could have called the town New Jerusalem, and it would have got my vote.

To get them suckers, we had to have the railroad, and it was coming. The track layers had started again and was throwing down two miles of rail a day, the Masterson brothers, Bat and Ed, who was afterwards them famous lawmen, doing the grading and leveling, and a gang of Irishers belting the rails down after them, and a feller told me that the way they was making that railroad, it would be a miracle if a train could actually run on it.

That worried me, you know, and I mentioned it to a feller called Hermann Fringer, who'd opened a drugstore, but he just laughed at me.

"Kid," he said, "sure, a train is going to jump the track now and then, but as long as some gets here, it's okay. Now, how about buying a ticket in the draw we're having."

The thing there was, when the first train pulled in, we was going to have a big celebration, same as we had for the Fourth of July, with mule racing and shooting competitions and with brawling thrown in for free, but Hermann's notion was a dandy one. You paid a dollar and got a ticket saying who'd get off the train first, and if you was right, you won the whole pot.

There was lots of tickets with names on, such as soldier, traveling man, hunter, and such-like, which was fine, but I drew an English duke, which I didn't even know what it was, but when I was told, I near went crazy. Hermann tried to calm me down, saying them dukes was coming over all the time for the hunting, but I was so mad he said I could have another for fifty cents, and I got a whiskey drummer with ginger whiskers and a green necktie, which made some kind of sense.

"And we'll know in a week," Hermann said. "Just one more week, is all."

I believed him, but it was hard to believe, if you get me. Just seven more days and we was going to be joined up to civilization, and all depending on a bunch of Irishers who didn't speak no more American than Mrs. Besser, from what I heard, out there with their own traveling saloon, toiling under the blazing sun, and give or take a couple of days, there'd be passengers coming who drank Champagne wine!

And I don't know if I did really believe it, until one evening I wandered out onto that low bluff. From there you could see a mighty long way, except there wasn't nothing to see, saving the prairie rolling away with never a tree or cabin to break it, just buzzards floating overhead waiting for you to drop dead, which you could do easy in the smothering heat, or maybe get chewed up by wolves or jumped by Indians who was feeling bad-tempered.

I was up there thinking, thinking how to make more money, that is, and looking out into that gathering darkness which was all dolesome and dreary, with never a light gleaming, sort of saying, "Folks here. If so be you're lost, ain't no need to lie down and die. Just make it a couple more miles and have some grub." Or if there was a light it was more like to be a gang of horse thieves and bandits who'd kill you for the boots you were wearing, but there wasn't even that, just the land getting that dreary purply color I always did find depressing. And I was just going to beat it back where there was lights and folks, when I heard a sort of piping, which might have been a night bird but wasn't, because that piping, you heard it once and you never mistook it for anything else ever. And I thought, Holy Moses, now the world is going to change for sure, because way out there, but not too far way out, there was a train, giving that old whistle a blast.

I slept the sleep of the blessed and the just that night, dreaming of my own store and the money I was going to make, and how when I made it I was going to dress fancy and maybe go back to Clement County and show the folks what a real predator looked like—and maybe getting even with old Tyler, too. But ain't it the truth, just when you think you're all settled comfortable, something comes out of the chair and bites you where it stings most. And there were two things stung me, as it were.

First off, that train I'd heard was a shunting train, carrying stuff for the railroad, not a real one, and it jumped the track, so the work got held up, and then the town plan ran into trouble.

The thing was, we was in Ford County. Well, we was going to be in Ford County when it got organized, but the state legislature in Topeka wouldn't recognize us because there wasn't six hundred folks living where the county was going to be. So, not being a county, we couldn't get no judge to sign the plat for the town!

I was sure burned up about that, but Bob Wright, the sutler, told me not to sweat.

"There's a way around every little difficulty," he said, and I thought yeah, and it's amazing how you law-abiding respectable citizens know them. "Just wait till the first train comes."

"Bob," I said. "It seems like I've been waiting for that for ten years."

Wright laughed. "I know how you feel. But take it easy. Those track layers will be coming through any day now. You'll see."

I'd see, he said, and didn't I just! Them Mastersons came

grading and leveling, and following them came the track layers. They worked like demons, but come Saturday night, lightning, they was like human volcanoes. That camp had seen some whooping up, but compared to this, it had been like a ladies' sewing bee. It was them and the teamsters going at it, the teamsters seeing their occupation vanishing before their very eyes, as they say, which was plumb ridiculous because all the fighting in the world wasn't going to stop the railroad. In fact, when some of the fellers said the track would never get to the Colorado state line because the Comanche would jump it, well, seeing them Irishers, I felt kind of sorry for them Indians, is all.

And then the great day came! A train, a real, special train, wrapped in flags and bunting, came puffing in with important folks and bringing a regular band all blowing fit to bust their brains out. The chairman of the mighty Atchison, Topeka and Santa Fe made a speech about how his glorious company was bringing peace and prosperity to the Golden West, the soldiers banged off a cannon from the fort, and then the train steamed back.

But that special train wasn't the point. We was waiting for the first regular train, and when that came in, we celebrated like all get-out, especially Hoodoo Brown, who won the sweepstake, having the first feller to get off who was a land agent. And, would you believe, there *was* an English lord! Leastways, that's what he said he was, although he didn't look no different from anyone else, saving he spoke kind of funny. Come for the hunting, he said, and he wasn't the only one. There was fellers reckoned they could make a fortune at it, and gamblers who figured they could make a fortune out of them.

Still, that's what we was all there for, and the railroad was doing it for us. In fact, we was having a boom! Three more stores opened, and a couple of fellers, A. J. Anthony and Bob Wright, brought out their wives, and Charlie Rath and a feller called Fred Zimmerman followed suit. You could go call on them and have tea, all genteel, just like the North Side in Abilene! In fact, they was already talking about doing some reforming! In that joint!

I'm not saying they was wrong, neither. Them trains was bringing other types in, too. Hard cases, and I don't mean hard cases like we was used to. These new bozos, it was like they was having a spring clean back East and beating them all the way to us.

There was plenty of them, too, holed up in a joint called the Essington Hotel, so-called after the feller who banged it together, and which was like their fort. They'd hole up there, doing unreformed things, which you can guess at because I ain't telling you, and lots of unreformed things started happening again. Horses and mules got a hankering for the wide-open spaces and wasn't where they should be the next morning, and there was robberies, so it wasn't safe to walk about at night, and a couple of hunters went missing, which them bozos said was Indian doing, although Indians didn't usually run off with a wagon and a load of hides.

And them fellers was sickening. They tied firecrackers to a dog's tail and drove it insane, and the feller that put that dog out of its misery, they beat him up. Just senseless cruelty. And they got bolder, demanding stuff on credit, booze mainly, and there was that hint behind them requests that if they didn't get it, why, you might get something for free, like a dose of lead poisoning. But the saddest thing was a tailor got killed. He was as meek and mild as buttermilk and should have stayed at home, but he got his, robbed and shot dead.

It was amazing, at that. There we was, building a town with a railroad and all, and five miles off there was United States Cavalry, but they might as well have been on the moon, for all the good they was to us.

Some of the newcomers, A. J. Anthony and Dan Wolf, went to see the colonel, but when they got back, they was bluer than when they left.

"Goodness." Old Anthony had been a preacher once and spoke in that comical way. "Goodness, the colonel won't do a thing unless Washington orders him!"

"Sure," Charlie Rath, who hadn't been a preacher, said. "What the hell do you expect? He ain't going to move against civilians."

"We could petition the state governor," Anthony said.

"Yeah." Charlie half laughed. "And while we're waiting for an answer, which could be in the twentieth century, we're getting robbed blind and bullied, and next thing, one of us is going to get plugged."

"But what do we do?" Anthony asked.

"Maybe I got an idea," Charlie said.

He told us the idea that night. There was a sort of meeting, saving it was mainly the old gang having it, some of them newcomers not getting invited. That meeting was in our tent, and the boys sat around the barrel while Charlie told us his notion.

"The thing is, boys," he said, having a drink to keep his throat clear. "The thing is, them bozos, there's too many of us to do like what we used to do"—not saying what that was, but us not needing to be told. "And they ain't really got nothing to lose, so they're walking over us. But we got something they ain't got."

"And what might that be?" Sam Fuller asked.

"We got money," Charlie said.

He didn't need to say no more. What he meant was, we should use that money to hire us some hard cases of our own. Like he said, if that fool legislature had let us be a real town, we'd be able to hire lawmen all legal, like Hickok back in Abilene.

"I don't know." George Smith, who ran a grocery store

with J. B. Edwards, shook his head. "The law allows that, but hiring on our own . . ."

"The hell with that legal law," Charlie said. "We got to fight fire with fire, is what."

"Yeah," Hermann Fringer spoke up. "But you play with fire, you can get your fingers burned."

Well, there was a lot of jawing and argufying, but in the end the fellers decided to go along with that notion, raising money, and that money was used to hire some more hard men, although it was all discreet. They didn't just go up to some gunslinger and say, "Here, Jack, you take this fifty bucks and plug that feller over there." No, sir, they just hired help like you would anyplace else to work in a store or saloon. Only the help, they didn't actually do no *work* in no saloon. They just sat in the saloon drinking and having free grub and playing cards—saying they never lost!

And it worked at that—at least, it did for us businessmen. Course, there was plenty going on, strangers waking up with a big lump on their head and finding they was poor all of a sudden, and there was a couple of real killings, but we could settle down to making money and sleeping safe.

I got a frame building, too. I laid out the cash and we stuck the tent at the back. Brusik asked me, kind of suspicious, who was paying for the frame, and I told him I was, out of my profits, and if he didn't believe me, he could check with his brother, old Brusik there being mighty sharp with a dollar when it was buying hides but kind of dim once them dollars got wrote down in a ledger, but he let it slide anyhows.

And I'll tell you, whoever got the idea of them frame buildings was more of a genius than Henry Ford is now. You just wrote off to a firm in Kansas City and they sent you a building any size you wanted, all the lumber sawed, planed, and numbered, so you just stuck up the frame and nailed plank 1 to beam 1, and so on, and in a couple of hours you had a dandy building that could be a house or a store or anything you wanted, and brother, what a difference that made. And if you don't believe me, try living in a dugout or a sod hut for a while like most of them sodbusters did, with snakes and beetles and insects, not to mention water pouring in.

I was surely glad I'd laid out on that building, too, because the winter of '72 through to '73 was just about the worst one there'd ever been. Jupiter, it was like them goddamn Britishers up in Canada was paying us back for beating them in the Revolution, sending down all the snow and ice and wind they'd got.

It snowed and blizzarded and froze, then blizzarded again, and I'll tell you, it was something to be in the store with the stove glowing, knowing we was safe, chewing the fat, or me going through my accounts, seeing how the dollars was piling up. But I couldn't get any of the fellers to play chess.

It was crazy, at that. We was rough, sure, but knew our manners, and we'd sit talking, or visit the respectable ladies, listening to them talk about the church they was going to build on Spruce Street and First Avenue, which wasn't nothing but prairie with gophers living under it, while outside there wasn't just bad weather, there was bad men. And they was bad. Some kid, just about my age, wandered into town and a real brute called Sherman shot him dead, just on a whim, and Tom Essington, who owned the Essington Hotel, he cursed his cook once too often and that cook shot him dead!

So, what with this and that, the winter wore itself out, and it passed about one million times better than any winter I ever had in Clement, because even if I got bored in camp, I was bored with money, whereas back home we'd been bored all the time without money, and I'll leave you to guess which is the best state to be in for a pilgrim passing through this mortal vale of tears.

So, the geese came flying north, flowers was opening and budding or whatever they do, the trains was running near enough on schedule, har-har, that being a joke, you could start shedding clothes and walking around like a human being instead of an old bear, but it wasn't just the weather was warming up.

I'd been down at the depot one day when I ran into Sam Fuller, who was looking real grim, and it turned out he'd been robbed of fifty dollars, and the feller who'd robbed him was a feller called Cox, who was actually one of them hard cases who was supposed to be looking after us!

That night, there was one of them meetings which wasn't a meeting, in George Smith's store, and Charlie said to Sam not to worry, we'd get his cash back and move Cox along.

"And how do you aim to do that?" Sam said.

Charlie shrugged. "We get the other fellers to do it."

"Sure," Sam said. "But they is all in it together."

"So"—Charlie shrugged—"we get more help, same as we've done."

"And we're right back where we started," Sam said, and cursed a mighty bad curse.

It was true, and there was no denying it, and didn't the fellers look gloomy, because they'd jumped clean out of the frying pan into the fire. Then Hermann Fringer spoke up.

"Fellers," he said, "I'm not suggesting we did the wrong thing, doing what we did. But the way I see it, we get this town platted, which can't be long now, for Jesus Christ's sake, the money we're paying that probate judge, and folks moving in, and then hire some real law. I hear that Hickok, who was marshal in Abilene, is down in Arizona doing nothing but playing poker."

291

"Kid"—Charlie turned to me—"go outside and stand by the door. Don't let no one in. You got that?"

I said I had and did what I said, saving I had my ear to the keyhole, you bet. They was speaking low, but not so low as I couldn't hear them. In fact, I near shouted that they should speak lower! But what I heard sure was interesting.

"It's that law you're talking about," Sam said. "See . . ." He coughed like his throat was dry, and I heard a glugging sound which I didn't need to see to know what it was. "See, Cox, he didn't wave no six-gun at me. But . . . but . . ."

"But what, for Christ's sake?" Charlie said.

"He"—Sam hesitated—"he did some talking. About fellers who've left here past few months."

"So what?" That was George. "Jesus, there's fellers coming and going all the time."

"Yeah." Sam sounded real grim. "But he was saying he knows where them fellers is *now*."

There was a dead silence for a minute, then George said, "Jumping Jesus!" And the others in there said the same or something similar, and I'm telling you, they was hard men in their own way. Like they wintered out on the prairies, and some of them had fought Indians or been soldiers in the war, but they was scared, and I knew why. Them fellers Cox had mentioned to Sam, they wasn't camping out *on* the prairie, they was camping out *under* it, and they wasn't going no further, saving someone came and dug them up. And if they ever was, say by a feller with a star pinned to his vest, why, it was wild and woolly out there, but it was still part of Kansas and under state law, and who knew but some goddamn reformers might start squawking that us terrible liquor sellers had paid murderers to put poor innocent men to death—and that could lead to more than a slap on the wrist. It could lead you, if not actually to a rope with a fancy knot in it, then to some rotting years in the State Penitentiary.

So them fellers in there had a bobcat by the tail and didn't know how to let go, and they was worried as all get-out, for which I didn't blame them, and there wasn't nothing they could do but all say they'd think about it. So they all vowed silence and secrecy and beat it, worried as all hell.

I beat it, too, but the truth was, I wasn't too worried. I hadn't never been out with them vigilantes and I hadn't never even talked to any of them hard cases. Sure I'd handed over money, but I reckoned I could always say I'd thought it was for sweet charity. It all going to show that there was something to be said for being just a kid!

But wasn't it something? There was that town growing before your eyes, and folks talking about schools and churches and civilization, while all the time there was regular businessmen walking the street, there being only the one, worrying about corpses moldering away out on the lone prairie! And I'll tell you something. I wasn't exactly what you'd call religious, not real religious, that is, but it made me think of something we'd talked about in Bible class in Abilene. It was in the Bible where the Lord said if you was going to build a house, you'd better make sure that house was built on rock and not on sand, otherwise you was going to be in trouble. Course, like the Reverend had explained, that meant living right and being in with the Lord and His doings, but it meant as well that if you was running a business you'd got to make sure you was running it right, making sure the books balanced and all and you didn't give too much credit, and if you did, making sure you'd got security, like a feller's farm or whatever. By the which I mean them businessmen in town had sort of built their house on a burial ground, and I guess you know what happens to one of them in time. They caves in, don't they?

Anyhow, I figured that was the other fellers' trouble and got on with business and keeping clear of the scalawags, of which there was plenty, especially around the Essington Hotel, which was called the Peacock now after the feller who'd bought it when Essington got killed, and around Tom Sherman's bar, which was somewhat baffling, him being the toughest, meanest feller you ever did see. You'd have thought that them bozos would have steered clear of him, but they didn't. Like they say, I guess, birds of a feather flock together.

So there was plenty of action in town, especially between the soldiers and the ruffians. The thing there was that the colonel, he'd got so mad at the troopers getting drunk at the fort, he'd stopped Bob Wright selling booze, so them boys had to come into town when they was allowed, them being like schoolkids, only going out to play when teacher says they can, and spending what pitiable pay they'd got in the bars. There was always trouble when they came in, them being despised, but that trouble didn't never amount to more than brawling, with maybe a stabbing now and then, and the colonel turned a blind eye to it. But then something happened he couldn't turn that blind eye to.

At that fort there was black cavalry who didn't hardly ever come into town, not unless they wanted to see what the world looked like through a noose. But there was some black servants who did, doing chores for the officers, and no one minded that, no more than seeing a mule which you'd whop out of the way if it didn't move, although them blacks had more sense than a mule, getting out of a white man's way before they *did* get whopped, saving one who didn't.

It was just at the start of June, hot as hell, and that

terrible wind blowing and blowing which got everyone's nerves on edge. But I was feeling pretty good because I'd been at Fred Zimmerman's store and he'd told me that the Township Company had found a probate judge in Ellis County who thought dollar bills was happier if they was all together, together in his bank account, that is, and that judge was going to jump the gun and allow the town plat, which meant a mighty fine profit for me and Heaney, whichever way you looked at it.

So I was walking along Front Street, rubbing my hands like old Heaney, and thinking maybe I'd call on Mrs. Anthony and have me a free cooling drink, when I saw a crowd of rowdies outside Sherman's booze factory. They was climbing over a wagon run by a black called Bill Taylor who was Colonel Dodge's servant at the fort and who did haulage in his spare time. That Taylor, everyone knew him, and kind of liked him, he being a quiet polite feller and knowing his place, which meant not being anywhere a white man wanted to be.

Them rowdies was all drunk and making a terrible racket, so I was going over to the tracks to keep out of the way, when Bill Taylor came out of Hermann Fringer's drugstore. I didn't hear all that was going on because them drunks was cursing something terrible, but it seemed like they wanted Taylor to drive them someplace and he didn't want to, that being his right, but he wasn't showing too much sense there because two of the rowdies was Cox and his sidekick Scott, who was as mean as could be.

Cox had hold of the reins, bawling and cursing, and Taylor had hold of the bridle of one of them mules. Then Cox yelled, "Get your hands off that bridle, nigger boy."

I didn't hear what Taylor said, them coloreds always speaking low and humble to a white man, but he kept hold of the bridle. Then Cox shouted, "Tired, is they?" meaning the mules, I guess. "I'll give them a rest. A good long one!"

And would you believe, he jumped down, yanked out a six-gun, and shot one of the mules in the head!

It was just incredible, you know? But there was worse, because Taylor, he backed away, then dived back into Fringer's, but Cox and Scott ran after him and dragged him out, and Scott roared, "You black bastard son of a bitch," and stuck his handgun right against Taylor's side and shot him!

That poor Taylor went down. Then, while he was lying there, Scott stepped forward and he shot Taylor, too. Then them murderers slapped each other on the back like they'd done some glorious deed, and whooped and screeched, then shambled into the Peacock, followed by their gang of ruffians.

It was just cold-blooded murder without rhyme nor reason. You know, you could get a killing and maybe it was two drunks both armed, and like Henry had said, where you got guns you got killings because that's what guns was made for, but at least there'd be some reason behind it. But this . . . just a feller saying his mules was wore out and he got riddled for it, and it was no good saying Taylor was uppity and deserved what he got, because he wasn't. And what made it worser, if that's possible, is that there were respectable people on that street and they didn't do a thing about it, and that includes me. We was afraid, is what, afraid of them murderers. In fact, them days we was living under gun law, but them guns was in the hands of the wrong people.

And would you believe, when the Army tried to do something about it, there was more trouble! The colonel came into town with a whole troop of soldiers and Cox showed him the body, which was still lying there, saving some Christian had thrown a buffalo robe over it, and Cox actually said, "Right there, I reckon that's my shot!"

The colonel sure was mad. He arrested Cox but missed

Scott, who was hiding in the icebox in the Peacock. But Cox swore out a warrant against the colonel for wrongful arrest, saying as how a soldier had no right to arrest civilians, for which the colonel got into trouble! And when that colonel sent soldiers into town to patrol the place and try and get some peace going, they had to be pulled out because they was drunk all the time, and the colonel got into even *more* trouble.

But that killing did some good. Scott beat it someplace, and Cox was being held on a civil warrant, so with them ringleaders out of the way, them other bullyboys kept to themselves. And then, what with that judge finally signing the plat, which he did a couple of weeks later, there was a feeling that maybe we could get ourselves some real law and put the guns in the hands of the right men. And I know for a fact that Mrs. Anthony and Mrs. Wright was getting onto the state senators to see about us having a United States Marshal right in town, and having seen what them women did in Abilene, I reckoned it wouldn't be long before we got one.

So, although Dodge—well, Buffalo City is what we first called it but had to change it because the post office said there was another burg in Kansas with the same name—although it was still simmering, it had stopped boiling and we could get back to business.

The price of hides dropped somewhat, there being plenty of fellers blasting away, but there was still a mighty fine profit to be made, so I was real content, sitting in my dandy store, gloating over the money I was making in Dodge and the profits old Heaney was making for me investing back East, bossing Brusik about because I'd got more brains in my little finger than he had in that whole huge body, eating good grub, being genteel as all get-out with the ladies, and counting my lucky stars that I'd been a noble darer when I'd got the chance.

And all the time I was doing that, living high, wide, and handsome, there was a clock ticking away, but it was a clock like them Anarchs used, stuck on to a bomb, and it was two thousand miles away in New York City, and when it got to September 1873, that clock ticked round to twelve o'clock—and the bomb blew up.

▪ TWENTY-EIGHT ▪

That bomb went off, and it blew me away, and a lot more folks, and in the end it blew away the buffalo and the Indians, and the feller who made that bomb go off, why, I'd never even heard of him!

I was going to the depot to see if some stores had come in when I met Eugene LeCompt, that hide buyer for Lobenstein. He wasn't looking so good, so I asked him if he'd had too much red-eye, but he didn't do no joshing back.

"This ain't no time for fooling," he barked. "Ain't you heard? Jay Cooke has failed!"

He hurried off and I went to the depot, wondering who in Sam Hill Jay Cooke was and what he'd failed at. I asked the clerk down there about it.

"You being funny?" he asked.

"No, I ain't," I said. "Just asking a plain question, but if you can't give me a plain answer, that's jake with me."

"Yeah? Well, you'll find out soon enough," the clerk said. "And your stuff ain't come, and to hell with you."

"And to hell with you," I said and beat it, and going back there was a few fellers shouted at me that Cooke had failed, so I figured it was some kind of gag going around and forgot about it.

298

Brusik was outside the store haggling over some skins a feller had brought in. When he saw me, he jerked his thumb. "Feller wants to see you," he said. "Inside."

I said okay and went in and there was this jasper, in a store-bought suit, drinking some of our best whiskey that came out of a bottle, not the barrel, and smoking a cigar as long as a Springfield rifle. I figured he was a salesman of some kind, told him who I was, and he looked surprised.

"You're a mite younger than I expected," he said.

"Is that so?" I said. "Well, I'm me. What can I do for you?"

"My name's Stokes," the feller said. "Tom Stokes, out of Iowa. I've a little business to discuss with you. About this store. It is yours, right?"

I gave the feller the glim, thinking he was maybe from the land registry in Topeka, and asked what was it to him.

Stokes sat on a chair and teetered back. "I aim to open a store here myself, as a matter of fact."

"It's a free country," I said.

"Sure is," Stokes allowed. "But it ain't that free. Like you've got to buy land."

"Believe so," I agreed. "So you just go ahead and buy some land and build your store."

"I'm aiming to," Stokes said. "Got everything ready, frame shed and all, stored on order. There's just one snag, you know?"

"No, I don't," I said. "And between you, me, and Buffalo Bill, I don't give a damn, neither."

"Sure," Stokes said. "I understand. But I think you should—give a damn."

"And why in Sam Hill should I?" I said, sounding mean and tough, which was the way to sound in Dodge, although maybe it didn't work 100 percent, coming from me.

"Why?" Stokes did some more of that irritating leaning back and teetering. "Because this store is on my land!"

"What!" I said, my eyes sticking out like they was on stalks.

"It's a fact," Stokes said.

"Mister"—I leaned forward—"this land belongs to D. B. Heaney of Newton. And let me tell you, he's a shareholder in this town."

"That's his story," Stokes said. "Mine's another."

"Mister"—I took a deep breath, then yelled—"Brusik, you get in here, quick."

Brusik came in quick—for him—and loomed behind me. "Right, mister," I said. "Beat it, and you come playing them tricks again and they'll be the last you ever do. Now *get*."

Stokes looked up at Brusik, then raised his hand. "Okay," he said. "I didn't come here to get in no bear fight. But while I'm gone, you might take a peek at these." He handed me some papers. "When you've calmed down some, maybe we can talk. If not . . ."

"*What?*" I said, sort of growling. "Just what?"

Stokes shrugged. "There doesn't seem to be much law in this town, but there's plenty in the state. Anyhow, you can have a few days to think it over and let me know how you're going to pay me!"

He beat it and I stared at the door, too stunned to do anything else, until Brusik said, "What's he mean, Ben? You owe that feller money?"

"The hell I do," I said. "I've never set eyes on him in my life. Just some trickster trying it on."

That satisfied Brusik and he went out back, but I stared at them papers and I've got to say they looked *sinister*, all thick paper and legal-looking and stamped, and I began to get a creepy feeling, like when you just *know* you've seen some goddamn vermin, like a tarantula crawling out of a corner, but you don't want to take a real look, in case you're right.

I didn't want to look close at them papers neither, but knew I had to, so I started going through them, and although there were lots of words in there that even I didn't understand, like *costly easements*, there were plenty I did, and when I finished plowing through them papers, I was white around the gills, because what they added up to was that the goddamn engineer of the railroad, that A. A. Robinson, he'd surveyed the town wrong, so the plats was all mixed up, and the land we was on belonged to Stokes, and he wanted rent on the plat for the time I'd been there, and that rent was enough to buy half of Kansas City, Kansas, *and*, it was hard to believe, but there in black and white, he was going to charge me about one million dollars more—them costly easements, whatever the hell they were.

I was scared, you know? Trembly, so's them blamed papers was shaking like leaves in the wind. Course, I knew there wasn't nothing real to be scared of, old Heaney owning the land and all, but it sure didn't seem like Christmas, neither. It was them legal papers . . . and that Stokes feller, he'd seemed mighty sure of himself . . . and then I thought, what the heck was *I* worrying for? I'd let my business advisor know and get him to earn his corn. And you know what I did? I sent him a wire! Yes, sir, a regular telegraph wire. I went down to the depot and I felt mighty important, too, it being the first time I'd ever sent one. I was sick, though, when I saw how much it was going to cost, but Keith Willis, the operator, he showed me how to cut out most of the words and said I could hear back in maybe a couple of hours and he'd let me know.

"And say," he said, "you hear about Jay Cooke?"

I said I didn't give a hoot in hell for all the Jay Cookes in the world and went back and started racking up some stores. But my mind wasn't on the chore, and that's the truth. I was getting beans mixed up with dried peas and .45 shells and I don't know what-all, until a feller stuck his head around the door and said there was a wire waiting for me.

I *ran* down to the depot, thinking my cares was over, and snatched that wire off Keith, and what did it say? It said: "Stall. Send papers. Urgent."

I stood under the lamplight wondering what in Sam Hill it meant. What did I have to stall for? *And* that wire had been sent collect, so I had to pay for it! Back in the store, I had real bad feelings. I brooded away and half made up my mind to go see one of the founders of the Township Company, maybe Henry Sitler, or even Colonel Dodge, but figured I'd be better off playing my cards close to my chest for the time being.

Seeing as how them legal papers was about money, I figured I'd see just how much I *was* worth, so got to looking at the accounts. We sure had a lot of debts, money owing to firms back East. Course, we had a heap of credits, too, money owing from hunters and such-like, and that cash I'd got invested through Heaney, but somehow them credits didn't seem as convincing as them debts, if you get me.

And that "Urgent" in the wire worried me. I'd wanted a message like "Take it easy," to get the cares off me, but the more I thought of it, the more urgent the whole shoot seemed. I lay awake most of the night, worrying worse than I had with them hats, and, come dawn, I thought what the hell, why worry yourself into an early grave? There's a goddamn train today!

So I dug up a pickle jar, took forty bucks, stuck them in a bag with the legal papers, put a Colt six-shooter on top, and told Brusik I was going to see Heaney. He did some goggling his sister would have been proud of, his sister-in-law, too, but I got it stuck into his skull he wasn't to leave the store on no account and that I'd be back on the next westbound train, then went to the depot to get the eastbound to Newton, and would you believe, some of the fellers on the street yelled had I heard about Jay Cooke, but I still figured it was just some gag going around town, and I sure wasn't in no mood for jokes right then.

It was around twelve hours to Newton, if the train didn't jump the track, thirty days if you was a settler in a wagon, but nothing at all sitting in a railroad car, even if all the seats was slashed, the windows broke, and it full of drunks. And simply being on that train made me feel better, like, just moving, I was leaving cares behind and getting to someone who'd do the worrying for me. Anyways, it was the first time I'd been out of Dodge for near two years, so the trip was doing me good, and as we swayed and bucked on that God-awful track, I thought of all the money I'd got invested, so by the time we hit Newton, I was real cheerful.

Getting off the train was like old times, which is to say Abilene before it closed down, with them huge stockyards, riders sashaying the streets, and music crashing out of a dozen dance halls. I felt somewhat homesick as I stretched my back, coughed out a couple of sacks of cinders, and asked the clerk where I could find old Heaney.

His place was a shack, the same one he'd had at Abilene, I guess, and he was in, sitting at a desk piled high with papers and documents, his bald head shining like one of them hen's eggs he liked eating.

"Howdy, Mr. Heaney," I said.

"Howdy," he said, then looked up and his eyebrows near climbed over his head and met his back collar stud. "Ben!" he said. "Ben!"

"Hi, Mr. Heaney," I said. "Hi!" Like we was two echoes, echoing at each other. "I brought the papers."

"Papers?" he said.

"Yeah, about the store. You said you wanted them urgent. Hey"—I took a step forward—"you ain't forgot them, have you?"

"Forgotten?" He did some more echoing. "No, no. Certainly not. No, indeed."

"I sure hope not," I said. "This is real serious."

"Serious. Oh, yes. Yes, it is. Serious. Very serious."

Old Heaney, he had a look on his face I didn't like one bit, twitchy as might be, and then he took out a bottle of rye whiskey and poured himself a shot old Brusik might have looked twice at. Him that was against drinking and a reformer and all! I stared hard at that bottle but figured it was his business and got back to mine.

"Mr. Heaney," I said, "there's hundreds of dollars riding on this legal stuff and you said you wanted them papers urgent so I come on the train, *which* cost me ten bucks, and this Stokes feller, he's talking about compound interest, and *costly easements*, whatever the hell they are—*and what in hell are you laughing at!*"—because he was, laughing fit to bust, only it wasn't real laughing, more like one of them hyenas you hear tell about. Did I see red! "Cut it out!" I yelled. "You hear me? Cut it out!"

"Heeee-heeeh-heee"—a terrible whinnying came out of him. "Ten dollars, did you say? My, my. Ten—didn't you hear?"

"Hear what?" I shouted.

Heaney, he caught his breath and took another slug. "About Jay Cooke!"

Did I fly off the handle! "Goddamn," I bellowed. "What is this Cooke stuff? I don't give a goddamn for no goddamn son-of-a-bitching Cooke." And would you believe, I pulled that Colt out of my bag and pointed it right at him. "You don't cut out this goddamn joking, I'll blow your head off!"

No kidding, I was there like a crazy man, waggling that Colt, which I could hardly hold straight, under Heaney's nose like I was a nervous holdup agent on his first job! And Heaney, he just looked straight at me and said, "Go right ahead. You'll save me the trouble!"

"What!" I put that fool gun down. "Mr. Heaney," I said, "will you kindly tell me what in Sam Hill is going on here?"

Heaney yanked at his collar like he was choking, then poured himself another drink and took a huge swig. "Yes," he said. "Me, drinking! Dave B. Heaney!" And suddenly he looked like an old man, a real old man, haggard and shrunk up and beaten. "Ben," he said, "Jay Cooke, he's a big financier in New York City. A big one, Ben. And he's gone broke, and we've gone broke with him."

I didn't actually get what he was saying, like it was Besser jabbering, but I did some laughing myself, not hearty, just showing goodwill like a salesman with a tedious customer. "Yeah, sure," I said. "Broke, Jay Cooke, ha-ha. Now about these here papers . . ."

Heaney was looking at me and I got a terrible prickly feeling. "You are kidding me, ain't you?" I said.

Heaney shook his head and took another drink, his hand all trembly, and I watched that rye slide down him like I was in some kind of dream, him joshing me and that bottle really full of colored water.

"No, Ben," he said. "I ain't."

"But all my money," I said. "In the bank . . ."

That twitching started again, Heaney's mouth moving like he'd got no control over it. "*The bank's bust, too!*" he said, and started roaring with laughter.

Goddamn, I near jumped over the desk and strangled him, but I got hold of myself and said, real hoarse, "How in hell can a bank go bust? You tell me that, and sweet Jesus, you'd better make it good, because if you don't, I swear to God you've ate your last egg."

"Right," he said. "Okay. Okay, I'll tell you." And he did, saying as all the money I'd made and saved and hoarded had gone into the bank and into stocks and shares—"which I've got the proof of right here, Ben"—waving his hand over them papers. "I've been straight as a die"—then going

305

on as how that Cooke, he was a millionaire banker and financier running companies and speculating all over the place, but he'd gone bust and all them companies with him, so all them certificates and papers was worthless!

"And he was an upright man," Heaney said. "Pious and moral. A pillar of the church."

"The hell with that!" I was seeing real red there. "I didn't put my money with no pious churchgoing son of a bitch in New York. I put it with you."

"Ben." Heaney was doing some real twitching there, like all over him. "Ben, you didn't hear me right. I put that money from your partnership in the bank and the bank invested it with Cooke to make big profits. *Big* profits."

"Mr. Heaney," I said, my voice all raspy. "You see that desk? You see what's lying on it?"

"I see it," Heaney said.

"Right," I said. "That there is a Colt six-shooter, and it's saying right now that if the bank don't pay me my money back, then the feller who put my money in it is. You got that?"

"I got it," Heaney said. "But it don't make no difference, Ben. I'm broke, too. Wiped out, and half the United States with us!"

And it was true, and I had to swallow it, although I took some persuading. Heaney took me to the bank and it was closed up. He even took me to meet some other businessmen, and they was cleaned out, too. Even Besser up in Abilene had gone broke! And the sodbusters, well, they was just ruined, is all. Ruined and getting forced off their land by creditors!

But I couldn't believe it, at that. Like when Bo was killed, I *knew* it was so, but as we went around the town, I kept thinking it was all a mistake. Okay, that goddamn Cooke had gone bust, and all the other fellers with him, but *my* money had got saved somehow.

It started to sink in, though, when I saw them busted businessmen with the steam gone out of them, and it sunk in more when we got back to the office and I looked at Heaney. He sure had been full of that get-up-and-go and noble daring and all, but there in the gloom, brother, he looked ninety-nine years old, his face caved in, his body all shrunk up, and his hands trembling so much the booze slopped all down his vest.

I'll tell you, if I hadn't been so sorry for myself, I might have been sorry for him and just left him to get sozzled and forget his cares and woes, but I'd got my own, and I drove at him again.

"Okay," I said. "That investment money has maybe gone with the wind"—still not *actually* believing it, you know?— "but what about the store and this feller Stokes?"

"Ha-ha." Heaney did some more of that ghastly laughing, then coughed, trying to pull himself together. He pawed at the papers, which was littered across his desk. "The thing is, Ben . . . that Stokes . . . well, he's right. Dodge has been platted out wrong, and you've got the store stuck on his land, and unless you pay that back rent, he's got a lien on it—that means he can keep it until you do pay the costly easements!"

"I just don't believe it," I said. "I just don't."

"It's the law, Ben," Heaney said.

"But that rent he wants—Christ Almighty!" I shouted. "It's . . . it's . . ."

"It's a lot," Heaney said, as if it was nothing to do with him.

"Goddamn it, it's more than I could pay in years!" I yelled—and then I got a notion! Yes, sir, I saw light at the end of the tunnel. "Say, if our plats are in the *wrong* place, we've got to have plats in the *right* place, ain't we? I mean, we've got to own *some* goddamn land there, and listen, we got shares in the Township Company!"

Brother, that light there in the darkness was getting brighter by the minute, but like the man said, he saw light at the end of that tunnel but it turned out to be a train coming right at him, because Heaney shook his head. Well, he shook it more, it shaking anyhow with all the booze.

"Ben," he croaked. "Ben." And I swear he was actually shrinking there, getting smaller as I looked at him. "Son, I bought them shares on time."

"What the hell does that mean?" I said, feeling I was starting to shrink myself.

"It means"—Heaney gave a grin like a skull—"it means I only put five percent down. Just being careful, Ben, looking after our interests, that's all. A deposit, you know? The rest to be paid . . . to be paid . . ."

"To be paid when?" Well, I asked, and I sounded like my mouth was stuck full of mud and gravel, but I guess I knew the answer before I asked the question.

"Yesterday," Heaney said.

He reached for the bottle again, and I don't know, I could have got the Colt and blown his head off, I guess, and one gets you a hundred there wasn't a court in the state but wouldn't have let me go free with a pat on the head, but what the hell was the point. And I was just weary, just plumb wore out and all sad. In fact, as he gulped and swigged at the bottle, I actually said, "Mr. Heaney, don't you reckon you ought to go easy on that booze?" And he just said, "What for?"

I didn't have no answer to that, so, while outside the riders whooped it up, wild as mustangs and free as birds, and some band blared away, me and old Heaney sat in the dusk in that ramshackle office, two all-American businessmen, busted. I stayed the night in that office, and the next day caught the westbound back to Dodge. There wasn't nothing to stay for in Newton, anyhow. The next morning Heaney explained about them costly easements, which was just fancy language for building on another man's land, and he wrote a letter which he said might bluff Stokes, although he didn't hold out much hope.

"But sell everything you can," he said.

"And then what do I do," I said. "Go on the lam?"

He winced, standing there in that clapboard office, which was falling apart, like him. "Just make out as best you can. And, Ben, you're using some awful bad language!"

I'd nothing to say to that, unless I used even worse language, so I said nothing. Just nothing at all.

He saw me off at the depot. "What do you aim to do?" I asked.

"Me?" He laughed that uncomical laugh. "Why, I reckon Dave Heaney has it in him to make another go of things. This is a big country, big enough for a feller to make ten fortunes. We'll both make out, Ben. Yes, sir!"

The locomotive bell rang and the conductor yelled that "All *aboooard.*"

"Remember that, Ben," Heaney said as I got on. "All you needs is get-up-and-go. Them's the words. *Get-up-and-go!*"

But he didn't look like a feller with get-up-and-go. He looked like a feller ready to lie down and stay there, him all shabby and shaking and covered with dust, and he got covered with a lot more before the month was over, because he went out on the prairie and blew his brains out.

I was feeling that way myself as the train hauled across the country, and by them God-awful sandy badlands beyond Hutchinson it had really sunk in I was broke. Real broke. Jupiter, just a few days ago I'd been making money like that old king, turning everything he touched into gold, and now I was back where I started, just a kid on the loose with no more to my name than the clothes on my back— and owing, too.

It got to dark and the country looked even gloomier, hundreds of miles of it without a light anyplace, and if there had, it would have been a bunch of thieves, although if they was plotting to rob any banks, they was in for a shock.

We got into Great Bend, and although I was longing for coffee and some grub, I didn't dare get off in case there was any creditors of mine hanging around the depot, and after we did jolt and lurch off, the train was full of drunks singing senseless songs and arguing over a poker game, so I couldn't even get no sleep, just dozing on and off, waking wondering where I was, then remembering my woes and feeling sick clear to my stomach, and I don't believe there was a more miserable creature in the entire United States of America, if not the whole goddamn world, when I got off at Dodge, and it was pouring down with rain, at that.

I sloshed to the store and it didn't make me no happier to see Brusik there, a mug of red-eye in his mitt, grinning at me all hopeful, and it took some hammering to get it in his skull that we was broke.

"But we was doing good," he kept saying. "Real good. You told me"—like as if it was my fault Cooke had failed, going over it again and again, his face getting redder and meaner, so I was real scared, like he could be a real tough feller.

"Anyways," I said in the end, "you don't believe me, send a wire to that brother of yours, only don't send it collect, because he's bust, too."

He brooded over that, muttering in foreign lingo, then said, "But what do we do? What do we do now?"

"Brusik," I said, "what I'm going to do is get some shut-eye." Then I ate a can of beans, cold, and hit the hay.

It was some nightmare night, too. I kept having crazy dreams about Heaney and Cooke and money, and when I woke, I felt like I'd been trampled on by ten galloping herds.

It was some sight I woke up to, as well. Brusik was lying

on the floor, a half bottle of our best whiskey by him, and an empty one, too, and him snoring fit to shake the joint down. I let him lay, made some coffee, and sat listening to that rain drumming down, and hoping it would keep on, like that flood old Noah made, so's it would wash all my cares away. But that coffee started bringing me back to life and I got to thinking, and what I thought made sense.

The way I thought was, I'd sell everything we had, even if it was at *less* than cost, which was real blasphemous, and with that and the cash I'd got under my bunk, I'd have quite a bankroll. Then I could light out before the creditors arrived, and make a new start someplace far away, maybe go prospecting up in the Black Hills, or—and it came to me like a bolt from the bright blue yonder—I could go to New York City and see old Henry! Maybe even start printing, like he did. As for Brusik, it was sad and all, but he'd just have to make his own way through life.

And that's where I made the biggest mistake of my life up till then. What I did was start daydreaming, excited you know, about going to that city and seeing Henry, playing with his new cat and maybe beating him at chess! Gee whillikers, I even got to thinking that maybe them preachers had got it right, the Lord working out His ways mysteriously and all, and that maybe right then He wasn't paying much heed to old Heaney and to Besser like He watched sparrows, but He was keeping an eye on Ben Curtis.

So, although it was real gloomy in the store, I got to feeling cheerful, and I was just about ready to go and get me a big buffalo steak for breakfast and start selling off the goods, when the door opened and in walked Stokes!

I jumped, startled, like I was guilty of something, and he didn't miss that, you bet, but he didn't say nothing about it, just sat down on the cracker barrel and lit a cigar.

"Heard you were back," he said. He peeked at Brusik

lying flat out, but not like it was a sight worth noticing, which it wasn't in Dodge, then picked up the whiskey bottle. "Shame to waste this."

"Help yourself," I said.

"That's civil of you." He took a swig. "Get to see that business advisor of yours?"

"You bet," I said. "He's a mighty smart feller. In fact, he gave me a letter for you."

"Well, that's just fine." Stokes took another swig. "I just admire getting mail. Let's see it."

I handed it over and he read it through slow, not like he had difficulty handling the ABCs but savoring it as might be, and reading some bits out loud.

"Claim ill-founded . . . equity . . . due process . . . *pertaining*, that's a good word. Press with *diligence*—a real ten-dollar word, that. Therefore, claim denied . . . hmm, counterclaim ensuing." He finished reading and stuck the letter in his pocket. "That's some legal advisor you've got."

"Just the best there is in Kansas," I said. "Ask anyone."

"Yeah." Stokes looked at the bottle, saw it was empty, and went behind the bar, casual as might be, and got himself another.

"Remember whose store this is, mister," I said, tough as all get-out.

"Sure will," Stokes said. "I hope I know my manners." He opened the bottle and squinted at me through it. "Pity that legal advisor of yours has gone broke!"

"How the Sam Hill—" I stopped, but it was too late and didn't make no difference.

"Telegraph works both ways," Stokes said. "Anyhow, son, we've cut enough bait. Let's get down to fishing."

That suited me okay. He was going to make me an offer for the store, I just knew it. That letter, you know? He was being bluffed out of the hand. "Sure," I said. "Make me an offer and we'll see how them fish is biting."

312

Stokes smiled. "That's fine, I guess, but it isn't what I had in mind. I was thinking you'd be making me an offer!"

My jaw dropped so, I guess it hit the floor, leastways there was a thud, but that might have been my heart dropping clear to my boots, and then through them, heading for whatever was on the other side of the world. "Me?" I said.

"I reckon," Stokes said. "Son, you don't seem to have got the message. This store is mine, and everything in it. Course, if you're ready to pay, why, you can have it right back."

"If this is some sort of joke," I said, "I don't see nothing comical about it."

"It ain't no joke." Stokes had stopped smiling. "Why, I hardly ever joke about money."

"But that letter," I began.

"That letter don't mean a thing," Stokes said. "And you know it, and I know it, and whoever wrote it knows it, too. If you want to go to court, that's your affair. But, as of now, you're out."

"Mister," I said, and I was shaking with rage. "Mister, I ain't going, and if you try and make me, I'll—"

"You aren't going to do anything," Stokes said. "You're busted. But I'm not a hard man"—which would have fooled me—"so I'll give you fifty dollars so's you can have some elbow room."

He stared at me and I stared at him, and he looked cool and I felt hot.

"I ain't going," I said. "I ain't. I've starved most of my goddamn life and I ain't going to starve again. And, mister, when he wakes up"—pointing to Brusik—"you're going to wish you'd never heard of them goddamn easements."

Stokes sighed and gave that whiskey bottle a little ping with his finger. "Son, it's a hard world for us pilgrims, and I've done some starving myself. But out you go. And as for

313

that buffalo there, why, I've handled bulls like him before and I reckon I can do it again. And what I can't handle, I know fellers who can. Now, are you going?"

"No," I said. "I ain't."

"Okay." Stokes sighed like there was some tedious chore to be done. "Come in," he called, and in walked two men. "Guess you know these boys?"

I did. One was Jack Bridges and the other was Levi Richardson, who was one of the meanest men in town, a killer— and he *had* killed.

"Jack here," Stokes said, "he's a Deputy United States Marshal. You know that?"

I surely didn't and said so.

"Show your warrant, Jack," Stokes said.

Jack looked at me somewhat apologetic, but took out a warrant, and it was a real one, leastways as far as I could tell.

I laughed, bitter-like. "Jeepers," I said. "The law! There ain't been none when there's fellers been getting murdered, but when it comes to evicting an innocent businessman who's an orphan, too, why—"

"Save it," Stokes said. "Here's your money. Out, *now*."

There wasn't nothing for it but to go. Stokes let me take my belongings, but he was right behind me when I got them out of the dugout, and that's where I'd made that mistake. There wasn't no way I could get my dough out of there without him seeing, and he sure wasn't going to let me walk out with it. Yeah, while I'd been doing that foolish daydreaming about Henry and New York City, I should have been digging up the dollars.

So I had to go, and they threw Brusik out after me, him being so drunk he didn't know what was happening, and that was it. Amazing, ain't it? I'd lost the store and them dollars and there wasn't one blamed thing I could do about that goddamn situation.

Course, I told the fellers, thinking they'd take Stokes out for a prairie tea party, but would they ever! Charlie Rath told me that if that Stokes had been a robber they'd have seen to him soon enough, but his doings being all legal, they couldn't see their way to helping out. Anyhow, they'd got problems of their own with them plats, them *all* being mixed up and half the town claiming costly easements off the other half! And he told me something else.

We was in Hermann Fringer's drugstore. Charlie and Hermann had both been over to see Stokes a second time, seeing if he'd hand me some more cash, which he wouldn't, not a dime! And Hermann, he said, "Kid, Stokes showed us your accounts, and you sure owe a powerful lot of money."

"Yeah," I said. "But I've a lot of money owing *me*."

"That's so," Hermann allowed. "But them fellers that owe you money aren't exactly going to come looking for you, are they? Whereas them fellers you owe money to *is*. Get me?"

"So what?" I said. "It don't make no difference to me. I ain't *got* no money."

"Uh-huh," Charlie grunted, and Hermann stared at a bottle of Professor Blitzstein's Miracle Cure-All for a while. Then Frank said, "The thing is, kid, those creditors of yours, they might be . . . well . . . het up. And the truth is . . . well . . . if I was you, I'd rather be someplace else, is all."

That's what he said, and I knew what he meant—after he'd spelled it out for me—and after he'd done that, if I could have done what he advised, I would have. But there was them dollars under the store. I wasn't going to leave them, no, sir, but I couldn't see no way of getting at them, neither. Moses, didn't I curse myself for not digging them up! But cursing made no difference, and it made no difference to Brusik, neither, although he cursed non-stop when he came to. That's what I was told, anyways, because I

315

made sure that where he was, I wasn't, if you see what I mean, although why he should have been mad at me I didn't get. It was Jay Cooke, or Stokes, or Heaney he should have been mad at, but the one time I tried to explain it to him he said he was going to pull off my arms and legs and ram them down my throat. Just unreasonable.

That was the fork I was pronged on. If I stayed in Dodge, then if it wasn't Brusik, someone else was going to do what he wanted to, but if I beat it, I knew I could kiss them dollars goodbye, I just knew it. But after I'd mooched around town for a couple of days, that problem got solved for me, although—and I don't want to sound ungrateful—it was an answer I just didn't want to hear.

I was in Hermann's store, and he was beginning to look at me like he wished I'd find someplace else to spend my time, when Sam Dawson came in. He was that hunter who'd said he'd teach me the business when I first got to Dodge, and he was one hard hombre, but straight. He bought some medicine off Hermann and chewed the fat for a while, then beat it. As he was leaving, he jerked his head at me, like saying come outside. I followed him, being glad to talk to anyone them days, and knowing for sure I didn't owe *him* nothing.

"I hear you got yourself in some kind of trouble," he said.

"Sam"—I was real exasperated and put him right—"*I* didn't get myself in trouble. That goddamn Jay Cooke got me in it. Him and that goddamn engineer who laid out the plats for this town and got it wrong, and it's a wonder he didn't get the railroad running the wrong way. *Them's* the ones who got me in trouble."

"Yeah?" Sam didn't sound too believing. "Well, whichever way, what are you aiming to do?"

"I'll tell you the truth," I said. "I just don't know."

Sam looked hard at me. "I'll tell you, kid. I'm going out

316

hunting again in a few days more. If you want, you can come along. I'll pay you."

"Me?" I said. "Hunting!"

"No." Sam shook his head. "Not unless you've got a hundred and fifty bucks for a Sharps. I do the hunting, and you—"

"Now hold on, Sam." I did some cutting in. "I appreciate your offer, I sure do, but skinning . . ."

"Not skinning." Sam shook his head. "I *got* two skinners. What I want is someone to cook and look after the mules and what have you. Hell, you know the score."

I did, at that. I knew what I'd be doing was being like a slave, is what, but I didn't say so, because there was something in that offer. If I went with Sam, I was out of town but handy, and making some money. But there was a little question I needed to ask, and I did. "Why me?" I said.

"I ain't playing no nanny to you, if that's what you're thinking," Sam said. "The way of it is, I know you. Get me?"

I did, too. There was some things didn't need spelling. Out there in the real wilderness, with just two skinners for company, it was mighty comforting to have someone to look after your back—if you could get someone to do it, that is.

"What happened to your regular cook?" I asked.

"Gone mining," Sam said.

I pretended to be doing some pondering, but I'd made up my mind. It was paid work, it fitted the bill, I knew Sam, and there was worse fellers than him roaming around, so I took it on.

"Okay," I said. "What the hell."

"Yeah," Sam said. "What the hell, at that."

So a few days later I was on a big Conestoga wagon, lashing away at four giant Missouri mules, with two ter-

317

rible mean-looking fellers on the tailgate, Sam riding a big strong bay mare leading the way, splashing across the Arkansas and heading for the range where the buffalo roamed, not to mention the Comanche and the Kiowa and Cheyenne and about a million other fellers with feathers in their hair. Yes, sir, it was like the settlers' motto right enough: "In God we trusted, in Kansas we busted," and ride on, brother.

KILLING TIMES

▪ TWENTY-NINE ▪

So it was away, boys, away over the Arkansas River, and out to where the buffalo roamed, but we didn't wander across the Plains at random. We hunted the creeks where them buffalo liked to drink and wallow in the mud, or the salt licks, because they liked salt now and then, and when Sam had found his targets, we'd make a camp and be in business.

It was a piteous business, at that. Sam would set up a tripod and mount his big Sharps .50 rifle, sort out the leader of the herd, which a feller with his experience could do, shoot it through the lights, and it would simply flop over. Them other buffalo would mill around and Sam would shoot another, then another—a stand was what it was called, and them buffalo was just too dumb to get the message, so's they'd browse around until there wasn't none left standing.

I don't know why, but buffalo didn't pay much heed to a man on foot, so they didn't charge you, and that Sharps, it had a deep mellow boom, soothing almost, so it didn't startle the creatures. And that rifle, it could kill at an amazing distance, eight hundred yards, easy. In fact, you could kill a man a mile off, which is why the Indians said it fired today and killed tomorrow, so it was safe for the hunter. Them buffalo just didn't know what hit them, and it was about as dangerous and exciting as shooting cows in a farmyard would have been.

Then the skinning started. Course, I'd seen skinning before, most everything from a jackrabbit to a steer, but skinning them buffalo was something else entirely.

Them skinners slashed around the throat, the belly, and the legs, then hitched the mule to the hide, and ripped it off. But it wasn't that which was sickening so much, it being just a chore, but what was left, them mountains of flesh rotting away with their heads still on.

It sure was gruesome, and you could get the feeling that them heads was looking at you all reproachful, and that ain't as fanciful as it might sound. The buffalo, they just didn't seem ordinary creatures like deer or cattle. The Indians worshipped them. Maybe because they lived off them, but I ain't sure there wasn't more to it than that. You saw them, especially against the light—black, with huge shaggy heads, pawing and grunty—and they was like creatures from out of a dream, unearthly, you know? And out there, under the vast skies, why, I don't know but what anyone could have got around to worshipping them.

But creatures from dreams or not, a couple of ounces of lead knocked them over so's they wouldn't never get up again, and more cash went into the bank.

Course, them two bozos with us did the actual skinning, but I had to help get the hides back to camp and scrape them, which was disgusting, too, with all them gobbets of fat and flesh to get rid of. Then we'd got to peg them out— and if Sam had been lucky, we'd have *acres* covered with them—and douse them with poison against bugs, the which maybe stopped them having lunch off the skins but headed them our way. They just covered us, you know. Goddamn, it was like being *dressed* in bugs, and most of them were bad enough stinging and biting and chewing at you, but them screwflies, jeepers, if you was unlucky, they could lay their eggs in you and then, well, it don't need spelling out.

There wasn't no peace by day or night. In fact, it was worse at night because them skinners would be in camp with us. The thing was, not every feller would do that chore, and them that would tended to be what you might call walking horrors, and the two we'd got wasn't no exception.

One of them, Pike, was straight half-witted, and his partner wasn't exactly 100 percent in the brain-box department either, but he was crazy in a different kind of way. He was called Red Dog, would you believe, although it ought to have been Mad Dog. But them scalawags all had nicknames, mainly because they didn't dare use their real ones, them probably being on a wanted poster someplace, but maybe also because they was turning away from being human beings with human names, or, I've got to say, like bums and hoboes I've lived with—having nothing, they pined to have something no one else had, and a nickname was all there was going.

But be that as it may, them two fellers was terrible, talking about women like *they* was animals, and killings, and things they'd done to Indians, or said they'd done, and which was truly awful, like nothing I'd ever heard of nor even dreamed of, and which, even if they'd never done them things, showed what was in their minds. And I had to cook for them! Me, who'd had his own business!

You know, it was clear weather then, in the late fall, crystal clear, and the sky at night, why, you couldn't have begun to guess how many stars there was glittering away. I'd always liked the stars, wondering what they was really and whether there was folks like us on them, working and worrying and maybe getting busted by a bank. Down in Clement, I'd looked out for them, and on the trail, too, them all friendly, like they was neighbors calling in for a visit. But them nights out there, they was more like the cold eyes of a gambler or lawman, staring you down and not giving one goddamn what happened to you. And them huge buffalo wolves howling out in the dark didn't help make things more homely, neither.

But them clear days and nights slipped away and we started getting rain, which sure made things cozy, and then, one miserable, soaking afternoon, we was hauling over a long swell, and we heard a gunshot.

Me and them skinners looked at each other, and for all their tough talk, they looked as scared as I felt, because that shot didn't come from no Sharps. It was a rifle, sure, but then some of the fellers out there that used other types of rifles wasn't the type to say come into the tepee and have a drink.

Sam had his horse reined in, and he'd got his head cocked, listening. Then that rifle cracked again.

"You boys stay here," he said. "I'll go take a peek."

He moved up the swell and climbed off his horse just below the skyline and moved forward on foot. I was licking my lips, which had gone dry for some reason, when Sam lifted his hat and waved it in a big circle, meaning okay, come on up, which we did, feeling one million times better.

By the time we reached the skyline, Sam had mounted and ridden on down into a shallow draw, and it was kind of hard to figure out what was going on. He was talking to a couple of fellers who was throwing their arms, like there was some kind of argument going on. So, thinking if I looked out for him, he'd look out for me, I got the shotgun out and slogged down to him, and it was baffling at that, because down the draw was a rig, like an old buggy that would have had trouble making it down Texas Street, Abilene, and an old horse that didn't have long to suffer. And if I was baffled, so was Sam, who was talking to them fellers, who was gaunt and yellowy-faced, wearing battered old hats and old U.S. Army greatcoats.

"Hunting?" Sam was saying. "You're hunting buffalo?

Starving is what you're going to do. Starve and freeze to death."

"Mister," one of them fellers said, "starving and freezing is what we was looking at where we come from."

"And where might that have been?" Sam asked.

"Grant County," the feller said. "We was farming but got wiped out, them banks failing and all, so we come out here."

Sam shook his head. "Do you know what you're letting yourself in for? How in Sam Hill do you think you'll get through the winter?"

"Same as back home," the other feller said. "Make a dugout."

"And you're going for buffalo with them?" Sam pointed at the weapons them two was carrying, one being an old Springfield rifle and the other some kind of bird gun. "You'll wing fifty animals before you get one kill."

"Yeah," the first feller said. "Well, that'll be money in our pockets, which is more than we get anyplace else."

Sam sucked his teeth. "You know there's Indians out here . . ."

The second feller laughed, except he wasn't laughing, if you get me. "We got skinned by white men, so we'll take a chance on them red men." He stared at Sam real sharp. "You're doing a lot of warning, mister. You wouldn't be aiming to warn us off this here prairie, would you? Because this here land don't belong to no one, nor do them buffalo."

"I wouldn't say no different," Sam said.

"Okay, then," the feller said.

"Okay." Sam climbed on his horse. "Best of luck. By Jesus, you're going to need it."

We moved on, Sam shaking his head, and it was something to shake your head about, them two farmers, busted like I'd been, struggling to make a living out of buffalo, which was like me, too, but I was out with a real outfit and a feller who knew what he was doing. But them two, Jupiter! Spending a winter out there with that rig!

Not that I was looking forward to it neither, and I looked forward to it less as we sloshed around, the weather getting worser, sleet and hail lashing at us, and them hides all soggy and even more disgusting. I got down to brooding, thinking how I could get my money out of the store. Then I got a notion. It wasn't the best of them brain waves I got, but it was better than nothing, and I was just about ready to take a chance and hand in my time, when that brain wave got knocked right out of my head.

We'd got pretty far south, heading toward where there was a creek Sam knew of, along which plenty of buffalo liked to pass the time, and Sam could sit behind some old cottonwood and knock them off, easy as kiss your hand, when who should roll up but Charlie Rath.

He'd gone into buying hides, and like some of them agents, he'd come out buying and bringing supplies, which saved us hunters a long haul into Dodge or Adobe Walls or wherever.

Charlie had come with a string of wagons and some roughneck teamsters all hung around with knives and pistols, and them and our skinners tapped a barrel of lightning juice Charlie had brought out, and indulged in genteel conversation, such as who'd stabbed who in Dodge. I rustled up some coffee and took it to Sam and Charlie, who was shaking hands on a deal, and if you'd heard the price you'd have known why business out there was done that way, because if Sam had got the cash, me and him might have lasted five minutes after Charlie hauled out, but I doubt it, because Sam had knocked over more than two hundred buffalo in the month we'd been out—at $1.50 a hide.

They gulped their coffee down, then Charlie opened a bottle of genuine Kentucky bourbon he happened to have on him, and we three settled down to chew the fat, talking of the big wide world and how much money we could make out of it, and Charlie mentioned that goddamn Jay Cooke.

"Sure hit the farmers," Charlie said. "Fellers getting foreclosed and losing their land. It's happening all over the country."

"Yeah." Sam savored that bourbon like it was liquid gold. "We met a couple of hayseeds sometime back."

"Scrawny fellers," Charlie said, "with a broken-down horse and buggy?"

"That's them," Sam said. "How was they doing?"

"Doing!" Charlie burst out laughing. "Jesus, they was doing as good as a one-legged man in a swamp. I ain't seen nothing like it since the war. They'd got but a hatful of flour left, no beans, no pork, no coffee. They eat any more buffalo hump, Christ, they'll have horns growing out of their goddamn heads."

He laughed again, and Sam laughed with him, but not what you'd call wholehearted.

"They get any hides?" he asked.

Charlie pursed his lips, like he didn't want to do no hasty judging. "Yeah . . . I'd say so. Some all riddled, and some so badly cured they looked like a coyote had gnawed at them. But they had some I bought. I got to say, though, it's a good job there's plenty of buffalo because there sure is plenty of fellers out hunting, you know?"

"Sure." Sam agreed, but he looked mighty thoughtful, and his expression didn't change much even when Charlie broke out another bottle.

The boys made a night of it, there being general agreement that one moon wasn't enough, two was better, but if you stuck at the red-eye long enough, you'd get to see three, which meant bedtime. So there was some sore heads the next morning, but we got the rest of the hides stuck on Charlie's wagons.

Then Charlie mounted his pony. "See you next time around," he said. "Oh, Sam, you ain't seen . . ." And he made a funny kind of gesture, putting his hand on his belly, then wriggling it up to his chest.

Sam looked annoyed, although why beat me. "Nothing like that," he said.

"Okay." Charlie walked his pony a few steps. Then, like it was a day for doing curious things, he pulled up and called me over. "I got something to tell you, kid," he said.

They say hope keeps jumping up in the human breast, or some such poeticizing, and I felt mighty hopeful when Charlie said that, thinking he was maybe going to give me some good news, like maybe Stokes had got shot dead and I could have the store back. In fact, that hope was welling right out of my ears, but when I heard what he had to say, jeepers, it just welled right back again.

"Kid," he said, "it ain't no business of mine, but I ought to tell you. There's a feller been asking about you in Dodge." He bit a chunk of tobacco off a plug and leaned down, all confidential. "Thing is, kid, that feller, he's making out to be all innocent, but he's a Pinkerton man!"

"A Pink—asking for me?" I yelped. "What in hell for? I ain't no Anarch. All I do is owe some money."

"Sure," Charlie said. "But that agent, he's been asking about other fellers in the same boat."

I laughed, all bitter. "It don't make no difference, nohow. I ain't got no money, so if he finds me, it won't do him no good."

Charlie spat out a big stream of tobacco juice. "Kid," he said, "it ain't like that. Them money men don't like bad debtors wandering around loose. It gives other folks ideas. They get you, well, they might stick you in the pen."

"Goddamn," I said. "It's that Jay Cooke ought to be there."

"Maybe," Charlie said. "But ain't nobody said where you are. They ain't going to turn you in, there being no reward for you. Even Stokes kept his mouth shut."

"So he goddamn should," I said. "Seeing as how he stole my store off me."

"It's a point," Charlie admitted. "Anyhow, kid, the word is, stick it out here until the heat's off."

He rode off, and, brother, was I cheerful! Stick it out there! Jupiter, I could be on the run forever, just like I'd said to Bo back in Lookout, wandering in the wilderness for forty years, and even then, waiting on the other side of Jordan would be a goddamn Pinkerton man to stick me in the pen. I was blue as can be, and that brain wave of mine, for getting my money out of the store, why, it just dried up, is all. And it started to rain!

I walked back to our rig, where Sam was mounting up to go looking for buffalo, and then something clicked.

"Sam," I said, holding the bridle of his horse. "That wriggling your fingers, what Charlie did with you there. What was it?"

"It ain't none of your business," Sam said.

"Okay," I said. "Just seemed funny, is all. Making them signs—oh!" I looked up at Sam. "Oh, signs. That was an Indian sign."

"So, what of it?" Sam tried to swing his horse away, but I hung on to the reins.

"You seen Indians?" I asked.

Sam cursed under his breath. "Keep your voice down," he said. "You want to scare them two skinners off?"

Jeepers, scare them off! It was me that was scared, and I said so.

"Okay," Sam said. "I saw some Arapahoe a week back."

"Arapahoe," I said.

"Sure." Sam pulled his hat down against the rain. "Nothing to worry about. Hell, they're more civilized than them two"—jerking his head toward the skinners.

Brother, I thought, that ain't saying much. And civilized—the way Sam was talking, you'd have thought them Arapahoe was going to start giving opera concerts. But it wasn't them worried me.

"But that sign," I said. "That Arapahoe?"

Sam cursed again, but I guess he knew I wasn't going to let go of the reins till I'd got a straight answer, so he half turned so the others couldn't see him.

"That"—he did that wriggling sign again—"that's Comanche—*don't jump*, for Christ's sake. I ain't one. They worship snakes, cunning, and striking without no warning, and that sign is a snake. But hell, I ain't seen none. They don't wander up this far."

"Then why did Charlie ask you?" I said.

Sam looked real mad. "Jesus, did you never get told it ain't smart to ask too many questions. He just asked, is all. Now let go them reins or I'll . . ." And he didn't need to say no more.

Moses, that was some day. My brain wave busted, Pinkerton men after me, maybe goddamn Comanche roaming around . . . I said I was in a wilderness, and goddamn it, I was, and I was being kept right in the n iddle of it by folks I'd never even clapped eyes on!

They was some thoughts there, pressing on me all the time, so I didn't pay hardly no heed at all to what was going on around me, just doing the chores and trying to ignore them skinners, but as the days wore on, I started to heed them, the reason being they was doing a lot of bickering and arguing. Course, that was as normal for them as snarling is to dogs, them not being able to speak like human beings, but the way they was going on was getting worser and worser.

I heard them one day, out on a skinning ground where Sam had made a big killing. Pike was whining away about how he was doing all the work, and Red Dog was snarling back at him.

"Shut your goddamn mouth," he said. "I ain't feeling so good with this goddamn bellyache."

That figured, living out there and bellyaches going naturally together, what with bad water and worse grub, but he didn't look so good at that, kind of green under his sunburn, and when he was eating that night, I noticed he couldn't hardly get his hands to his mouth, they was shaking so much—and he was a feller who ate *with* his hands.

He wasn't no better the next morning, neither, and wouldn't get out of the tent, so I had to go out with Pike, which made me mad. Sam had moved on, but there was some hunters not far off, and we could hear their Sharps booming, so I wasn't too worried right then about Comanche.

We worked till dark, then beat it back. Sam was already in camp, taking his ease, which was a mighty fine way to live if you'd got enough dough to lay out on an outfit. There wasn't no sign of Red Dog, but I rustled up some grub, just mush, fat, and beans, which we crammed down, and I was getting coffee when Red Dog crawled out of his tent.

I didn't pay no heed, thinking maybe he was feeling better, when he kneeled up and, goddamn, he had a pistol in his hand!

Jupiter, we stared at him, thinking he'd gone crazy, or crazier, I should say, because as well as waving that six-shooter he was muttering and cursing, real bad ones, too.

The truth was, none of us knew what to do, saving get as far away as we could, but the way Red Dog was waving that pistol about, we was too scared to move, in case we caught his eye, you know.

But someone had to do something and Sam tried. "What the hell is this?" he said. "You having a nightmare? Put that gun down."

That's what he said, but I guess he wished he hadn't, because Red Dog swung on him, holding that pistol with both hands.

"You son of a bitch," he croaked. "You thieving son of a bitch. You think you can kick me around? You got another think coming. Pike, get the shotgun. We'll finish these two off and get rich!"

Well, I don't know about Red Dog having a nightmare, but it sure was like I was. That crazy feller there, waving that gun, and the firelight flickering on him like a picture out of them religious books, showing the sort of place it seemed me and Sam was about to visit.

"Pike!" Red Dog shouted. "You do as I say, you goddamn mule, or I'll let you have it, too."

Pike moaned, as scared as the rest of us. Then Sam said, "You do as he says!"

I figured we'd got two crazy fellers when Sam said that, but I figured wrong because when Pike stood up, his legs all wobbling, Red Dog looked at him, taking his eyes off me, and I let him have the coffee in his face. That coffee wasn't boiling, and I wouldn't have wanted to throw it if it had been, but it was hot and it sprayed his eyes long enough for Sam to jump over that fire like a goddamn kangaroo, kick the gun out of his hand, and give him a bang on the head that sent him flying, and before he hit the ground, *I'd* got the shotgun and was covering Pike, just in case.

Pike's hands went up so high he was near grabbing the moon, and he did it like he had some practice, and while he was shouting, "Don't shoot! Don't shoot!" Red Dog was moaning on the ground, and Sam was cursing like blue blazes.

"What in hell's going on here?" he roared, and would you believe, Pike got down on his knees, praying! Praying for his life!

"Wasn't me," he gabbled. "I swear to God it wasn't"— jabbering away until Sam said if he didn't shut up he'd get shut up, permanent.

Red Dog was out, but we tied him up all the same, then got to work on Pike, and from what we could get out of him, Red Dog had wanted the two of them to kill us, then take the outfit and hides down south to Fort Supply.

Sam heard him out, then said, real grim, "You didn't let on, did you?"

Pike was stammering so bad he couldn't hardly speak, but he did some more piteous pleading, ending up saying, "I didn't pay no heed to him. You know how fellers talk. And, sweet Jesus, I didn't help him, did I? I didn't *do* nothing."

Well, he hadn't, and that was a fact, and I guess Sam believed him because he let him be and went to look at Red Dog, and one look was enough to tell you he wouldn't be no trouble for a while. He sure looked sick, and it wasn't just that bang on the head, neither. He was twitching real violent, and his face was a funny color. But Sam wasn't taking no chances. We dragged that feller over to the wagon and lashed him against a wheel, chucking a robe over him.

Then Sam turned on Pike. "Get in your tent," he said, "And, by Jesus, I hear you so much as breathe, I'll put a load of buckshot in you."

Pike cowered away and just dived into the tent. Then I made more coffee, and me and Sam sat around the fire, sticking some whiskey in the drink.

"The crazy son of a bitch," Sam said. "Pulling a stroke like that, and me near taken for a sucker." He brooded for a while, real mad, then said, "You did all right there, kid.

If you hadn't been quick, Christ knows what would have happened."

I reckoned I'd done pretty good, too, but I just shrugged, like there hadn't been nothing to it. "What are you going to do with him?"

"I'll think about that tomorrow," Sam said.

"And Pike?"

"Him." Sam was contemptuous. "I reckon he was telling the truth for the first time in his life. Anyhow, he sure ain't going to try no fancy strokes on his own. Turn in, anyways. We got things to do tomorrow."

That tomorrow was another dreary morning, gray and windy, with big clouds scudding over, and cold. Not real icy, but that thin cold you got with winter heading your way, and I was glad to get by the fire, which Pike had made up, and get me some coffee, which he'd made up, too, him jumping, ready to do anything you wanted. Jumping and cringing.

I got warmed up some, then went to the wagon, where Sam was looking at Red Dog, and, jeepers, wasn't he in a state. That twitching was worse, and there was black stuff coming out of the side of his mouth.

"What is it?" I asked.

Sam shook his head and turned to Pike, who was lurking behind us. "He get bitten, do you know, by a skunk maybe?"

"He didn't never say so," Pike said.

"Then it ain't that hydrophobism," Sam said. "Lucky for him." He lit a stogie. "Could be that poison off the hides. I've seen it before, but never as bad as this. Usually you just get a bellyache, but this feller, you've seen the way he eats, and never washing . . . Well, let's dose him."

He rummaged in the wagon and got some medicine and whiskey.

"That make him right?" Pike asked.

"How in hell do I know," Sam said. "I ain't no saw-bones."

He mixed the stuff up, and that medicine, it was powerful stuff. I'd tried it once, and it was enough to blow your head off, although it made you mighty sleepy afterwards.

"Here," Sam said, holding it out to Pike. "Stick it down him."

"Me!" Pike was shaking near as bad as Red Dog.

"He was your buddy, wasn't he?" Sam yelled. "Now do it or—"

He didn't need to finish, Pike being more scared of Sam than that sickness. That skinner leaned forward, keeping as far off as he could, pouring about a quart of the mixture down Red Dog's throat and near choking him to death.

"Okay." Sam stepped back. "Let's have breakfast."

I went down to the creek and washed my hands, and didn't I wash them, too. I scrubbed them so hard there wasn't hardly any skin left on them, scared of that poison, you know? And Sam made Pike do the same, him not having the sense to do it on his own. Then we had the grub, and that medicine was real good stuff, because by the time we'd finished eating, Red Dog was sleeping like a babe.

"Okay," Sam said. "Stick him in the tent, and let's get some work done."

Pike went to get the rig, and Sam looked at me. "We got a little problem here," he said. "I'm a skinner short."

"I kind of noticed that," I said, sarcastical and knowing what was coming.

"Okay." Sam was mollifying. "I know you didn't hire out as one, but how's about it?"

"Gee," I said. "I don't know about that. Skinning . . ."

"Don't let that poison bother you," Sam said. "It don't hardly ever happen if you're careful."

"Maybe," I said. "I just never figured on being a skinner, is all."

"I never figured being no buffalo hunter, neither," Sam said. "I was heading for California when I got here. But what do you say?"

"It ain't a job I care for," I said.

"It ain't a job anyone would, with any sense. I don't care much for killing buffalo, neither, but it's a job and it pays. Look, I'll get another skinner as soon as I can—and I'll do some cooking."

I took my time answering. Not that I was going to turn him down, because there wasn't nothing else for me to do, not and stay anywhere near Dodge and them pickle jars. But I figured if I played hard to get, why, I'd get a raise, and I did at that, twenty cents a hide instead of fifteen, so I said I'd stick it out and started on a whole new career. As a goddamn skinner.

▪ THIRTY ▪

I said we was in a wilderness, but it was more like being dragged into a swamp, what with that slime and blood, the terrible sucking noise them hides made when they was tore off, rain sweeping across that desolation so we was never really dry, and listening to Red Dog moaning and vomiting. He was dying, is what, just dying, while we dragged him across the prairie, and the truth is, all we wanted was for him to get that dying over and done with, so's we could get rid of him.

Terrible, ain't it? But that's the way it was, and it's sure the way I was. What the hell was that feller to me? Just a bum who'd tried to kill us and who was probably wanted for murder and torture in a dozen places. Anyway, there wasn't nothing more we could do for him, and we'd got enough on our hands, being a skinner short.

In any case, all I'd got on my mind was them Pinkerton men—and them twenty cents a hide. I sure drove at that skinning, not letting myself ease up, nor Pike neither. Every buffalo Sam shot we was going to skin and cure, every last one. In fact, it got so I was resentful if Sam took time off, because that meant so many less cents for me.

Pike made a feeble protest one day, saying we was doing too much work, but I drove him down. And I made him do all the dirty work, spilling out the entrails and guts, and I made him do the dousing with that poison, you bet. He tried to protest about that, too, but I'd got the whip hand over him, not that there was much in that. One stamp and he scuttled, and if you don't know the type, go in any bar on the wrong side of the tracks in your town and you'll get acquainted with them. Course, you might get acquainted with the type who make *you* scuttle, which is a different story.

Then Red Dog died. We'd had our grub, and Pike went to give him the medicine, and as it went down him, he gave a big snort and he'd cashed in his chips, and the only things we felt was relief he'd beat it for good and resentment about having to dig a grave, and it wouldn't have taken that much for us just to leave him out there.

But we did—dig a grave, that is—and wrapped him in a blanket, and I'll bet there wasn't one of us who didn't think it was a waste of a good covering, and rolled him in. I guess Sam thought he had to say something, so he mumbled the Lord's Prayer, and then he said, "Well, I guess you've skipped some judges in your time, but you're going to meet one you can't skip. So long, whatever in Sam Hill your name was."

Pike filled in the hole, we stuck some buffalo horns on as a marker, and the next day broke camp and moved on.

We drifted south, following a long, winding creek, heading south same as the geese, which were coming down, honking across the sky, and I wouldn't have minded flying with them at that, because the weather sure was turning, the rain at times being more like flying ice. But Sam, he went out every day now, rain or not, us having found some rich pickings there, and me and Pike hacked and slashed, and I was looking forward to the stage where I could turn my credits into cash, when Charlie rolled up again.

We was sure glad to see him, it being as how we was getting low on grub, and glad to see other human faces, too, and old Rath there, he brought out newspapers and magazines for us to while away the hours.

There was the usual whoop-up, but I got hold of Charlie and asked him how things were with that little problem of mine back in Dodge.

"Why," he said, "that Pinkerton feller, he's gone. But that don't mean your owings have gone with him. If I was you, kid, I'd stay out here a while longer. In fact, I'd stay out as long as you can. What the hell, you're making a living. Anyhow"—he gave me a sharp look—"just what in hell do you want to go back for? If I was you, I'd forget the place. It's a big country, use it."

It was an awkward question, about going back, because I didn't aim to tell him about that money I'd got buried and which was part of the notion I'd had which he'd knocked out of my head the last time he was out, and I was trying to think of a believable lie when he laughed.

"You ain't in love, are you? Got your eye on Nell Saintclair?"

I blushed and he guffawed and moseyed back to Sam to settle the accounts, and he was still guffawing at me next morning. Some of them fellers sure did have a simple sense of humor. But he stopped laughing when he told Sam he'd try and find a feller ready and willing to come out and share the work.

"See you next time around, boys," he said. "The Lord and the weather willing." And him and his men got them big bull teams moving.

And then I played a little card from the bottom of the deck, me having been doing some thinking during the night. "Did I hear him say next time around?" I asked.

"Yeah," Sam said. "Why?"

"That'll be kind of late in the year, won't it?" I asked.

"So?" Sam stood there, the hail bouncing off his face and him not flinching, like he was made of rock.

"So, when are we going back in?" I said.

Sam rolled his stogie around his mouth, and it was a miracle how he could keep it alight in that weather. "Talk about it tonight," he said.

"Okay," I said. "Tonight."

He rode off, scouting for buffalo, while we got to work turning hides until dusk, when Sam came back in, made some grub, us now sharing the chores, and called it a day. Pike crawled into his tent and me and Sam got in ours. Sam had a bottle of good Kentucky whiskey Rath had brought along, and he stuck some in his coffee, lit a cigar, and leaned back, making himself real comfortable, which I kindly allowed him to, before I said, "About what we was saying this morning."

"That," Sam said. "What about it."

"I asked when we was going in someplace," I said. "Seeing as how it's nearly winter."

Sam didn't answer, lying back there with his whiskey and cigar, and I got somewhat exasperated. "We is going back, ain't we?" I said. "I mean, you don't intend spending the rest of your life wandering around out here."

"No." Sam allowed he didn't. "But here is where the

buffalo is, so now's the time to make money." He poured some more whiskey into his coffee, being a moderate sort of feller. "You want out?"

"Well, I sure don't want to lose my hands and feet with frostbite," I said.

Sam snorted. "Won't be like that. Them fellers that get hurt that way, they're just foolish. No, come real bad weather, we hole up."

"Hole up!" I said.

"Yeah." Sam was a mite testy. "It ain't what you think at all. There's a creek I know where I got me a dugout, lived in it all last winter. Good range there, plenty of buffalo. Clear days, we go out working. Bad days, we stay in there all snug."

I snorted then. "Snug! I lived in a dugout when I first got to Dodge. If that's snug living, I've got two heads."

"This dugout is fine," Sam said. "All lined with hides, and I got a regular stove and a bunk"—going on making that hole in the ground sound like a goddamn king's palace out there on the prairie, while I thought, Jeepers, Sam, you're in the wrong business. You ought to be a newspaper editor, because he could have given old Vear Porter Wilson points. "Hell, what's your aim in life, anyways?" he ended.

"Keeping on living," I said.

"Goddamn it!" Sam was getting riled. "You ain't going to die. Ain't I just told you I've spent winters out here. And how do you think them Indians go on? They just sit in them goddamn tepees, fine and dandy, smoking them goddamn pipes and havin a good time and—"

"And plotting how to murder us," I said.

Actually, Sam laughed at that. "I ain't saying they don't," he admitted. "But any raiding they do is in summer. Why, the winter is the *safest* time to be out here"—making it sound like we was out there for our health. "What the hell more do you want?"

340

Well, I knew what more I wanted, which was more money, but I didn't want to raise that direct. I wanted Sam to say it, then we could haggle again like we did last time, so I just said, "Thing is, I sure don't like this way of earning a living."

"You think I do?" Sam said. He sighed. "We went through all this when Red Dog died."

"Sure," I said.

"Well, I told you then this wasn't my idea of a life, shooting buffalo. It ain't no more than being a butcher, at that."

Brother, I thought, here we go. I was telling him my problem and now he's telling me his! That being a thing that happens all the time in life. And I was just going to say I appreciated his delicate feelings and how bad it was for him they was hurt, when he said, "Now, hear me out, kid. Just hear me out." He stuck more whiskey in his coffee, doing a kind of miracle there, changing one thing into another. "I told you back there, when you started skinning— I was on my way to California when I got into this shooting."

"Sure," I said. "California"—that being a tale I'd heard before.

I guess Sam heard the disbelief in my voice because he sucked his teeth, like his patience was being stretched. "I was," he said, "and I'm going. But let me tell you how I'm going."

I near did some teeth-sucking myself, like I was talking there to get another cent a hide, not listen to some goddamn daydream, but I let it ride, saying nothing.

"What I'm going to do," Sam said, "is, I'm going to shoot through to next year, then cash up and go out there and get me a spread."

"Cattle, you mean?" I said, pricking my ears up.

"Yeah, cattle. Real cattle, not longhorns. Do some breeding, and raise fat stock. Them folks out there like beef as

341

much as they do back East. Real climate, too, damn near perfect. Fruit . . ."

His voice trailed off, and I thought, maybe you *was* an editor sometime, and I was just going to say that was fine and dandy but let's get back to business, when he turned and said, "I was thinking you might come along."

I'll tell you, if ten Indians had jumped in the tent waving tomahawks, I couldn't have jumped more. I near brought the damn tent down on us. "Me!" I said. "Go with you to . . . to . . ."

"That's it," Sam said.

I lay back and listened to the hail rattling on the tent, and it maybe sounds crazy, but I felt all sad, depressed, like you might if some friend played a cruel trick on you— say, if you'd put your last quarter on a long shot and he said it had come in first, and it hadn't. Crazy, ain't it, but that's how I felt. In fact, I turned away, until Sam poked me in the back.

"What in hell's wrong with you?" he said.

"You mean it?" I said, not turning around.

"What the hell! You got ears, ain't you?" Sam poked me again.

"Yeah," I said. "I hear you. Sure."

"Well, okay." I heard that whiskey bottle tinkle again against the coffee mug. "Suit your goddamn self. You don't want the deal—"

"It ain't that," I said.

"Then what the hell is it?"

I turned back and looked at him. "Why me?" I said.

Sam sighed. "All right. Look, you ain't a bad kid, although maybe somewhat disbelieving for your age. But I don't know as how I blame you for it, seeing as how you've been bitten a couple of times. But you're a worker at that, you've been around cattle, and you did us both a favor with that Red Dog. Yeah, we could both have been moldering away like old John Brown if you hadn't shown some sand. But okay. Just to show you I *am* being straight with you, it pays to have a buddy in this world *and* we're going to need every cent we can get. That's the straight deal. Now, what do you think?''

Well, what I was thinking was that Father Christmas had come in, that's what, because that stuff about the money was eyewash. What I was making wasn't nothing compared to what he was, so maybe it was true at that, maybe I wasn't a bad kid, and maybe it was a chance in a million to get to California. And you know, I'd been dreaming about that place ever since Keeler lit out for there. It sure was supposed to be some place, sunshine and good water, that Pacific Ocean sloshing around, no savage Indians, just a bunch of harmless greasers to kick around, and all them oranges and stuff, and that's what fellers said, not them goddamn lying railroad agents.

Yeah, I thought that, but before I could say anything, Sam shrugged. "No hurry," he said. "Think it over for a couple of days. In fact, you can think it over as long as you like, because I'm going come what may, but you might just go thinking about it for so long, I'll find another buddy."

"No!" I jumped in there. "No. Hey, I'll go with you. Sure thing."

"Yeah?" Sam said. "You sure you know what you're letting yourself in for? We shoot clear through to next winter. No backing out."

"Sure thing." I said. "Sure."

Which is what I said. "Sure." But I'll tell you the truth. I didn't mean it. It's so. I was kind of lying. I say kind of, because I was ready to go with Sam, but if I got my money out of the store, well, that was maybe a different story. With that I could go to New York if I wanted, easy as eating pie, and maybe that would be the thing to do, because hunting for another whole year was a sickening thought.

Course, what I could do with that money was buy myself a gun, too. Then me and Sam could really make money. But, whichever way I jumped, the way I saw it, I was going to end up in a bed of roses. So moving on through that worsening weather wasn't so bad and we could really get down to what we were there for, killing.

Killing and killing, knocking down them buffalo, with the cold getting colder and that wind cutting into you so you blessed the Lord for making wolves so's you could have a wolf-skin coat. Killing our way down to that dugout of Sam's.

Like most everything else out West, that dugout wasn't really nothing like it had been made out to be, but it wasn't bad at that, and when we'd got the stove fixed and going and hung up some buffalo robes, it wasn't no worser than when I'd first got to Dodge. In fact, with it getting cold, it was better, seeing as how the bugs and vermin died down and there wasn't so much water pouring in.

There was other hunters down there, so it was kind of like a huge camp. Most of them wasn't exactly the sort of fellers you'd find in a parlor Sunday nights singing how they longed to cross Jordan and get themselves a harp. They was more like the types who wanted to send other fellers over. But they wasn't bad on the whole—company, you know—and there was enough of us to make any Indian think twice before jumping us.

And there were days out there when it was clear and still, the air dry so's a few snuffs of it in the morning would set you up quicker than a slug of red-eye, and you felt good, full of life, and with the bugs killed off, even skinning wasn't such a terrible job.

Well, I say that, but I guess it was, and couldn't be nothing else, it was just I was getting hardened, as folks do. Like a feller told me once who'd been in the Army during

344

the war. The first time he saw a dead man, at Antietam, he threw up all over the place, but after he'd seen a few more, they didn't bother him no more than cords of wood. And that's how I was with them buffalo. Just plain getting used to seeing them dead, and not giving a goddamn, saving I thought it was a pity we couldn't find some way of using the heads.

And when the weather did turn, when Old Man Winter really got down to it, and them blizzards come down from Canada, why, we did like Sam had said we would. Holed up, and while Pike goggled at nothing, me and Sam chewed the fat, or played chess! Yeah, I taught Sam, and would you believe, he got so he could beat me! Yeah, and it was me taught him! And he beat me at checkers, too.

Charlie Rath came in, too, and he brought in another feller for us, one of them silent wanderers glad to do most anything for a few bucks. Hack, he was called, so he said. He didn't get in the way and he took some of the weight off our backs, although I still went out skinning—for them dollars, you know?

Rath had news, as well. "You know them two fellers you met last fall? Them hunters?"

"Yeah," Sam said. "How are they getting along?"

"Fine," Rath said. "Just fine and dandy. Why, they ain't got a care in the world."

I was thinking maybe they'd found some gold or whatever, but Sam shook his head.

"Like that?" Sam said.

"Like that," Rath said. "Stiff as boards. What was left of them."

"Wasn't . . . ?" Sam touched his hair.

"No," Rath said. "Sides, them red devils is holed up for the winter. Look like they just got caught in a blizzard, is all. You know what we found on them? Take a peek!"

345

He handed over a fly sheet such as the railroad company sent all over the States, and I don't know who wrote it, or who in Sam Hill he thought would understand it, because most of it might as well have been written in foreign, but Sam could get his tongue around them words.

"Listen to this," he said. " 'Come to Kansas, the Italy of America, where Hoary Winter has yielded permanent possession to Laughing Spring!' Jesus H. Christ. The feller who wrote that is a bigger liar than Ananias! Laughing Spring! Have a look!"

He gave a bitter laugh, and I did too, taking a look around there, snowdrifts ten feet deep and a wind howling cold enough to cut you in half. "And them two fellers paid for it."

"Guess that's so," Rath agreed. "Well, so long. See you next time around, if you ain't come in by then."

We said so long back, and went in the dugout, and Pike, who'd been doing some light drinking, har-har, said, "Them fool fellers. Guess they got et up by wolves, if they didn't eat each other." And he laughed that foolish stupid laugh again, as if that was funny.

But Sam wasn't having it. "It's no joke," he said. "It's two poor devils dead because of some lying writer, is what."

Pike pulled his face. "They was asking for it, wasn't they?"

"They was trying to earn a living," Sam said. "And they've probably got folks waiting for them. Women and kids starving on some goddamn piece of land that ain't worth plowing."

That shut Pike up. He was surprised how sharp Sam was, and I was myself, him not being what you call sentimental. But talking of them fellers' kin—that wasn't something you hardly thought of, out hunting. There wasn't hardly any women and kids in west Kansas, and most of the fellers you met was just drifters of one kind or another, like Pike, or Hack, or Sam, or me, come to that. When you got down to it, all of us lonesome in that lonesome country.

And it was a lonesome country, and you could get sad out there, what they call melancholy, just the sheer size of it oppressing you, getting into your brain so you could feel sad all the time, no matter what, which is why so many fellers hit the bottle or just went plumb crazy. Women too, come to that. And that sadness got into me that night. I lay wrapped in about ten buffalo robes, with the fellers snoring around me, and I thought of them two fellers out there, dead and cold, and their womenfolk waiting for a letter. And then I got to thinking of Bo, and I wasn't far off weeping, and maybe if I'd been on my own, I would have done, too.

But come next morning, I was out there skinning and flaying, and I wasn't thinking of them two fellers. What I was thinking was I wanted to make enough money so's I would never be like them. Just never. That's what I was thinking, and I went right on thinking it as that winter wore on, and wore away, too, which out there you figured it never would do. But like that fly sheet said, Hoary Winter gave way to Laughing Spring, which is to say it rained and the dugout was slopping with mud. But some flowers came poking their heads out, like drunks who'd been chucked out of a saloon sticking their heads through the door to see if they was forgiven, and me, Pike, and Hack began looking at each other, like signaling maybe it was time for a break at that. Saying it, too, while Sam was out, hunting and hunting as if he aimed to wipe out the entire buffalo population of the United States on his own, until one day he came back in, threw down his Sharps, and said, "Get them hides skinned and cured, and when they're ready, why, we'll take a look at Dodge."

We whooped, just plain whooped, me and Hack, and Pike, he said, "Want to live it up, hey, boss?"

But Sam stared him down, the way he could, like Jack Shears, and said, "Live it up, hell. The only reason I'm going in is the Sharps is worn out."

And that's what had happened. He'd done so much shooting, the rifling in the muzzles had just got worn out, so they wasn't much use no more. It was kind of hard to believe, them Sharps being the finest rifles that ever was made, but it was true, which showed how many buffalo he'd killed, and which I could tell you exactly from Sam's tally book, so we left behind us 1,043 dead buffalo, as he headed back to the Arkansas River, and the wonderful, brilliant, miraculous godforsaken line of shacks and false fronts called Dodge.

■ THIRTY-ONE ■

We crossed the Arkansas River and hit the Santa Fe Railroad tracks to the east of Dodge, so we missed an interesting sight which I'll tell you about later. But the thing was, I'd got real worries. Maybe it was true, what Charlie had said about the heat being off, and no Pinkerton men waiting to clap the irons on me, but maybe it wasn't. Anyways, I wasn't taking no chances, so I yanked my hat right down over my eyes and pulled my bandana up over my nose.

Sam looked at me all amazed. "What in hell are you doing that for?" he asked. "You look like a goddamn bandit."

"Well . . ." I hesitated for a moment, then thought, what

the heck, he might as well know the story, so I told him, and he burst out laughing!

"It ain't funny," I said. "Goddamn, I could get hauled off to Leavenworth."

Sam choked that laughing back. "Don't worry, kid," he said. "I guess we can get you clear."

"But what about that money I owe?" I said.

"That's okay, too," Sam said. "No one can take money off you that you ain't got!"

My face sure changed, and Sam held up his hand. "I said you were a disbelieving son of a gun, and you sure are. You got money coming to you, but if I hold it, no one can take it off you, can they? Now, come on, for Christ's sake. You was the one howling to get off the range."

We hauled the wagon out of the mud and headed down Front Street, along the railroad track, to Charlie's place, and that was a surprise. Not long ago, it had been nothing but a shack, and now, jeepers, it was a real big building with *two* floors, like the place I might have been owning but for that goddamn Stokes.

There was a stable around the back, where we handed in the mules to a feller, then got the hides off, and Sam and Charlie went through the business.

"Okay," Charlie said, after the usual haggling. "I got your account up to date and you can see all the paperwork when you want. But here's a hundred on account"—fishing out a roll of bills that would have choked a goat—"and I reckon you'll take a drink with me?"

"Sure thing." Sam handed Pike and Hack twenty each and said he'd see them later, because although he needed them fellers on the range he wasn't going to sit drinking with them, and neither was I. Keeping up standards, you know. Then the three of us went to the Peacock.

"Some changes in town," Charlie said. "Another store,

Fred Zimmerman is expanding, and two fellers called Cutler and Wiley built that huge place over there. It's the warehouse for the railroad. You'll see it all, but I reckon refreshments first, hey?"

He could say that again, but as we dogged down the block to the Peacock, it wasn't so much the buildings that was strange as the folks. There was the usual riffraff hanging about, and hunters and skinners, but most of the fellers there, they'd still got straw in their hair, real Reubens straight off the farm, wandering around looking lost, and dressed like they was going to milk the cow.

"Told you the place was busy," Charlie said, when we'd got settled in the Peacock and him and Sam was having a snort and me having a beer. I was surprised to see that for sale, but Charlie explained that, with the railroad arriving, you could bring in beer easy, which you could never do on the old wagons, and which is why that whiskey-drinking habit had grown up in the West.

However, we got a drink down us, then Sam shook his head, all amazed. "What the hell's going on out there?" he asked. "Who is them fellers? They settlers?"

Charlie laughed. "They is *ex*-settlers. In fact, you might call them *un*-settled"—which was a mighty clever gag. "They're just flooding in, on the railroad, carts, wagons. Christ knows how they made it here. In fact, some of them have hoofed it from wherever. Jesus, it would make a cat laugh. Take a look!"

He pointed to the doors, which was pinned back to let out smoke and smells, some of which I've got to admit was mine, and it sure was some sight out there. The street was just crowded with fellers walking and milling, shouting and bawling at each other, some of them sticking their heads in the saloon for a second, nervous, like they was afraid of getting shot, or maybe what was worser, being charged for looking.

350

"Jesus," Sam said. "They're just hayseeds. What in hell are they doing?"

Charlie roared for another bottle. "What you're seeing, boys, is a parade. The most amazing parade in history."

"Okay," Sam said. "Parade of what, for Christ's sake?"

Charlie grinned and banged the bottle on the table. "Hunters!"

Sam swallowed his drink the wrong way and near choked to death. "Quit joshing"—and he snorted.

"I ain't joshing." Charlie beamed at us. "Them Rubes out there have come out hunting. Hunting buffalo!" He laughed, a big belly laugh, being partial to his own jokes. "And they is bankrupt before they begin! They started drifting in last winter. You remember that bank crash, when Jay Cooke failed?"

Remember! It was something I wouldn't never forget. If it hadn't been for that upright, sober, pious, churchgoing, God-fearing son of a bitch, I'd have been sitting in my own store right then.

"That crash sure hurt folks," Charlie said. "And them hicks out there, they've lost their farms, so they've come out here to try their luck."

Sam was real disgusted. "Jesus, how are they going to get to the range, and how in hell are they going to live when they get there? It's just suicide, like those fellers who got froze to death last winter."

"Sure," Charlie said. "But it's spring, and summer's coming, so they reckon they can make out. All you need is a rifle. The way they talk, there's about a million more of them heading this way. Just desperate, is all. Desperate to make a living. You can't blame them." He stood up. "I've got some business to tend to. I'll see you later—maybe after you boys have had a bath."

He laughed again and moseyed out, backslapping most

351

everyone in the bar and shouting and laughing, leaving the bottle, me, and Sam, and didn't *he* look thoughtful.

"Anything wrong?" I asked.

Sam shook his head. "Not so's you'd notice." He finished his drink and stood up. "Time for that bath and a haircut, and you need both as much as me. Let's go."

We went out and it's a funny thing, there was a couple of fellers I knew real well, and Mrs. Zimmerman passed me by, but none of them said "Hi." I figured they was cutting me because I wasn't on the social register no more, but in the barbershop I looked in the big mirror and I didn't recognize myself! Jeepers, staring at me was a filthy, raggedy, greased-up, bloodstained creature with hair down to its shoulders and a face all black with windburn and smoke—it would have scared the pants off Stonewall Jackson, and it near scared them off me.

It was a shock at that, seeing myself as no better than Red Dog or Pike, and when I walked out of that shop an hour later, I'd made up my mind I wasn't going to be like them skinners no longer. No, sir. I'd decided that I was going to use that notion I'd had back on the range which Charlie had knocked on the head, and if it worked, I was going to quit hunting, and to hell with dreams of California. I was going the other way, to Henry and a civilized way of living, because it wasn't just that I looked like a skinner, I'd got a feeling that if I carried on, I was going to end up *being* one, by the which I mean a dirty-mouthed, whiskey-boozing, fighting savage, and winding up with a knife in my belly.

So I left the shop, told Sam I'd see him later, took a deep breath, and went looking for Stokes.

He wasn't hard to find, being in the store, and wasn't I mad seeing him in there! He'd done it up, like I would have done, building out and carrying a big line of goods, everything from Sharps to skillets, and he was in there, too, all duded up and prosperous-looking, but, under them fancy duds, looking twice as hard as nails.

"Why, now," he said when I walked in. "It's the kid. You look like you could do with some new duds. I can do you a mighty fine deal"—speaking like he was the rightful owner!

"I ain't looking for duds," I said. "And if I was, I sure wouldn't come here."

Stokes half smiled and took a drag on his cigar. "You sound sore."

"Yeah," I said. "I'm sore."

"It's understandable." He nodded. "But there wasn't anything personal in what happened, just business. You didn't expect me to lose money—"

"Forget it," I said. "Just forget it."

"Okay." Stokes sounded agreeable. "But if you ain't buying and you ain't complaining, what are you doing here?"

I took another deep breath, and I was beginning to sweat, because I was going to start playing with fire and I didn't want to get burned. "I want to make a deal," I said.

"A deal?" Stokes cocked an eyebrow at me, poured himself a drink, and offered me one, which I turned down. "I'm listening," he said.

"Okay." I took another deep breath, and the way I was deep-breathing, I was going to use up all the air in Kansas, but I told him the deal, and when I finished, Stokes was doing some deep breathing on his own account.

"I don't get it," he said.

"You don't need to," I said quick, hustling him because I didn't want to give him time to do no figuring out. "You just say yes and you get twenty-five bucks and it ain't nothing illegal. But you got to say yes right now."

Stokes stared into his whiskey glass and I could see his mind was racing away there, trying to work out what the catch was, and he might have been the coolest customer this side of the Missouri, but he was beginning to sweat, too. Like, twenty-five dollars for nothing and all would have baffled a real-life college genius. I was doing more sweating as well, but I've got to say I kept my nerve.

"Okay." I made for the door. "You don't want it . . ." And I had my hand on the latch when he cracked.

"Right. Right!" he said. "I don't know what in hell is going on, but if it's legal, I'm in."

"Your bounden word," I said.

He swallowed hard. "Bounden word. Now, what's the score?"

"Why," I said, really enjoying myself for once. "Why, you just open that door to the dugout and you'll see."

And then he got it, and his jaw dropped. "I'll be damned," he said. "You've got money stashed in there."

"Yeah," I said, and thought, Swallow that, you son of a bitch, you.

Stokes looked as mad as a feller can be, but he took a big key out of his pocket and unlocked a huge padlock on the dugout door. "Let's get it," he said. "You cunning coyote."

He waved me in, but before I went, I lied, casual-like. "Just so's you know, I got a couple of buddies across the street who know I'm in here. Skinners. Savvy?"

"I savvy," Stokes said. "You've got a real open nature, haven't you?"

"Sure," I said. "And you meet the kind of folks I do, you'd have one as well." With which piece of mighty good sarcasticism I went in, and did I get a surprise. "Jupiter," I said. "You've changed it!"

He had, too, it being three times bigger than when me and Brusik lived there, and all planked, with shelving, a ceiling, and a wood floor.

"Yeah, I changed it," Stokes said. "I'm running a real store. Now, where's this goddamn buried treasure?"

"Let me think," I said, although it was hard to. I paced a couple of steps one way and a couple more sideways, until I was standing right over where my bunk had been and where the dough was buried, and, Jupiter, didn't I feel good! I could see myself on that train to New York already, and drinking pop and beer all the way. "Get me a shovel and crowbar!"

Stokes handed them over, and I got to work, thinking as how the Good Book had got it wrong in saying don't bury your treasures in the ground where the moths will eat it up for supper. "Here we go," I said, and started ripping up the planking.

I got a space clear and dug down. Then I dug down again. "Must have stuck it deeper than I thought," I said, and dug again, but there was nothing there! "Maybe it was over here," I said. "A mite this way"—and I started ripping and digging there, then farther away, then on the other side of that, digging faster and faster, hurling myself at it, ripping up more planking and digging deeper, while Stokes looked at me amazed, and he might well have, because the way I was going at it, I was heading clear out of sight!

"What the hell!" Stokes roared. "Just what the Jesus do you think you're doing? This some kind of fool joke?"

"Joke!" I was madder than a hornet. "No, it ain't no goddamn joke. I buried that money right here, under my bunk."

"You sure you slept that side?" Stokes said.

"Sure I'm sure," I yelled. "I know where I slept. I stuck that dough right here."

"Well, it ain't here now," Stokes said. And when he said that, I got a terrible notion. *Real* terrible. I got a tight hold of that crowbar and glared up at Stokes. "You . . ." I said, but Stokes shook his head.

"Not me. You think I'd let you ruin my store if it was?"

355

Then he clicked his fingers. "Goddamn! It must have been them fellers I got in to do this work."

"And what fellers was they?" I asked, ready to get me a shotgun and go looking for them right then.

"Off the railroad," Stokes said. "Jesus, I thought they was looking mighty pleased with themselves when they beat it."

And that was the end of my amazingly brilliant notion. The Good Book had been right, at that. Them goddamn moths had come in the night, doing their rusting, and they'd got them dollars and flown away, saving they was goddamn Irish moths and was probably halfway to Denver by now.

I could have bayed at the moon, and wasn't Stokes sore with his room looking as if a pack of lunatics had been whooping it up in there, and missing out on his twenty-five bucks. But he wasn't half as sore as me, *and* I had to fill in the holes and stick the planking back, cursing. Cursing non-stop and mad-dog mean, and when I left that store I did something Red Dog stupid. I went to George Hoover's liquor tent and drank whiskey, lots of it, and I don't know exactly what happened next but I woke up at the back of Nell Saintclair's shack, my head feeling like it had an ax stuck in it, my ribs aching, and my face all numb, which wasn't as strange as all that, since it seemed I'd got into a brawl with some human giant who'd given me a beating like them Jack Johnson hands out.

Eugene LeCompt found me and took me around to the Peacock and handed me over to Sam. He was real sympathetic and fatherly, saying as how I ought to have my backside kicked clear to Wyoming for being such a fool. Soothing, you know? But he poured coffee down me and made me eat some scrambled eggs, which made me throw up again, then stuck me in our room, where I just slept the clock around.

I was feeling brilliant when I did wake up, though. Amazingly brilliant. I had a huge lump on my forehead, my lips was all puffed out, my eyes was blue and black and yellow, and my side hurt so's I could hardly walk. And no money! Moses, I was sick all over again. It was fitting, though, seeing as how I'd lied to Sam about California, although right then I was glad I had. At least, I'd got some kind of future still beckoning.

It was beckoning quick, too, which was by no means all bad, it taking my mind off things, because when I got hold of Sam in Sherman's barroom, he told me to get myself new duds and whatever else I needed quick.

"We're moving out tomorrow, early," he said.

Truth to tell, I didn't mind hearing that. You know how it is, a place can get bad associations for you so you never want to see it again, which was how I felt about Dodge. So I said okay but what was the rush for.

"You'll see," Sam said. "Now, get your buying done, stick some real grub down you, and hit the hay."

I did all them things, although I had to take some joshing about the way my face looked, and I suddenly had a notion that maybe it was Brusik who'd beat me up, but when I asked about him, it turned out he'd gone to work for Lobenstein at Leavenworth.

But come the next morning I was feeling somewhat better and managed to get breakfast down me, steak and eggs, canned tomatoes, browned spuds, and hot biscuits, then beat it down to Charlie's place.

"And I ought to dock you some pay," Sam said, "seeing as how we had to load up without you. Still . . ." He let that fade away. "There's one thing. Hack's coming out, but Christ knows where Pike is. Anyhow, I got me a new man. He ain't got no experience, but—"

He didn't need to say no more, because that new man came around the wagon.

"Jeepers!" I said. "A goddamn Rube!"

He sure was, at that, lanky and sallow, with big hands making up for him having no teeth. I mean, if you was putting on a play and you wanted to have a feller playing a farmer, he's the feller you would have hired to pretend to be one, if you see what I'm getting at, which I've got to admit is more than I do.

But Sam said he could handle mules, and skin, having done that with cows, and although he hadn't never been on the range, he was used to living hard, not to mention that he was probably cheap—Sam not mentioning it, I mean.

"He seems a decent enough feller," Sam said, speaking as if that hayseed wasn't there. "Honest and all. You'll get along. So."

He climbed on his horse, me and Hack got on the wagon, the Rube grabbed the mule bit, we said so long to Charlie, and Sam said, "Let's go."

And that was the end of my amazing visit to Dodge. Forty-eight hours of pure misery!

▪ THIRTY-TWO ▪

Sam had decided to try our luck on the western ranges, so we headed out down Front Street, and that's where I saw that interesting sight I told you we missed, going into Dodge. There was some tangle on the street, wagons and teams all over the blamed place, but when we got to the river, it was worser. There was a couple of real good outfits like ours, but most of them was the craziest collection you ever did see. Anything with wheels on that you could name was there. Some of them rigs had chickens on board and goats tailing behind, and one of them actually had kids staring out the back! Jeepers, it was like the Camptown races down there, them busted farmers going out hunting, like Charlie had said.

"I'll be damned." Sam shoved his hat back. "I ain't seen nothing like this since I saw a Mormon wagon train, a couple of years back, heading for Salt Lake City. Well, crack that whip, Hack."

We lashed the mules across the river, driving right through them pathetic rigs, shaking clear of most of them on the far bank, but we hadn't gone a mile when we came on a wagon crashed over, with a couple of fellers looking as bewildered as may be.

"Look at them," Sam said. "Bust already!"

We laughed, except the Rube. "We a-going to lend them a hand?" he said.

Sam looked down at him, amazed. "Lend a hand?"

"Surely," the Rube said. "Be neighborly. We do it all the time back home."

"Neighborly!" Sam near fell off his horse. "Well, you ain't back home in goddamn Starvation County or wherever the hell you come from. This is a hunting trip, mister, not a goddamn charity expedition. 'A-going to lend a hand.' Jumping Jesus, you got plenty to learn."

"All right," the Rube said. "Maybe I have. But there ain't no need to go a-mocking me, and I don't like no blasphemous talk, neither."

"You don't—" Sam started, then laughed and turned to me. "You'd better tell him the facts of life, kid."

I'd got time to do that, seeing as how we had to get to the buffalo before we could start shooting them, so Sam would ride out scouting and we'd follow, and there was plenty of them rotting carcasses but there wasn't no sign of what we was after.

In fact, Sam got to be looking mighty thoughtful. "Ain't hardly a thing," he said one evening. "Last year I was knocking them down here without no trouble at all."

"It's them goddamn new hunters," Hack said, pointing at the Rube.

"Don't think so," Sam said. "They've hardly started. Guess the herds have moved to better grass or whatever. We'll just move on, is all."

Well, we did at that, and it wasn't a bad way to move, riding on the wagon, with the sky pure blue and the birds warbling away. In fact, it put me in mind of when I hurt my leg on the drive north, and I got to thinking, maybe I had lost that stash of mine, but I was still better off than back in Clement, and plenty to look forward to, at that. And I was *on* the wagon, and there was something mighty fine about being up there while the Rube plodded along on foot, mumbling away.

And couldn't he just mumble. His name was Abel, would you believe, being named after that feller who got bumped off by his brother in the Bible. And if I'd been old Abel's brother I might have done the same thing to him, because although he wasn't a bad feller—in fact, he was a good one—could he talk! He damned near talked our legs off, him plodding along and droning away about himself like his life was the most important one ever lived since Creation.

He'd been a farmhand in Ohio, and tried his luck on a homestead in east Kansas, but his luck ran out when that Cooke failed, although any fool could have told him it would have done anyhow.

"T'warn't like them posters said," which is how he spoke, saying "t'warn't" and such-like, which was truly comical. "Broke my plow, so's kern't get ner kern in, an the caow deed, so it did, and kern't grow ner greens ner nothing, ser hed to leave the misses arn kids bek theer"—on and on, but which was okay, it being a free country, until one night Hack pulled out a bottle of the old juice and Abel said, "I'd be erbliged iffen yer"—well, that's enough writing the way he spoke: "I'd be obliged if you didn't drink that hard liquor while I'm here."

No kidding, that's what he said, and Hack, whose blood was about 90 percent pure alcohol, stared at him bug-eyed. "What's that?" he said.

"Drinking." Abel wagged his head like a sunflower in the wind. "It's wicked sin, that is. Just brewed by the devil"— rambling on like them temperance reformers back in Abilene. "You drink that, and you'll go straight to hell, and I don't want to get mixed up in no wickedness—"

But he didn't get no further, because Hack had the cleaver out and was going to send Abel to hell before him.

But Sam stopped it. "Break it up," he said. "We're here to kill buffalo, not each other, if we can find the goddamn things."

And that was the thing. We'd been out a time and hadn't seen any worth making a camp for. To do that, we needed a good stand—just picking one or two off at a time was hardly worthwhile for a professional outfit like ours.

Then one evening Sam rode in looking more cheerful. "There's some at the head of the next creek," he said. "Being hunted, but I reckon we're on the edge of a real herd. So turn in, we'll hit them tomorrow."

We was all more cheerful, hearing that, especially Abel and Hack, who hadn't earned a dime. And we was sure more cheerful the next day when we went out and found a heap of buffalo browsing in broken country with little creeks running through it.

So it was "boom" time, sure enough. Sam had his tripod up and knocked off them beasts, and it was candy all the way. Down they went and we skinned them, and piteous it might have been, but there wasn't no pity in our hearts, 'cepting that first day when me and Abel was ripping the hide off one, and it was a buffalo cow in calf. And that *was* piteous to see, that little creature in its ma, and it not hardly formed properly.

I felt kind of sick myself, but Abel, he near went on strike. "T'ain't right," he said to Sam. "T'ain't right at all"—and saying that to Sam's face.

Sam sure blew up, hearing that. "The hell it ain't right," he yelled.

He sure was mad, but you had to hand it to Abel, he stood his ground there.

"T'ain't right to kill an animal carrying," he said, stubborn as a mule.

Sam got even madder, and I guess it wouldn't have taken much for him to belt Abel in the mouth. "Don't give me no goddamn tear-jerking," he shouted. "What the hell, them calves gets born and grow up, they going to get knocked over anyhow, ain't they?"

"Maybe," Abel said. "But it ain't even *sensible*, killing like this. You kill cows in calf, where's the next generation coming from?"

"Goddamn it!" Sam's shoulder dropped, which is a sign someone *is* going to bust you one. "I don't get them buffalo, someone else will, but, you don't like it, get the hell out of here."

And that was it. Old Abel there, he had to put up or shut up, and for a moment I thought maybe he'd hand his time in. He stood there, bloodied and greased up already, a skinning knife in his hand, and he was a decent fellow at that, feeling the way he did, but he didn't quit. No, sir, he was doing what the rest of us was, thinking of the dollars and cents, and finally shrugging, not uncaring, but more hopeless. Resigned, as they say.

"Right." Sam glared at him. "Now get skinning, and

for Christ's sake, stop that goddamn endless mumbling."

He stomped off, burning like all get-out, and me, Hack, and Abel got to work, him still muttering it wasn't right, but doing it, just like me.

And it was strange, at that. When Sam came in at dusk, he shoved his grub aside and pulled out a bottle, which he didn't do much out there, and got stuck into it, and when he'd killed that soldier, he started in on another!

"T'wern't right, t'wern't right," he said, mocking Abel. "Ain't no goddamn hayseed going to tell me what's right or wrong"—glaring across at Abel. And that fool, instead of letting the storm ride out, he said it *wasn't* right!

I kicked his ankle, giving him a friendly warning, but that cluck was so dumb, he turned on me!

"What you do that for?" he said. "What for is you kicking me?"

"Kicking you, is he?" Sam shouted. "By Jesus, *I'd* like to kick you, and by God, when I've finished my drink, I'll maybe do just that."

It sure looked like trouble coming, so I tried to do some pacifying. "He don't mean nothing, boss," I said. "He don't know the score yet. Just a dumb hick, is all."

I was taking the heat off Abel, but would you believe, he was riled again! "Who are you calling a dumb hick?" he said. "I'm a peaceable feller, I am, and I don't hold with violence, but I'll throw you, so I will. You take that back, you hear me?"

Jeepers! I was trying to help him out, and he was threatening to bust me one! And Sam joined in!

"Yeah," he said. "Keep your goddamn mouth shut, or I'll give you a hiding worse than you got in Dodge. You ain't so goddamn smart yourself."

I got mad myself then, but not liking violence any more than Abel did, and figuring anyhow that I was likely to get

363

roughed up if I stayed, I walked away real disgusted and went and stood by the mules, and them being calm, like big animals can be, they helped calm me down.

It was a wondrous night, too, such as you get in west Kansas and which I ain't seen noplace else. There was millions of stars and the old moon was up there, looking so close you felt you could reach up and squeeze it, and silvering the prairie, which was strange, the moon being yellow, and it reminded me of what Ma used to say: "The earth is silver, but the heavens is gold"—whatever the Sam Hill that meant.

Anyhow, I did get calmed some, and then, always being afraid that a goddamn great rattlesnake was going to take a chunk out of me, I went back to the fire.

That fool Abel had hit the hay, and Hack was asleep on the wagon, but Sam was still up, doing serious damage to the bottle. I was wary, though, and I was stalking around him to the tent when he called me over. I went, but I was ready to jump out of the way, you bet. But Sam's mood had changed, as some fellers' do when drinking, like some drunk hanging around your neck sobbing about how sorry he was he never told his silver-haired old ma how much he loved her, and then suddenly deciding your nose is pointing the wrong way and he's going to change its direction.

But Sam wasn't in either of them moods—someplace in between, I guess, brooding over his drink. He told me to get myself some coffee, which I did, not wanting an argument over that, too, and we sat some, watching the fire.

Then Sam spat out his stogie. "He's right, at that," he said. "Goddamn it. I've been hunting out here five years, and I know what we're doing here ain't right. Jim Bridger sure thought so."

I didn't need to ask who Jim Bridger was, him being just about the finest scout and hunter there ever was, saving

maybe Kit Carson, the so-called—so-called by himself—
Buffalo Bill Cody coming nowhere behind them two.

"Yeah," Sam said. "Jim saw some goddamn duke out
on a hunting trip and that duke and his buddies killed near
three thousand buffalo! Bridger said it wasn't right. In fact,
he wrote to the Governor of Kansas about it, but nothing
happened. It's a slaughter, is all, but what the hell can I
do about it? If I don't hunt, there's plenty of fellers will.
Goddamn, it seems like half the United States is out here.
Well . . ." He brooded some more, watching the fire go
down. "Get some sleep," he said at last. "There's work
tomorrow. Plenty of buffalo about. I can smell them. Yeah."
He finished his bottle. "But it's just slaughter, at that."

He was right, too. Slaughter is what it was, and slaugh-
terers is what we was, living in a blur of blood and heat,
and all the time the boom, boom, boom, of that old Sharps,
calling out like it would never end.

And we was just one outfit in a firing line that stretched
for five hundred miles, and behind us there was fellers too
poor even to have a rifle—and they was collecting bones!
Whole families of goddamn scarecrows doing it because
they was worth money, just a few cents a ton, but there
was a market for them. Them bones would get ground up
for fertilizer, and, would you believe, for them fancy cups
and saucers. Yes, sir, there was many an old lady back East
saying as how the poor buffalo ought to be saved who was
drinking tea out of a cup made of them!

Yeah, it sure was some killing. There was thousands of
carcasses out there, thousands and tens of thousands, and
tens of tens of thousands, rotting in the sun and crawling
with maggots. Buffalo wolves and coyotes gorged so they
could hardly get their bellies off the ground, and the sky
so full of hawks and buzzards you could near sit in the
shade under them. And us butcher boys was adding more
carcasses every day. Then Charlie Rath came out.

365

We stopped shooting and skinning. Sam put down his rifle and we put down our knives, dazed, looking at Rath like he was a creature from another world.

"Howdy, boys," he said. "Looks like you've been busy."

"What's that?" Sam stuck his hand to his ear, like a lot of them hunters, going deaf from the booming of his rifle.

"Busy!" Rath rubbed his hands together. "In fact, you look as if you boys would appreciate a spot of you-know-what, which it so happens I've got a barrel of. How's that sound?"

Well, it didn't sound no worse than dollar bills crackling, so we had a few, me as well, although I was cutting it with water so much it nearly was.

"Well, now," Rath said, after we'd had a few and was all relaxed. "Got me plenty of hides? If you'd seen some I've been offered this trip, Jesus, them Rubes' grandmothers could shoot better, and they sure spoil more hides than they cure."

"Goddamn farmers," Sam said.

"Them's the ones," Rath agreed. "And more coming out all the time."

"Jesus," Sam moaned. "More of them! There ought to be a way of stopping them."

"How are you going to do that?" Rath said.

"Hell, I don't know." Sam took a big swig. "Make them get a license. Use the Army—"

"The Army!" Rath spluttered over his booze. "Them fellers ain't out to *stop* fellers from killing buffalo. Christ, they'd stop folks who tried to stop them, if you get me. Hell, they say that down in Fort Supply the soldiers is giving out free ammunition to anyone who wants to go out shooting. Grub, too."

At that word, Abel pricked up his ears. Didn't he just! "Free!" he squawked. "Free food! You all telling me that the Army is giving away food for nothing?"

Rath grinned. "You fancy some?"

"No, I don't," Abel said. "I ain't never taken charity in my born days. I don't hold with it. Feller should earn his own bread. I reckon it's a disgrace, the Army giving out free grub! That's money out of the taxpayers' pocket, that is, and just encouraging idleness."

Rath stared at Abel like he was a human freak. "He for real?" he said. And it was crazy at that—Abel, all raggedy and without more than a few cents to his name, haranguing us about taxpaying, like one of them Prophet geezers in the Bible, with Hack sitting guzzling red-eye like one of them Heathens who didn't care none.

"Pay no heed to him," Sam said. "He don't know the score."

"And what score is that?" Abel said. "Just tell me what score it is, tell me—"

"If you'll for Jesus Christ's sake shut up for one minute, I will tell you," Sam yelled. "They want the buffalo gone, see? The government and the Army. Get rid of the buffalo and you get rid of them fellers with feathers in their hair— and I ain't talking about lunatics. Starve them out. I heard that the Army is thinking of giving hunters weapons. But I don't know but what them Indians has a point, complaining about the slaughter."

"A point?" Rath gave Sam a hard look. "You ain't going soft, is you?"

"The hell I am," Sam said. "But the way this hunting is going . . . And what's happening north of here?"

"Same thing," Rath said. "And along the railroad, why, they come across a herd, they stop the train and shoot buffalo through the windows. Sport, they call it. They don't even skin them. No kidding, the Santa Fe and Kansas Pacific Railroad, they run buffalo specials for folks coming from back East for a vacation. Europe, even."

"Well, something ought to be done," Sam said.

"They've tried." Rath poured out more red-eye. "Bills in the state legislature, in Congress, but they just gets tucked away and sort of forgotten. And there's a point at that. Goddamn, there's millions of folks wants to come out here. They ain't going to let a few thousand savages stand in the way."

"Guess you're right at that," Sam said. "Pass the red-eye."

They drank on, steady but not hogging it, and I drank, too, till my head was spinning, and the stars, and I spun right into the tent.

We loaded Rath up next morning and waved him off, and Sam wasn't in no good mood, neither, and it wasn't only the whiskey was biting him, it was the price Rath offered for the hides. Sam cussed and swore, but it didn't make no difference. The price was down, and for all Rath said what good old buddies him and Sam was, he wouldn't raise it by a cent.

"Supply and demand," he said. "Supply and demand. If you can get a better price off some other dealer, you take it. But you won't do better. There's more supply than there is demand right now."

It was an argument at that, and there wasn't no answer save to get back to work. Well, I call it work, but like a union organizer told me once, there's a difference between work and labor. Work being what you like doing, labor being what you've got to for a living, and what we was doing out there was labor, nothing but that.

We was back to that madness again, and didn't we go at it. We'd moved out of that broken country and was onto the High Plains, and wasn't there just some buffalo there, and we got at them like greedy fellers stuffing themselves before the grub runs out, and I guess that's what we was doing at that, grabbing at what was going while it was there, just like everyone else out there. We'd meet them, and although some of them fellers used to boast how many kills they'd made, for which they'd have needed a Gatling gun to do, there was others, hunters like Sam, and they'd maybe talk about buffalo, but not look each other in the eyes, like they was ashamed of themselves, almost.

And then, as if the heat and the bugs and the stench of rotting flesh wasn't enough to put up with, the grasshoppers came.

There was always plenty of them around, but they was just some more bugs, and being as they ate grass and stuff and not us, we didn't give a hoot for them, but these, jeepers! They came in clouds, billions of them, huge clouds, twisting and turning in the sky like cyclones, and when they landed, they was everywhere, crawling over you, in your grub, in your hair, all over the hides, hopping away and, goddamn it, you could *hear* them munching away, all them millions of jaws. I'd grown up with bugs of one kind or another, but these were something else entirely. In fact, we met a feller who said he'd near died of thirst because they'd choked a water hole he was counting on!

Then Abel stuck his nose in. "I hope they don't go to east Kansas," he said. "It'll be just terrible for the folks there."

"I don't give a goddamn where they go," the feller said. "They can *eat* the goddamn farmers, so long as they leave me alone."

We guffawed some, but Abel didn't join in.

"It ain't so funny," he said. "Why, it's like them disasters in the Good Book. Them banks failing, and now these, plagues all coming from the East and the West. Them poor farmers that's stuck it out will just be ruined."

"What the hell's that to you?" Hack spoke for once, and real brutal, too. "You ain't got no goddamn farm."

"Not now, I ain't," Abel said. "But I'll get me another, so I will. These here animals we is slaughtering won't last forever, but then we'll grow things. 'Blessed is the fruit of

369

the earth'—that's what the Bible says. There won't be no more hunters, but there'll always be farmers."

"Farmers!" that feller said. "Here? Jesus, take a look."

Put like that, it sure was ridiculous. You only had to take a look around at that wilderness blistering under the sun, with them millions of grasshoppers hopping about.

But Abel stood his ground. "Laugh away," he said. "But laughing won't alter it."

And I don't know but what, for all he was real dumb, I didn't get the feeling that he was right. It reminded me of Old Hobs, that squaw man we'd met on the drive, and what he'd said. First the railroad would come and the buffalo would be wiped out, and the Indians, and then the settlers would arrive, and that would be the end of an entire world. We'd laughed at him then, and he didn't get it altogether right, but looking at Abel there, that long raggedy goddamn whining streak of water, I wasn't so sure. He was just stubborn enough, and stupid, to try and scrabble a living out of that prairie and them Plains. Him and millions like him.

Well, that hunter left and we moved on, and as the sun beat down we got them mirages, seeing buffalo roaming and browsing, saving they couldn't be doing that because they was dead. And then one day I saw something that I truly hoped was one. Truly, with all my heart and soul.

I was out with Sam. He said I should go with him and try my hand with the Sharps, figuring if two of us was shooting we'd make more money, which made sense at that, another Sharps being a hundred and fifty bucks that stood between me and killing buffalo. But he was reckoning it would be worth maybe investing in one for me, if I could use it. I hadn't pressed him teaching me, because after that cow in calf I was sickened by the thought, but that feeling had worn clear away again and I was ready to shoot human beings, if so be they was woolly and had horns on their heads.

370

Sam had found a herd of buffalo, maybe thirty or forty, in a draw. We was on the Great Plains then, which you'll maybe hear folk tell are flat as a billiard table, which they mostly are. But you get these swells and folds, and it was in one of them that the herd was, nice and compact, and no one around to spoil the shooting.

We circled around the herd till we was downwind, got the tripod up, and settled, while Sam studied the herd, looking for the leader, and when he'd spotted it, boom, down it went. And the rest went, one after the other, as good a piece of shooting as you'd ever see, until there was just one left. Just the one. Then Sam let me get behind the Sharps.

I squinted through them sights at that buffalo, which was standing there like it was a tin target in a shooting gallery. I pressed the trigger and, Jupiter, that gun went off like two cannons, smoke pouring out of the barrel and leaving my head ringing like a church bell. And that buffalo, I'd gone and done as bad as any sodbuster, just maiming that creature, which was half down and making a bubbling, grunting sort of noise.

Sam cursed and grabbed the rifle and reloaded, then walked forward and put the buffalo out of its misery. I walked after Sam, who made a nasty remark about my shooting, but I didn't pay no heed to that. I just stood among them buffalo and it got to me in a way it never had before. A couple of hours ago, there'd been that herd, peaceful as might be, grazing and snuffling and grunting at each other, the calves too, and now there was just them huge dead bodies, and not a sound saving the buzzing of insects. And I don't know, I felt bad deep inside me. Kind of sad, like when Bo had got buried and I knew I'd never see him again, ever. Crazy, ain't it, but it's the truth. I felt I'd lost something, but the real awful thing was I didn't know what it was I had lost.

I handed Sam his horse, expecting more cursing for that terrible shot, but I didn't get that. He grabbed me and swung me against the flank of the horse while he stood staring over the saddle, and I looked, too, and I surely didn't like what I saw because what we was looking at was a mounted man on the skyline.

■ THIRTY-THREE ■

"Can you make him out?" Sam asked.

I shook my head, it being hard to see anything but a black shape, that feller having the sun behind him. He sure looked sinister, though, and even more so when he turned his pony around two or three times.

"Jesus," Sam said. "That's an Indian calling up his goddamn buddies. Oh, Christ!" Cursing again because more riders appeared, and wasn't they scary, black against the light, not moving, just sitting up there like they'd got all the time in the world to spare before they came down to murder us.

"Maybe they won't see us," I whispered, not knowing why, because them fellers was half a mile off.

"And maybe goddamn pigs can fly." Sam slid his Sharps over the saddle. "Let's hope to Christ they ain't hostiles, because here they come."

Them riders dipped off the skyline, heading straight for us, and I thought I'd got a frog where my heart ought to be, it was jumping about so much. But Sam was right and wrong, because they wasn't hostiles but they wasn't white, neither, one of them being a Pawnee scout who looked tougher and meaner than a railroad cop with a hangover, and the other two fellers being buffalo soldiers. And maybe that wasn't the most amazing thing in the world, lots of them soldiers out there being black, but what was amazing, the kind of amazingness that shakes you clear to your boots, was I was able to say to one of them, him being a corporal, "Well, I'll be goddamned. It's Tom Carney!"

It was, too, Tom slouched in his saddle, blinking at me as amazed as I was.

"It's the kid," he said. "Ben Curtis! What in hell are you doing out here?"

"What in hell are *you* doing?" I said, grinning as wide as he was. "You a soldier boy! Jeepers, what happened to Dutton?"

"He got thrown," Tom said, "like you did on the drive up, remember? Now he can't keep up with the riding, so he's moved down to Galveston. Reckons he can make money out of that kerosene oil. Crazy, hey? Anyways, I came up with another herd, then thought I'd try my hand soldiering, and being as how I can read and write, they made me a corporal. And how's about you, kid?"

Out of the corner of my eye I saw Sam stiffen somewhat, and I just knew he didn't like the way Tom was talking to me, all free and easy. But what the hell, this was Tom, although I don't know but there was something different about him at that. On the trail, for all he was big and tough, well, he'd been like Dutton's shadow. But now it was like he was his own man. That sounds strange, I guess, him being a soldier, but maybe it was because he'd got two stripes down his sleeve, and that sleeve being Uncle Sam's dark blue. Sort of a conqueror's uniform, I guess, seeing as the Army in that color had beaten down the poor Southland.

Anyways, I told Tom the story and he shook his head. "Well, I'll be." Tom took a swig of water from his canteen. "I heard that Kessel got his."

"Sure did," I said. "But where's the rest of the boys?"

Tom grinned. "McCann's still poisoning riders. The rest, they is scattered, you know? But say, you remember Jack Shears? Seems his real name was Jack Madigan and the Rangers was after him. But would you believe, he went as a lawman up in Denver and got killed."

"Judas Priest!" I whistled. "I wouldn't have thought there was many fellers could have got the drop on him."

"Shot in the back," Tom said. "Like most everyone. Well, real good to see you, kid, but we've got to get moving or the lieutenant's going to bite us where it hurts most." He looked down at me, and sitting up there, he sure seemed a somebody. "You fellers out here on your own?"

"What if we are?" Sam was real edgy, like he didn't care to be questioned by no nigger.

"Kind of dangerous, is all," Tom said.

"No more than usual," Sam said, speaking loud and slow, like he was talking to an idiot.

"Oh?" Tom spat over his saddle and gave Sam a look, and I thought, Sam, if you knew the man you was up against, you'd sing a mite smaller. "You ain't heard?" Tom said, speaking exactly like Sam had.

"Heard what?" Sam said, looking white around the lips.

"Mister!" Tom shook his head. "You ain't heard what happened at Adobe Walls?"

"We ain't heard nothing for weeks," Sam said. "And if you've anything to say, spit it out, you—" He cut himself off, and I guess it was lucky for him, at that.

"Sure." Tom took his time answering. "Mister, there was some hunters down at Adobe Walls a couple of weeks ago, and about a thousand hostiles tried to wipe them out."

"Jesus!" Sam jumped and so did I.

"Sure did," Tom said. "Seems they had a big council meeting, Comanche and Kiowa and Cheyenne, and them chiefs, Lone Wolf and Quanah Parker and Satanta, they

374

brought out the dog soldiers. They've had enough of the buffalo slaughtering. That's why we're here, sweeping for them."

"So they finally done it," Sam said. "They came out."

"Yeah." Tom looked around the draw, nodding, like he was counting them dead animals. "They finally done it. You want my advice—"

"I don't," Sam flashed out, and it was clear as day he wasn't going to take that advice because Tom was a nigger. And that was crazy. There was Tom and them other buffalo soldiers guarding us white men from them red men, but Sam wouldn't listen to a corporal of the United States Cavalry just because he was black!

Not that Tom was fazed. In fact, he half smiled. "Suit yourself," he said. "But you, kid—"

"Yeah?" I said.

"Get off the Plains. Pronto. You savvy?"

"I savvy," I said. "I sure do."

"That's the way. I always did think you was smart. Okay." Tom raised his hand. "See you around, kid."

Him and them others moved off, back into the sun, and we was silent, thinking, and while I was thinking how amazing it was meeting Tom, it wasn't the main thing I was thinking, and you sure don't have to be no head doctor to know what I was really thinking about.

Then Sam broke the silence. "Well, Billy be damned," he said. "They did it. They come out."

"Seems so," I said.

"Okay." Sam got all brisk. "Go get Abel and Hack. We got work to do."

I just couldn't believe what I was hearing. "You mean, start skinning?"

"What the hell do you think I mean?" Sam barked. "We ain't going to start square dancing."

"But . . ." I said. "But you heard what Tom said."

"That buck?" Sam spat. "I heard him. What of it? So there's some hostiles out. Hell, Adobe Walls is a week's ride from here, and I ain't leaving these hides."

"Sam!" I said. "Goddamn, it'll take three days to cure these hides."

He didn't like my arguing, not one little bit. He cursed and swore, but it was plain sense. A few dollars wasn't worth risking our hides for, and Adobe Walls might be a week's ride away the way a white man rode, but them Comanche and Kiowa . . .

In the end, for all his cursing, Sam saw sense and agreed we'd get to where there was company, company that didn't want to spend their winter sitting in a tepee combing your hair, and not needing to ask if you wanted some more off the back, you not being there *to* ask.

So we left them hides to rot and went back to camp, and if it hadn't been so scary, it would have been comical, the way Hack and Abel jumped. Lightning, we had the stuff loaded and was on our way inside a half an hour!

We headed north, toward the nearest point on the railroad, where there was white men, and for a day or so, that was some scary trip. The air being so dry, things out there, like it might be some scrubby plant, or, more like, them buffalo bones, they'd seem to flicker and move as if they was alive. When you started seeing that, they said you'd got prairie fever, and we sure had a double dose of it. Every flicker was some huge Indian waiting to jump us, and them mirages, we wasn't just seeing buffalo upside down, or lakes or woods or palaces, we was seeing the entire Comanche Nation heading our way.

And about the third day, we saw something that wasn't a mirage. Judas Priest, we stood behind the wagon, the Sharps out and the shotgun, Sam biting his lips, Hack cursing, old Abel calling on the Lord, and me urging him to call louder. And maybe that day the Lord was in a listening mood, because them riders heading toward us wasn't no painted savages but a whole pack of hunters who'd got the message, too, and was heading the same place we was.

Weren't we glad to see them! Not much more than a drunk finding a bar open on Sunday, we wasn't, because together we made up quite a bunch, over twenty armed men, and we could stand off a war party, given that there weren't too many braves wanting to get to the happy hunting grounds before their natural time.

But although we was all glad to see each other, none of us was in what you'd call a good mood. We didn't so much as keep slogging our way north as curse it, curse it and shoot it, because them fellers, they saw any buffalo that had got left out, they blasted them down, not even trying for a clean kill, or even a kill at all. Just leaving them animals lying there, or wandering around, wounded and dying slow, like they was taking out of the buffalo what they couldn't take out of the Indians.

I didn't care to see that going on, nor did Sam, come to that, but Abel was plain horrified. He asked one of them hunters, who looked kin to that hairy feller Henry had got stuck up on his wall in Abilene, just what he was doing it for.

"For?" that feller said. "What in hell do you think for. If I can't have them, I'm making sure no goddamn Indian does."

It was plain stupid, stupid and mean, but I kept my mouth shut, him not being the kind of feller to mention that to. But if I didn't do much talking on that trip, I did plenty of thinking. Not just about that senseless waste, but lots of things. Like Tom Carney, meeting him again, and Jack Shears getting bumped off, which figured, them that lived by the Colt .45 dying by it, and the boys I'd come up the trail with, all scattered like Tom had said, and Dutton going and selling oil! That was crazy. He should have stuck to herding cattle, where there was real money to be made.

But, I guessed, that was America. There was plenty of it. Plenty of it to move around in, plenty of it to make a fortune in, to go broke in, too, come to that, and plenty of it to die in. And maybe it was just because there was so much of it—America, that is—that made folks restless. Thinking which amazingly brilliant thoughts, I lay back on the wagon, sweat pouring clear out of my boots, them being full of holes, until we hit the railroad at Bailey's Halt.

That had once been a staging post on the old Santa Fe Trail, but the railroad had turned it into a stop for the trains. Not that there was anything for anyone to get out for, there just being a stack of wood for the locomotives and a huge barrel of whiskey with a shack built around it. But it was doing plenty of business when we got there. Lots of hunters had got the message, same as us, and come in, all cursing and mad, which was calming in a way. Like they say, a trouble shared is a trouble halved—well, it is for the feller with troubles. For the feller who didn't have none, it's doubled, as you might say.

Still, we could all join in together, cursing and drinking and gambling, and we got the lowdown on what had really happened at Adobe Walls.

The best anyone knew, the Kwahadi Comanche, them who worshipped snakes, and the Kiowa had done some worshipping, like a big campground prayer meeting, and got enraged about the buffalo being knocked off and all them hunters coming and breaking the treaty I told you about, the one made at Medicine Lodge back in '67, and Lone Wolf, Satanta, and Quanah Parker, their war chiefs, had led about a thousand braves out to do some hunting, and since there wasn't many creatures left with four legs, they was ready to try their hands on them with two, starting off at Adobe Walls, that being, like the name says, an adobe shack built by greasers once, but used as a saloon and store by hunters.

A feller who'd come in late told us about the attack, and when we'd heard the full story, we was absolutely disbelieving.

Sam shook his head. "Let's get this straight," he said. "You saying that a couple of dozen hunters stood off a thousand Comanche and Kiowa?"

"Sure thing," the feller said. "I spoke to one of them. Two hunters was jumped outside and got scalped, but the rest just stayed inside and picked them savages off."

It sure sounded like someone someplace was stretching it, but it turned out to be true, would you believe, which didn't say much for them so-called fearsome warriors, although it sure did for the old Sharps.

"And where's them Indians now?" someone asked.

The feller shrugged. "Who knows? Scattered, I guess, one day here, next day there, roving around. They left it kind of late, though, coming out. Them buffalo . . ."

He didn't need to finish, us all knowing what he meant. What they called the southern herd, them buffalo south of the railroad, well, it wasn't wiped out, but it was heading that way, them animals being blown away like leaves in the fall. You know, one day the ground is thick with them, the next day they is gone, save for some in corners where the wind hasn't found them.

And that kind of bothered me, because Sam there, he knew where them corners was, and I'd got a bad feeling he was thinking about going out and doing some poking about in them.

He'd look at me and I'd turn away, thinking them Indians might have scattered but they knew the Plains as well as Sam did, if not better, and if they was after buffalo, we was all likely to end up in the same place, and that was one place I didn't want to be. So I tried to keep away from

379

Sam, playing hide-and-seek around that shack—even, when it got to sundown, walking down the track a way, and that was more scary than being out with the Indians, because a couple of them busted farmers was holed up there collecting bones, and them bones was lined up along the track, millions of them. In fact, one of them fellers said them bones stretched all the way back to Dodge, which wouldn't have surprised me if it had been true.

But there was no real getting away from Sam, and he was just biding his time anyhow, drinking and gambling around the barrel, and doing all them things the preachers say you shouldn't do, which is bad for you now and will be worser when you've cashed in your chips, which hardly seems fair.

So one morning he grabbed me and said we was heading out. "And don't look like that," he said. "You ain't going to lose your hair."

"I know I ain't," I said, "because I ain't going where I *can* lose it."

Sam snorted. "There ain't *no* chance of it."

"Is that a fact?" I said. "You going hunting in Chicago?"

"Don't get smart," Sam said. "It's going to be safe."

"I guess that's what them hunters at the Walls figured, too," I said. "And what is they now? Two bald-headed ghosts, is what."

Sam sighed. "Kid, you remember that rancho in California we talked about?"

"I sure do," I said. "In fact, I *dream* about it"—which was true—"and I want *all* of me to get there, which is why we shouldn't go out no more."

"Okay," Sam said. "*Okay!* And if you'll stop talking and being so goddamn chipper for a moment, I'll tell you *why* we needn't bother about them Indians."

"Right," I said. "I'm listening"—and I did, and he was near enough right at that, because the way we did go out was enough to scare off the Indians and the Russian Army put together, there being near enough fifty hunters with wagons and skinners, and like Sam said, if we didn't scare them Indians off, there was something wrong with them because we was real wild. Wild and woolly, whiskered and red-eyed, and toting a regular armory. And if we wasn't enough on our own, there was plenty of cavalry around, sweeping the prairie with Pawnee scouts, and from what they told us, there wasn't hardly one Indian to be seen.

A sergeant told us that. Him and a troop of cavalry was bedding down by a creek where we was going to stop, and he came over to chew the fat and sample the whiskey.

"Yeah," he told us, after a few slugs. "Old General Crook, he's got something in mind, though. Him and Sheridan and Custer. There's a full regiment moved into Dodge, and another down at Fort Concho."

"Is that so?" That was a hunter called Kemp. "Manners" Kemp he was called, being as how he had no more than a hog. "Don't say the Army's actually going to do something about them red bastards."

"We'll deal with them," the sergeant said, sounding tough, like he didn't appreciate the delicate way Manners had made his point. "We got to find them first, though."

"Find them!" Manners laughed and said something about the Army not being able to find a stray dog.

"What was that, mister?" the sergeant rounded on Manners, edgy, the way soldiers usually is around civilians, knowing they is despised and all. But before Manners could say more and us start fighting each other instead of the Comanche, Sam struck in and cooled things down.

"Here." He poured the sergeant another drink. "Where do you reckon they're at?"

"I don't know," the sergeant admitted. "But them Pawnee figure the Cheyenne went north and the Comanche and them Kiowa are heading for some goddamn great canyon in Texas. Kind of a secret hiding place they got down there."

"Secret! Jesus Christ!" Manners said.

"You know that place?" The sergeant was real mad. "Because if you do, you'd better open up about it."

"He don't mean that." It was another feller, Manners's partner. "But we've heard of it. A trader told me about it once. Palo Duro, it's called. Mighty pretty place, he said. Never been there myself, though, not on calling terms with them Comanche."

"Yeah," the sergeant said. "Well, we'll get to them. But it's a big country."

He had some more booze, then went off to his boys, leaving us to hit the sack. But I lay awake, thinking of what that soldier had said, about it being a big country. Course, it didn't take no genius to figure that out. In fact, fellers was saying it all the time. "Yes, sir," they'd say, if they didn't have nothing else to talk about, "it's a big country"—like as if they'd made it personal or something, or as if it being big made *them* big, too. But it didn't, not the way I saw it. It made them smaller, if anything, tight-fisted and narrow-minded, like them reformers back in Dodge, as if they was getting dwarfed just by the size of the place and turned inward just to protect themselves.

But be that as it may, it *was* a big country. Jeepers, I thought of them Comanche and Kiowa, thousands of them maybe, all shacked up in a hidden canyon and no one being able to find them! Not even what sounded like half the United States Army! That made it a big country, sure enough, and wasn't I looking forward to seeing more of it. Crossing the Rocky Mountains and riding down to California, raising creatures instead of slaughtering them . . . Yes, there were times ahead for me in the big country, that was for sure.

But before I got to them times ahead, I had to get through

them times now, if you get me, and they wasn't nothing to write home to Ma about. We dragged across the Plains, finding some buffalo here and there, small herds, which we knocked over without hardly thinking about, but if we didn't find many live buffalo, we sure found plenty of dead ones, mile after mile of rotting carcasses, and no matter which way the wind blew, you got a reek in the air, a taint that you could smell and taste.

Then one day we was dragging along, and even Sam was beginning to wonder whether it was worthwhile carrying on, when we saw Manners and his partner, who'd been riding point, scouting as might be, heading toward us. Seeing them coming, we thought maybe they'd found buffalo, which made us feel pretty good. But we didn't feel so good when Manners put his horse to a hand gallop and raced at us, shouting "Indians!"

Judas, the fellers had their rifles out before you could blink, and I was looking for someplace to hide, when Manners bust out in one of them senseless laughs.

"Haw-haw!" he guffawed. "Don't get heated up. These is *good* Indians. Come and take a peek. T'ain't but a step."

It wasn't, neither, just a pull over one of them swells, and there, by a muddy water hole, was them Indians right enough. Two men, four women, some kids, and a few ponies.

■ THIRTY-FOUR ■

I'd got to thinking, and maybe you do, as well, that them Indians out on the Plains ran around with big headdresses of feathers and all, and maybe some did, but these weren't. They was dressed in buckskin, just ordinary, saving their ponies, which was them pretty piebalds they fancied, was painted with stars and moons and suns. In a funny kind of way, they made me think of the buffalo, like they wasn't real animals, just like the Indians didn't seem like real people, not actually living in our world of land plats and banking and credits. More as if they'd come out of some world of their own, maybe a dream world, one they'd dreamed up for themselves, a long time ago, a long, long time since, and when they'd started to dream the dream, all the clocks had stopped. And one thing was sure, the clocks was never going to start for these Indians again, not ever, because they was dead. All of them. The men, the women, the kids, even the ponies and a couple of dogs.

"Told you they was good Indians," Manners said. "Let's go take a look."

We went down into the fold, through a flock of crows that hardly bothered to flop out of the way, and it was a sorry sight to see. Well, it was to some of us, but not to others. They was walking around the bodies, poking at them like they was buying meat in a market, and them Indians, they didn't have no eyes, but it was like there was still something in them holes, something peering out at us.

"They's just Arapahoe," Manners said. "See them paint marks on that buck? They've got different markings so's they can tell each other apart, and they needs to, because they all looks the same, har-har."

"What do you reckon happened?" someone asked.

"Got jumped, looks like," Manners said. "Three, four weeks ago, I guess, the way they is shriveled up"—the which being probably a good guess, that hog being used to seeing dead things. He spat, then said, "Well, look here, guess this tells the story."

He bent down and picked something up. "See this?"

We crowded around as he held out his hand, and what he had probably did tell the story, because what he was holding was a brass button with crossed sabers and *U.S.* stamped on it.

"Yeah." Manners flicked the button up and caught it. "Cavalry. Must have caught them with their pants down, only they don't wear no pants, har-har."

It wasn't everyone laughed at that, but we stood around, staring at the button like we was bound in a spell. But then Abel, who'd been standing there real dazed, like he'd been hit on the head, spoke up. "You saying United States soldiers did this?"

"Sure," Manners said. "Cavalry. That's a cavalry button."

Abel took a step forward. "You trying to tell me that American soldiers just come along and shot these women and children?"

Manners frowned. "You deaf or something?"

Like I've said, old Abel was a stubborn cuss. He stood there, his head down like a goat butting at a tree. "You telling me them soldiers did this killing?"

That frown of Manners turned into a real mean scowl. "I told you twice, didn't I. You making me out to be a liar? Is you? By Jesus, you step back or you'll goddamn join them Indians, so help me."

Well, would you believe, Abel stepped *forward*, his jaw jutted out, and the Lord knows what would have happened if Sam hadn't moved in.

"Break it up," he said, sounding just as tough as Manners. "He don't mean you're a liar. He just don't understand, is all. Anyhow, let's get the hell out of here. Get moving, Abel. You, too, kid. This ain't no place to be."

He grabbed hold of Abel and shoved him back up the

slope, and I was following with Hack, being glad to get out of there, when my foot got tangled in something in the grass. I got hold of it and called Sam over.

"Well, I'll be," Sam said. "A bow."

That's what it was, a bow, about a couple of feet long.

"See that, kid," Sam said. "That whole thing is made out of buffalo. That's buffalo horn, sliced and stuck together, and that string is buffalo tendon, and that grip, it's buffalo hide." He shook his head. "Not much against an Army Spencer repeater, hey?"

It wasn't, at that. It was just a bow, is all, saving it was somehow more than that. It had a feel to it, a balance, so just holding it, you felt like giving it a twang. A real good tool, but like Sam said, not much against a carbine. Not much to go up against a huge buffalo with, neither, come to that.

Some of the other fellers had come across to take a look, and one of them whistled. "Say, kid," he said. "You'll get a couple of bucks for that most anyplace that's civilized."

"Jesus!" One of them skinners slapped his leg. "What the hell's wrong with us? There's money lying around here."

"Too goddamn right!" Manners let out a whoop. "Let's get at it!"

He went down to them bodies but started cursing, shouting the soldiers must have taken what there was going, while other fellers was wandering through the grass, all laughing and joking, like it was hunt-the-thimble. And one of them, who was some kind of human genius, pulled off a moccasin one of them women was wearing which had that pretty beadwork on it, and all the time them Indians, it was like they was peering at us through them eyeholes.

Sam and me, and a couple of other fellers, sure was unhappy at what was going on down there, while Abel looked like he was in some kind of nightmare, which I did myself. But even that wasn't the worst of it, because Hack said, "Take a look at that."

We turned and there was Manners leaning over one of them bodies with his skinning knife out. He looked at us, grinning all over his face. "Jesus," he shouted. "We was looking for keepsakes and they're right beneath our eyes!" He yanked at that Indian's hair, the head coming half off. "Goddamn, you can get five bucks for a real scalp!"

"Well, by Jesus, if you ain't right," a skinner said. "Hey, they ain't all yours." He pulled out his knife, then stared at us. "What in hell are you looking so holy for? They is Indians, ain't they—and they is dead."

Manners and his buddies whooped it up that night, drunk as all get-out. There wasn't nothing unusual in that, but they was real wild, and I don't know, maybe it was because they knew they'd done something real bad back there, something so bad they was trying to blot it out. Maybe. And I say maybe because there wasn't nothing strange about taking scalps out on the Plains. You could sell an Indian scalp just like any other curiosity, and them Indians themselves liked to have them in their tepees, showing how many enemies they'd killed. I don't know, maybe it was because them scalps had been lifted from corpses, and them women and kids . . . It just didn't seem decent, is all. And it sure didn't to Abel.

He went on and on about how it wasn't right and he was going to let his senator know, and General Sherman, and the President, on and *on*, until Sam, who'd been mighty silent, just told him to for Christ's sake shut up. "There was Indians roamed back where you come from, wasn't there?" he yelled. "What the hell do you think happened to them?"

"They was given reservations," Abel said. "Land of their own to live on."

Sam looked like he didn't know whether to burst out

laughing or bust Abel in the nose, but he took a deep breath, sort of counting ten, then said, "*This* is a reservation! We're on one. You're making a living on it, and if you don't care for trespassing, get to hell out of here. Only *shut up!*"

That should have been the end of it, because we was back then to shooting buffalo and working too hard to brood over a few savages, but Manners had them scalps nailed to a pole on his wagon, curing them, so everywhere we went, they came with us, and it sure was eerie, seeing that hair waving and riffling in the wind, like them Indians wasn't dead at all, or if they was, their ghosts was following us, dogging us across them vast Plains.

Once I was in Oklahoma, which used to be that Indian Territory where me and Bo had ridden up the Chisholm Trail. Me and an Indian bunked down for the night under a culvert. It was winter, but neither of us wanted to go to a hotel, him because there wasn't none that would take Indians, and me because I was organizing labor and there was a whole pack of deputy sheriffs out wanting to play baseball with me—them having the bats and my head being the ball, that is, and besides, there wasn't no hotel near fancy enough for us, ho-ho. And this Indian, he told me his pa had said that Indians didn't ever die. Not die like white men did. In fact, he'd had this notion that white men wasn't real. That we was ghosts, and them cities, Chicago and Oklahoma City, they wasn't real neither, and the tribes, the Comanche and Cherokee and the Sioux, the Kiowa, Arapahoe, Blackfeet, and Crow, them and the buffalo was still roaming the Plains and it was only because *us* white men was ghosts that we couldn't see them. And I don't know but that out there, with them scalps following us, I didn't get the feeling sometimes that it *was* us that was unreal, at that.

It was getting late into fall then, which was a blessing

and relief, the sun relenting, the air clear and crisp, and I began to keep an eye open for the geese, which I always liked seeing, coming and going twice a year, honking and calling way overhead, and it maybe sounds crazy, but I used to think they always sounded dolesome heading north but cheerful flying south, like they was looking forward to some easy living.

I mentioned that to Sam one night. Abel was snoring away and Hack had gone into Bailey's Halt, our teamsters taking it turn about to haul what hides we'd got in there.

"Yeah." Sam sat brooding by the fire, smoking a cigar. "Maybe something in that." He brooded some more, rubbing his chin. "Kid," he said, "I've been doing some thinking."

"Okay," I said, not having any objection to that, and it not making any difference if I had. But I was hoping he'd say something I wanted him to say, and I *willed* him to say it, and he did!

"It's that rancho," he said. "In California."

Well, Jupiter, that's exactly what I'd wanted to hear! It was like I'd got them hidden powers, sending out brain waves and making folks do what I wanted them to. In fact, I thought I'd work on it some and try it out, making folks give me money. So I did it some more, brain-waving at Sam like all get-out, although, just to make sure, I spoke up, too.

"Yeah," I said. "The rancho. Why, it would be mighty fine to be there right now. In fact"—hinting as might be— "in fact, for what buffalo we are getting, we might as well be there now."

Them hidden powers worked, too! Well, almost, because Sam, he took a big drag on that cigar, prodded the fire, then said, "Tell you what I'm thinking"—not knowing I was doing the thinking for him. "These Plains is just about shot out . . . Remember last winter, when I said we'd hunt until it wasn't worthwhile or the first blizzard came?"

"I sure do," I said.

"Well." Sam looked at the end of his cigar, the way fellers do when they're pondering. "I reckon we got enough money coming to us to spring it!"

Jehoshaphat! Them was the words I wanted to hear. I was ready to start for the railroad there and then, but Sam told me to cool down.

"There ain't no big hurry," he said. "What I've got in mind is to go to the Halt and I'll send a message in to Charlie Rath, saying we're coming in. But till them blizzards do start, we'll take a look north of the railroad and see if we can't find a herd or two. I know a couple of places up there might be worth looking at. And we might as well make what money we can while it's wandering around. But if there ain't nothing worthwhile, we beat it. That suit you?"

Suit me! Not much more than a store-bought suit, it didn't. Jupiter, I hardly slept at all that night, thinking of California, of them green fields and running water, and trees a hundred feet tall, or so Sam said, stretching it more than somewhat, I reckoned. And why, I might even meet up with Keeler, and maybe he'd struck it rich and was a millionaire, which would be mighty handy.

There was a harvest moon out, round and full and red, like one of them oranges you could get as easy as pie out in California. It was hanging in the sky so close you felt you could just reach out and pluck it and cram it in your mouth, the cool juice running down your chin, and I guess I'd got prairie fever because I got to thinking the stars was like grapes and such-like ridiculous poeticizing, so I closed my eyes—but, would you believe, I dreamed of that far country. Just like them Indian savages, dreaming their dreams, too.

THIRTY-FIVE

That summer out on the Plains, time had kind of vanished. Not having any meaning, saving when the sun got up and started frying your brains so you counted the hours till it went down. So days hadn't counted, days and weeks, nor months, neither. But after Sam said we was really going to California, why, time sure meant something to me again.

I just couldn't wait for Hack to get back from Bailey's Halt, and when he did and we'd loaded up, I just couldn't wait to get to the railroad, as if *we* hurried, then time would, too. And tell you another thing. The only time of the year them Plains was really fitting for a human to live on was fall, but I'll bet I was the only person in the entire West longing for it to end, so's winter would come and we could head off to that promised land.

But it's just the way of it. Even though time had got back in our lives, it sure went slow! Dragging into the Halt, every minute was like an hour, the old sun hanging overhead. I got to wondering whether old Joshua wasn't out there someplace stopping it.

I sat on the wagon watching the wheels go round and round. One of them had a crack on the rim and I started counting that crack, going up to a hundred, then starting over again, mumbling to myself as bad as old Abel.

We was all the same, just mindless and heedless. Once, far off, we saw a column of blue with a pennant flying, cavalry, maybe them that cut down them Indians, but we hardly bothered raising our heads to look, just plodding on through them miles of boneyard—the prairie, you know, strewn with the bones of buffalo—me watching them wheels turn—and then they stopped, and we was at Bailey's Halt, and there was actually a train there! It wasn't much of one, being just a locomotive, one car, and a caboose, and it didn't have no steam up, just standing there looking abandoned, and mighty strange, too, in that place, like some lunatic had stuck it there.

"Well, Billy be damned," Sam said. "What in Sam Hill is that doing here?"

That question was understandable, there being nothing there for a train to do, but it was answered when we got into the shack and surrounded some red-eye—me and Hack, that is, Abel saying he *liked* looking after the mules, which just showed his head was stuffed with straw, and anyhow wanting to go talk to them bone collectors about such fascinating topics as grasshoppers and bankruptcy.

A soldier told us about the train, him being one of a handful who was hanging around. He was one of them fellers who are dumb, not being able to speak unless they get a miracle cure, that being a big glass of whiskey.

"You don't know?" he said in that irritating way folks do when you've just asked a question. "It's an ambulance train."

Sam raised his eyebrow. "First time I ever heard of one. What sort of an ambulance train?"

"Army," the soldier said. "For wounded. That's why we're here, to take them wounded back someplace where there's hospitals and such-like."

"Wounded?" Sam said.

"Sure." The soldier toyed with his glass, discreet-like, such as banging it on the table, holding it upside down, peering through it, and so on, until Sam got the message, and him another drink.

"Yeah," the soldier said. "Wounded from that fight."

"And what fight might that have been?" Sam asked, sounding like he'd be amazed to hear the Army had actually done any fighting.

"Why," the soldier said, "there was a big fight with the Indians down south of here. We got the news a few days ago. I'm surprised you boys didn't hear."

"Well, we didn't," Sam said. "And *I'd* be mighty surprised if you got another drink before telling us what this fight was."

"I'm getting around to it," the soldier said. "The way we've heard, old General Mackenzie and the Fourth Cavalry, they found a heap of Indians in some big canyon—"

"Palo Duro?" Dave cut in.

"Something like that," the soldier allowed. "Seems they wiped out a whole tribe or something, so we've come for the wounded."

"Wounded Indians?" Sam was somewhat incredulous.

"The hell!" That soldier was real offended. "Our boys."

"Seems a mighty long way to haul wounded," Sam said. "I'd have thought they'd be taken to Fort Concho."

The soldier looked at Sam and gave sort of a dry grin. "Clear you ain't never been in the Army, brother."

That was the story we heard, and it was true, because a couple of days later some cavalry came in who'd been down there, and for a few drinks they was ready to fill in the details, it seeming some Tonkawa scouts had found that canyon and Mackenzie had attacked and caught them Indians napping.

A corporal told us that. "Hell," he said. "Them Kiowa put up a fight so their women and kids got away, and them Comanche, who was farther up the canyon. But we got all their supplies, burned the tepees, and shot the ponies. Must have killed a thousand." He shrugged. "Had to be done, I suppose."

"And where's them Indians?" Sam asked.

"Just scattered, is all. We're rounding them up now. I heard tell that Little Wolf got clear with a few braves, mounted that is, and maybe Quanah Parker. But most of

393

them is on foot and there ain't no place for them to go but to some reservation. Yes, sir, you can all rest easy. There ain't going to be no more trouble with the redskins."

"Guess not." Sam stood up. "Reckon I'll stretch my legs down the track. Come on, kid."

I went with him to the door, but Sam stopped for a moment. "What about them wounded? Them that train is for?"

The corporal toyed with his mug there. "Wasn't no wounded," he said. "Didn't have no casualties at all."

It was a clear, fresh night, with millions of stars glittering like they'd been fresh polished and them bones along the track shining white. And away from the Halt, where them soldiers was whooping it up, it was real quiet, just the wind sighing and little rattles coming from the bones where some kind of vermin was burrowing around.

Yeah, it was quiet and peaceful as we walked along the track, and it was hard to believe that out there, in all that vast night, there was thousands of Indians hobbling around, no ponies, no tepees, no nothing, I guess, winter coming on, and nothing waiting for them except, like the soldier had said, a reservation, and nothing for them there, neither.

I guess the same thoughts had been running through Sam's mind, too, which was natural enough. Anyhow, he stopped and lit a stogie, that match flaring yellow and showing his hard face, which wasn't so hard when you got to know it.

"Well," he said. "Seems like they got them, at that." He puffed away. "You ever see a horse Indian, kid? I mean a real one, out riding?"

I allowed I hadn't, and the which was amazing, having been out on the Plains two years. Like I'd seen Arapahoe and Pawnee scouts, and them bucks back in Indian Territory, but never a real *wild* Indian.

"That's not so surprising," Sam said. "We ain't been that far south. But I have. They was some sight, them painted horses and that beadwork. They had kind of breastplates, you know? Made out of porcupine quills, all dyed red and blue. They used to trade. You know that? All across America."

"Trade?" I said. "You mean like us?"

"Sure," Sam said. "Furs and beads, shells, that stone they make the peace pipes from." He smoked for a while, that cigar smoke scenting the night. "I ran into a war party once. It was something to see. That war chief, he'd got a full headdress, them eagle feathers. And them braves . . . they was proud. Yeah, that's the word. Proud. Like they owned the world."

"Lucky you wasn't scalped," I said.

"Hell, no." Sam shook his head. "They was out after another tribe, horse stealing. They didn't want no trouble with us. We gave them some tobacco and they was okay. We wasn't doing them no harm, just hunting buffalo, and there was plenty for everyone then. You wouldn't kill a feller for pulling a few blades of grass out of your field, would you? No, when I came out, them buffalo, I don't know, it was like they was a huge river. We was on one bank and they was on the other, so no harm done. But they've gone now, buffalo and Indians."

"You reckon?" I said.

"Sure, on the Plains, anyhow. You heard that soldier boy? They ain't got no ponies and there's no way they can get more. You any idea what it's like out there without a mount? No, the buffalo has gone and they've gone with them. Had to happen, I guess, but I don't know . . ."

"Don't know what, Sam?" I asked.

Sam waved his hand. "Just . . . just, although they could be murderous bastards, it's like . . . like a loss. Hell—" He got all brisk. "What am I talking like this for. It ain't nothing to me. Anyhow, them mules is all rested up, so I reckon we'll go on that hunt."

"The last," I said, getting that in quick.

"Sure." Sam grinned and flicked the butt of his stogie onto the track. "Sure. Starting tomorrow."

We headed back, and I was full of the joys of spring, even though it was a week into October. But I guess you know what I mean. Just a few more weeks, then farewell to that goddamn butchery, and hi there, California. Yeah, I felt real good, walking back along them rattling bones.

The next morning we moved out, following the railroad for a while before we went north, going to broken country, where Sam reckoned there was land that hadn't been shot out. Two other hunters came with us, there being safety in numbers, and which we was glad of, what with Lone Wolf roaming around somewhere, but we didn't see a thing until we got to that hunting ground, there being a regular camp there, with maybe fifteen or twenty hunters dug in along two creeks. And what was funny about them creeks, it was like Abilene, there being what you might call a north side and a south side, fellers like us living up one creek and, well, *other* fellers living along the other. Birds of a feather flocking together, as they say. Course, there wasn't exactly dance halls or saloons on that other creek, and there wasn't exactly no churches or temperance groups on ours, but there was a difference, and it was comforting to be with our own kind.

Anyhow, we got there, said hello to the fellers, scraped ourselves a dugout, rough as may be since we wasn't staying long, rested up the mules, then moved on.

It was mighty fine, too. It was golden weather and buttermilk skies, and even them dead buffalo didn't seem so terrible, the weather and the vermin having cleaned them up some.

And there was the other kind of buffalo, too, them that

could still use their four legs for walking on, and Sam knew where to find them in draws and broken ground, and say what you like, the first time that Sharps sang out, and the first time a buffalo fell, and the first time a dollar went into the account, all pity went flying out the window.

And, without that pity, they was days to be living through, them golden days and nights like you couldn't begin to imagine, the moon so big and the stars so bright the whole world seemed washed with silver and gold. And even skinning, them days had a lazy kind of easiness, warm so you'd enjoy the chill of night, and nights chill enough for you to enjoy the smell of woodsmoke, and look forward to the sun on your back next day. It was real Indian summer at that, a hazy dream where everything seemed right. Just right.

Then it was winter. But that winter, it sure seemed an awful long time coming, and there were times it seemed it had made up its blamed mind to stay at home that year. But then the geese came honking down, all shining in the sky, like they was coming from darkness into light, and I waved at them, saying, Hi there, girls, be seeing you soon, and I was ready to swear they honked back, calling, Right on, Ben!

Winter came behind them geese. It started to get colder, and there was days when the wind had a new edge to it, and nights, there was crackling frosts. And then the wind started coming at us steady, poking at you like a feller giving you a warning. There was cold rain come, too, sleeting across the range, and lightning, huge cold-weather thunderstorms, the weather there saying, Don't you go thinking this here balmy weather is all I can do. No, sir, I got an ace up my sleeve, and you'd better believe it, mister.

Then the snow came, but Sam wouldn't have it that some flakes made a blizzard, saying he'd decide that.

"You get me?" he said, real mean.

I got it. I got it the day of that first snow, and I got it a lot more the days following. It rained and hailed and the wind screamed down, but to Sam it seemed like they was them laughing breezes of verdant spring, and I got a real bad feeling he wasn't never going to give up while there was buffalo to be got. And there was, goddamn it. They wasn't thick on the ground, but there was enough to make it worthwhile hunting, and Sam did. He kept at it, them beasts falling, falling, falling while the Sharps boomed out. And then there wasn't none.

I say there wasn't none, but I don't mean there wasn't none left in the world, nor even in the United States. Just there wasn't none where we was, so if we wanted more hunting, we'd have to move on, and to this day I'm not sure he wouldn't have done so, that being how dollars grab you. But the light was getting funny, dark but bright, if that don't sound ridiculous, like gun metal, and we both knew what that meant. But even then Sam hesitated, walking from the fire to his horse, and his horse to the fire, drinking coffee, puffing away on a stogie, and looking mad, too!

Abel and Hack stood against the wagon, looking at their boots, glum, and I stood by the fire, staring at the sky, meaningful, you know, just staring at it and not batting an eyelid, and that riled Sam. He came over to me, mean as prodding. "No good, you standing there like a goddamn statue!" he shouted. "I know what's in your mind."

I didn't answer none, just kept standing there, staring north, and Sam, well, I guess he didn't know whether to burst out laughing or bust me on the nose, although he didn't do neither.

"All right," he said. "*All right!* That's a goddamn blizzard coming." He chucked the butt end of his stogie in the fire. "Right. Well, why the hell not. Okay, let's get out of here."

Jupiter! I could have jumped over the moon! I could have wrestled a buffalo to the ground with my bare hands. I could have pulled that wagon on my own. I could have done damn near anything at all, and not even broken sweat. Because that was it. We'd finished. Finished and done. Done with shooting and skinning. Finished with blood and guts and grease. Done with eating rotten grub, and being ate up by bugs, and finished with being scared, because we was going at last, all the way to where the sun shone and the birds sung sweet, and the only thing that puzzled me was why in Sam Hill we wasn't there already.

But we was going, and we went, heading back to camp with that blizzard behind us, and it caught us, too, and it was a killer blizzard, man and beast, raging for two days and nights, but we got through it and, lucky for us, it froze hard after instead of going somewhat warmer, which could happen, so's we could get across the prairies instead of being trapped in that deep, soft snow, which the mules would never have got through, them being plumb tuckered out.

But we got through, back to the creek and that dugout of ours, stuck the animals in a rough corral there was below us, and give Sam his due, he made sure they was as comfortable as could be, sticking blankets over them and feeding them as best we could. Then we got in the dugout and we made *ourselves* as comfortable as may be, which wasn't much better than the mules, and Sam fished out a bottle of whiskey he'd been cherishing. He sloshed out the drink, me having some too, although he cut it with water so much it was more like drinking root beer, and we settled back.

"Boys," he said, speaking to Hack and Abel. "I guess you know this is the end of the line. Me and the kid is going back into Dodge. If you want to come in, okay, but if you want to stay out here, maybe one of them hunters up the creek will take you on. I can give you a credit note and you can cash it with Charlie sometime. But suit yourselves. In the meantime, I'm going to have me a party."

It was fine, you know. Fine and dandy. It was snowing again, and we was sitting in a hole in the ground, but I'd got a real buddy and a future, so that hole was as fine to me as the Drovers Cottage back in Abilene. But I've got to say, I felt somewhat sorry for old Abel. Hack I didn't give a hoot about, him being the sort of feller that drifts in and out of your life, never saying much, just doing a job, then beating it. In fact, I didn't know no more about him than the day he'd started. But Abel there, squatting in a corner, his knees up past his ears . . . he was kind of pathetic at that, with his wife and kids back in Starvation County or wherever, and with them crazy dreams he'd got for getting another farm. Yeah, I was real sorry for him for about five minutes, but after that, and another slug, I wouldn't have given a can of beans if he'd sunk through the ground and disappeared, and since I didn't intend doing nothing for him, it didn't make no difference anyways.

And that party we was having didn't end that night. It sort of went on and started again the next day. The word had got around that we was pulling out, and fellers came down the creek, giving us mail and messages, and one thing led naturally to another, such as fellers inviting us up to their dugouts, and then, it having stopped snowing, we got a big fire blazing. More whiskey got magicked up, and we sat around the fire broiling buffalo meat, and would you believe, one of the fellers had a fiddle and scraped some music out of it for us! It was real good, we had music and grub and whiskey, and saving the lack of dance girls, there wasn't a thing we was lacking, which sure was a fine way to celebrate stopping being a butcher.

Not that we was orgifying. Apart from that fiddle music,

it was just a straight around-the-fire drinking session, with plenty of talk about Indians, and how there was silver in Colorado and gold up in the Black Hills, where most of them fellers was aiming to go as soon as may be, and to hell with the Sioux doing their worshipping up there, the Army being ready to fix them like they had the Comanche, and seeing as how we was heading back, talk about Dodge.

A feller said a church had got built, which was news to me, and how it was turning into a real regular town, although there was others saying it was just a buffalo camp too big for its britches and it would vanish, just like hundreds of other towns, even though it had a depot and a Town Council and they was going to hire a regular lawman.

But the talk drifted away from Dodge, which no one cared a damn for anyways, and onto lawmen in general, and no matter how tough they was, or how good with a gun, they was likely to get it in the end.

"Like Bear Thompson in Abilene," a feller said. "They reckon he was the hardest man alive, but he got blasted, didn't he? And Hickok, he might be the best thing with a gun that ever walked, but someone's going to get him, sooner if not later."

There wasn't no gainsaying that, but I had something to stick in there, and I stuck it in. "Hickok wasn't no marksman," I said.

It didn't need no brilliance to know what was going to happen, and it did, them fellers hollering me down, shouting what did I know, as per usual, but I'd moved on some during the past year and I was ready to do some hollering back, and when a feller tried to shout me down by saying what the hell did I know, I just said, "Mister, I know because I saw Hickok, is what. And I saw him shoot down Phil Coe and Mike Williams, outside the Alamo."

"You saw that?" another feller asked, incredulous.

"I sure did," I said. "And my own brother was shot dead in Abilene."

If there'd been an earthquake, it might have caused more excitement, but I doubt it. Them fellers was at me, wanting to know every last detail about them killings. Strange, ain't it? Them boys was real hardened men, but they was hanging on my every word like kids listening to a fairy tale. In fact, if I'd said I knew fellers from Mars, they couldn't have been more interested.

I reckon it was tedium. I guess that sounds crazy, like there we was, out on the wild frontier, shooting buffalo and with savage Indians on the loose, but most of the life was just plain hard toil, and most of the fellers you met was the same, having the same thoughts and saying the same things, just like folks most anyplace, so they was looking for romance, I guess you'd call it, in other people's lives, just the same as talking about prizefighters or ball players when you get down to it. In fact, Bat Masterson, who was one of the most famous bandits ever to wear a marshal's star, was a sports writer in New York, and if what he wrote about sport was as fanciful as what Wyatt Earp has written about Tombstone, Arizona, it ain't no wonder no one ever won a bet.

Be that as it may, them fellers was all hushed while I told them about Hickock and Bo and all, which wasn't much when you got down to it, but I spun it out so I could be the center of attention.

"And I'm goddamn sorry that Kessel got his someplace else," I said. "By Jesus, I am. I wanted to plug that dog myself."

It was that booze talking. Just the booze. Me sitting by that fire all set to go to California and I was shooting a line about venging, which I hadn't thought about for more than five minutes ever since I'd left Abilene!

But while I was doing that ugly, senseless boasting, I wasn't really meaning it. I just wanted to be the center of attention, is all, and I don't know but what when the fellers got tired of me and moved on to talking about other bullyboys and murderers, I wasn't glad at that, even though, and it just shows how mixed humans are, I felt somewhat sour, too, sour and excluded.

But you let Jack out of the box and it ain't so easy to stick him back again, because while I was leaning back against a wagon wheel, a feller came over to me with a bottle. "Have a drink, kid," he said.

I said I didn't want none and he didn't press, just hunkered down next to me, taking a swallow himself. "That true, kid?" he asked. "What you was saying there?"

"About Hickok? Sure it is," I said, real surly. "You making me out to be a liar?"

"Why"—the feller kissed the bottle—"I wouldn't do that, and if I did, I'd say it straight out. I'm talking about your brother. You really the Curtis kid?"

"If I ain't," I said, "I don't know who the hell else I am."

"And that Kessel—"

But I didn't want to talk about him no more. Just talking about it gave me a bad taste in the mouth. I wanted to leave it be. Just forget it. Stick away. It wasn't a burden I wanted to carry no more, and I told the feller that. "Forget it," I said. "Let it be."

"Okay, buddy." The feller stood up. "I'll sure do that. But I ain't sure Kessel will!"

"**R**eckon not," I said, sour, with that bad taste in my mouth, and then my head started to prickle. "What do you mean, *will?* You got a telegraph to hell?"

"Don't know about that," the feller said, the firelight flickering on him like we was at the front door of that place. "Just telling you what I know, is all."

"Yeah?" I struggled to my feet. "Don't come trying no fool jokes on me, mister. I ain't in the mood for none."

It's a wonder that feller didn't slug me, but he just shook his head. "I ain't joking," he said. "Hell, it ain't a thing to joke about."

"But," I said, "But . . ." groping for words there, like drunks do. "You saying that son of a bitch is alive?"

"Just as alive as you or me," the feller said.

"But, goddamn it—" I grabbed hold of the wagon to steady myself. "He was killed. Shot dead in . . . yeah, in St. Louis. Hickok told me."

"You got told wrong, kid," the feller said. "He was maybe shot but sure wasn't killed."

I pawed at the air like I was scraping spiderwebs away, but I was trying to wipe away what that feller was telling me. I didn't want to hear that stuff. I didn't want for Kessel to be alive and me to have to think of him drinking and gambling and having women. I wanted him to be dead. And I didn't want to think about venging no more, neither. And I reckon that was the worst part. Instead of them golden dreams, I was being pulled back into some goddamn nightmare.

And I got mad, too, mad at that feller for telling me. "How in hell do you know?" I said. "How the hell do you know he's alive?"

"Why"—that feller looked at me real steady—"why, because he's here!"

Jesus, it was a nightmare. I mean the worst you could ever have. "Here!" I said.

"Yeah." The feller dropped his voice. "Kid, he's been holing out on the other creek. The way I heard it, he killed a settler outside Larned. There's a warrant out for him, which is why he's here. And, kid, like I say, it ain't none of my business, but he's got buddies been at this here party and you was talking mighty big just now. So if I was you I'd start making plans. Pronto."

He moved off, and when what he'd said had sunk in, I moved off myself, double pronto, and grabbed hold of Sam, who was helping some hunters make a bottle lose weight.

He was sore about being pulled away from the fire and the whiskey and said so. "This had better be something serious," he growled.

"It's serious," I said, and told him the story, and when I finished, he gave one of them whistles without a sound.

"Jesus!" he said. "Jesus H. Jumping Christ! Who told you this?"

I pointed him out and Sam went over and started talking to him while I stood where I was, shivering even though I'd got a wolf-skin coat on, and feeling sick, and that wasn't just whiskey and half-cooked buffalo meat, neither, until Sam got back.

"Okay, kid," he said, "Now listen to me and don't start jumping. Got me?"

I said I had, although he'd got *me*, holding the back of my coat and pulling me back slow, out of the light of the fire and into the dark.

"Now listen," Sam said, still easing me back. "That feller, I reckon he's on the level, and he's positive that murdering bastard is around here."

"So, what do we do?" I said, croaked more like.

"It's what *you* do," Sam said.

Yeah, I thought. One minute *we're* all brotherly love and *we're* going to make a new start and a new life, but the minute Old Man Trouble knocks on the door, it's *you* and *your* troubles. But I'd read Sam's hand wrong there, showing you shouldn't jump to conclusions, especially the wrong ones.

"The thing is," Sam said, "that Kessel, he ain't alone"— which figured, them rats running in a pack—"and we sure as hell don't want to get in a shoot-up."

You can say that again, I thought. Sweet Jesus, just the thought of it made me heave. "So, what do we do?" I asked. "Get them hunters together—"

"The hell," Sam said. "You think they're going to get involved?"

"But he's a murderer!" I said. "Okay, I'll *keep* my voice down. Goddamn it, there's a warrant out for him. He murdered that settler and he murdered my brother!"

"Yeah," Sam said. "And them hunters don't want him murdering *them*. And that warrant, out here it wouldn't be worth the paper it's written on."

"So, what the hell do I do?" I asked.

"You beat it," Sam said. "And quick, before that Kessel gets to hear of you shooting your fool mouth off. So *listen*"— hissing because I was near ready to fall down. "He's going to come gunning for you as sure as God made little apples, so you're going to take my horse and get moving, but quick. You get to Bailey's Halt but don't stop there. Keep going. Get to Dodge and wait for me. I'll follow with the wagon, but you get."

"On my own," I said, because riding over them prairies in the winter wasn't the place to be anyhow, leave alone without company.

"I know," Sam said, not needing to have that spelled out.

"Kid, I know how you feel, but it's the best I can think of. We sure don't have much of a chance against a pack of murdering coyotes. Come on, I'll help you saddle up and give you some grub."

We eased away from the crowd and moved down the creek to the rig and that rough corral that was down there. It was some night at that, the frost crackling under our feet and a white moon staring down so bright the entire world was just black and white, the white parts whiter than you ever saw them, and the black parts blacker, like all the color in the world had been drained away. And them shadows, so black you felt you could touch them, goddamn, I was balking in case Kessel was lurking in one of them, ready to jump out and send me to meet Bo.

But nothing happened. No Kessel came out, and we got to that corral and moved among them peaceful animals, cutting out Sam's horse, and as we was doing that, Sam muttered something.

"What's that?" I whispered.

"This pony," he said.

I moved over and there was a pony I hadn't seen before, all saddled up.

"Someone fresh in," Sam said. "Goddamn, you'd have thought he'd have unsaddled it."

Moses, I thought, here was me, near getting a one-way ticket to the great blue yonder and Sam was sorry for a goddamn pony! But it wasn't the time for a debate, so I just got hold of Sam's horse and led it out.

"Okay," Sam said. "We'll get the saddle and I'll let you have the Sharps. Come on."

The dugout was upstream from the corral and we stole up there, the horse breathing warm on my neck, and crossed the frozen stream to the east side. In that glittering moonshine, the dugout was just a black hole, with the embers of the fire outside glowing dull red, and that dugout sure looked scary, like that cellar door you never wanted to go through when you was a kid.

Sam stopped. "Abel," he called, low as may be. "Abel, it's me and the kid."

There wasn't no answer, just that black hole, like it might have been a blind eye in a dead white face. The horse moved behind me, jittery, like they can be, and like I was, too, but Sam just cursed.

"Sung his goddamn hymns and gone to sleep. Abel, I'm coming in."

He walked forward, just a step or so, and there was a weird yell, a screech more like, a flash of flame, and a huge bang. Sam gave a terrible cough, like someone retching, there was another bang, and he went down, all crumpled and twisted, and a shape came out of that black dugout into the moonlight.

It was Kessel, you know, who else. Him who'd dogged me in my waking hours and in my dreams, come back from hell, right enough.

"You bitching bastard son of a whoring mothering son of a bitch," he said, and he said it slow. Slow and deliberate, like he was choosing his words and relishing them. "Out you go."

There wasn't no way he could miss, and he fired right at me, saving he didn't fire. I heard the hammer click, like a latch opening the gate that leads to that place you don't ever want to go to, but nothing happened!

It was like a miracle at that, saving there wasn't nothing miraculous about it, just a misfire, but it was enough to wake me out of my shock, and while Kessel was cursing and clicking away on that pistol, I was around the horse and across the stream into the blackness.

Brother, did I move! I went down that creek like a jackrabbit, and right then I had about the brains of one. I ought to have been going up the creek to that goddamn party, but you don't think straight when you've just seen your partner blasted in half, and there's a 100 percent mad-dog killer after you with a six-gun as big as a cannon. You just ain't being reasonable, you're taking the quickest way out, and that was down, but even as I was skidding down there I had a thought because down that creek there was a way out, and I took it.

I got to the corral and, brother, did I bless the feller who was unkind to animals, because I was on that saddled-up pony and heading out like greased lightning, and did I bless the day I went riding herd! Not that the pony was like them I'd ridden, them jumping like cats and with a sprint in them. In fact, it was so wore out and bad fed that if I'd been much bigger I could have carried it quicker than it was carrying me. I had a third blessing, too. I didn't have no spurs, but I did have my skinning knife, so I used that, jabbing that pony into a trot until I was out of that broken country and onto the prairie, where the creeks ran into a sort of river. And it's a crazy thing, that river was frozen solid so it wasn't no kind of barrier, but I crossed it to feel safer, then let the bridle hang loose.

I slid off the pony and leaned against it, although I don't know but it was leaning against me. I could feel its heart pounding against its bony ribs, but it wasn't pounding no harder than mine was. Moses, I couldn't believe what had happened. I just couldn't. Goddamn, Sam cut down, Kessel back, and me out there on that vast plain in that eerie moonlight. And them names kept going around in my head. Kessel and Sam, Sam and Kessel. And Jesus wept, why had Kessel come back and why had he come to just the spot we was at, and why hadn't we moved out a day earlier, and why, and why, and why, around and around, them thoughts scraping at my skull.

And I don't know, maybe I'd have just stood there until

me and that horse both froze together, but it was the horse brought me around, it moving all restless, pricking its ears, and when I heard what it heard, mine pricked, too. There was a wolf howling out there, some goddamn great buffalo wolf howling at the moon, and there was another answering, but although they was scary, them wolves being able to pull down a buffalo when they was hungry, they didn't scare me as much as that human wolf did.

Okay, I said to myself. *Okay*. Grab hold of yourself. You got to get back to humans—which was easier thought of than done. There wasn't no way I was going to make it to Bailey's Halt without grub, but Kessel was back there at the creeks . . .

I stood there for a while, listening to them wolves howl, pretending to myself they was getting farther away, then decided to do the only thing I could do, which was go back across the river and swing around the creeks so's I got to them from the north. That way, I could maybe get to human beings without Kessel seeing me, maybe get help, maybe, but, anyhow, get a gun.

I climbed back on the pony, and it near collapsed under me, and I had a look around, it being amazing how much farther you can see from a saddle than from the ground, and way off, in that whiteness, I saw a black shape move.

It was just a black speck under the moon. I thought it might be a wolf, but it was too far off for me to have seen it if it was, and the way it was moving, it was more like creeping. Jupiter, it was the most frightening thing I ever did see, creeping toward me, creeping and crawling—then it stopped. And I ain't sure that wasn't more frightening, that black shape out there stopped, like it was a creature that had scented something, and me stopped on that pony, two black specks motionless on that snowy plain under a sky glittering with stars and a cold moon.

And then, as I was wondering what in hell was going on,

there was a boom, the mellow boom of a Sharps. And I'll tell you something you won't hardly believe. When that rifle sang out, I looked around me! No kidding. I looked around to see what was being shot at!

That rifle shot echoed and died away, and it dawned on me that *I* was being shot at, and that black shape was Kessel. And it wasn't a bad notion to try a shot, even one as long as that. It was as bright as day out there and he might have been figuring that if he didn't hit me he'd get the pony, and for all he knew I had a rifle or six-gun, so it paid him to keep his distance. And although I figured he was well out of range he clearly thought different, and for all I knew, he was a better judge of distance than I was.

But him being there and coming at me, there was only one thing to do, so I did it. I wrenched that pony's head around and jabbed at it with my knife until it started moving and headed south again, out onto that dazzling plain, under that dazzling light.

I didn't try to make the pony run, or even canter, and I don't think it could have done if I'd tried to. It was in a sorry state, breath rattling in its lungs and its head slung low. And I was in a sorry state, too, sweating and shivering at the same time and gasping in that still, icy air, like a dying man. Which I thought I was, too, dying with every minute that passed and every yard of ground we covered. It was bitter, at that. Bile swilling around the back of your throat, and the bitterness of knowing your time's run out and none of them dreams you had is ever going to come true, that you was never going to have the girl you dreamed of nor the life you wanted, and that in a half hour at most you was going to be nothing but a bag of flesh and bones lying on the prairie for some wolf to gobble up. Just no different from your horse or any other creature that died out there on them Plains.

I looked around, though, like almost out of curiosity. I

could see Kessel clear enough, but he didn't seem much closer and he wasn't trying to gallop me down, just content to follow me, which made sense. He was going to get me sooner or later, and he wouldn't want to have his pony blown—seeing as how he'd be going back.

But, Jesus, it was worse than any nightmare, the way we was moving. Slow, slow, me having no time left, and him all there was in the world. That Sharps boomed out again, and when I turned, I could see him remounting, like he'd got the time to climb down and stick up that tripod. That's how much time he had.

A slight wind blew up, stirring the snow, sending little feathers scurrying past. It made it more nightmarish, the whole plain stirring and moving. The light was changing too, that pure whiteness changing into a funny kind of yellow, evil as you might say. At first I didn't even think about it, just saying to myself as it were, the light's changing, going yellowy, yeah. Then I looked up and there was a cloud over the moon.

It was just a cloud. Just that one hanging over the moon, changing its color. But someplace at the back of my mind something flickered, like saying, you've seen that before, you dummy, and I looked north and there wasn't no Big Dipper up there, and there wasn't no North Star neither.

There was more cloud coming down on that wind, and for a moment there I felt some hope. Enough cloud and there wouldn't be no light for Kessel to shoot in, and then . . . But that hope didn't last long because there wasn't no "and then," or there was, but it rhymed with *amen* because there wasn't no place for me to run to. Just the bare Plains and Kessel catching up to me with every step. And just to remind me he was back of me, the Sharps boomed out again, and maybe it was lead and maybe it was that wind, but I thought I heard something whine past my ear, and if you translated that whine into American, it said, "I'm getting closer, you son of a bitch. Getting closer."

And maybe it was that whine that stirred me, but I thought okay, okay, you're going to get me, but you'll goddamn have to work for my hide, you blackhearted bastard.

I jabbed at the pony with the knife, forcing it on, thinking I was going to run it till it dropped dead, then get behind it and make Kessel get in close, and then, maybe, I could stab him. Something foolish like that, anyhow.

That poor pony moved on. Then something mighty strange happened. I was turning a lot to see where Kessel was at, and I turned and he wasn't there! God Almighty! For a moment I thought he'd thrown his hand in, just given up and let me go free. Then I realized I couldn't see nothing at all back there. I rubbed my eyes and looked again and there still wasn't nothing. Nothing at all but a blur. And then that hope didn't just flicker, it flared up like a forest fire, because that blur was snow.

Goddamn! I had half a chance, at that. I could maybe throw Kessel off my trail, circle back to camp, even jump him! And if I couldn't do them things, if I froze and choked to death in a blizzard, that was better than being gunned down by Kessel.

The snow reached me, small flakes, spinning before that wind, and I turned, keeping that wind on my left cheek, hoping to get behind Kessel. I had to fight to get that pony around, too. It wanted to drift before the wind, if it had to move at all. I had to saw the bit, and I didn't like to think what I was doing to that creature's mouth, but it turned and we made some little distance. Then the snow moved on, the moon shone down, and I was a sitting target again.

But I figured I had a couple of things going for me. Me and the pony was plastered white with snow, so we'd be hard to spot, and the other was the snow itself. What we'd had was just a flurry, but it could be the start of something bigger. And I was right on that but wrong on the first notion because that Sharps boomed out again.

Jesus, I thought, that goddamn murderer's got eyes like an owl, and I used that knife again, forcing the pony on, me crouching low in the saddle, as if that made any difference. Then the snow came again.

It was thicker this time, dense as it were, huge thick flakes, and coming on a howling wind that hit you like a hammer. There wasn't nothing to do but stop, and, in any case, that pony just couldn't move no more in that weather. I slid out of the saddle and leaned against the pony on the side away from the wind. I'd have pulled the pony down, saving if I did, it wasn't never going to get up again, and I guess it was a good thing at that, because if I'd laid down, I wouldn't never have got up again neither. That's how fellers went, I'd heard, laying down in a blizzard and going to sleep, and not waking up never again.

I was scared of that, too, so I *tied* myself to that pony, lashing the reins to one arm and sliding my other through the stirrup. And I near went to someplace else, at that. I'd find my mind wandering, drifting like the snow, thinking I was at home in Clement, or being in the store with old Besser, crazy random pictures. Then I'd start to fall and get jerked away with that stirrup cutting at me. A couple of times I reckon I did fall asleep and was only woke with the pony dragging me along as it moved before the wind. I came near to letting it happen at that, letting myself get dragged along like a hide. Just surrendering.

Then the snow eased up. It was still coming down but nowhere near as thick, and there was kind of a sickly pale light behind it. Dawn coming, and I'd woken to some bad mornings in my time, but never one worse than that, because whichever way you looked at it, I was going to start my last day on this earth.

But that hope, you know, the one that jumps up and down in the human breast, it was still there, maybe not fizzing around like a firecracker but not totally snuffed out, neither. Fellers had been caught out in blizzards before and come through, and I wasn't like that feller Charlie Rath had found, all froze to death. I'd got the right clothes on, and if the worst came to the worst, I could start eating the pony. There was just two things I wanted. That snow to stop, and Kessel to be missing.

And the snow did stop. Well, it drifted away south, and what I ought to have done was turn into the wind, trying for the camp, but I just couldn't do it. Not me, and not the pony. In fact, it made the decision, which is something, ain't it, a pony making up your mind for you?

I let it wander. I didn't even mount up, just holding the reins and letting it haul me along, step by step, hoping to Jesus it *would* hold up and that maybe we'd hit a camp, or the railroad. Fantasies, you know. Just fantasies. But they was all I had to hold on to, and I did. I held them as tight as I held them reins as we lurched and staggered on into nowhere as the light got stronger and there was even a hint of sun, which gave that hope a prod, at that. And then I heard the boom again.

It was Kessel, not a half mile away, coming out of one of them snow flurries and shooting from the saddle, which was no way to use a Sharps, and if he'd taken his time and stuck it on the tripod, I'd have been dead meat.

And I near enough waited for him. I near enough stood there, hoping for that one chance, but I didn't. I got on that pony, still hoping. Hoping against hope. And you never knew, at that. His pony could step in a gopher hole and break its leg, and maybe his neck with it. And like the man says, if there ain't but one thing to do, that's the thing you *have* to do and you ain't got no choice in the matter, so I jabbed that pony again, slicing it to ribbons, heading for one of them snow flurries, hoping to hide. Hoping hopelessly, and I near enough got there. I was near enough there when the pony gave up. It didn't fall, just sank beneath me, its neck stretched out, its eyes rolled back, and blood-stained saliva dripping out of its mouth.

But I kept going, would you believe? Even then, on foot and with just a skinning knife. I scrabbled out of the stirrups and shambled on, plowing through the snow, waiting for a bullet in the back, and no more than a hunted animal at that, some poor creature being hounded down, saving I'd got no burrow to run to nor hole to hide in. Nothing but that flickering snow, hiding in which would be like hiding behind a spiderweb.

I looked over my shoulder and there hadn't been no miracle. Kessel was still coming on, and I don't know that it was because I was on foot and he was mounted, or maybe it was just a trick of the light, but he looked gigantic, looming up like one of them mirages, like he was unreal, and I couldn't really believe he was real, I couldn't believe it was me, neither. And I couldn't believe it was all happening. It wasn't Ben Curtis out there on the Plains, not that yellow-haired kid who'd hauled his way from Clement and run a store, and who'd learned *Store Keeping Made Simple*, not him about to get his head blown off.

No, it was someone else it was happening to, someone I was just thinking about. Not me moaning and cursing and shambling on, shrinking inside my clothes as a gun cracked out, and realizing that gunshot was from a six-shooter, meaning Kessel was close enough to use one. And it wasn't me pulling out my skinning knife and turning, ready to face and run at that shadow what had darkened my life in Abilene.

But like someone in a dream, I turned, my knife out, and watched him come at me, slow, slow and easy, in no hurry at all, saving his pony, and he stopped being just a black shape, his face showing under his hat, and showing he wasn't a dream at all. And then something moved behind me, something huge and plastered with snow, all snorting and grunting.

Yeah, it was buffalo, and there was more of them, a small herd come from God knew where, maybe drifted south before that blizzard and missed out by hunters, but there, and there for me. One last chance, and I took it. I stopped thinking it wasn't me out there because it goddamn well was. And I knew one thing maybe Kessel didn't. I was on foot and buffalo didn't pay no heed to a feller like that. It was a horse they'd charge, and one of them buffalo did. It went for Kessel, not a real killing charge, more threatening, but enough to throw him off his stride and give me time to run into that herd.

It was hide-and-seek, you know. Hide-and-seek through that herd, saving if you got caught, you wasn't on, you was out. Out for good and ever.

There wasn't much hiding room, neither. There wasn't more than a dozen animals, and they was spread out, so Kessel could get at me, if he had the nerve, and he did.

I could see him, you know, in and out of the flurries of snow, trying to get into the herd, and he could see me, dodging around them creatures. A couple of times he did get in back of me, but I was quicker than that pony of his and kept a buffalo between us and him. And it was like we'd gone back into that dream world—them huge animals, like something from times long past, all white with snow, looming up out of the snow, and Kessel white too, and me, coming and going like we was ghosts sure enough, ghosts in a ghostly world, as if we'd already crossed that line that divides you from here and there, and there being that place where you won't never taste coffee in the morning again, or smell spring flowers, or take your ease, come dusk.

But as we darted through the herd, them buffalo was getting restless, moving about, pawing the ground and grunting, and while I was thinking, sweet Jesus, don't let them run, I heard the crack of a handgun, and another, and I could hear Kessel yelling, and then the heart really started to go out of me, because he'd got the notion clear enough. Run that herd. Just stampede it, and if I wasn't trampled down, I was left all isolated, and in that entire country, that huge big country, big like all them fellers kept saying, three thousand miles from sea to sea, I was left without no more space to run to.

And like, I guess, it was fated to, it happened. Slow at first, sort of ambling, but then as Kessel whooped and blazed away, them buffalo began to run, and they run until there wasn't none left, saving one which was half down and coughing up blood, and I was left alone as Kessel walked his pony toward me.

There wasn't nothing I could do no more. There was nowhere to run to and nowhere to hide, so I just stood there, holding my knife, as Kessel walked his pony toward me, taking his time, like he'd got all there was in the world, and knowing mine had run out, and holding his six-gun casual, like he knew there wasn't no need for fuss, because all he had to do was raise it and pull the trigger.

He got within a few feet of me and then he spoke. "Lights out for you," he said. "Lights out, you son of a bitch."

It's crazy to say I was scared since I hadn't been anything else for the last twelve hours, but looking at Kessel there, I was. Like until then I don't know but that at the back of my mind there hadn't been a feeling that even if he did catch up with me I'd be able to do *something*. If not stab him, then *appeal*, and I couldn't believe that he wouldn't listen, it being incredible that anyone would want to kill Ben Curtis. Anyone else, sure, but me? That flesh-and-blood

Texas kid who never did no real harm to anyone in his life and just wanted to be left alone to make his pile . . .

It's right, I hadn't believed it, but I did then, looking up at Kessel lounging on his pony, them snowflakes swirling around him. He looked crazy. I mean, all them killers was, but he looked like he'd win the world's prize for craziness, and he sounded it, too, when he spoke again. "You," he said, in a cracked voice that sounded all wrong, like a piano being played out of tune. "You. You've haunted me. You've been on my back for long enough. Goddamn Jesus, I should never have let you be. I should have hunted you down and finished you off."

And that *was* crazy, the two of us out there in that snowy waste and desolation, a buffalo dying and spewing blood onto the snow, and Kessel raving at me. I wanted to tell him so, to say we wasn't doing neither of us no good, and it wasn't me that had haunted him but him that had haunted me. I wanted to say why didn't we just call it off so's he could go his way and me mine. To appeal to reason there. Sweet reason, and his better nature. But he hadn't finished, at that. He'd got more to say, more to spew out, like a festering boil bursting.

"Yeah," he said. "I've been waiting for you. Everyplace I went to. Every bar I ever went in. Every time I opened my eyes, I expected to see you standing over me. Yeah. But it's over now, and you can go join your bitching, goddamn —— brother."

He half leaned over his saddle, sighting down the muzzle of his pistol, real careful, like shooting in a competition, and I heard that *click click* as the hammer was drawn back, and I knew that this time there wasn't going to be no misfire, and I was going to throw that knife at him and jump sideways, when he suddenly straightened, his jaw dropped, and he said, "Jesus Christ!"

I couldn't help myself. I didn't want to turn my back on him, not even in my last moments, but my neck screwed around like someone else was turning it, and then my jaw dropped, and "Jesus Christ," I said, too, because coming out of the swirling snow was a sight I'd never seen and didn't think I ever would see.

Once, like a million years ago, I'd been told I wouldn't need no telling, and I didn't, neither. They wasn't dressed in no fancy beads and didn't have no feathers in their hair. In fact, they was all muffled up in buffalo robes, but they didn't need no signs to tell you who they were. I guess it was the way they was balanced on their ponies, haughty you could call it, like they ruled the Plains still and every creature on it, and the whole world they knew, same as they had before us white men came and blew them away, away into a world of dreams and visions and two-bit shows, no more real than a cloud of cigar smoke in a cheap saloon bar.

I guess Kessel didn't need no telling, neither, because he blasted away with his six-shooter, and blasted again, but he didn't get no chance for third time lucky, because one of them horse Indians danced his pony at him and skewered him in the ribs with a lance. And I didn't get to see no more, because while I stared at them specters, one of them, whited up with snow, passing me, swung a club backhanded, and you won't believe it but I was laughing, laughing at how crazy it all was, and thinking, now I'm going to see the elephant, too, and laughing still when that club crashed against my head and I went down into the snow, yeah, and into that darkness, too.

EPILOGUE

I've lost plenty of hair since, but I didn't lose any that dawn, in the snow, since them braves let me be, although it wasn't from no sweet charity but because they was worried about their own, being as how they was being hunted down by the United States Cavalry.

I heard after that it was Cheyenne, on the run from Palo Duro, saying there wasn't noplace for them to run to, if you get me. Most of them surrendered a while later when their ponies foundered, although they say some of them made it to the Black Hills and was with Crazy Horse and the Sioux when they wiped out Custer and the Seventh Cavalry at the Little Big Horn. The last victory of the horse Indians, I guess.

For the rest, it was just oblivion, is all. Course, some of them are still kicking around. You can maybe see them in a carnival along with the freak shows, or maybe *in* a freak show, or you go across America and come across the worst land there is and see a pile of junk, old jalopies and the like, with mangy dogs wandering around, why, that'll be a reservation, and them drunks shambling around, they're the descendants of the horse Indians.

But what they thought they was, and maybe *what* they was, lords of the earth and the sky, and brothers and sisters of the sun and the moon, and the rain and the wind, why, that's gone, clear gone like the buffalo. In fact, they went *with* the buffalo, and getting rid of *them* didn't take more than ten years when the boys got down to it. Yeah, maybe twenty million animals. It just goes to show what the U.S. of A. can do when it has a mind to.

As for me, I got picked up by the cavalry patrol who was hunting them Indians. They was buffalo soldiers and one of them was Tom Carney, so I got treated right, and although I'd got a busted head and frostbite some, I made it back to Dodge. But, although everyone in town knew I was rightly Sam's partner, I didn't get them credits for the hides. No, sir, what I got was fifty bucks to see me on my way.

I didn't argue about it. I was just plain sick of arguing about money. I was sick of the West, too, so I took the handout and headed for New York City and old Henry, and like he'd said in his letter, he was glad to see me, even though I hadn't made a million.

I shacked up with him on the Lower East Side, with a nice cat he'd got, sort of gingery, got used to seeing that hairy picture on the wall, and learned me printing. After, I moved around, working on them lying newspapers and doing some labor organizing. I got my head busted a few more times by gents who figured unions was thought up by the devil, and I saw the insides of a few county jails, although I never did get to see California.

It's strange, at that. While we was roaming around, and the Indians and the buffalo, too, at the back of us, fighting droughts and blizzards and cyclones and grasshoppers and bankers and the railroad companies, stubborn as all getout, them settlers kept drifting in, and sticking at it. In fact, it was some foreigners who brought in a strain of wheat, that Turkey Red seed, that could stand the weather in Kansas, and them immigrants knew how to handle the weather, too, so that laughing I did about farming out there was on me, seeing as how Kansas feeds half the world. And while we was living like savages, that feller Glidden was inventing barbed wire so's you could fence off your land, and McCormick was making them reapers so's the crops could be got in, and most of all, I guess, that plow was invented that could cut deep through the buffalo grass. Like they say, the plow that broke the Plains.

Still, it's all history now, history and dreams, and dime novels and motion pictures. Although what ain't a dream is what's happening right now. The stock market has gone bust again, just exactly like it did when Jay Cooke failed and me and them other suckers got busted. There's fellers like old Heaney jumping out of skyscrapers, and fellers like poor old Abel, in rags, selling apples on the streets, the which you can't walk down a hundred yards without getting bummed for a dime. Only now there ain't no big Wild West to roam around in and make a fresh start. There's just us, is all, and what we can make of ourselves.

So there they is. Joe McCoy, Wild Bill Hickok, the Reverend Christopher, Colonel Dodge, Charlie Rath, Cox, who shot that black in Dodge, Little Wolf—they was real at that, realer than what I've writ down, but they've gone, all of them, gone with the buffalo and the tribes, the Comanche and the Kiowa, Cheyenne, Arapahoe, the Sioux and the Blackfeet, the Crow and the Nez Percé, and all the rest. Them who tried to make it in civilization and them who didn't. But they was doomed, as they say. Doomed the moment the first white man put his foot ashore. There just wasn't no way a couple of million Indians was going to hold on to that vastness, not with them millions and millions and millions of folks in Europe pining to get here. So maybe it worked out as it should. Maybe.

But I'll tell you a funny thing. I was in a bar in New York City a while back, and I heard a feller singing. Well, he was singing before he got chucked out. I followed him, but

423

he'd gone, just lost in all them folks milling around. But I remembered the song. It was kind of nice, at that. Maybe you know it. It's about a rider selling his pony and moving on someplace, anyplace.

Goodbye, old Paint, I'm a-leaving Cheyenne,
I'm a-leaving Cheyenne, and I'm off for Montan';
Goodbye, old Paint, I'm a-leaving Cheyenne.

And that was something to hear in a barroom on Union Square West, New York City, wasn't it?